THE KILLING FROST

SCOTT GAMBOE

Gold Imprint
Medallion Press, Inc.
Printed in USA

THE KILLING FROST

SCOTT GAMBOE

DEDICATION:

For my mother, who lost her battle with cancer before this project saw its final success.

Published 2006 by Medallion Press, Inc.

The MEDALLION PRESS LOGO
is a registered tradmark of Medallion Press, Inc.

Cover Illustration by James Tampa

Typeset in ITC Galliard

Printed in the United States of America

10 9 8 7 6 5 4 3 2 1
First Edition

ACKNOWLEDGEMENTS:

First, I would like to thank Beth for her ideas and suggestions, which helped to keep the story rolling. I would also like to thank Marti for her technical and grammatical assistance, which helped bring this whole project to a successful conclusion. And of course, I would like to thank my wife, Jill, who supported me in this effort, as she supports me in everything I do.

CHAPTER ONE

ARANO LAKELAND MOVED STEALTHILY ALONG THE wooded bluff near his home, picking his way carefully and soundlessly through the darkness. Although it was a moonless night, he moved with confidence through the tree-covered landscape. Some of his colleagues thought it odd that he kept coming back to his homeworld on these short breaks from work, but this forest paradise was his greatest love. Untouched by the wars and petty bickering of the outlying systems, his home here helped him to escape from the harsh realities he had to face every day.

He was wearing his usual hunting garb: loose-fitting, camouflage-patterned clothing that allowed him to move without being seen by the object of his hunt. Arano was in excellent shape, his body kept lean and fit by decades of hard physical training. Small scars were scattered across his body, memoirs from battles long since forgotten. While he was still a young man by most standards, the experiences he had been through had removed all traces of youth from his countenance, leaving behind a serious face, the eyes stubbornly trying to hide his emotions.

His breath steamed in the cool autumn morning air and the frozen grass crunched soundlessly underfoot. He stopped for a moment to consider his surroundings.

Laying aside his hand-carved longbow, the only weapon he ever used for hunting, he knelt and felt the icy layer of frost beneath him. He sniffed at the air and nodded in satisfaction. The killing frost had come, making his quarry safe to eat. Now, the hunt could truly begin.

He shouldered his longbow and continued along his chosen path for the better part of an hour, making absolutely no sound as he went. He finally arrived at his hunting grounds, sat on a frozen tree stump, put his back up against an outcropping of rock, and waited. He knew should he keep moving; the super-sensitive ears of his prey would pick up his movements, despite his uncanny ability to move silently. He removed his hat and ran his fingers through his close-cropped brown hair before pulling the hat firmly back into place.

Although his family held a hereditary title and consequently had substantial wealth, Arano lived a simple life. He had steadfastly refused to use his family's position to get ahead; instead, he prided himself on getting everything he had through hard work and dedication. He had a passion for working with his hands, a pastime he'd picked up from a woman he'd been close to years before. In fact, with a bit of help from a few close friends, he built his own house on Leguin 4, clearing the trees from the area and using the wood harvested from those trees for the construction. Arano had seen enough bureaucratic waste in his time to have developed a strong dislike for excess and waste, and tried to make the most of resources at his disposal. When he had a successful hunting season, he gave away what food he wouldn't use himself.

He shifted his weight slightly, trying to find a more comfortable position. While he waited, his thoughts naturally drifted back to his work of the past few weeks. Since the brief occupation of his homeworld a few years prior by the Bromidian terrorist group, Rising Sun, he had attempted to prove a link between Rising Sun and the government of the Bromidian Empire. He had finally made some headway recently, finding a likely financial link between Rising Sun and the Bromidian High Command, but it had been to no avail. The rulers of the United Systems Coalition knew if a definite link were established between the terrorists and the Bromidian Empire, it would mean a second titanic war with the Bromidians. This was something the Coalition High Council wanted to avoid at all costs, even if it meant turning a blind eye to what was plainly in front of them.

And the Grand High Councilor, Balor Tient, was the greatest obstructionist of them all. If anything angered Arano more than waste, it was those who couldn't be trusted, who betrayed their loyalties to others in order to better their own positions. He fumed in frustration at the last thought and forced the matter from his mind. Worrying about it now would do nothing to change the situation.

He stretched his legs slowly to the front, muscles stiffening in the cold air despite his superb state of physical conditioning. He leaned back once more, watching unmoving as the sun climbed slowly above the ridgeline. Unbidden, his thoughts drifted back to the dark days, years before, when this peaceful world languished under Rising Sun occupation.

The door to Arano's tent parted with a snap, and a messenger hustled inside. He was breathing hard and, judging by the way the man sweated, Arano surmised he had run quite a distance.

"What is it?" Arano asked.

"Rising Sun . . ." he gasped. "They've . . . they've found the Giona site!"

Arano dropped onto his chair, his leaden legs suddenly unable to support his weight. His heart pounded, and each beat resonated to the furthest reaches of his limbs. His chest felt so tight he could scarcely draw a breath.

"My family?" he asked softly.

"Your parents were taken to the square in the center of town, along with the other families hiding at Giona." The man paused, choking back tears. "They started the executions immediately."

Arano rose and moved woodenly to a supply cabinet. He hung a spotting scope from his neck before picking up his sniper rifle. "Show me."

An hour later, Arano lay on his belly and crawled to the edge of an outcropping of rock. He knew the area well, and in fact he and his fiancé, Erlinia Drontas, had frequently come to this place to admire the view. From here, he could use his scope to look out over the city where so many of his family and friends had managed to hide for so long. In the town square, plainly visible from Arano's high vantage point, about fifty people sat huddled in a tight group, their hands secured behind their backs.

To Arano's everlasting horror, he saw row upon row of bodies, the gaping holes in their chests giving mute testimony to the savagery of their captors. Almost reluctantly, he zoomed in his scope for a closer view. Tears came to his eyes when he recognized the faces of people he had known his entire life. But the tears turned to white-hot anger when his scope showed him the faces of his parents, their features contorted with the agony of death.

Hatred so intense it almost overwhelmed him filled his heart. With a certainty that defied logic, Arano knew he would avenge them. But the death of one Bromidian would not suffice to calm his rage, not even a hundred. He wouldn't rest until the resistance he led had killed every Bromidian on the planet.

New resolve swept over him as he finished looking over the bodies of the fallen. He felt a small measure of relief when he didn't see Erlinia among those executed at the hands of the Broms. When he didn't find her among the prisoners who yet lived, he grew puzzled. Had she somehow escaped the Bromidian assault on Giona? If so, she might need his help. Arano lowered his scope and turned to leave, but a lone figure at the center of the square caught his eye. His scope confirmed what his heart already knew: Erlinia was being held prisoner, tied securely to a post as a message to

Arano; he must surrender, or she would die.

For three hours he sat in silence, watching the forested hillside in anticipation. He had studied the signs in the area for two days, and he knew his prey would return. Finally, he was rewarded as the object of his search came lumbering into view. The furry, horned animal weighing in excess of 100 kilograms was larger than he had anticipated, but he still felt confident he could bring it down with one shot. He fingered the tip of his arrow, waiting for the beast to come into range.

The Comm at his belt gave a telltale twitch. Annoyed, he briefly considered ignoring it, but knew he couldn't. He inserted the speaker in his ear and activated the link. "Lakeland here," he whispered.

"Captain Lakeland, this is Sergeant Drowt with Avengers Command. Sorry to bother you during your leave time, but this is an emergency. The Disciples of Zhulac have killed again."

"Damn," muttered Arano. "All right, be there as soon as I can." He snapped off the Comm, then loudly gathered his gear. He looked longingly after his prey, which had moved off upon hearing Arano crash about. Sighing, he shouldered his pack for the long walk back to the spaceport. After a moment's consideration, he retrieved his Comm and activated the subspace link, the tiny device instantly contacting a member of his squad hundreds of light years away on Immok 2.

"Lieutenant Videre Genoa here," a voice announced.

"It's me," Arano responded. "Do you have any details on the latest Disciple killing?"

"Nothing yet, Viper," Videre replied, using Arano's nickname. "Lain is trying to find out the specifics right now. He should return within the hour. Squad B is doing a presentation for the High Council Committee on Special Military Units, so they'll be tied up for a while."

"Understood," muttered Arano. "I'll see you when I get there. Lakeland, out." He replaced the Comm in the holder on his belt, then resumed his march. Even with such weighty matters on his mind as the ongoing serial murders by the Disciples, his enthusiasm for the beauty of the forest could not be dampened. Something small and unseen off to his right scampered away at his approach, ducking into a large briar patch for protection from its perceived threat. Overhead, the trees bent reluctantly under the unyielding force of the wind, scarcely felt by Arano on the forest floor.

Sighing once more, he picked up his pace, knowing he needed to get back to his ship as quickly as possible. Despite the chill in the air, his efforts brought out beads of sweat on his forehead, and he loosened his jacket, and relaxed. Lieutenant Lain Baxter was very thorough, as were most Kamlings, since that reptilian race based their society on a military hierarchy. Arano knew Lain would have all the information gathered long before Arano's arrival back at headquarters.

Five hours later, Arano had arrived at the spaceport and boarded his personal ship. Though not large, the Eclipse was fast and highly maneuverable. He had added modifications not typically found on civilian ships, like an advanced targeting computer, a torpedo bay, and three independently controlled plasma battery beam weapons.

As the ship hummed to life, Arano breathed a sigh of relief. The Eclipse had not been the most reliable ship, even though it was only a year old. He and the dealer had gone round and round about the problems, but there seemed to be no resolution. The ion engines roared, and the Eclipse lurched obediently toward the heavens.

On a whim, he activated the ship's subspace link, similar to his portable model but with the addition of a video display. After a few moments, Lieutenant Genoa's Gatoan, feline face appeared on the screen, the large, fur-covered ears twitching in irritation at the interruption, then relaxing when he saw it was Arano

"Anything yet, Videre?" Arano asked him.

"Not much," the Lieutenant replied, shuffling through a stack of papers. "Rumor has it the victim was a Human female Coalition employee. No confirmation on that yet."

"If the police tell you the victim was Human, make sure the medical examiner double checks to be certain she isn't Padian."

"There hasn't been a Padian victim yet," noted Videre. "You Padians and your danger senseit really keeps you from being easy targets."

"We're funny that way." Arano had to laugh inside. Videre frequently made light of the fact many Humans looked down on Padians, who they thought of as a race of primitives who would still live in the dark ages if Humans hadn't provided them with a technological boost. Arano felt no particular animosity toward Humans in general, but found it amazing such an enlightened people could judge someone based solely on their race. He shook off his reverie and returned to his Comm.

"Keep me posted. It's about a sixteen-hour jump from here to the Immok system. I'll be there as soon as I can."

Arano closed down the subspace link and returned to his flight controls. He monitored the ship's sensors until he confirmed he had cleared the planet's gravity well, then calculated the jump to the Immok system. He touched a final control, and his Rift Drive engines instantly came alive. The stars before him, which had been mere pinpoints, stretched into larger and larger globes of light. They exploded in a white flash, followed by an eruption of color. Irregular shapes, most of them various shades of reds and blues, rushed outward. A dark field, colored a deep blue-black hue, formed a tunnel and rushed out to greet him, the swirling colors morphing into different shapes as they spun around the tunnel's surface. His Rift Drive engines had opened an artificial wormhole linked to his destination, and the swirling vastness in front of him swiftly devoured his ship.

"Captain Lakeland," greeted the duty sergeant. "You arrived more quickly than we had anticipated. The rest of your team is in your ready room. They have all the details." The sergeant paused, then added, "Sir, the lab has confirmed this was not a copycat killing. It was the real thing. The victim was a civilian who worked down the hall here in intelligence. Pisada Casan."

"Thank you, Sergeant." Arano moved through the seemingly endless corridors of the United Systems Coalition Military Headquarters building. He wondered briefly at how many thousands of people of different races all worked here, and the fact that despite having been assigned here for several years, most of these people were just faces in the crowd. Some were soldiers, men and women who had proven themselves either at the training grounds or on the field of battle. Others were simply time-serving bureaucrats, many of whom were self-important people whose assessment of their own self-worth was inestimably higher than their actual achievements.

His Comm twitched once more, and he activated the link.

"Captain Lakeland, this is Corporal Heatherly. I've been asked to pass along new orders for you. You'll get a full report shortly, but I can give you an overview."

"Go ahead."

"The Grand High Councilor has assigned one of his aides to study your team's interaction with your civilian advisor and determine if that arrangement is worth the expense."

Arano rolled his eyes to the ceiling and gave a great sigh. "What's his name?"

He continued through the sprawling complex, eventually arriving at the computer-filled room that had been set aside for Avengers Team 5. When he entered, he noted that the rest of his team was assembled and poring over documents and photographs on the planning table, assisted by their civilian advisor.

Arano and his team tended to ignore some of the more inconvenient military formalities when no one else was around and his arrival was greeted with little more than smiles, nods, and words of welcome. Military protocol called for the soldiers in the room to rise upon his entry, but Arano and his friends were informal about those matters. As he took his place with the team, the door slid open behind him, and an official-looking Tsimian entered, his diminutive form contrasting with the large, bestial features and hawk-like beak common among the members of that race.

Arano cleared his throat to get his team's attention, and announced, "Everyone, this is Cono Vishturn. He's one of the closest advisors to Grand High Councilor Balor Tient. He will meet with us and observe as we investigate this case. Cono, I'd like to introduce everyone. Welcome to the headquarters for Avengers Team 5. I'm Captain Arano Lakeland, team commander and squad leader for Squad A. I also pilot my team's Assault Class Fighter, the USCS Specter. This is"

"Specter?" interrupted Cono. "How did you arrive at such a dreadful name?"

Arano glanced sideways at Cono, scowling at the interruption. "We enter systems unseen, and leave the same way. It seemed appropriate. The Gatoan to my left is Lieutenant Videre Genoa, of Squad A. He's our communications and computers expert."

Videre nodded in greeting, bearing his long, pointed eyeteeth when he smiled at the newcomer. Videre's short, coarse fur was a light brown that contrasted with the green of the military's duty uniforms. Even as Gatoans went, Videre was considered muscular, and his uniform struggled to contain his powerful arms.

Arano breathed an inward sigh of relief when Videre didn't make an attempt at humor. Videre was in the habit of trying to show everyone he could be funny, and occasionally did so at inappropriate times. Despite this shortcoming, he could always be counted on in a tight situation, and Arano knew of no one who could do more with computers.

"The Kamling next to Videre is Lieutenant Lain Baxter, also of Squad A," Arano continued. "He's our demolitions expert, and he also works with SIG INT. He"

"SIG INT?" cut in Cono.

"Sorry," answered Arano, reminding himself that Cono wasn't well versed in military terminology. "Signal Intelligence. He intercepts enemy messages, decodes and analyzes them. He's one of the best in his field." Lain smiled at the compliment, thin lips seeming to stretch even thinner as he absently rubbed his fingers along the single row of bumps lining his forehead, a facial feature common to the Kamling race. His deep blue eyes, set wide in his face, displayed a vast intelligence. Lain tended to be quieter than his Gatoan teammate, but still managed to surprise his friends with an occasional light-hearted jab.

"The woman to my right"

"Which woman?" asked Cono.

Videre opened his mouth to make a witty comment, but Arano quite deliberately stepped on Videre's foot to silence him.

"The Human female," sighed Arano, giving a look to Videre that spoke a thousand words, "is Captain Alyna Marquat. She's the Squad B leader and pilots her team's assault class fighter, the USCS Summerwind. She's also our leading tactician."

Alyna nodded at the praise, and Arano's heart caught in his throat when she fixed him with her beautiful smile, her brown hair pulled neatly together behind her head and her tight-fitting uniform clinging to her every move. Alyna tended to have a much more optimistic view of life than Arano did, but then, Arano thought, she hadn't seen the harsh cruelties the universe could throw at someone. Alyna was also more supportive of the United Systems Coalition's bureaucratic government than Arano, believing as long as you had the right angle on a problem, anything could be accomplished. Arano forced his mind back to his work.

"The Tompiste female to her right is Lieutenant Kish Waukee." The small, gray, leathery-skinned lieutenant approached Cono and shook his hand in greeting, her large almond-shaped eyes studying him intently as the double eyelids opened and closed rapidly. As with all members of her race, she had no hair, and her head was somewhat large in proportion to the slight frame of her body, making her appear deceptively fragile.

"She specializes in the repair of electronic equipment, and also works with communications. She has a photographic memory, so watch what you say around her. It could come back to haunt you."

Kish acknowledged the last comment with a faint smile. Most Tompiste had superb memories, the race having followed an evolutionary path emphasizing mental abilities rather than physical accomplishments, but Kish carried this tendency to an extreme. She could carry on a conversation with someone, and an hour later write down a transcript of not only her conversation, but the one going on behind her as well. The ability had proved useful during many an intelligence-gathering mission.

"And the Tsimian?" prompted Cono with an impatient wave of his furry hand.

"He's Lieutenant Pelos Marnian," replied Arano, stifling a grin. Pelos was a constant source of trouble for corrupt politicians, always digging up information on their illegal activities. One of his main targets was the Grand High Councilor, Cono's boss. As was the case with most Tsimians, Pelos was highly superstitious, although it didn't stop him from being an invaluable member of the team. He stood well over two meters tall, and was by far the physically strongest member of the team. Although his body was covered with a fine, light black fur, the muscles beneath the hairy mass rippled when he moved, giving mute testimony to the power they contained.

"He specializes in encryption and has made a serious study of the physiology, sociology, psychology, and history of the various races. He was the one who discovered Bromidians experience some disorientation from inertial nullifier fields generated aboard starships, which is one of the primary reasons we've always been able to outgun them ship to ship."

Pelos nodded in greeting to the Grand High Councilor's aide, the clicking of his fierce beak showing the irritation he felt at the perceived interruption of their work. He scratched at his fur-covered neck with a sharply-clawed hand and said nothing. Pelos' extracurricular investigations of the Grand High Councilor had made him instantly suspicious of anyone who worked in the Grand High Councilor's Office. Arano judged by the big Tsimian's scowl and his abrupt greeting that Pelos had taken an immediate dislike to Cono Vishturn. Pelos looked back to his work, obviously determined to continue his efforts despite the presence of the annoying interruption.

Cono looked puzzled. "Studies of the Bromidians? But why is that important? The war you Humans had with the Bromidians ended over a hundred years ago."

"First of all," corrected Arano testily, "that war saw the birth of the United Systems Coalition. It started as a war between the Humans and Bromidians, but expanded to include the other races. Second, just because we aren't fighting the Bromidian Empire now doesn't mean we won't fight them in the future, and there's always the Bromidian radical faction called Rising Sun to consider. And remember, the military is constantly finding information linking Rising Sun to the Bromidian government. Mark my words: within a year, we will be at war with the Bromidians once again. I, for one, am ready to wipe out the entire race." Almost as an afterthought, he added, "Besides, I'm not Human, I'm Padian."

"You Humans and Padians all look alike," complained Videre, eliciting chuckles from some of his teammates.

Arano permitted himself a brief laugh before continuing. "And of course, the Tompiste in civilian clothes is Cadron Stenat, our new advisor. With his demonstrated ability to sort through mounds of evidence and find what is relevant, he has been very helpful in making headway with this Disciple business." Cadron stared impassively at the newcomer, his gray-skinned face showing no hint of what he was thinking. He was short, even for a Tompiste, with the diminutive build common to the race. Cadron didn't possess Kish's photographic memory, but he did have a keen sense of deduction and an eye for detail. He seemed to be able to look at problems from a fresh perspective and find new resolutions that had evaded the team's previous efforts.

"All right," said Cono pompously, "let's get down to business. I'm here to study your group and evaluate your performance, because the Grand High Councilor believes we need major changes in the Avenger teams. I'm also here to decide if it's prudent to continue having a . . ." he paused, adding a disdainful sniff, ". . . civilian working so closely with a military unit."

Cadron started to reply, but Alyna coolly beat him to it. "What do you consider yourself? You certainly don't look like you have it in you to last for long in the military."

"Let there be no doubt about it," snapped Cono, "I may not be a member of the military, but I'm certainly no civilian."

"Let's move on," interrupted Arano, trying to head off the unproductive argument. "We've got a lot of work to do. Do you have any specific agenda for us, or are you just going to watch as we go on with business as usual?"

"Just do as you normally do; I'll watch and ask questions as they come up."

"Okay, what do we have on this latest Disciples killing?" Arano glanced over a compiled list of the information.

"Here's what we've got at this point," replied Cadron. "The victim was a thirty-seven-year-old Human female, killed in the usual ritualistic fashion. Her name was Pisada Casan, and she worked in Coalition Intelligence for the last seven years. No family here on Immok 2. Two nights ago she was jogging home from her fitness club when she was attacked. As usual, no witnesses. Park employees found the body the next morning."

"Pardon my ignorance," chimed in Cono, "but the news reports have been sketchy about the details of these killings. Can you fill me in?"

"They are sketchy by our design," replied Cadron. "That way, we can more easily differentiate between the real Disciple killings and the handful of copycat killings we've found. Pelos, the history of this group is more up your alley, if you could fill in the details for the good Grand High Councilor's aide."

"Certainly," replied Pelos professionally, leaning back in his seat. He paused, closed his eyes for a few moments and rubbed his face while he gathered his thoughts. "Sometime around the year 1150, Standard Human Calendar, an occult group calling themselves the Disciples of Zhulac formed on the Padian homeworld of Leguin 4. They worshipped the evil god Zhulac, who was the ruler of Martok, the Padian version of Hell. A portion of their rituals included massive quantities of Human sacrifices, which involved torture and dissection. The victim was stripped naked and tied to an altar, spread-eagle. A red-hot knife was used to carve a rune into the victim's chest. The rune was the ancient symbol used to represent Zhulac. Next, they cut out the victim's tongue and remove his eyes. It was believed once the victim died, when the victim's soul began its trek to Padian Heaven"

"Giona," corrected Arano.

"Ah, yes, thank you," said Pelos. "Once the soul of the victim began the journey to Giona, it would be unable to find its way without eyes, and unable to ask for entrance without a tongue, and would therefore be damned to Martok, the Padian version of what Humans call Hell. This served to strengthen Zhulac by increasing the number of souls he owned. Eventually, around the year 1900, the Padians had had enough of this cult, and they sent a special task force of their elite troops, the Daxia, who eliminated the cult to the last man.

"It was thought the cult had been permanently destroyed at this point. Then, in 2210 here in the city of Immok, a twenty-two-year-old Tsimian male was murdered in the same sacrificial fashion. His corpse was discovered the next morning by a jogger. The nude body was tied down spread-eagle, on its back, with a hideous symbol burned into the chest. The eyes and tongue had been removed and, according to the autopsy, it was all done while the victim was still alive. The cause of death was a virulent poison he had been forced to ingest, although his wounds were such that even without the poison he wouldn't have lived long without medical help.

"The victim, a local business owner, was just the beginning. Averaging just over one victim every three weeks, the Disciples went on a killing spree. The second victim, an unemployed Human female, was killed in the same fashion three weeks later. After the third victim, a female Kamling who worked in a high security position for the Coalition, was found, the Avengers were called in. There was some criticism of this decision, as it made it appear that the Avengers wouldn't have been called in had not one of the victims been a Coalition employee.

"Now, over two years later, there have been forty-five murders confirmed to be the responsibility of the Disciples. Our primary means of discerning real Disciple murders from the handful of copycat killings we've seen are the measurements of the rune burned into the victim's chest. Instead of using a knife, the Disciples use a metal brand in the shape of the Rune of Zhulac. The copycats can't get the measurements exactly right, so we can eliminate them from consideration in the bigger picture, and can reassign the investigation of these cases to the regular police department."

"So," remarked Cono snidely, "the vaunted

Avengers have been on the case for . . . let's see . . . the first murder was in 2210 . . . so it's been two years . . . and no suspects? You guys do need help."

"The whole reason we're able to solve most other mass murder cases is because of the patterns the killer establishes," explained Kish, her gray skin getting darker as she became aggravated.

Pelos leaned across the table, pushing aside a document he had been examining. "I've made a study of serial killings. The typical serial killer stays within one specific demographic group, meaning the victims are all the same race, the same ethnic group within that race, the same gender, and usually are similar to each other in appearance. Additionally, with the exception of gender, the demographics of the victims are usually similar to that of the killer. With this in mind, and by looking at the killer's methods of operation, we're able to get a fairly accurate psychological profile. This gives us an idea of what type of person to look for, as well as when and where the killer might strike next, eventually leading to the killer's capture.

"Not so in this case. We've seen a variety of victims who cross the demographic spectrum. We haven't been able to find even one item of similarity among the victims. In most cases, we can find something in common a church, a health spa, a place of employment. But in the case of the Disciples, the victims cross the socioeconomic spectrum, coming from all over the city of Immok. The city itself, being over two hundred kilometers across, is too large to use the location of the victims' residences as a clue.

"We've developed a theory based on the physical

evidence at the crime scenes. We believe there are at least two people involved, each having a distinctly different personality. We also believe they share a sense of bitterness toward society due to a failure in their personal lives, a failure they attribute to society at large. Because of the violence involved in the blitz-style attacks, as well as the torture common to each murder, we believe one of the subjects feels a need to show his dominance. His failure would be of a physical nature. Perhaps he was turned down for a position on some type of elite military unit. The extensive planning and preparation involved definitely point to someone with a military background.

"On the other hand, the second subject is more passive. Since the removal of the eyes is done with a certain amount of care, we believe he's had some type of medical training. He may have been a doctor and had his license revoked, or he may have been turned down for his license before his medical career even began. In either case, he's more passive, but still very dangerous.

"At any rate, after the seventh murder, I discovered references to the Disciples of Zhulac in some old history texts I was reading. That's how we figured out who these people are imitating. The fact remains there has to be an ulterior motive. There has to be a reason for a Padian cult wiped out 200 years ago to appear to resurface now on the Coalition homeworld."

"Couldn't some of the cult members have escaped from the Padian homeworld and reestablished themselves elsewhere?" asked Cono.

"Not a chance," replied Pelos confidently. "Humans developed Rift Drive engines in 2075 and gave the technology to the Padians in 2104 during the war with the Bromidians, but the cult was wiped out in 1900. There's no way they could have escaped the planet."

"Additionally," added Cadron, "we've discovered an interesting piece to this puzzle recently. I've been crunching numbers, trying to find some type of pattern. One of the more interesting items I've found is that while none of the victims were Padian, there have been a few Human victims. The reason there are no Padian victims is simple: with his danger sense, a Padian would know he's going to be attacked and could possibly thwart the attempt on his life. The question, then, is this: since it's impossible to tell a Human from a Padian without a medical exam, how could the killer be certain the intended victim is Human and not Padian?

"One obvious answer was medical records. All of the Human victims were Coalition employees, so they all had to go to the same medical facility since the Coalition regulates medical care. The killer could be a person who works in the medical office and has access to the patients' records. But the fact all are Coalition employees sets up another possibility. The killer could be someone who has access to Coalition personnel files and would therefore know the race of each intended victim."

The morning continued in much the same fashion. On more than one occasion, Arano had to draw a deep, calming breath following another of Cono's seemingly endless interruptions and personal attacks. He firmly reminded himself of the need to be civil and avoid the harsh remarks hovering on the tip of his tongue as he needed a positive recommendation from the High Councilor's aide in order to keep his team intact. The morning dragged on, and at one point Arano would have sworn the clock was running backward.

"Well," noted Arano, "it's time for lunch." He was getting closer to the point of saying something he might regret later, and knew he should break up the discussion. They were wasting valuable time explaining, for Cono's benefit, things about which his team had drawn conclusions long ago. Another perfect example of bureaucratic waste, he thought. "Alyna and I are to meet with some of the other Avenger squad leaders during lunchtime, so the rest of you are on your own. Cono, you can either come with us or join the rest of my team."

"I'll come with you," decided Cono. "I'd like more information about the Avenger teams."

The group of Avengers squad leaders sat around a narrow metal table, talking loudly among themselves to be heard over the din created by the other diners in the crowded hall. The aroma drifting from nearby tables reminded Arano of just how hungry he was.

While waiting for the food to be served, Arano and Alyna explained the history of the Avengers and the role they had played in Coalition history. Seated around them were several other Avengers team leaders, including Lon Pana, a longtime friend of the members of Team 5. He was a tall, thin Human with a mischievous smile continually playing around his lips. His blond hair was thinning on top, which he attributed to too many years of keeping an eye on Arano. Lon and Arano went way back, and frequently helped each other out on missions. And when the work day was over, it wasn't uncommon to see the two of them out finding some sort of entertainment together.

"Originally," Arano explained, "we were called Special Operations. That's a polite way of saying that on every mission you'll be outmanned and outgunned, but you're expected to succeed. Following the Bromidians' biological attack on Earth, we were renamed the 'Avengers' in memory of the billions of people who lost their lives."

"You say 'we' as if you were there," said Cono. "That is conceited, don't you think?"

"It's called esprit d'corps," replied Alyna, setting down her cup rather abruptly. "It helps keep morale up by building unit pride. When one Avenger completes a successful mission, we all share in the victory." Arano glanced at Alyna, noting by her pursed lips that her patience with Cono was wearing thin as quickly as his own.

Cono looked away, distracted by a commotion near the door. Arano took advantage of the respite and gave Alyna a sympathetic look, smiling at her when she rolled her eyes in resignation.

"Anyway," Arano continued, "once the Humans became established in the Subac system, set up Subac 3 Prime as their new homeworld, and built a new shipyard, they went on the offensive. Most of their fleet was out killing Bromidians, although some had to stay behind and protect Subac 3 Prime, or Sol as it came to be called. Despite massive Bromidian casualties, the supply of Bromidian warships seemed inexhaustible. Avenger teams were sent out in secret to find the Bromidian shipyards and try to locate the Bromidian homeworld. One of our teams found both in the Rystoria system. When the final Coalition attack on Rystoria came, that same Avengers team stayed on the ground on Rystoria 2 staging hit-and-run attacks on Bromidian command and control centers. It was that team's successful attack on a ground-based planetary defense system that enabled the Coalition fleet to punch a hole in the Bromidian defense grid and land several brigades of ground troops. That landing cost the Bromidians their planetary defense system, effectively ending the war when their ships lost the covering fire from the planet's surface. That one Avengers team set the standard for all Avengers to come. The surviving members of the team were the first to receive the Coalition Star of Courage, our highest award."

"So how is it this great military Special Forces group finds itself investigating murders in the civilian world?" asked Cono.

"You should know the answer to that," chided Alyna. She poured herself another glass of water, her distraction over the presence of the Grand High Councilor's aide obvious when she spilled water on the table. "It was your boss, the Grand High Councilor, who cut military and police funding so drastically it forced the government to assign us double duties in order to save money. We're now used as a sort of major case squad. Since intelligence gathering is right up our alley, they figured we should be able to help solve crimes. On top of that, we have to help with the investigation every time some terrorist from Event Horizon so much as sends a letter to the media going off on some diatribe about their anti-Coalition, anarchist ideas. And don't get me started about what happens when Event Horizon actually plants a bomb. We're stretched a bit thin."

Cono shrugged nonchalantly. "Sometimes cuts have to be made."

As the conversation continued, Arano cast more frequent glances at his watch. The single hour spent on lunch seemed to be dragging on for an eternity. His disapproval of the uppity Cono was mirrored in the scarcely concealed scowls on the faces of the other Avengers at the table. He furrowed his eyebrows and gave a barely perceptible shake of his head, thinking to himself how unlikely it was Cono had ever accomplished anything of worth himself. He found it much more likely Cono tended to ride the coattails of others who had been doing the real work. It was with some measure of relief Arano pushed away from the lunch table.

They returned to Avengers Team 5 Headquarters and continued poring over the mounds of data on the Zhulac cases. Soon the door to their meeting room opened to admit a sharply dressed Human officer bearing the rank of major. His large frame seemed to strain the buttons on his jacket when he walked, and the cluster of medals on his chest bore evidence this was an experienced combat soldier. His clean-shaven head gleamed under the room's bright lights, providing a perfect counterpart to the glisten of his well-polished shoes. Cadron stood respectfully at attention, and all six Avengers immediately stood and saluted smartly. The newcomer returned the salute crisply and said, "Carry on. How's it going in here?"

"Major Alstor," greeted Alyna, taking her seat. "Just reviewing our data right now. Have you met the Grand High Councilor's aide, Cono?"

Major Alstor came forward briskly, and Arano could see the veteran's instincts quickly assessing the conceited Tompiste in front of him. Arano and the Major had been together for Arano's entire career, and in fact had spent a good deal of time serving on the same teams together. The times of combat they'd shared had brought them together, and the two had become close friends. Major Alstor tended to reject military formalities as quickly as Arano did, but when outsiders were around he felt obligated to put on a show of following the proper procedures.

"No, I haven't," Major Alstor answered, extending his hand in greeting. "Major Laron Alstor, Team Commander for Avengers teams 4 through 6."

"Cono Vishturn," replied Cono, taking Laron's hand. "I'm here to observe your procedures and see if it's advisable for you to continue with a civilian consultant attached to this team."

"Well," replied Laron, "you'll get your chance to see them in action."

"They have a mission?" he asked. Cono's eyes came alight with curiosity.

"That's affirmative, sir. The Avengers teams are frequently used as opposing forces for the conventional ground warfare units. For today's mission, this team is supposed to hold a ridgeline against an infantry platoon that's on a mission to secure the area."

"What's the scenario on this one, sir?" asked Arano.

"Your team will be inserted into Area J by parachute. You're playing the part of insurgents who are attempting to commit acts of sabotage and guerrilla warfare against a Coalition stronghold and highway supply line. Coalition forces will spot you parachuting into the area and will send a patrol to find you. Your equipment has been loaded onto your transport ship. Cono, since you're not parachute qualified, if you wish to observe the mission we'll have to drive you out there in a land vehicle. Let's move out, people. Wheels up in two hours."

Laron left the room, and the Avengers began their preparations. Documents on the Disciples of Zhulac were packed away neatly, and battle gear was gathered into packs the team carried.

"What did he mean, 'wheels up'?" asked Cono.

"It's an old expression from the early days of airborne units," commented Pelos as he gathered a few small items he wanted to bring with him. "The transports they jumped from were required to have wheels, because they had to attain a certain ground speed before they became airborne. Although we no longer use those types of craft, the expression has stuck around. It's sort of a tradition."

For the first time since Arano had met him, Cono smiled. "Esprit d'corps?"

"Exactly," replied Pelos.

Arano and Alyna surveyed the area surrounding their intended defensive perimeter. They prowled silently through the woodlands, noting places of interest such as "dead spaces", those areas direct fire can't reach due to terrain conditions.

As they walked along, Arano glanced over at Alyna. Though she had been on the team only a few short months, she had already proven a valuable asset. She knew the tactical side of the job inside and out, and she always seemed to have an angle on whatever problems cropped up. She was extremely enthusiastic and, unlike Arano, had great confidence in the bureaucratic policies of the Coalition. He also found her physically attractive, another advantage she had learned how to flaunt, flirting outrageously with Human and Padian males to gain information, information they might not have revealed under other circumstances.

Finally, Arano was forced to admit this last facet, her physical beauty, stirred feelings in him he had not felt since the death of his fiancé during the invasion of his homeworld by members of Rising Sun eight years before. Since then, he had been consumed by hatred of all Bromidians. Arano had always been cynical about bureaucracy, but that hadn't stopped him from accepting then-Captain Alstor's invitation to join the Coalition military, and ultimately the Avengers.

The pair finished their sweep and returned to the others, where they finalized a plan of operations. Arano would simulate the guerrilla warfare tactics for the scenario by taking his squad on a scouting mission to watch the enemy's likely avenue of approach and staging hit and run attacks to keep them off balance. In what he felt might be a vain attempt to head off more questions from Cono, Arano explained the whole procedure. "Both sides will use weapons set for stun only. If the shooting starts near you, you might want to stay down. Getting stunned is a little uncomfortable.

"At any rate, I'll take my squad on ahead, while Alyna's squad sets up in a defense here. You'll notice we're high up on this ridge, giving us the advantage of higher terrain, but we're not far enough up to be silhouetted against the skyline. There are also enough trees to give us a moderate amount of overhead cover. We've set up a five-point contingency plan between the two squads. This plan covers the majority of incidents that could arise during the mission: where my group is going; when we will return; what Alyna's squad should do if we don't return; what each squad should do if my squad gets hit; and what each squad should do if Alyna's squad gets hit. That way there's less guesswork and improvisation later if things go wrong.

"We've established a system of challenges and passwords as a means of recognition when we return, a running password in case we come in with the enemy hot on our trail, and even a far recognition system in case we're spotted at a range beyond convenient verbal communication. My squad is leaving now; you'll be staying here with Squad B. We'll return in approximately three hours." Without waiting to answer the questions he knew Cono would have, he shouldered his pack and moved out, Videre and Lain in formation with him. As they stealthily picked their way down the hill, Arano heard Videre chuckling softly as Cono's interrogation of Alyna began.

The terrain was fairly hilly, interspersed at regular intervals with small creeks that gurgled noisily along their well-worn paths. The trees, a tall, thin variety, were spaced far enough apart they could move between them easily, but close enough together to obstruct Arano's line of sight. He led his team for a short while until Lain, keeping the pace count, indicated they'd traveled as far as was needed. Putting away his compass, Arano motioned his squad to take a knee. He edged off into the treeline in the gathering darkness, shielding his eyes from the glaring red rays of the setting sun. All around him, Arano heard the sounds of birds singing and the whisper of the wind in the trees.

After traveling a short distance, he located the rock pile Alyna had pointed out during their earlier leaders' reconnaissance. He moved back within sight of his squad and indicated for them to follow. They reached the large pile of man-sized rocks and immediately took up positions. There was a streambed about a hundred meters downhill from their position, which the enemy forces would likely "shadow" as a means of keeping their direction. Since the terrain on the far side of the creek was much rougher and covered with springy thorn bushes, Arano felt this was the most likely route the enemy would follow.

After putting his squad members into position, Arano moved further up the hill and into the direction of travel expected from the enemy. From there, he could provide some measure of cover for his squad.

Once Videre and Lain opened fire on the platoon's lead elements, the rear was likely to try a flanking maneuver. Since the creek was downhill and too open, they would likely come up the hill a short distance. After they were settled in, Arano would hit them from behind. His squad would pull out, occasionally stopping to fire at the advancing forces to keep them cautious. At a set time, the squad would cease fire and rendezvous at their rally point for the return trip to meet up with the rest of their team.

Settling into position, Arano surveyed the area. Although he didn't expect to see the enemy for another hour, he began his vigil. He was amazed at the resemblance between this area of Immok 2 and the forests where he grew up on Leguin 4. As he sat in silence, his thoughts drifted back to his home

For three long days, Arano maintained his positioned on that small rock formation, watching the town square as Erlinia continued her slow march to oblivion. She continued to waste away as dehydration took its deadly toll. The part of Arano's heart that refused to accept defeat continued to believe her captors would decide she was worth more alive than dead, and would therefore not allow her to perish. At times, hope gave way to despair, and he found himself praying to the Four Elementals she might have a swift, painless death, but such was not to be.

He watched as the remainder of the prisoners from Giona were summarily executed, their bodies left lying in neat, orderly rows, a warning to all who might oppose Rising Sun. If the deaths no, Arano corrected himself the murders of these people had been intended to stop the Padian insurrection, then it had been a miserable failure. The ranks of Arano's force were now growing by the hour, as outraged citizens who had previously thought to wait out the situation saw the peril facing them all.

Rising Sun's treatment of Erlinia had also backfired. Apparently, their leaders believed by threatening her life they could force Arano's surrender. Arano didn't believe for a moment his arrest would save Erlinia's life; on the contrary, he believed she would be murdered in front of him, just prior to his own death. Any rescue attempt would be equally foolhardy, as evidenced by the almost aggressive lack of security around Erlinia. Without a doubt, there were hidden Bromidian forces waiting for anyone foolish enough to try to save her.

Late on the evening of the third day of Erlinia's confinement, Arano realized her time was near. Her face, which had been a flushed, ruddy hue, slowly changed to a grayish pallor Arano knew could mean but one thing. He stared at her face for those final minutes, fixing her beloved features in his memory and fueling his fires of hatred. Her head, which had sagged against her chest, slowly raised to stare blankly out at the surrounding hills, almost subconsciously facing the spot where she and Arano had spent so many happy times. It seemed to Arano she was looking straight at him as her heart struggled with its final beats. She mouthed the words, "I love you," then her body sagged limply against the restraints.

Arano gave a howl of pain and loss, his hands clenched into tight fists and pressed against his forehead. Moments later, after a lone Rising Sun soldier had checked Erlinia's body, Arano saw a full platoon of Bromidians emerge from surrounding buildings to converge in the square. He raised his sniper rifle, his blood boiling with rage as he sighted in on his first target.

As Cono's questions to Alyna continued unabated, Pelos groaned inwardly and began pulling the burrs from his fur, trying desperately to shut out the droning voice. Using his thumb and forefinger, he made the Tsimian sign for good luck and mentally prepared himself for the upcoming battle. Whether the combat he was facing was real or simulated, Pelos always tried to put himself into the live combat mindset. A slogan he lived by was, "You perform as you practice." If you slacked off during training, there was no way you could be fully prepared for actual combat, and that was a good way to get yourself or your teammates killed.

"I assume that you Avengers find some advantage in those obsolete projectile weapons," Cono continued, "even though laser weapons are lighter and fire faster"

"Laser weapons are generally better, but there are no absolutes," Alyna replied. "Everything depends upon the specifics of each situation. A hand-held laser rifle is effective only out to about 400 meters. I've seen Arano use a sniper rifle to shoot his target from three times that range. We still use laser technology, but we don't automatically abandon all else in favor of it."

"Is that why Arano has become such a widely sought consultant among Coalition military commanders? There are other Avengers with more time on the job and more combat experience."

"They really didn't tell you anything about us, did they? He's a Daxia. And before you ask, the Daxia are members of an elite Padian military organization. Their trainees go through several years of intensive training, becoming spies and assassins for the Padian government. No one in their right mind crosses one of the Daxia."

Kish snapped her fingers, held up her hand for silence, and listened to her FM radio through the earpiece. "Captain Lakeland says his squad has made initial contact and is preparing to pull back." Kish paused, then laughed. "Affirmative, out," she said into the radio. She turned back to the others. "Captain Lakeland also reports the enemy forces have already lost almost half of their platoon. They tried a flanking maneuver and walked right into the trap you guys set up."

"Why do you continue to use that antiquated FM radio when there have been portable subspace radios available for years?" Cono interrupted again.

"Because subspace radios that are portable have no encryption on their signal, and have a range of only about five clicks .. sorry, Cono, kilometers," said Alyna. "The reason we can use portable subspace radios to communicate over longer ranges is because our ships are all equipped with repeaters which boost and rebroadcast subspace signals. Also, although the planets with major settlements have a grid of repeater towers covering the settlements and the surrounding areas, we often get out of the range of the towers. We train with FM radios because we never know if we'll have access to a repeater, and because we can encrypt the signal with the FM. The drawback is that FM radios are limited to the speed of light, making interstellar FM communication impractical.

"Look, the time for the battle is getting close. They may have scouts in the area at any time. We need silence until this thing is over." Alyna noticed the thankful looks from her teammates, and gave them a quick wink before turning to study the surroundings.

Down in the valley, she saw the top of a tree shake gently back and forth, despite the lack of a strong breeze. Then another tree shook, and still another. The disturbance, about 500 meters away, seemed to be headed in the direction of her position. She gave a low whistle to Pelos, who had also noticed the disturbances. He nodded, then moved slowly down the hill, flanking whoever was moving toward them. After a few minutes he returned, carrying an unconscious Human soldier over one massive, furry shoulder. "Got him with a stun stick," he noted. "He never saw it coming. I think he was looking for our tracks, because he was looking down. He forgot to look up."

Arano ran silently down a hill to his rally point and was relieved to see two members of his squad had made it there safely. Although this was just a drill, he still took it as a personal failure if someone in his squad didn't make it through a mission. He had run over two kilometers through the sparse undergrowth, agilely leaping over fallen branches, and was only now winded. Although the terrain was uneven, he managed a swift pace without any mishaps or undue noise.

Lain and Videre, seeing Arano's approach, shouldered their gear and moved out with him, Arano having slowed his pace to a brisk walk. "Good job, men," he told them. He knew some Avengers thought it odd he always gave compliments to soldiers under his command after successful action, but Arano knew it was just as important to tell people they'd done something right as it was to tell them when they'd done something wrong. Consequently, morale in his teams had always been high. Arano retrieved his compass and navigated their path back to the others.

"Subspace radio message coming in," announced Videre. "Training mission is terminated. We're to report to headquarters ASAP. We have an emergency."

Arano nodded, checked his map, and adjusted their course to bring them back to the transports.

CHAPTER TWO

ARANO AND CADRON ENTERED THE AVENGERS Team 5 planning room. The din immediately quieted down while everyone took their seats. Arano moved deliberately around the long table, taking his customary place at the far end. He briefly looked over his scribbled page of notes, ignoring the hum of the computers and monitors surrounding him, then looked up at his teammates.

"Here's the situation," he told them. "According to new intelligence, Rising Sun is going to meet with a Coalition traitor on Codian 3 who has been selling them critical data on our defense systems. We can't just send a task force because too many ships will chase them off. Avengers Command has been instructed to eliminate this traitor, and our team has been selected for the mission. We'll parachute onto the planet's surface from a meteorological survey ship, eliminate patrols we encounter, and I will take him out." He hesitated. "The traitor is General Handron from Immok Defense Command." He tossed his pen onto the table with an angry snap of his wrist, feeling the rage and sense of betrayal boiling within him.

The room was filled with the heated protestations of his teammates, and Videre slammed a furry fist on the table in frustration.

"Even if you do manage to kill the general," Cadron said slowly, his leathery face crinkled in concentration, "won't Rising Sun still be able to obtain the data he's going to be bringing?"

Arano shook his head with a smile. "The Galactic Bureau of Intelligence provided him with false data once they suspected him. The information he's selling this time is false."

A short time later, they'd laid out a tentative plan. A satellite surveillance map had been overlayed with their airborne insertion point, target location, and other points of interest. Codian 3 had only one major landmass which allowed severe weather conditions to build almost every night. For this reason, the survey ships flew only during daytime hours since their sensors would be reduced in efficiency by the heavy cloud cover. This required the Avengers to go in during the daytime. Complicating matters, according to intelligence reports, Rising Sun frequently used the region as a meeting place, indicating a high likelihood of encountering regular patrols.

Arano pointed to an area of the map. "We'll have to eliminate these guards here"

"Why must you kill them?" asked Cono. "They have technically done no wrong, and you're planning to sneak up on them and murder them in cold blood. Why can't you find other means? Captain Tient of Team 1 always manages to keep from inflicting many casualties."

"Yes," snapped Arano, "I'm quite aware of the record the Grand High Councilor's daughter has achieved. She uses stun weapons on guards and patrols rather than more lethal methods. Consequently, she's leaving live enemies behind her. These enemies have to wake up sometime. In the last two years, she has managed to get more Avengers killed than half the other teams combined. She also has the highest mission failure rate in the history of the Avengers. Her team has the lowest morale and the highest turnover rate."

Arano thrust a finger at Cono. "My methods are just that: mine. My job is to complete the mission and bring my entire team home alive. If it means someone on the other side has to die, then, by the Four Elementals, they will die."

Cono shrank back under Arano's onslaught, and looked like he might run out of the room when Cadron intervened.

"Point taken," he said. "We've worked out the generalities here. You can finalize while you're enroute. Alyna, what is your ETA at Codian 3?"

Alyna tapped a few buttons on her computer. "Forty minutes to clear Immok's gravity well, approximately fifteen hours in the wormhole, another fifty minutes to arrive at the planet. Approximately sixteen and a half hours. We're going in a civilian craft, so we have to be further from the planet's gravity well before the Rift Drive engines can open a wormhole, and we have to exit the wormhole farther from our destination."

Cono's eyes narrowed, and his beak opened slightly as his face took on a perplexed expression. "I guess no one briefed you about military Rift Drives," Arano told him. "A Rift Drive is actually capable of operating in higher gravity than what most people believe. The Coalition's Council on the Environment decided even though there was no evidence of environmental damage from Rift Drives, just the possibility was enough to regulate where a Rift Drive can be activated. Military engines are exempt. Unfortunately, just with civilian craft, we still have to deactivate our shields before entering a wormhole." Arano let out a silent sigh of relief when Cono nodded in understanding without adding any further questions.

The meeting broke up, and Arano's teammates prepared for departure. Equipment, gathered from various lockers within their planning room, piled up around the table. Arano scowled when he noticed Cono gathering his notes into his briefcase, looking for all the world as if he intended to go with the Avengers. "Sorry, Cono," Arano informed him. "This is a real mission, so I can't allow you to come along. We will contact you upon our return." Cono nodded, apparently cowed into submission by Arano's earlier tirade. From behind Cono, Alyna winked at Arano in gratitude.

In less than thirty minutes, Arano's combat-ready soldiers bumped along on a troop transport, their Assault Class Fighters sitting prepped and ready in the distance. Arano looked around at his teammates, a sense of pride swelling in his chest at being a part of this elite unit. Alyna was double-checking her power packs, ensuring they were fully charged. Videre was leaning back in his seat, eyes closed. Arano knew even without looking that Pelos was running through his battle rituals to bring them luck and success. Kish and Lain chatted quietly together, their voices lost in the rush of the wind.

Lain nudged Arano's foot. "Hey, Viper! Thanks for dumping Cono. He was getting to the point where I was going to have to strangle him."

"I could bring him back," Arano offered with a sly grin.

"Don't you dare," Alyna warned him, checking her hair was securely tied back. "I've had enough of him to last me a lifetime."

"Yeah," agreed Videre. "At least we can relax military protocols while he isn't here. No offense, my omniscient captains, but 'Viper' and 'Alyna' flow so much easier than 'Captain So-and-so'. I was getting tongue-tied."

"Ten minutes to drop point," intoned the ship's jump computer. The cargo bay doors ground noisily open to display a panoramic view of Codian 3 as it passed serenely beneath them. Away to the West, deceptively passive-looking clouds gathered in anticipation of the coming storm. The forested patches of dense green on the planet's surface contrasted sharply with the deep blue of the nearby sea. Arano found it somewhat disconcerting to see the thriving trees below them, but to smell only the stale odor of the various compounds keeping their ship's ion engines running. The six Avengers paired off and checked each other's equipment, then paired up with another and checked again.

"One minute to drop point," announced the computer.

Arano gave a vicious grin. "Okay, Lain. Take up the first jump position and prepare to jump on my mark." The Avengers lined up, one behind the other, and waited while the computer's countdown continued. Arano glanced around at his teammates, absently noting Pelos was going through his pre-jump good luck ritual. He glanced over at Kish Waukee and saw that, as he had expected, Kish was calmly awaiting the signal to jump. As a people, the Tompiste had abandoned all forms of religion generations before and felt no need for prayer or superstitious rituals. She made an interesting contrast to her squadmate, Pelos, who seemed to have a superstition for just about everything.

The computer indicated they'd reached the jump window, and on Arano's signal Lain stepped out of the ship, his reptilian form falling toward the planet far below. Arano did likewise, stepping out into the void and feeling his stomach lurch as gravity's inexorable pull took hold. His adrenaline soared as he felt the wind roaring by, and he exulted in the freedom of the air.

Spotting Lain below him, he guided his falling body in Lain's direction. The other members of the team eventually joined them. Arano checked his altimeter and saw they still had some time before they needed to deploy their parachutes. He spun around, taking note of the location of some of the more prominent land features on Codian 3. For the most part, the landscape was covered with a seemingly endless forest, broken here and there by an occasional clearing.

Sparkling rivers wound their way through the trees, one leading away from an enormous lake. Arano used the lake as a landmark and spun to find their intended landing area.

He turned again and came face to face with Alyna. It was a sight he knew he would remember forever: Alyna's perfect face framed against the horizon with the sun setting behind her, her long brown hair streaming out from under her helmet, her eyes fixing his with a look that nearly stopped his heart. His sense of regret was almost palpable when he heard the altimeter beep its warning, and the team members separated to deploy their parachutes. He felt that familiar momentary sense of vertigo when the parachute slowed his descent from the howling winds of terminal velocity to the absolute silence of a barely noticeable drift in a matter of seconds. They floated almost imperceptibly down to an uneventful landing.

On the ground, they assembled rapidly and concealed their parachutes. After a quick equipment check, they were ready to begin. Arano moved over to Lieutenant Waukee. "Kish, you have the point. Heading is one-one-two. I'll keep the pace." Turning to the others, he whispered, "Let's move."

They moved out at a cautious pace. They had about thirty kilometers to cover in about ten hours. They hadn't wanted to jump in any closer to their objective; to have done so risked detection by the sentries. Arano found himself wishing they could have jumped in at night, but with the survey ships flying almost exclusively on the daylight side of Codian 3 jumping in at night would've drawn unwanted attention. They walked on in the growing darkness, their eyes adjusting to the conditions and allowing them to see the gigantic trees of the primeval forest that covered the planet's landmass.

Soon, the sound of distant thunder came to Arano's ears as the storm he was expecting drew nearer. The enormous ocean covering this still-developing planet produced some violent storms, but the Avengers counted on that to keep enemy patrols to a minimum. First, a strong, chilling wind began to blow, and Arano correctly assumed they were within the storm's gust front, and the more violent part of the storm wasn't far behind. The rains came as a slow drizzle at first, but soon became a deluge drenching them to the bone. Deafening cracks of thunder echoed through the trees, and sporadic flashes of lightning lit the skies, ruining their night vision. They walked through the downpour for two hours until Arano called their first halt. He and Alyna checked on their squad members, then consulted on their location.

As they continued on their way, the night seemed to have no end, just near-complete darkness and perpetual rain. The wind howled through the trees, adding to the din of the storm. Arano's cold, clammy uniform, dripping water, clung to his every move, doing nothing to ward off the storm's chill air. After hours of marching, they arrived at the last checkpoint before their final position.

The rain had slowed to a mere sprinkle when they called a halt. Arano nodded to Alyna, then slipped on silent feet from the group. He moved cautiously forward, immediately spotting two Bromidians on patrol leaning casually against a tree, the bipedal insect-like bodies creating an immediate and overwhelming sense of hatred within Arano's heart.

He couldn't use an energy weapon to kill the guards; the Bromidians in the valley below might detect the weapon's energy signature. He edged gradually closer until he could hear the hissing and clacking noises of their guttural language. He briefly thought of sending for another member of his team but decided against it. He positioned himself as near as he dared, then charged. When the two Bromidians looked up, Arano's hunting knife took one of them full in the throat. While his first victim dropped gurgling to the ground, Arano leapt onto the second Bromidian, his momentum knocking the sentry down. Before the surprised guard could call out, Arano's hands closed firmly about the insectoid neck, his grip tightening inexorably until the Bromidian stopped struggling. He kept the stranglehold in place for another minute to ensure the guard was dead, and retrieved his knife. He checked the area but found no other Bromidians, then called his team forward and they set up a base camp. As soon as the camp was established, he called everyone in for a meeting.

"Okay," he began, "here is what we'll do. Alyna is going to go with me to that outcropping of rock. I'm going to take my shot from there, and she will be my spotter.

"Lain, Videre, I want you two covering our left flank," he continued, indicating the area off to the south. He turned and pointed northward. "Kish, Pelos, you have our right flank."

As his team took up their positions, Arano considered their tactical situation. We'll have several advantages here, he thought. The sun would come up behind his team, making them harder to see. Also, the Bromidians were in a valley, causing the sound of the sniper rifle to echo, confusing efforts to locate the source of the shot. Arano believed his best advantage was the thicker atmosphere. Bromidians were used to the thinner atmosphere on Rystoria 2. In this atmosphere, sound traveled so much faster than it did on Rystoria 2 they wouldn't be able to determine the direction of the sound with any certainty. It was similar to being underwater, he reminded himself. Sounds were heard over a long distance, but the direction of the source couldn't be determined.

"Okay, let's do it. The meeting should begin in a little over an hour. Standard signals and procedures, and we all know the rally points. Let's make it happen."

No further words were necessary as skills and training took over. While the four lieutenants took up their flanking positions, Arano and Alyna moved forward to a small rock outcropping which afforded an excellent view of the fertile valley where the meeting was to take place. Although he couldn't see it from his vantage point, Arano instinctively knew a river wound its way through the lush green bottoms before them. While Alyna changed into dry clothes, Arano sighted his rifle in on different objects in the valley. Satisfied, he waited until Alyna was ready, then, following her example, switched to a dry set of combat fatigues.

As the sun slowly brightened the morning sky, a Bromidian transport arrived on a low approach pattern, settling into a field about a kilometer from Arano's position. Several Bromidian soldiers quickly disembarked, each wearing the distinctive logo and uniform identifying them as members of the Rising Sun faction, a group bent on the destruction of the Coalition. Arano briefly sighted in on each Bromidian, looking for high-ranking officers as a target of opportunity should the traitorous Coalition general fail to show. Next to him, he felt Alyna stiffen and draw in a sharp breath when she peered through her spotter's scope.

"Viper," she whispered excitedly, "look on the ramp to their ship. It's General Dralak, from the Bromidian High Command. Isn't he with their intelligence bureau?"

His heart suddenly racing, Arano swung the rifle around to the ship, and spotted the general. "That's him. More proof of the collusion between Rising Sun and the regular Bromidian army. Alyna, I could kiss you!"

Alyna gave a wicked laugh. "What do we do now? We don't have any video recording equipment."

"Don't worry," he assured her. "I'll take care of it."

"What are you going to do?"

"I don't want to spoil the surprise. Call it a birthday present. Happy birthday, by the way. I owe you dinner when we get back."

Alyna smiled at that. "Oh, really?"

"Yep. It's something of a tradition on our team, which goes back . . . about . . . well, I guess you're the first. I still owe you."

Alyna laughed again, and they turned back to wait

for the arrival of the general's ship.

The morning continued to slip past, and the day grew hotter. The dampness left behind by the previous night's rainfall evaporated, and the resulting humidity made the air noticeably uncomfortable. Remarkably, Arano noted a decided lack of biting insects in the air. Judging by the frequent glances the Bromidians cast at their watches, Arano guessed the General was late for the appointment. He cursed under his breath, hoping the long trek through the rain had not been in vain.

As noon came and went, Arano began to get nervous. He knew the time for the meeting was long past, and he figured the Bromidians would soon leave the area. If he was going to shoot the alternate target, he needed to do it soon, but as soon as that shot was taken, the chances of seeing General Handron would be nil. He glanced again at the Bromidian ship and saw General Dralak emerging with an aide. They spoke briefly with another soldier who stood nearby, then all turned and faced west.

Alyna looked over at Arano and saw him sighting the rifle on General Dralak. "You thinking of taking that shot instead?" she asked.

"Possibly. But I have a feeling they just got word Handron is inbound from the West. I'm going to wait a little longer."

A few minutes later, he was rewarded by the arrival of a new ship. It settled in near the first ship, and its ramp opened to allow a Human to exit. Arano looked through the rifle's scope and saw it was indeed General Handron emerging from the newly arrived craft. He was met halfway between the two crafts by General Dralak, and the men shook hands before beginning their conversation. Arano checked for effects the wind had on trees, bushes, and the loose-fitting garments worn by the soldiers in the area. He made a few final adjustments on his scope, then indicated to Alyna he was ready.

Alyna zoomed her scope in on the wayward general and waited. She found she was actually holding her breath and forced herself to relax. She heard Arano's breathing become regular and smooth, and knew the time was at hand.

Even though she was prepared for the shot, she still jumped when the rifle cracked with a loud report. There was a ringing in her ears as she looked back through her scope in time to see General Handron drop lifelessly to the ground, half of his head missing from the impact of Arano's shot. The Bromidians around him stood dumbfounded for a moment, then dropped into a defensive crouch and looked desperately around, hands on their weapons. Alyna was about to congratulate Arano on the shot when the rifle fired again. She looked out into the field once more and saw General Dralak lying on the ground, as dead as General Handron.

"You got them both!" she exclaimed breathlessly.

Arano gave her a quick grin without looking away from his scope. "I'm not done yet," he announced. As the Bromidians scurried about looking for cover, Arano fired off three more shots before stopping to reload, and Alyna informed him one more Bromidian was down. Arano reloaded, and looked as if he would continue firing. Alyna laid a restraining hand on his shoulder.

"We have to go," she told him. Arano turned his hate-filled eyes from the scene below, and she saw the anger slowly drain away. Without a word, he rose to his feet and moved off. Alyna followed him, the look on his face still embedded firmly in her memory. In the back of her mind, she was glad she wasn't a Bromidian.

The Broms were still in a state of confusion, but it wouldn't last. Alyna knew they needed to leave the area in a hurry. As the other four Avengers gathered around and fell in, Arano checked his compass and confidently moved toward their first rally point, having established Videre as the point man.

They'd gone barely a kilometer when they encountered their first resistance. Word of the assassinations had apparently been passed over the Bromidians' Comms, so the patrols were actively looking for them. They topped a small hill and saw Videre waiting for them, crouched behind a tree. Videre held up a fist, indicating for the others to stop, then held up four fingers and pointed in their direction of travel. Arano saw nothing at first, although as soon as he moved up for a better view, his danger sense warned him something was out there. Alyna moved to his side and pointed out the Bromidian patrol.

"What do you think, Alyna?" he asked her. "Do we go around them or through them?"

"There probably aren't any other patrols close enough to cause a problem if we go through them," she offered, brushing at a lock of brown hair that had somehow escaped her efforts to keep it pinned back. "But I don't know . . . something about these guys being right on our chosen escape route, and being here ahead of us, just doesn't sit right with me."

"I agree. I've got a funny feeling there's something else going on here."

"Danger sense?"

"No, that won't tell me anything unless I actually start a course of action. Just thinking about it doesn't set off the danger sense since I'm not actually in any danger. This is just intuition." He let out a long breath, nodded, and motioned to his team. "Let's go around them."

The group moved out cautiously, flanking the unsuspecting patrol and moving off into the forest. Once they were well out of earshot, they moved more quickly, confident they'd left the Bromidian patrols floundering around behind them. Arano frequently cast glances at both his map and his compass to reassure himself they were still on course. They weren't going to be at the rendezvous point for the initial pickup, but if they didn't waste time they could make the second time window. The more he thought about it, the more he became concerned their mission wasn't as secret as they'd hoped. The part confounding him most was the fact he had been able to accomplish his objective almost without opposition. If someone had leaked the plan to the Bromidians, why hadn't they stopped him from killing the two generals? In fact, why would General Dralak have presented himself as a target at all? Shaking his head, he forced his thoughts back to the task at hand: getting his team off the planet.

Arano eventually called a halt and put his team into a defensive perimeter. He called Pelos over to him. "I want you to check the rendezvous point. We're about a click due south of it right now. If you head north, you should come out on a ridgeline at the edge of the trees. From there, you should be able to scout the area and make sure we don't have any more surprises waiting for us."

"Yes, sir," came the stoic reply from the always-serious lieutenant. He disappeared into the surrounding trees while Arano and Alyna tried to work out a plan of action in case there were more Bromidians in the area. Soon, Pelos returned with a look of towering rage etched on his bestial Tsimian features. Settling to the ground next to Arano and Alyna, he filled them in.

"The area is heavily patrolled. I got close enough to hear some of them talking. They were wondering where we were since this was supposed to be our pickup point. It appears someone briefed them on our mission, although they didn't get the information in time to stop us. I was able to see four groups of three-man patrols, but there are probably more. The area is pretty well covered. We could maybe sneak in, but we'd be discovered if we tried to signal our transport."

"Thanks, Pelos," Arano responded. "Good work. Go ahead and take up your position while Alyna and I work this out."

As Pelos moved away, Arano turned to Alyna. "I don't like this. We have to make the rendezvous window. This stretch of the woods is beginning to get a little too crowded, and it will probably get even worse." He paused and closed his eyes, considering his options. "The Bromidians are expecting us to try sneaking past them, so I believe we need to do the opposite. When we're just a few minutes out from the transport's next pass, let's signal them from here. We can hold this position and fend the Broms off until help arrives."

"I agree," she said. "As rocky as this ground is, we have great cover. We can use the higher ground as a fallback position, if we need to."

They passed the plan to their squad members. Almost an hour later, Kish activated the beacon which broadcast the signal that would call the transport to pick them up. It wasn't long before the first Bromidians came into view. A quick shot from Lain proved deadly for one of the Bromidians, who screamed and fell twitching to the ground. As more Bromidians streamed into the area, they fell into a murderous crossfire. The Avengers' positions had been carefully picked, preventing the Bromidians from sweeping through the area. Instead, they were forced to crawl forward, relying upon the cover fire provided by their comrades.

From high atop the battlefield, Arano peered down between the enormous branches of a towering tree, watching the approach of the Bromidians and feeling the familiar hatred begin to boil. The feeling had become so common to him he scarcely paid attention to it. He braced his sniper rifle on a man-sized branch, took careful aim, and fired. Seeing his target collapse in a writhing heap, he selected another Bromidian and fired, then another, and yet another. The radio on his hip squawked, and he heard Alyna's voice. "Viper, there are too many of them now. We have to fall back to our secondary positions."

"Right," he answered. "I'm coming down." He gathered his gear and started to descend, but stopped when he felt a twinge from his danger sense. Looking out to the west, his heart dropped to his toes when he saw at least a hundred Bromidians moving tactically toward his position.

"Alyna," he called into the radio, "hold what you've got! At least three platoons coming up from your rear! I'll try to provide cover! Where in the Hell is that transport?"

"If they don't get here soon," she responded, "they won't need to come at all."

Arano feverishly fired his sniper rifle, almost every shot claiming a Bromidian life. As the toll his team inflicted on the advancing Bromidians mounted, the attackers slowed their advance. Once they moved more cautiously, however, they closed the distance with alarming efficiency.

Finally, a group of four Bromidians broke through the perimeter. As Arano desperately brought his rifle around, he heard a deafening roar go up from Pelos when the powerfully built Tsimian leapt into hand-to-hand combat. Swinging his laser rifle, he crushed the skull of the first Bromidian. Seeing his teammate was going through the Broms like a scythe through wheat, Arano returned his attention to the still-approaching armies. Two more Broms burst through, but they were met by Videre, the hackles on the back of his neck twitching as his Gatoan muscles rippled beneath his fur.

Just then, there came an enormous explosion amidst the Bromidian ranks, followed by the roar of ion engines as a Coalition transport and its fighter escort streaked low over the treetops. The wing of fighters fired another volley of missiles, and lethal eruptions of fire ripped through the enemy ranks. The advance of the Bromidian army slowed, then reversed when they fled howling back into the forest, several more falling under the unabated fire from the Avengers.

Moments later, the transport lowered gracefully to the springy turf of a nearby clearing. Major Alstor stepped out quickly, laser rifle in hand, and fired off a few shots at the fleeing Bromidians before greeting the exhausted Avengers team. There were tight grins and a few handshakes, and their equipment was quickly gathered. Shortly, the craft launched into the skies, the pilot already preparing the necessary calculations for the Rift Drive jump back to Immok 2.

In a small meeting room onboard the transport, Arano and Alyna met with Laron, and they sketched in the details of the mission. Laron, who quite obviously longed for his days of combat operations, hung on every word, sitting on the edge of his seat with a boyish grin on his face.

"So, you got Handron and Dralak?"

"Oh, Laron," laughed Alyna, feeling comfortable using the Major's first name. "You should have seen it. Viper sniped Handron right away. Then, while the Bromidians were just staring at the body, Viper dropped Dralak. I've never seen anyone shoot like that. I have to admit, though, the second shot really caught me off guard."

"I couldn't resist." Arano grinned. "The Bromidian High Command can't even file a formal complaint about this since they deny having ties with Rising Sun. Instead, they'll probably find a way to twist it around to make it look as if they were the ones who killed him after finding him in league with Rising Sun. You know how they are."

"That brings up a problem," noted Laron. "Someone passed on information that could have cost all of you your lives. I've already contacted Lon Pana. By the time we return, he'll have a list of everyone who had access to the information about your mission. His team will be tasked with finding the spy. Dar Noil, one of our intelligence analysts, will assist Pana's team."

"Thanks, Laron," Arano told him. "Too bad we haven't officially declared war on Rising Sun." Seeing the puzzled looks on his friends' faces, he continued, "Lieutenant Marnian was doing some historical research for me and found a little-known law from the early days of the Coalition. During a period of war, if a captain or higher ranking officer finds irrefutable evidence someone has betrayed us to the enemy, that officer is allowed to execute the spy on the spot, justifying his actions later in an official hearing. That way, spies don't just sit in prison for thirty years waiting on their appeals. The law had expired, but it was recently reinstated by Grand High Councilor Tient."

"Tient passed a law like that?" wondered Laron.

"Not without a little coercion," laughed Arano. "He wanted to grant exclusive iridium mining rights in the Leguin System to a company called Garanth

Construction. He claimed they're environmentally conscious, but it appears there's probably more to it than that. At any rate, I assume Tient spread some bribes around, but there was a group of lawmakers who refused to vote for his resolution unless he attached this anti-espionage rider onto his bill. It seems they got their way."

"Why was Pelos doing history research for you?" asked Laron suddenly.

Arano rolled his eyes. "I've somehow been chosen as the guest speaker at a seminar at Immok University."

Alyna smiled wickedly. "Enjoy!" she told him.

Laron laughed out loud, shaking his head. "Anyway, the sum of this whole mission is that you were successful despite overwhelming odds, and I attribute that largely to stealth. Even though they knew you were coming, you got in there and made your hit, then escaped with your team intact. They didn't know where you were until you were ready for them to know."

"That, and some of the best damned shooting I've ever seen," added Alyna with a sidelong glance that made Arano blush.

"Uh, Laron," Arano asked, changing the subject, "are you going to be in hot water for coming out here? You know Avengers Command gets steamed at you for doing that, and this time there was shooting going on."

"What can they do to me?" Laron laughed. "I've done a lot worse than this, and they still know better than to do anything but gripe at me."

The meeting broke up, with Laron returning to the bridge, and Arano and Alyna returning to their team's quarters. There was an awkward silence between them as they strolled through the short corridor to the room the whole team would share for the next few hours. When they arrived, they found the room empty, their teammates apparently having left for a meal. Arano dropped exhausted into his chair and looked speculatively over at Alyna.

"Now," he said hesitantly, "about that dinner I owe you."

CHAPTER THREE

THE NEXT MORNING, ARANO WAS UP WITH THE morning sun at his modest rented house on Immok 2, working on getting the yard ready for the cookout his team had planned. It had become a tradition for him, the day after a successful mission, to give his team the day off and invite them to his house for an informal gathering. Sometimes Avengers from other teams or even higher ranking officers stopped by briefly, as it was widely known the cookouts frequently turned into parties and just about anything could happen.

In fact, Lain Baxter had been nicknamed "Rock" after one of the wild shindigs. The beer was flowing, and Lain had consumed more than was really good for him, especially since Kamlings had swifter and more exaggerated reactions to alcohol than the other races. He told everyone he was a rock, and that no one could move him. He challenged a very large Tsimian to try to knock him over, resulting in some cracked ribs and a trip to the hospital.

Despite technological advances that made doing lawn work by hand unnecessary, Arano still insisted on manual landscaping, taking great pride in the appearance of his lawn. The physical labor involved allowed him time to let his mind drift to mundane matters and dismiss the more pressing worldly matters that occupied his thoughts at work. It was not unusual for him to be seen spending hours meticulously mowing, trimming, and edging his yard.

As he trimmed the grass behind the house, he stooped beneath a tree, pushing an offending branch out of his way. Moments later, he felt a sharp stinging pain on the back of his neck. He heard a buzzing sound growing louder, and suddenly knew he was in trouble. He dropped his tools and raced for the house, feeling several more stings while he ran. As the swarm of insects he had disturbed drew close to him in greater numbers, he decided simply running was not going to save him. He added screaming and cursing to his defensive strategy until he finally reached the safety of his garage. He slammed the door behind him, swatted the few remaining insects that had entered the garage with him, and went into his house to get something for his stings.

Alyna arrived an hour later, followed closely by Lain. Their laughter filled the sunny afternoon while Arano related his encounter with the unfriendly swarm. "What I can't understand," he complained, "is how they were able to pick me as their target. Some of my neighbors were outside, but none of them were stung."

Alyna managed to choke back her giggling long enough to answer him. "Most stinging insects inject their victim with a hormone. The other insects can smell it, and they'll zero in on that scent. I wouldn't advise you to go anywhere near their nest for a while, unless you want to show us how well you run and scream."

Lain chuckled softly. "Arano, I've got everything under control here, if you want to take off."

"Where are you going?" asked Alyna. "I thought you were staying for the cookout."

"I won't be gone more than an hour or two," replied Arano. "Today is the day I'm speaking at the university about the Coalition's war with the Bromidians."

"How did they ever get you to agree to do this, anyway?"

"It's my latest rampage. I'm trying to undo the damage being done at our learning institutions. The other day, one of my neighbors showed me his son's history book. Would you believe this book claims the Coalition was far too aggressive in the final assault on the Bromidian homeworld? They actually describe the Broms as being innocent victims in that war. I'll tell you what it all boils down to. That son-of-a-bitch Grand High Councilor hates the military. All of his policies are antimilitary. Now he's trying to rewrite history to cast us in a bad light. I can't believe our people actually voted that criminal into office."

Lain gave a broad, reptilian grin. "Arano," he chuckled, "why don't you tell us how you really feel?"

"If you don't mind," Alyna said, "I'd like to come along with you. I'd love to hear you tell it like it is."

"Sure. You going to need anything, Lain? The others should be here in an hour or so."

"I'm fine. Get outta here and give them hell."

"Today, as our class begins its study of the Bromidian War, I have a guest speaker to give you an overview of the titanic events that gave rise to the birth of the United Systems Coalition. I'm sure you'll find his insights into the war to be stimulating. Without further ado, I give you Captain Arano Lakeland of the Coalition's famous Avengers."

Arano looked over at Alyna, who was seated next to him. She leaned over and whispered, "Good luck!" He moved to the podium, taking his place in front of the microphone.

"Good afternoon," he began. "I want to thank you all for inviting me here, and for giving me this opportunity to place history in the proper light. I also want to assure you I do not have the plague; these red marks you see on my face and neck are the result of a slight misunderstanding I had with a family of stinging insects. They made some valid points, so I agreed to leave them alone." The assembled crowd chuckled.

"What I'm about to tell you is an historically accurate version of the events leading up to and occurring during the Bromidian War. Many of you may disbelieve with what I reveal here today, and you may even want to dispute these facts. I assure you, however, this is the story as it really happened. What you have been taught is a version of the truth tainted by people with political goals, and whose aspirations would be hampered if these truths were widely known. But, as it has been said, 'The truth shall set you free'. At any rate, here are the events as they actually occurred, and as they are recorded in military documents.

"In the year 2099, Humans first made contact with the Bromidians. Despite Human attempts at diplomacy, the Bromidians were aggressive and attacked Human shipping lanes. The Bromidians attacked only Humans since the other races were much further away. The Humans sent diplomats to try and put an end to the violence, but these diplomats were captured and summarily executed.

"At this point, the Humans declared war on the Bromidians. This decision was, to put it kindly, hasty. Due to some ill-advised treaties among Human communities, they had no weapons in space other than a laser defense system covering less than half the Earth's surface. They had the technology to arm themselves, but the process of building armed spaceships took time and put them on the defensive. During the next year, as the Humans built their ships of war, several Human outposts were destroyed.

"They split their ships into three fleets. The First Fleet was assigned to protect the earth plus the colonies on earth's moon, on Mars, and on a few assorted moons orbiting other planets in the system. The Second Fleet was assigned to protect the colonies in the Subac system. The Third Fleet, the largest of the three, would go on the offensive. The military leaders wanted to divide the third fleet into smaller task forces to keep from over-committing, but they were overruled by the political leaders of the various Human governments who had taken command of the military.

"The Human political leadership ordered the

Third Fleet to attack a reported Bromidian fleet rally point. When the fleet arrived, they found the Bromidian force much smaller than they'd been led to believe. They easily overwhelmed and destroyed the lesser force.

When the battle ended, they received a distress call from the Earth System. A huge Bromidian fleet had executed a classic backdoor maneuver, attacking the Earth System while the more powerful Third Fleet was out on a wild goose chase. The Third Fleet was unable to immediately return, of course. Their battle had lasted less than an hour, and the Rift Drive engines on capital ships have to cool for six hours before making another jump, or the engines could experience a meltdown. This delay was critical.

"After a fierce battle, the First Fleet was beaten, although the Bromidian fleet suffered heavy losses in the process. The Bromidian task force then bombarded Earth from orbit, attacking with standard planet buster bombs as well as a horrific biological weapon, a standard Bromidian battle tactic. Due to the orbital defense system, North America was protected from these attacks, but the rest of the planet suffered genocidal losses.

"The third fleet finally returned to the Earth System, and the Bromidians pulled out upon their arrival. For the next two years, parts of the Third Fleet harassed Bromidian patrols and supply lines while the remainder shuttled the surviving Humans from North America to other Human settlements in the galaxy, mainly the Subac system, which the Humans had designated as their new home. The plague let loose by the Bromidian attack had completely wiped out Human life on the rest of the planet, killing over 7 billion people. Indications were the pestilence had the staying power to be carried to the surviving North American population by normal wind currents. Studies estimated that the strain of microorganism used in the weapon would kill its host within twenty-four hours, was highly contagious, and could survive in the earth's atmosphere for several decades. It appeared to have been bioengineered to be safe for Bromidians.

"While the evacuation of the earth was ongoing, a new shipyard was constructed at Sol in the Subac system. The other races secretly provided parts and supplies, but their ruling councils were reluctant to go to war.

"During the following year, 2103, the Fourth Fleet was commissioned. It was more advanced than anything either side had ever used, the Humans having added their own innovations to the new weapons and shield technology obtained from the warlike Kamlings. The Third Fleet was reassigned to protect the supply lines to the Fourth Fleet and to act as a reactionary force, if needed. Meanwhile, the Fourth Fleet methodically wiped out Bromidian Forces in the surrounding systems.

"For the first time, the Humans pushed the Bromidians back from Human space. However, although the Fourth Fleet inflicted heavy losses, the Bromidian supply of ships seemed inexhaustible. Several of the small teams of Human special forces, redesignated 'Avengers' in honor of their crusade to avenge the losses on their homeworld, were assigned to locate the

Bromidian shipyards. Six months later, an emergency communication was received by the marauding Fourth Fleet. The Avengers had located the Bromidian Homeworld at Rystoria 2. They'd also discovered a massive shipyard orbiting the planet.

"While the Fourth Fleet and parts of the Third Fleet gathered in preparation for the assault on the Bromidian Homeworld, the Avengers stayed in the system, wreaking havoc in small hit and run attacks at Bromidian command and control centers and other important facilities. They also continued to send intelligence information. The fleet guarding Rystoria 2 was at least twice the size of the entire Human fleet, and there was also an extensive planetary defense system. These ground-based outposts became a favorite target of the Avengers.

"It was at this point the Humans received some unexpected help. Representatives of the other races met at Sol, where the United Systems Coalition Pact was signed. In addition to sending fleets of their own to help, the other races agreed to allow the Humans to give technology to the Padians, who at the time were still in an early industrial, though tribal, state. The Padians were invited to join the USC, which they did, bringing the total number of races in the pact to six. The Padians came to be known as fierce ground fighters, which became their forte during the war, although they did contribute significantly to the fleet. In addition, the decision was made that, in the name of expedience, all forces fighting under the USC banner would use Human systems of weights, measures, and time. Since Human elements were already in the field, it would be easier to leave them alone and change everyone else. After the war, the decision was made to make this a permanent arrangement, thereby establishing Human standards as the guidelines for the Coalition.

"At last, the fleet was ready. The USC juggernaut attacked Rystoria 2. During the second day of intense fighting, a detachment of Kamling fighters and light cruisers managed to punch a hole through the planetary defenses, aided largely by repeated attacks from the Avengers team, still attacking ground installations. Coalition transports landed several divisions of Padian soldiers, who separated and destroyed Bromidian ground-based planetary defense systems. This hastened the destruction of the Bromidian fleet as they lost the cover fire they'd received from the surface of Rystoria 2. Finally, with over 90 percent of their fleet destroyed, including their flagship, and their shipyards falling toward the planet and burning up in the atmosphere, the Bromidians surrendered.

"The destruction wrought during this five-year war was unbelievable. Over half of the Coalition fleet was destroyed in that final battle. Earth was a total loss, the microorganisms from the Bromidian biological weapons having spread across the entire surface of the planet, leaving it uninhabitable.

"In an attempt to show mercy and try to bridge the chasm between the Coalition and the Bromidians, the USC permitted the Bromidians to retain a military force capable of defending their empire. The Bromidians have since abused this right, building a fleet well in excess of what is required to defend their interests.

A group of them has separated from the Bromidian Empire. Calling themselves Rising Sun, they have dedicated themselves to the destruction of the Coalition. Although we have no proof, we believe Rising Sun is cooperating, at some level, with the terrorist organization known as Event Horizon.

"There have been accusations that Rising Sun is still connected with the Bromidian Empire, but no solid evidence has been presented to, or at least accepted by, the Coalition High Council. Rising Sun's most notorious activity was their occupation of Leguin 4 eight years ago, in 2204. They brutally crushed all opposition and executed a large number of civilians, some because they were leaders and others in an attempt to gain information through torture. The Padian resistance, assisted by covert forces from the Coalition, managed to drive the Bromidians away.

"In a nutshell, that is an overview of our history with the Bromidians. I want to emphasize the dangers posed to the Coalition by the complacency we're now seeing. An alarmingly large number of people feel since there has not been any open armed conflict between the Coalition and the Bromidian Empire in decades, everything is sweet and cozy. Somewhere along the way, the message has gotten lost.

"We must keep our guard up. When you hear our leaders and educators telling you how cruel we were to the Bromidians in the final battle at Rystoria, I want you to remember the billions of people they killed on the planet Earth. I want you to think of all the diplomats they executed when the Humans tried to negotiate a peaceful settlement. I want you to think of all the unarmed Human settlements the Bromidians wiped out without a thought about the lives they ended. I want you to remember the innocent Padians who were ruthlessly murdered at the hands of Rising Sun operatives during an invasion conducted solely to obtain iridium for their Rift Drives. I want you to think of my mother and father, mercilessly executed in front of hundreds of other Padians during the Rising Sun occupation. I want you to remember the woman I was supposed to marry, who was tied to a post in the town square for three days until she died of dehydration, all because they were trying to draw me and the resistance movement out of hiding. Event Horizon also boasts Bromidians among its members, and there have been rumors some of these are Bromidian military advisors.

"That is the Bromidian Empire we're dealing with. If they were really interested in peace, they would integrate with our society and allow us to integrate with theirs. That's just not happening. So remember all this . . . and keep your guard up. Thank you."

Arano turned and walked back to his chair amidst the stunned silence and awed stares of the students. After a few moments, the applause started, and it soon cascaded into a waterfall of sound, quickly becoming a standing ovation. At his table, Arano was greeted by a hug from Alyna. She kissed his cheek and whispered, "I'm sorry . . . I didn't know."

"It's okay," he whispered back. "Very few people do. It's just something I don't talk about."

After a quiet return ride, Arano and Alyna arrived back at the ongoing cookout. Arano invited her to join everyone, and told her he was going into the house for a few minutes and would be outside shortly.

Alyna felt as if she drifted in a fog. She had learned something about Arano that afternoon, and she knew she needed clarification from someone who had been with Arano from the beginning. She spotted Lain and quite deliberately moved to his side. He was talking with a couple of Kamling ladies who worked in the intelligence division at Coalition Headquarters, and appeared to be drinking enough to be well on his way to another "Rock" incident. "Sorry to interrupt, Lain," she told him, "but I need to talk to Laron. Have you seen him?"

"Umm," replied Lain, swaying slightly, "I think he's running the grill."

Alyna mumbled her thanks and headed toward the side of the yard with all the smoke. She saw Laron frantically trying to control the growing flames engulfing the food, to the laughter of the intoxicated onlookers. "Major Alstor, can I talk to you?" she asked.

Immediately seeing the opportunity, he plopped his chef's hat on a nearby Tsimian. "Take over," he said. "Duty calls." He escorted Alyna off to one side, away from prying ears. "What's up?" he asked.

"Laron, it's about Arano. Is he . . . ?"

"Available? Yes, please, ask him out. I haven't been able to get him to take any initiative in the dating arena since I met him."

"Well, that's not exactly what I meant." She briefly recounted the fiery speech Arano had delivered earlier that day. "If I know my Avengers history, you were leading an Avengers team on Leguin 4 during the Rising Sun occupation. Exactly what happened to Arano and his family there?"

Laron sighed, then guided her over to a pair of chairs. "What I'm about to talk about I've not discussed with anyone in a long time. Don't let Arano know I told you this. The only reason I'm telling you now is because I think there's some chemistry between you two." Seeing Alyna blush slightly at his last comment, he gave her a knowing smile before he continued his narration.

"Of course, you're aware Arano is a Daxia. That is a story in and of itself Arano will have to tell you on his own. Suffice it to say he's one of the best. In his second year of service as a Daxia, he discovered the clan leader of the Waya Plains Clan had been selling information to Rising Sun. The compromised information included data about the Daxia, about the Whelen Academy where the Daxia are trained, names and families of current Daxia, and other items associated with the Padian government. Arano was sent in to silence the leak, and he did so with a large-caliber rifle from over 1,500 meters away.

"About three months later, Rising Sun forces invaded Leguin 4. Of course, the Bromidian government claimed no responsibility, but they wouldn't help to fight the invaders, either. The only motive we've been able to determine for the invasion is that Leguin 4 is the only inhabitable planet in the system, and it's fairly close to a large asteroid belt containing iridium.

"The Coalition, afraid they might aggravate Bromidian civilians by openly attacking Rising Sun, decided to send a couple of Avengers teams to train the indigenous forces to fight the Broms themselves. I was with Team 5 at the time, and when my team arrived, we found Arano. I have to tell you, I've seen the look of death in a man's eyes before, but I've never seen anything like the look in his eyes." Laron paused, haunting memories crossing his face before he continued. "When Rising Sun occupied Leguin 4, they put their spy's information to use quickly, rounding up all governmental leaders and Daxia. The people were herded out into a central square and executed, one at a time, while thousands of Padians were forced to stand and watch. Among those executed were Arano's parents.

"When the Bromidians discovered there were some Daxia unaccounted for, they imprisoned family members of the missing Daxia and tortured them to death, trying to get information about the Daxia's whereabouts. After that, Arano led a few successful raids against Bromidian supply dumps, weapons caches, and prison areas. These attacks strengthened the resistance by adding weapons from the stockpiles and more soldiers from among the more able-bodied prisoners. Soon after, the Bromidians discovered Arano was close to a young woman named Erlinia Drontas."

"During his speech at the university he mentioned something about having had a fiancé. Was that her?"

"Yes. They arrested her and took her to the square in the center of town. They tied her to a post as a sign to Arano he needed to surrender. Arano refused to take the bait knowing to do so would be his death, as well as Erlinia's. For three days, Erlinia was tied to that post. She eventually died of dehydration.

"That didn't have the effect the Bromidians had

hoped for, and Arano and I began a campaign of terror of our own. We showed the Broms there was no place safe for them, and no time day or night they could relax. Eventually, when their losses became unacceptable, the Broms pulled out. Of course, their leaders were conveniently 'captured' by Bromidian Empire forces and were promptly executed. We believe this was more a punishment for their failure than anything else. At any rate, Arano was given a release from his Daxia service, allowing him to join the USC military and become an Avenger. His clan leaders gave the usual flowery speeches about how this was for the greater glory of Leguin 4, but we all knew it was a move that put him in a position to get revenge. Remember, the Padians are still fairly primitive, socially speaking, and honor and vengeance are major driving forces in their lives. Since the day I met him, he has had an obsessional hatred of Bromidians. Given the circumstances, I can't say I blame him."

Alyna stared at the ground, trying to take everything in. "Thank you," she said simply. "You've given me a lot to think about." She moved off among the revelers, reviewing what she had been told. She now understood the origin of Arano's hatred of the Bromidians, although she couldn't help but see the irony in the situation; he expressed a strong dislike for all Bromidians out of hand, but at the same time condemned Humans who felt similarly about Padians.

Arano emerged from his house a short time later and

found Kish Waukee sitting in a group of people of mixed races, debating religion. Arano had to smile at that, in spite of himself. As a race, the Tompiste tended to be completely secular, having become convinced centuries ago that religions were a tool created by people in positions of authority to strengthen their hold on a given society. Arano grabbed a beer and sat down to watch the show. By now Kish was in her element, arguing enthusiastically with several members of the group.

"But look at the blatantly illogical conclusions religions come to," complained Kish. "Let me give you an analogy I want you to follow. Last year, terrorists from Event Horizon bombed the Arena in downtown Immok City. Hundreds of people were killed, and less than a hundred escaped unscathed. Afterward, people were quoted over and over thanking various gods for saving those people who made it out alive, saying this was proof their god is all-powerful and all-loving.

"Now, let's try this twist to the story. Let's say I'd received an intelligence brief that warned me about the bomb ahead of time. However, instead of evacuating the building, let's say I went in and pulled people out in small groups. I managed to pull a thousand people out in this fashion before the bomb detonated, killing everyone left inside. Am I now a hero for saving a thousand people, or am I a criminal for not saving the rest of the people inside when I had the chance?"

A Human participant in the discussion named Dar Noil, the intelligence analyst who had assisted Lon Pana in his search for the spy at Coalition Headquarters, started to voice his objections, saying this was a different case, but Kish stopped him.

"Think about it," Kish told them. "Your god, the all-knowing, all-caring, all-powerful god knew this bomb would explode. He had to, being all-knowing. He could have saved everyone, either by stopping the bomb from going off or by keeping it from being planted in the first place, since he's all-powerful. He should have saved everyone, since he's all-caring. But he did none of these things because he's not all-anything. Were the victims not worthy of life? If so, I guess your god isn't all-caring.

"At least the Gatoans are more honest. They're a money-grabbing people, and they're extremely bureaucratic by nature. Their god, Launyr, promotes wealth and encourages Gatoans to accumulate as much money as they can. Launyr has an enormous hierarchy of angels as his servants, which also encourages his followers in their formation of large, inefficient bureaucracies. It's all nonsense, if you ask me."

Arano couldn't restrain his laughter anymore. "You guys are biting off more than you can chew. I learned long ago not to argue religion with Kish. She knows more about the various religions of the Coalition than all of us put together. I just admit my religion has flaws and let it go."

Videre stepped up from behind Arano. "Did I ever tell you the one about the priest, the bishop, and . . ."

Arano moved on through the crowd, finally spotting Pelos off to one side with a group of fighter pilots from his last unit. As was usually the case with Pelos, he was talking about investments. There were times when Arano felt lucky some stock brokerage firm didn't steal Pelos away from the Coalition military. He certainly had the knowledge and the instincts to make a fortune in the stock market. But, like most members of the military, amassing a financial fortune was not a driving force in Pelos's life.

"My latest find is a company called Transcorp. I noticed their number of shipments into the Navek system had recently increased dramatically. I wasn't able to determine who is paying for all these shipments, but they appear to have established a major trade route between Navek and Ervik. I'm sure there might be some under-the-table deals involved, since Ervik is in a nebula and therefore the cargo can't be scanned before it leaves the system, but they have quite a lucrative business going out there. Their stock is up 15 percent just in the month since I bought in." There were murmurs of approval from the group surrounding Pelos as Arano stepped up.

"Pelos," he began, "I need to ask your advice. I bought into that medical research company, Biomek, just like you suggested. Today, I was checking into their activities and found something that doesn't make sense. They've been pouring almost half their research funds into live organ transplant technology, including research to allow transplants of organs between the different races."

"Why would they do that?" asked a nearby Tompiste pilot, scratching absently at one leathery-skinned hand. "It's been over a century since we developed the genetic technology to quickly grow new organs and body parts in a laboratory setting. What possible purpose could such archaic technology serve now?"

"That sounds pretty bad," commented Pelos, his brow furrowed in thought. "I may have led you astray here. You'd better dump that stock as soon as you can. When word of this gets out, Biomek's value will head to the cellar."

The conversation moved on, and Arano continued to circulate among his guests. He had been in a slightly pensive mood following his speech earlier in the day, but that was to be expected. Anytime he brought up those terrible days of the Occupation, he felt the pain and sense of loss all over again. The friendly banter of fresh conversation was doing him wonders, however, and he was beginning to feel like himself again.

A group of fighter pilots and an Avenger were arguing about the efficiency of the Coalition bureaucracy. The Avenger, Arano's friend Lon Pana, spied Arano and called him over. "You want to see how bad things are?" asked Lon. "Arano can tell you."

Arano smiled, shaking his friend's hand. "Lon."

Lon nodded. "Arano, how many Coalition hoops did you have to jump through to have this party?"

"Well," mused Arano, thoughtfully scratching his head, "I had to start with the Bureau of Licensing. They sold me a license to obtain permits. Then I had to get a food service permit, an outdoor fire permit, a large party gathering permit, and an alcohol permit. Then there was all the insurance I was required to buy. The permits are good for six months, so I plan to take full advantage of them."

Lon laughed out loud, raising his eyebrows and looking around the group. "See what I mean? All that for a cookout?" Arano laughed with him and moved over to the grill to get his dinner.

By late evening, Arano was cleaning with the help of Alyna, Kish, and Laron. They were nearly finished when Arano finally broached a subject he'd been thinking about all day. "Alyna," he asked, absently stepping over the comatose form of Lain, "I was wondering if you could help me out of a tight spot. Next week I'm supposed to return to Leguin 4 to attend a meeting between the Clan Leaders of Leguin and representatives of the Coalition High Council. I'd like you to accompany me, as a friend, when I go. You see, I have an aunt there who's the closest thing to a family I have left. I love her dearly, but every time I see her she starts bugging me about how I'm not dating anyone. She's getting old, and I don't want to give her anything else to worry about. The Four Elementals know she's been through enough.

"What I'd like to do is have you pretend to be my date for the weekend. It won't be an easy deception to pull off, because she's shrewd, but I think we can manage. It'd make my aunt feel a lot better, plus I think you might see some things that will really open your eyes to Padian society as well."

"Well," said Alyna, "I don't have anything else planned. I guess it all depends on one thing."

"What's that?"

"If you're planning on taking me there in the Eclipse, you can forget it."

Arano glared at Laron, who was laughing uncontrollably. "Okay, Laron," Arano complained, "it wasn't that funny."

"Yes, it was," giggled Laron. "Go on, tell her the rest."

Arano sighed. "No, we probably aren't going in the Eclipse. It's back in the shop for repairs again, and they aren't sure if it'll be done in time for the trip."

Arano tried to scowl at his companions, who were hopelessly lost in hysterics, but he couldn't contain himself. He too joined in, their laughter filling the deepening twilight of a gorgeous, star-filled night.

CHAPTER FOUR

THE NEXT MORNING, ARANO AND THE REST OF Avengers Team 5 assembled in their main room, and Arano prepared to lead them through an extended training exercise. He saw the curiosity on his teammates' faces as he placed a rather bulky box on the planning table, rummaged around inside briefly, and looked out at the Avengers standing before him. "I like to call this the 'Game of the Stones', named after an ancient tradition back on earth. On Leguin 4, we had our own version of it in our ancient times, with a similar name. We use a similar technique during Daxia training. It's an excellent way to enhance your memory.

"Here's how it works. You all see the box on the table. I will remove the lid from the box and give you five minutes to study the contents. In ancient times, they used stones of varying sizes and colors, hence the name, but I'm using small military devices you'll all recognize. At first, there won't be many items in there, and you'll have ample time to memorize the contents. As your skills improve, I'll add items to the box and decrease your allotted time for memorizing the contents. By the time we're done, with a simple glance you'll be able to tell me not only the box's contents, but also the location of each item within the box."

"I really can't believe this one," complained Cono with an exaggerated sigh as he scribbled notes on a notepad. "You're telling me you're going to waste valuable time looking at toys in a box when you could be out there tracking down the Disciples? This is unbelievable."

"As my mother used to say," intoned Arano, leveling a finger at the Grand High Councilor's aide, "sit down, sit back, and shut up. You have no idea what is going on here, do you? The Disciple killings aren't the only thing we're working on. In fact, being mainly a police matter, their crimes are secondary to us. Our primary function is still military, and we need to conduct military training."

"What possible military usage could this idiocy have?"

Arano scowled darkly, leaning forward against the table. "Let's say I send Lieutenant Baxter out on a scouting mission. I need to know what kind of force we're up against. Obviously, he'll write down what he sees, if possible. What if he doesn't have writing supplies? What if his notes are lost or destroyed? What if, as has happened in the past, this is an underwater scouting mission? He'll need to use his memory. Watch, and learn."

"Yeah," added Videre. "You should remember to keep your mouth shut and let us think you're a fool, rather than open your mouth and confirm it." There were a few chuckles Arano silenced with a shake of his head. Cono opened his mouth as if to protest, but apparently changed his mind and kept silent. Arano returned to the business at hand.

"First," he told his team, "I'll test you. There'll be ten items, and you'll have ten seconds to memorize them. We'll see how many items each of you get right. At the end, we'll retest with the same standard, and I'll show the skeptic here how much you've improved."

The testing began. Despite their military training, all Arano's teammates scored poorly, with the exception of Kish Waukee, whose photographic memory recorded everything at a glance. Then the game began, with Arano starting at a very basic level but gradually increasing the level of difficulty. As the morning progressed, Arano added items and deducted time, but his team was still able to score well.

After awhile, Arano changed his line of questioning. "All right," he told them, "you've all observed the box for this round. Get ready to write your answers." They snatched up their pens, ready to show Arano they had his game mastered.

"Now, write down a description of the colors and patterns on the inside of the box." His teammates looked at each other in stunned silence, and only Kish was able to write a response. "Don't miss the forest for the trees," he told them.

Major Alstor laughed at them from the open doorway. "Never a dull moment with Arano in charge."

Arano smiled. "What's up, sir?"

"We have a situation developing in the Seoran system. You can check it out on this data disk. I've got to get back to a command briefing, but I'll meet with you before you leave. Cono, I realize you have a high enough security clearance for this information, so I won't ask you to leave. Just remember, this is a very sensitive issue involving undercover agents. Please be vague in any reports you make. Grand High Councilor Tient won't be the only one who has access to what you write."

Seeing Cono nod in acknowledgment, Major Alstor spun on his heel and left the room. Arano looked briefly at the data disk in his hands, then moved to the data terminal on the nearby wall. He inserted the disk and waited for a response.

After a brief pause, the computer hummed to life. "Identify yourself," commanded the computer.

"Captain Arano Lakeland, USC Avengers," Arano replied before entering his password.

"Retina identification," came the next order. Arano complied by positioning his face in front of a slitted viewer where an infrared beam scanned his retina for the telltale signs that would verify his identity. "Identity confirmed. You may proceed."

Arano perused the information in the disk, pulse quickening when he realized the intensity of the mission. He could sense the impatience of his teammates behind him as they shuffled their feet and fidgeted in their chairs. He finished reading through the report and turned to the other Avengers.

"This is a pretty desperate situation. There was a freighter in the Seoran system that was attacked by a Rising Sun ship. They managed to guide their escape pods to Seoran 4. The only known survivors are a group of USC operatives who were on a classified mission in that system. The other escape pods were destroyed. When these operatives saw the Broms attacking the other escape pods, they guided their pod in the general direction of Seoran 4 and shut down all power. The Bromidians picked up their distress signal, though, and they're hunting for them. We need to get in there, rescue them, and get out as quickly as possible.

"The Military High Command can't send in a regular military force, for two reasons. First, it might compromise what the agents were doing. Second, the star in that system is unstable, and the High Command is unwilling to risk a large number of troops in such a mission. Our best estimate is that the star will go supernova within a week, but probably sooner. That's why there's a time factor involved.

"Let's get loaded, people. We're leaving within the hour. We'll have plenty of time during the trip to plan a course of action, so let's move like we have a purpose. We have a twenty-two hour jump to the Seoran system." He moved over to the terminal, slapped a button on the control pad, and yanked the disk from its slot before securing the personal gear he would take to their waiting ships.

As Arano finished packing for the mission, he noticed Cono glaring, his beak twitching in disapproval. Following the Grand High Councilor's aide's gaze, he spotted Pelos as the big Tsimian finished his usual pre-deployment superstitious ritual, involving several "lucky" hand signs and his tollep's tooth. Arano started to explain Pelos' actions, but Kish beat him to it.

"Pelos always does this before a mission," she told him quietly. "As a Tsimian yourself, I thought you would understand."

"Not all Tsimians are a bunch of primitive superstitious fools," answered Cono, a bit tartly. He cast a cautious glance in Pelos' direction to see if the big Tsimian had heard him. "Surely you don't approve, Lieutenant Waukee? Aren't all Tompiste a bit more secular in their beliefs?"

"Totally secular," she answered plainly. "We have no use, ourselves, for religions or supernatural beliefs of any kind. However, if Pelos believes these rituals help him, then they'll help him. By boosting his confidence, he can improve his performance. So in a way, the superstitious rituals have their benefits."

When Arano turned to leave, he saw Alyna was waiting for him. She gave him a questioning look, eyebrows raised in concern.

"Are you angry over this mission? Especially a rescue mission?"

He motioned for her to walk with him. "I'm not mad that we're trying to rescue someone. I just don't like being in a no-win situation. I've always been of the mind that there's a way out of any situation, as long as you use your head. If that star goes nova while we're in-system, we don't stand a chance."

She nodded, and they walked on in silence. Arano, lost in thought, led his team to the hangar where they boarded their ships. After a brief video conference with Laron Alstor and Cadron Stenat regarding their strategy upon arrival in the Seoran System, they requested and received clearance from the control tower. The two Assault Class Fighters lifted gracefully into the air and surged upward toward the stars. Arano checked with Videre, who sent him the Rift

Drive instructions from the navigational computer. Arano transmitted them to Alyna in the USCS Summerwind, and she signaled her acknowledgment. At Arano's signal, both ships activated their Rift Drives and disappeared into their twin tunnels of light.

Arano sat mesmerized by the swirling vastness of the wormhole. Varying shades of reds and blues chased each other around his ship in an endless game of tag, swirling into combinations of colors that boggled the mind, all the while staying just on the surface of the dark tunnel surrounding his ship. No matter how many Rift Drive jumps he made, Arano was always fascinated by the sheer beauty of these artificial wormholes.

They had left the Immok system nearly a day earlier and were now closing in on their destination in the Seoran system. The planning for their assault was complete, so there was nothing to do but wait. They wouldn't be able to acquire a sensor reading of Rising Sun sentry ships while they were in the wormhole, so that portion of the mission would be improvised. Videre was busy monitoring the Rift Drive navigational computer, and Lain was analyzing the latest data from the Seoran star, trying to get a better idea of when the star was going to explode.

Once more, Arano mulled over their plan. The Avengers had an advantage over their Bromidian adversaries because the Avengers had a very close approximation of the location of the lost agents, while the Bromidians had only a general idea. Upon their arrival in the system, the Avengers would have to eliminate Bromidian fighters, then proceed directly to their destination. They had an area approximately 4 square kilometers they'd need to search. Any Rising Sun operatives found on the planet's surface would have to be neutralized immediately.

To expedite their escape, one Avenger from each squad would remain behind and fly the ships to their comrades' location as soon as the agents were located. To prevent friendly fire accidents between the trapped agents and their would-be rescuers, the Avengers had been given the encryption codes necessary to call the agents and notify them that friendly forces were in the area, facilitating the link-up. Once everyone was aboard, the two Avengers ships would rendezvous on their way out of the planet's atmosphere, calculate the rift jump back to the Lican System, and exit as quickly as possible. If there were signs the explosion of the star was imminent, the mission would have to be aborted.

Arano was awakened from his reverie by a signal from Videre it was time to exit the wormhole. He wouldn't be able to contact the Summerwind until they'd returned to normal space, so there would be no advance preparations for the coming dogfight. He touched a few controls, and the engines hummed as the ship prepared to drop into the Seoran system. The swirling color scheme of the artificial wormhole seemed to stretch and fade simultaneously, tenuously holding its grasp around the ship, then with startling suddenness it was gone, replaced by the stark blackness of normal space. Arano spotted the Summerwind off to his port side, positioned right off his wing. The jump had gone perfectly.

The sensors came online, and Videre immediately began a scan of the area as Lain moved to the weapons controls. Arano could only utilize the forward firing weapons since he was the pilot. Lain would have access to the side mounted weapons, a feature that made the Avengers' assault class fighters even more deadly in combat.

"Viper," announced Lain, "weapons are online and charged. Ready for combat."

"Acknowledged," noted Arano. "Videre, what do we have on sensors?"

"Six fighters, Meridian Class, closing in from 113 mark 25."

"I have them. Moving to engage." He activated the ship-to-ship radio. "Alyna, you with me over there?"

"Roger," responded Alyna. "I see the fighters; we're moving in. I'm on your wing."

"Moving to combat speed," said Arano as his ship raced ahead. Lain tracked the closest fighter, getting a computer targeting lock. He fired a torpedo, and moments later the fighter exploded in a brilliant ball of flame. The second fighter also exploded, and Arano noted automatically that Pelos, Alyna's gunner, had scored a torpedo hit.

The remaining fighters immediately scattered, trying to come at the Avengers from all directions. Arano fired his forward plasma battery, more to keep the Bromidians off balance than to actually score a hit. By now they were too close to get a target lock with the torpedoes, and Lain had switched to the two secondary plasma batteries which could be turned and aimed, unlike their forward-mounted counterpart. One fighter closed in from above Arano, scoring two hits on the Specter's rear quarter. A plasma blast from the Summerwind silenced that threat in a brilliant explosion. Arano swung the ship about in an incredibly agile maneuver, bringing a fourth enemy fighter in line for Lain, who easily destroyed the Bromidian ship with his plasma battery.

"Videre, how are my shields holding up?" Arano called out.

"Just fine," came the reply. "Neither hit was direct. Shields are at 91%."

But the remaining two fighters had stayed in formation with each other and now closed in from the rear of the Avengers' craft. As Arano and Alyna turned their craft to meet the latest onslaught, a barrage of plasma battery fire from the lead fighter struck the tail of the Summerwind. Even as the impact shuddered through the craft, Arano expertly guided his ship into a position where he could protect Alyna's craft. Eventually, under a murderous stream of covering fire laid down by Lain, the fighters banked off, preparing to come in for another pass.

"Damage report, Summerwind," Arano ordered.

"We've lost our rear shields," replied Alyna. "Any more hits back there are going to cause some serious damage."

"We'll cover you," Arano answered.

Alyna hit the throttle, accelerating away from the combat. Arano banked the Specter hard, veering away from the Seoran system as if to make a run for the safety of outer space where he could jump back to a secure system. The two remaining fighters turned and pursued the Summerwind, floundering helplessly, heading deeper into the system.

With a warning to his team, Arano turned back toward the fight, far enough now from his targets to acquire a torpedo lock. Lain fired the first torpedo, then moved to get a lock on the second fighter without waiting for the first torpedo to impact. He fired a second time just as the first torpedo found its mark, and within moments both remaining fighters had been destroyed.

The two Avenger ships regrouped and moved toward their destination on Seoran 4 as Alyna's two crewmembers began emergency repairs. After descending into the planet's atmosphere, they landed gracefully in a clearing near a woodland stream. Arano and his team disembarked, met in a few moments by Alyna.

"My crew is going to have to stay here and work on the ship," she informed them. "My Rift Drive took a direct hit back there. As it stands right now, our best guess is that it'll take them between twelve and twenty-four hours to get us operational again."

Videre gave a visible start. "I took some readings on the Seoran star after the battle. According to the data I gathered, we have less than eighteen hours before this sun is going to explode."

Alyna's eyes went flat at the news. "It was going to be a tight fit trying to squeeze our crew plus half of the USC agents into either ship. I doubt we could fit the six of us plus the ten agents into the Specter, not to mention the problems that would cause, logistically speaking, for the life-support system. I think we're in trouble." She turned and hurried back into her ship to inform her crew of what had developed. Arano studied his map intently, trying to find way to conduct their search and still repair the Summerwind. Alyna returned shortly, a worried expression on her face.

"Here is what we're going to do," announced Arano. "Lain will have to stay here and offer whatever assistance he can to Alyna's crew. Those repairs must be finished within sixteen hours. Alyna, Videre and I will have to split up and search for the agents separately. Stay in touch on the FM radios, and don't use any subspace frequencies. If you find them, alert the rest of us and set up a defensive perimeter. The agents should be armed, so they can help out. The rest of us will hurry back to the ships and come and get you. We may have to finish the repairs to the Summerwind on our way out of the system. Let's move out."

Lain moved inside while Arano, Alyna, and Videre split up, each having a designated search area marked on their map. Arano darted agilely down a hillside and inside the treeline, eyes alert. The densely-forested region had sparse undergrowth, allowing Arano to move about with a minimum of effort and noise. The sun was setting, but fortunately he had the sun at his back, making it easier to see ahead. As darkness fell, Arano felt along his utility belt for his night vision goggles. He briefly considered donning them, but discarded the idea, preferring to allow his eyes to adjust to the darkness. There were no clouds, and although the stars were fairly bright, the darkness beneath the trees was very thick. A sudden crashing to his right brought him about sharply, gun in hand, but he relaxed when he realized he'd scared up a group of animals that were bedded down for the evening.

He reached a second clearing, a hilltop spot that afforded him a dim view of his surroundings. He saw several prominent land features from this vantage point, enabling him to triangulate his position on his map and confirm his location. Reassured, he continued his search.

He left the clearing and started down a nearby hillside. He was about halfway down the slope when he saw a light come on briefly, then disappear. He froze in his tracks, waited a few moments, and edged behind a nearby tree. He peered off into the darkness, but was unable to find the source of the light. He sighed in frustration as he retrieved his night vision goggles, and activated them with the press of a button. He placed them on his head and again looked in the direction of the light. At first he saw nothing, but then his sharp vision caught a bit of movement. The figure was perhaps 150 meters ahead, making the shape tough to discern. Resolutely, Arano edged silently closer, and his danger sense immediately sounded its warning. He closed to within fifty meters, lay on the ground, and again tried to make out what was ahead.

At that moment, a Bromidian soldier stepped into view, briefly activated a small light, and searched for something on the ground. Arano blessed his luck realizing the light kept him from stepping unknowingly into the soldier's view.

Creeping closer yet, Arano eased his knife from its

sheath. He wanted to see if the Rising Sun soldier guarded something important, but he also knew the only way past this soldier would be through him, not around him. He waited patiently for his chance to come. The lone sentry turned his back and sat on a nearby log in apparent boredom.

Arano started to step from his place of concealment, intent on taking the guard by surprise, but pulled up short. Something clicked within him, his danger sense warning him all was not as it seemed. He decided to bide his time to see if there were any other Bromidians in the area. Just then, two more Rising Sun soldiers emerged from the darkness and approached Arano's intended victim. It appeared there was a changing of the guard in progress.

After a subdued discussion, the original guard moved off into the darkness with one of the soldiers while the other took up the vigil, scanning the nearby forest. Arano cursed his timing. He would have to wait for the soldier to feel comfortable and relax his guard. Arano found the opportunity he wanted, however, a few minutes later when the sentry sifted through his pack.

In a sudden flurry of speed, Arano seized the sentry from behind, pulled back his head, and jammed his knife into the Bromidian's throat, angling upward toward the brain. After struggling weakly for a few seconds, the soldier slumped lifelessly in Arano's arms. He surveyed the surrounding area and made certain he was alone, then activated his Comm and contacted the Summerwind.

"This is Viper," he said after Lain acknowledged

his transmission. "Just took out a Bromidian sentry. I'm inside their lines now."

"Acknowledged," replied Lain. "Videre broke through about ten minutes ago. He thinks he might be close to the target. Alyna's line of approach brought her close to too many sentries, so she's trying to flank them. They've narrowed their search and set up a perimeter. Lain, out."

Arano returned his Comm to his belt and resumed his search. He spotted three roving patrols, but was easily able to hide from them. Arano now used his skills at stealth and evasion to the utmost of his abilities, staying out of sight but moving as swiftly as he dared. He grew concerned time was running out on the mission. When the sun came up, daylight would make it next to impossible to sneak out past the sentry line. He wondered if they might have to rethink their search plan when the radio at his hip gave a warning twitch. Glancing about the area, he took a knee and activated the radio.

"Viper here," he whispered.

"This is Videre. I've found the agents. They've established their own perimeter, and are well-hidden. The Bromidians haven't found them yet, but they're close. There's no way I can sneak over to them, let alone get them out. What do you think?"

"I'm going to have to provide the Broms with a reason to look elsewhere," Arano replied. He made a quick check of his map, nodded to himself, and returned to his radio. "Take a look at your map. In my search sector there's a clearing about a click due east of a small lake. That's where I want to meet the ships.

On my signal, you and Alyna need to link up with the agents and get back to the ships as quickly as possible. Try to have the ships come to you. As soon as you're onboard, come and get me and we'll get out of here before this whole system goes up."

"Got it," came the reply. "What'll you use for a signal?"

Arano laughed. "I think you'll recognize it."

Videre groaned in reply as Alyna's voice crackled on the radio. "Viper, I copied the plan. Videre and I are only about two hundred meters apart. Give me ten minutes to get into position, and we'll be ready."

"Acknowledged," Arano answered. He was about to switch the radio back to standby mode when Lain's voice broke the silence.

"Viper, we have good news and bad news."

Arano could almost see Lain's smile over the airwaves. "I hate it when you say that."

"Why do you think I say it? At any rate, the repairs are coming along as scheduled. I think the Summerwind should be ready to make a rift jump within three hours."

"Okay," Arano replied apprehensively. "What's the rest?"

"The star in this system just experienced a major solar flare, and this planet was right in the path. We only have about two hours to get off the planet before the resulting firestorm reaches this continent. I don't need to tell you what'll happen if we haven't left yet. On top of that, my best guess is that the star will explode very soon, probably within the same three hours we're going to spend repairing the Rift Drives."

"Then you had better pick up the pace," retorted

Arano tartly. "Let's do this quickly. We have a tight timetable. Viper, out." He returned his radio to its holder on his utility belt and moved back toward the Bromidian defensive perimeter. He moved much faster now, the prior need for stealth having run its course. By the time the agreed upon ten minutes had passed, he was in the general area he felt most useful to his team.

He knew it was time for another roving Bromidian patrol to pass nearby, so he crouched down and waited. He subconsciously noted the locations of the stationary Bromidian guards, as well as the hole in the defensive line he had made by dispatching a guard on his way in. He forced his breathing to slow, calming himself and thinking more clearly. Now he was the predator at hunt, waiting patiently for his prey. Soon, he heard the sounds of several soldiers crunching through the heavy underbrush. He removed the safeties from two hand grenades, and waited in silent anticipation. Moments later, a patrol of six Rising Sun soldiers came into view, moving along a route that would bring them within ten meters of Arano's position. His chest tightened and his hands tightened around the grenades as the hatred within him boiled.

He rose to one knee and tossed the two grenades at the Bromidians in rapid succession, then dove for cover. A concussive blast rocked the forest, followed immediately by a second explosion. Leaping to his feet and howling with rage, Arano charged the three surviving Bromidians, laser rifle firing rapidly. His heavy fire and surprise attack took its toll; three guards were killed by the grenade attacks, and two more were dead from laser fire before they could recover from their shock.

The last threw himself at Arano, and the two were locked into hand-to-hand combat. Arano leaned into the soldier and pushed him backward with all of his strength. The Bromidian sensed he was being controlled and tried to push back. Once Arano felt resistance, he seized his foe in a headlock, spun and threw him across his hip, flipping the soldier to the ground. Arano snatched his knife from its sheath and ended the fight with a slash to the throat.

Then there were other soldiers charging into the area, filling the air with their shouts. Arano retrieved his rifle and hurriedly made his way to the rendezvous point. A sense of elation filled his mind that seemed oddly out of place, given the violence of the previous encounter. He felt a sudden urge to lay in ambush for the pursuing Bromidians, but he thrust the thought aside.

Thunder rumbled violently on the horizon, and Arano realized there might be a storm brewing as a result of the solar flare that had baked the other side of the planet. He realized he might have less time to get to the rendezvous than he had anticipated, and forced himself to move faster. He had another short firefight with a two-man patrol before breaking through the Bromidian lines. He considered calling his teammates to check on their progress, but thought better of it and kept moving. He had to assume they had succeeded and would soon be enroute to the planned rendezvous. Checking his location, he moved out into the fading darkness.

Alyna checked her watch and signaled Videre it was time for their rescue attempt. She had been in radio contact with the missing agents, and they expected to be extricated by the Avengers at any moment. She sat in tense silence, waiting for whatever signal Arano provided. The seconds ticked by, and she was beginning to think something had gone wrong when she heard the distant sound of two grenades detonating, followed by the sounds of laser fire. Chuckling inwardly, she led Videre forward to their rendezvous. All the Bromidians were moving in the direction of the explosions, thinking a major battle was underway. Nearing the area where she had spotted the USC agents, she shouted, "USC Avengers! Let's go! We're getting you out of here!" She raised her hands and stepped out where the closest sentry could see her.

The bedraggled agents stirred from their hiding places to close about Alyna, shaking her hand in thankful greetings. Videre joined them, and they formed a single file line for their return trip. Without wasting time, Alyna contacted Lain and gave him a rendezvous location, then led the group to the pickup point on a nearby hilltop. The sky had grown noticeably brighter, and she knew they had precious little time left on the planet. She picked up the pace, checking to make sure those following her were keeping up. She found the anxiety building within her when she thought of what would happen if she failed to get back to the ships in time to rescue Arano. In a flash of insight, she forced herself to confront the source of her excessive worries about him. She'd been with teammates during near-death experiences before, after all. She realized that despite her efforts to bury her feelings deep inside, she'd begun to care for Arano as more than just a teammate. She forced the feelings aside and concentrated on the task at hand.

She managed to lead her charges back to the ships without incident, easily avoiding the disorganized Bromidian patrols, in a state of chaos following Arano's diversion. They boarded the ships, already prepped for takeoff. Pelos told her the repairs were proceeding quickly, but there was still much work to be done. Alyna dropped into her chair, dropped her helmet to the floor with a negligent flip, and activated her controls with a snap of her wrist. She rocketed her ship into the air and immediately headed toward the rendezvous with Arano, the other ship close behind hers.

Activating the Comm, she contacted Videre in the Specter. "Videre, I've got a mobile anti-aircraft battery on my scopes. It can't bother us now since we're flying so low, but it may be a problem on our way out. Why don't you continue to the rendezvous point and pick up Arano? I'll take out their guns and catch up to you on the way out."

"Roger that," answered Videre. "See you in a few."

Arano wiped the blood from his knife on the body of a fallen Bromidian soldier and looked around the clearing at the bodies of the patrol he had encountered. It could have turned ugly for him, had his danger sense not warned him of the approaching soldiers. Still, it had been a close call. He'd ended up fighting hand-to-hand with three Rising Sun soldiers, and things hadn't gone well. One had used a thick fallen tree branch as a club, striking Arano's right thigh during the scuffle. Now, as Arano again raced to his rendezvous point, he limped noticeably with a considerable amount of pain shooting down his leg.

He struggled on for several minutes before collapsing, the wounded leg no longer able to support his weight. He pulled his Comm from its holder at his hip, intent on changing the pickup site. One look at the Comm told him it was useless, having been damaged beyond use during the fight.

For a moment, despair set in. He realized if he didn't reach the pickup site, he'd be left behind to die in the ensuing supernova explosion that would destroy the planet. Then another reality set in: His team wouldn't leave him. They would search for him until it was too late to make their own escape, and they'd die with him.

Determination to survive boiled up within him, and he forced down the pain and nausea shooting through his body. He dragged himself to his feet and resumed his trek. Overhead, flashes of lightning lit the early dawn sky, accompanied by claps of thunder. Somewhere in the back of his mind, Arano realized the daylight was coming much too quickly, and knew with a deadly certainty the firestorm was probably going to factor into this equation as well. He made a few mental calculations, confirming he and his team were running out of time. Ignoring the sudden downpour of rain that assailed him, Arano concentrated on putting one foot in front of the other.

With less than a kilometer remaining between him and his destination, Arano collapsed again. As he pushed himself back to his feet, he heard the familiar hum of the ion engines from one of the Avengers' Assault Class Fighters. He pulled a smoke grenade from his belt and detonated it, sending a white pillar billowing skyward. The Specter roared overhead, circled once, and landed nearby. Arano had managed to drag himself most of the way to the ship when two of the rescued agents emerged and helped him inside. The ship's engines fired once more, and the Specter took off almost before the doors were shut.

"Where's the Summerwind?" Arano asked in a weak voice.

"Inbound," answered Videre tensely as he stared unblinking at his monitor. "Here they come. Unknown if their Rift Drive is repaired yet. Guess we'll find out shortly. I'm raising Alyna on the Comm now."

The Comm hummed, and Alyna's face appeared, looking concerned. "We still don't have functional Rift Drives. Our best bet is to run full speed on the ion engines and put as much distance between us and the star as we can. We're seeing a bit of good luck, though. One of the rescued agents specializes in Rift Drive repair. He's jury-rigging some replacement parts as we speak. We'll see you guys back at the base."

"Negative," replied Arano. "One of us might be able to offer some advice if your repairs hit a snag. We're staying until the last possible minute. Keep us posted."

The two fighters ran at breakneck speed toward the outer reaches of the solar system. Arano moved painfully over to the weapons control panel and sat next to Lain, lightly massaging his injured leg. "At top speed, how long would it take us to reach a safe distance?"

"Without Rift Drives? At least a day. That star will be gone within the hour."

Arano nodded and turned to stare toward the front of the ship where Videre sat at the pilot's controls. The conversation in the ship was subdued, mirroring the concerns they all felt for their comrades in the other ship. Arano checked the time on his watch, tried unsuccessfully to read Videre's display from where he sat, then checked his watch again. Just when Arano thought he couldn't stand the silence any longer, the Comm beeped, and Alyna's excited voice crackled over the speaker.

"We think we have it! It'll take us a few minutes to warm up the Rift Drives, and then we can try it."

"Viper, you better take a look at this," interrupted Lain. "That star is starting to go. Impact with the first shock wave in fifteen seconds. Activating our shields."

Everyone grabbed for a handhold, bracing for the impact. Arano felt himself holding his breath, every muscle in his body tense. Seconds later, the ship was rocked by a severe hit that sent people and debris flying through the cramped passenger area. The Specter roiled violently for a few tense moments before its flight stabilized.

"Damage report, both ships," demanded Arano.

Lain turned from his controls, shaking his head. "We've lost our weapons systems, and the shields were damaged. Rift drives are still intact."

"We're in trouble," announced Alyna from the Summerwind. "We lost our shields. Another shock wave like that and we're finished."

"The next shock wave will hit in less than a minute," noted Lain, looking up from his screen.

"Videre, get us in position behind the other ship," ordered Arano. "Lain, can our shields cover both ships?"

Lain frowned, his thin, reptilian lips thinning while he considered the idea, and he checked his control panel. "I can push out the coverage area enough to protect them from the next shock wave, but our shields will probably be knocked out when the wave hits. After that, both ships will be defenseless."

"Do it," said Arano tensely. He watched as Lain manipulated his computer, carrying out the orders, while Videre notified Alyna that the Specter was going to offer shield protection. Arano heard the shield generator hum in protest as the added strain of covering both ships pushed the already damaged equipment to the breaking point. He secured a grip on the side of the ship and held on, waiting for the next impact. He looked around the room, seeing his white-knuckled handhold mirrored all around the ship as the occupants awaited the next crushing shock wave, not knowing if either ship would survive.

It finally came, slamming into both ships and tossing them around like flotsam in a raging river. When the turbulence ended, the warning beeps emitted by

Lain's computer told Arano all he needed to know about the condition of his ship's shield generator. He looked to Lain, who nodded in confirmation.

"Notify Summerwind about our condition, then prepare to activate the Rift Drives. There's nothing else we can do here."

"I copied that," announced Alyna. "We're getting ready to try our Rift Drives in a few moments. Get your people out of here. We're picking up serious contractions in the star's structure, so the supernova blast could come at any time."

"Roger. Good luck," answered Videre. "Specter out." Videre sat immobile for a few seconds, staring blankly at his panel as he, somewhat reluctantly, touched the final few controls necessary to activate the Rift Drive. The engines obediently roared to life, opening a small wormhole and propelling the ship toward the safety of the Lican system.

CHAPTER FIVE

THE RETURN FLIGHT SEEMED ENDLESS AS THE PASsengers and crew of the Specter worried, hoping and praying the sister ship had successfully jumped out of the system before the Seoran star went supernova. Arano would have paced the deck in nervous anticipation, but the cramped quarters prevented walking about. Besides, he thought glumly, he should rest his leg. For the entirety of the flight, he tried not to think about it, knowing if the Summerwind's Rift Drives had not been repaired, the ship and her entire crew would be destroyed. There was a possibility he would never see Alyna and his other teammates again. It was a bitter pill to swallow.

His crew members became active again, bringing the ship out of the wormhole in the Lican system. Time continued to tick away, and there was no sign of the sister ship. Scanners had been knocked out during the final shock wave back in the Seoran system, and they were reduced to the expedient method of repeatedly calling the Summerwind on subspace radio, hoping for an answer. It might take Alyna and her crew a few moments to get the ship's radios functional again once it dropped out of the wormhole, but hopefully they would contact the Specter with news of their safe arrival as soon as possible. Behind him, he heard Lain's voice endlessly calling for the Summerwind without results, but with hope still alive in his words. The silence that greeted them over the radio was almost palpable, and tension was thick in the confined crew area. Arano, along with the others who were crammed into the Assault Class Fighter, stared wordlessly at the floor while waiting for news.

"Long range sensors are back on-line . . . sort of," commented Videre dryly. "I should be able to pick up energy sources as long as they're concentrated forms of energy. I can't scan for ships yet, but I might be able to pick up a trace or two from their engines. Also, Fleet Headquarters reports the rescue group is enroute and should arrive within two hours." Arano nodded in acknowledgment while Videre struggled to get his damaged equipment to function. Arano glanced at his Gatoan teammate, and noticed a look of intent concentration on Videre's feline face, the light eyebrows furrowed and his eyes almost squinting as he manipulated his communication interface.

Suddenly, he bared his teeth in a broad grin. "I think I've found them! I'm picking up an energy source about 50 kilometers away. It appears to be a ship continually firing its plasma battery in a repeating pattern."

"Let me see it," commanded Arano, struggling to his feet and limping over to Videre's station. He laughed and clapped Videre on the back. "It's old Morse Code! They are requesting help. This used to be called an 'SOS'." Excited shouts ran through the ship as the Avengers and their rescued agents celebrated the successful search with gruff handshakes and firm pats on the back. Videre returned to the pilot's station and plotted a course for the source of the plasma blasts as Lain sent news of the find to Fleet Headquarters.

Late the next day, the Avengers Team 5 planning room was a scene of chaos. The team had returned immediately upon disembarking from their transports, and hadn't yet begun their equipment maintenance. Piles of hastily discarded gear lay about the room.

"Well, everyone," Arano said, "I understand the dining hall has prepared a meal for us, so let's not keep them waiting. We can finish gear maintenance later. We're all getting a few days off, so enjoy it while you can. We'll concentrate on this Disciple thing since our ships are going to be in repairs for quite some time. Let's eat."

They filed out of the room, Arano limping at the rear of the group as he read over a report from Cadron regarding the betrayal of their mission in the Codian system. There were seven individuals outside his immediate chain of command who were aware of the mission. One of those individuals was deceased. Arano didn't eliminate that individual from the list, but he decided if this was in fact the traitor, his death would eliminate the long court processes associated with espionage trials. He walked through the empty corridors, trailing behind five people who, although they were from different races and different backgrounds, he knew would never betray him.

Arano keyed the controls on the pilot's panel of his starship, the Eclipse, and the craft disappeared into the wormhole. He looked over at Alyna who was reading one of her favorite romantic novels. Irrationally, like an inexperienced teenager on his first date, he felt his pulse quicken when he cast his gaze casually in her direction. He hadn't been in a relationship since the murder of his fiancé, but Alyna brought feelings to the fore he'd thought were long since buried. Wiping the perspiration from his hands, he nervously licked his lips and looked over at Alyna for the umpteenth time since they left the spaceport.

"Thanks again for coming along with me," he said. "I told my aunt you and I only recently started dating, so she shouldn't ask too many questions. I hate lying to her, but at her age I hate seeing her worry about me even more."

Alyna gave him a knowing smile. "Well," she said hesitantly, "we don't have to lie to her. I know how Command feels about teammates going out with each other, but why don't we make it a real date?"

Arano's face lit up, despite his best efforts to hide it. "Why, Miss Marquat, are you asking me out?"

"That's 'Captain Marquat'," she corrected him with a smile, "and yes, I am. And accepting my offer is the least you can do, after I agreed to ride in this junk heap you call a starship. Especially after you led me to believe it wouldn't be ready in time for us to take it."

"All right." Arano said with a grin. "It's a date." He thought for a moment, then asked, "Have you ever seen one of the Padian rituals we go through with the officials from the Coalition?"

"No," she replied, her brows knitted in curiosity. "Why?"

"I don't want to spoil any surprises for you, but be prepared. The rituals, while different each time, may seem a bit strange at first. But whatever you do, don't laugh. I don't want you to alienate what little I have left of my family. By the way, before the ritual, I'll introduce you to my aunt, and then I'll have to disappear for a few minutes. Since my father was a clan leader, the hereditary title fell to me. I have to meet briefly with the other clan leaders and then we can join the festivities. The whole meeting will last another couple of hours and we'll be free to leave."

"Then why did we get released from duty for an additional day?"

"It's hunting season," Arano said slyly. "I never miss the opportunity to hunt padorsas this time of year." Alyna raised an eyebrow and looked at him askew, so he continued. "A padorsa is a small furry animal. They usually weigh about ten kilograms, although some weigh closer to thirty. At any rate, the last time I was there, the killing frost had come, so it's time to refill my meat freezers."

"Killing frost?"

"A Padian superstition, but one rooted in fact." He

opened a plastic bag containing crackers, and offered some to Alyna. "Have you ever heard a Padian talk about the killing frost?" She shook her head, and he glanced away briefly to gather his thoughts. "Most of the species of fur bearing animals on Leguin 4 carry a parasite through the summer months that would make you sick or even kill you if you ate an infected animal. Through the ages, experience taught my people the first killing frost of the year destroys that parasite, making the animals safe to eat. According to Padian religion, Vyper, the Padian god of autumn, brings the killing frost every year, which kills the parasite. It has become tradition among our people that the hunting season starts with the coming of Vyper."

"And you were nicknamed after the Padian god of autumn? Why is that?"

"That's another story, not directly related to the religion itself," he replied, expertly dodging the question. "How much do you know about our religion?"

"Just that you have four good gods and one evil god."

"Basically correct. The four 'good gods' are called 'Elementals'. Moran represents winter, Primae represents spring, Tera is Summer, and Vyper is autumn. Vandaar is the god of evil, and he has many powerful servants. Eons ago, he sent Sardon, the three-headed demon of the apocalypse, to guard the entrance to Giona, our version of what you would call paradise. This meant that Padians who died could not enter Giona and were doomed to wander the afterlife endlessly. After 500 years of this, the Elementals sent Neral, son of the great warrior king Krados, to do battle with Sardon. During their melee, Neral's sword shattered, forcing him to fight with his dagger in one hand and the shattered sword in the other. Neral finally slew Sardon, but soon died from his injuries. As a holy symbol, we use a crossed dagger and broken sword."

"What kind of holidays do you celebrate?"

"Well, I'm not very serious about the whole thing myself. I'm not as skeptical about religion as Kish is, but I'm not a religious fanatic either. I tend to follow the teachings of our religion as closely as the next person, but religion doesn't rule my life. Of course," he said with a sly grin, "I'm quite content to take our holidays off from work. We celebrate some similar to your Human religion. You celebrate your savior's birthday as Christmas. We celebrate Neral's birthday as Virendor and his day of death as Matandor. Each Elemental has his own holiday as well: Primandor in the spring, Terandor in the summer, Vypandor in the fall, and Morandor in the winter."

"For not being devoutly religious, you seem to have a pretty solid grasp of your theology."

Arano rolled his eyes. "Daxia training. Part of our studies included religion. That wasn't my favorite part. Maybe it's why I'm a little less enthusiastic about my religion. It always took time away from other things I wanted to do."

The conversation turned, and the voyage passed. After several hours, they exited the wormhole, and Leguin 4 slipped into view. Shortly, he was smothered in hugs from his aunt, who had been waiting in anticipation at the spaceport.

"Alyna," he announced when he managed to pry

himself loose, "this is Nebra. Aunt Nebra, this is Alyna Marquat, who I told you about on the radio." Alyna and Nebra shook hands, exchanged an enthusiastic greeting, and all three moved to the waiting transports that would take them to the ceremonial greeting between the Padian government and the Coalition officials. They passed the time by making small talk, and arrived at the Padian palace following a short ride.

Alyna saw Arano looking at the ostentatious palace, his pursed lips betraying his opinion of the need for such an opulent structure. Massive white pillars lined the front, and slender spires rose majestically into the sky. Numerous government officials scurried about, each looking as if his business was the most important in the Padian government. Of course, she knew Arano saw about as much use for these bureaucrats as he did for the excessive ornamentation on the massive structure in front of him.

When they entered the building, Arano excused himself, explaining he had to join the other Padian clan leaders for the ceremonies, and left Alyna in the company of his aunt.

Alyna couldn't help feeling there was something going on behind the scenes with the ceremony, but she couldn't quite put her finger on it. "You've noticed it, too," observed Nebra as she led the way to the audience chambers.

"Noticed what?"

"That look on Arano's face, for starters. I've been trying for years to get him to tell me why he gets so much entertainment from these meetings with the

Coalition Council. He normally hates going to political functions for the Padian government, and I'm sure you've noticed he has a strong dislike for the Coalition's bureaucracy. He's up to something."

"Definitely," agreed Alyna, turning the corner to enter a large, decorative room that housed the Padian Clan Council. "But doesn't he always have some scheme or another cooking?"

"Like his plan to get you to pretend to be his girlfriend?" asked Nebra with a grin. "He told me he was bringing you, and that you two had started dating, but he can't fool me. He's such a dear for not wanting me to worry about him, but he can't fool me."

"Actually," Alyna told her with a wink, "on the way here we made it official. We'll have to see where it goes."

Nebra started slightly, then sighed. "I have to warn you, girl. His intentions are good, and I have no doubt he will treat you right. But you have to realize he's carrying a lot of baggage."

A surge of sympathy welled up in Alyna's heart, and she struggled bravely against the tears coming unbidden to her eyes. "You mean the murder of his fiancé?"

"Yes, but not in the way you're thinking. He's over her death, for the most part, but he's not over his hatred for the Bromidian race or his desire for revenge. All Padians bear a strong dislike for Bromidians, but with Arano, it's a passion so strong it's almost unholy. Right now there's so much hatred in his heart there's no room left for him to love someone. He's going to have to deal with those feelings of hate before he can begin to deal with his feelings for you. I'm not sure what that will take."

Alyna was about to respond when a trumpet fanfare announced the arrival of Arano and the other Clan Leaders who took their places in their ceremonial chairs. A second blare of the horns brought the representatives of the Coalition into the room, dressed in multihued robes with feathers adorning their heads in a shocking clash of colors. As Alyna sat staring and speechless, the Coalition members shuffled in an odd gait to a long bench where they went through a ritual involving kneeling first on one knee, then the other, then making a strange sign with their hands before being seated. The meeting proceeded, matters of state interspersed with other ritualistic details the Coalition officials uncomfortably performed. Oddly, even from where she was sitting, Alyna could see the scarcely concealed grin creeping across Arano's face.

Following the ceremony, Arano met with Alyna and Aunt Nebra for the brief stroll to their waiting transports. Aunt Nebra gave Arano a hug, promising to be at his house for dinner that evening, then she entered her transport. Arano guided Alyna to another waiting groundcar, and the two rode away in the direction of a nearby, densely forested range of hills. As they drove along the meandering road, Arano pointed out various landmarks and government buildings, explaining to Alyna the significance for Padians and their heritage.

The hustle and noise of the city soon gave way to a vast wilderness. Arano noticed the awed expression on Alyna's face, and smiled in satisfaction. He had hoped she would appreciate the woodland he called home, and she hadn't disappointed him. One particular stretch of road displayed a serene view of such beauty that Alyna gave a startled gasp. Arano stopped the groundcar, and the Avengers walked to the edge of a sharply sloped hillside.

The valley stretched away before them, a forest of ancient oaks obscuring the valley floor. A cool, crisp breeze blew in from the North, a sure sign of the coming winter. The leaves on the trees had turned a golden brown, interrupted here and there by patches of red. Far below, over three kilometers distant, a wide, slow-moving river wandered along its lonely path to the sea. Arano felt Alyna's hand reach tentatively for his own, and grasped it gratefully.

They stood admiring the view for several minutes before Arano indicated they should move along. He'd heard there might be bad weather coming, and didn't like the look of the clouds moving in from the west. His instincts proved prophetic; before they'd driven ten kilometers, a heavy downpour was soaking the area. Brilliant flashes of lightning accented the drenching rains and blowing winds. Arano relaxed, listening to the heavy pattering of the deluge.

They finally arrived at Arano's home, a fair-sized house built in a secluded part of the forest. His ancestral home was much larger, a mansion left to him following the death of his parents, but he preferred to spend time in the smaller house. He had built the entire structure with the help of two other Daxia, classmates of his at Whelen Academy. Although it had taken a considerable amount of time and labor, he took great pride in the fact he had built it himself. Arano parked his craft under the covered walkway and led Alyna into the house while the storm still raged around them.

"I've always loved thunderstorms," commented Alyna as she watched the sheets of rain driving against the windows.

"Me too," replied Arano, his eyes distant, remembering times long past, times after he had joined the Coalition military, before he had become an Avenger.

"You're thinking of a story, aren't you?" Alyna noted. "I can see it in your eyes." She smiled. "Come on, let me hear it."

"There isn't much to tell," he told her, motioning for her to sit. "I was attached to a parachute infantry division, and we were assaulting a moon held by a particularly brutal band of pirates. The attack went well at first, but then a surprise storm moved into the area. Our laser rangefinders couldn't function in the driving rainstorm, making it hard to use our artillery. I was able to estimate the distance to different land features by using the lightning. When a bolt struck a prominent tree or cliff face, I'd time the difference between the flash of the lightning and the sound of the thunder. It's simple math from there to calculate the distances, based upon the speed of sound on that moon. It didn't take us long to have range estimates to their different heavy weapons emplacements. The battle didn't last very long after that."

"You amaze me sometimes," Alyna told him. "You don't look like much, but you can come up with some pretty creative ideas."

Arano was about to protest, a puzzled look on his face, but Alyna disarmed him with a laugh and a smile. "I'm just kidding you. That was a pretty innovative idea, though. It's no wonder you made it into the Avengers as soon as you did."

"I think Laron may have had something to do with that," answered Arano, accepting her compliment. "Once he saw me in action against Rising Sun, I didn't have a moment's peace until I was a graduate of the Avengers Academy."

They were interrupted by a ring of the doorbell as Aunt Nebra announced her arrival. The three talked briefly before Arano left Alyna and Aunt Nebra with a bottle of wine and went to the kitchen to fix their meal. Following dinner they lingered at the table, telling stories of times past. Finally, Aunt Nebra announced she needed to head home and said she'd stop by the next afternoon.

"We had better be getting some sleep, too," announced Arano. Seeing the puzzled look on Alyna's face, he said, "You're going hunting with me in the morning, right?"

Two days later, Arano entered the Avengers Team 5 planning room, ready to get to work on the Disciple murders. His teammates were already assembled, and datapads covered the main table as they reviewed evidence from the case. Noticing the Grand High Councilor's aide was not present, Arano's spirit lifted and he anticipated being able to get some work accomplished without all the endless questions.

"Good morning," he announced as he pulled out a chair. "Where's Cono?'

"We haven't seen him." Videre said, laughing. "We assumed he rode with you on the Eclipse, and you left him stranded on Leguin 4."

Arano sighed, looking over at Alyna. "I see you kept quiet about this one," he complained in a voice dripping with sarcasm.

"Oops,"Alyna said without conviction. "Actually, I tried not to tell them, but it was just too funny. The look on your face when the ship wouldn't start was classic. It's a good thing your aunt loaned us her ship. Did they say when the Eclipse would be ready?"

"At least a few days," Arano told her, smiling in spite of himself. "So, Pelos, I got your message about Grand High Councilor Tient. What did you find out?"

Pelos shook his head and rolled his eyes. "I can't believe that slimeball got re-elected. I checked out some rumors about the arrest of Balor Tient almost eight years ago. According to my sources in the police department, the rumors are true. In 2205, he made a very unpopular environmental decision concerning fuels used by certain land-based vehicles. He imposed regulations prohibiting the use of any type of fuel other than that made by a company called Alcon, citing environmental factors. Oddly, Alcon's fuel was less efficient and more expensive. A detective looked into it on his own time and found that during the previous election Alcon had donated some very sizable amounts of money to Tient's campaign. This detective arrested Tient on the charges, but they were dismissed and all evidence destroyed after allegations were made the detective was discriminating against the Grand High Councilor for being a Human. The information never went public."

Arano frowned, a sickening sense of certainty coming over him. "What happened to the detective?"

Pelos sighed, looking up from his notes. "The next time he took an interplanetary trip, the Rift Drive engines on his ship exploded, killing everyone aboard."

"Should I act surprised?" asked Arano, shoving a chair out of his way.

Pelos looked back at his paperwork. "During some unrelated financial research, I discovered a few more items of interest. I learned Transcorp has been participating in some unusual shipping practices, so I checked them out. They're still shipping items from the Ervik system to Navek 6, and, just as you mentioned, the cargo isn't being scanned because of the nebula in the Ervik System. Even stranger is their route through the Navek System, coming through the system in a flat trajectory along the same geometric plane as the planetary orbits."

"Through the Navek asteroid belt?" asked Alyna, her eyes going wide.

"Very close to it," replied Pelos, squinting slightly as he consulted some handwritten notes. "They drop off food supplies at Navek 6 and return empty to Ervik. It makes no sense. At any rate, I checked back into their expenditure history. Although they made some pretty serious attempts to hide it, they've been giving money to Tient.

"The other company we talked about that day was

Biomek, which was researching old technology on live organ transplants. They got their start in the field by buying the technology from Tient."

"But information on that technology is available for public access, right?" wondered Videre, his feline brow creased in thought.

"Public, yes," answered Pelos with a click of his beak, "but the fact that someone had made access to that information would also have been made public. It appears they want this to be kept secret, and they've paid a lot of money to the Grand High Councilor to keep it that way.

"The last bit of information I found makes no sense. Garanth Construction received the contract to build the new High Council offices last year. Garanth had both the highest bid and the oddest architectural design. Every office has a window, and there are no interior rooms. At any rate, they got the job, despite their high bid. I just can't figure out what their angle is. There's no evidence showing they gave the Grand High Councilor any money."

"Why don't you start checking into their background?" decided Arano after a moment's thought. "It's possible the owner is giving money to Tient through another company to keep it secret. He also gave Garanth exclusive iridium mining rights in the Leguin System, so there has to be a connection. Excellent work, Pelos. I'd love for us to dig up enough dirt on Tient to run him out of office."

"And into jail," added Pelos.

Just then, the door to their meeting room burst open and Cadron hastily entered. "The Disciples have killed again," he announced. "The body was found this morning near Wolf Lake. The victim was a Kamling female who owned a local restaurant. I've lined up transportation to take us to the crime scene, if you're able to leave."

"Let's go," responded Arano. "I take it the scene has been processed by the police?"

"They should be finished by the time we get there," replied Cadron. "They aren't going to remove anything until you get a look at it."

Upon arrival, Arano's team combed the crime scene, a grassy area of Wolf Lake Park, looking for anything the police might have missed. Arano considered the scene even as his eyes poured over the ground, searching for tidbits of evidence that might have been missed. This part of the park was well-manicured, with trees and shrubs showing signs of recent pruning. The close-cropped grass was interrupted only by a single meandering trail, perhaps two feet wide, encircling the entire lake. Off in the distance, a boathouse was plainly visible, and the lack of boaters in the area told Arano the police had cordoned off the park in the hopes that something might turn up. After fruitlessly searching the crime scene and the surrounding area, they backtracked the trail the victim appeared to have been following. Finally, Arano called a halt and gathered his team.

"Once again, we've found nothing. I think we need to change the thrust of our search. There never seem to be any witnesses or evidence left behind. Anyone have any thoughts?"

"Actually," Cadron said slowly, massaging his arm

in deep thought, "I've been developing a theory along those lines. The absence of witnesses in every case so far leads me to believe that the perpetrator knows when no one is around. It's possible the Disciples are using motion trackers to alert them to the presence of potential witnesses. Also, one of the newer handheld scanners would easily alert them to DNA evidence they might have been accidentally left behind, such as hair. That explains how they could be such perfect housecleaners at each crime scene."

Kish looked around thoughtfully, her leather-skinned face intent. "What we need is an eyewitness who can't be detected by their equipment."

"You have something in mind?" asked Videre.

"If I remember correctly," said Kish, her reputation for having a photographic memory eliciting a sarcastic chuckle from Videre, "I believe I saw a security camera on that boat storage building we just passed. If their camera was working at the time of the killings ." She trailed off thoughtfully, as Arano looked around the crime scene again.

"All right," said Arano, "Kish and I will go check this out. The rest of you finish up here, and we'll meet you back at the transports."

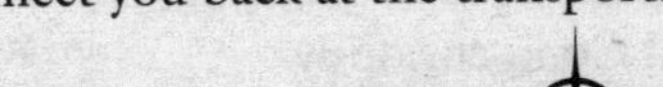

Arano leaned forward in his seat, peering intently at the screen before him. With the rest of his team, he was scanning several video disks confiscated from the boat storage facility. Finally, perseverance paid off as the latest Disciples victim appeared on the tape, jogging along the trail that wound around the lake. Arano found himself perspiring while he waited for what would follow. As the video continued to play, the door to the meeting room opened to admit Cono, who was motioned to silence by Kish Waukee. As the moments ticked by and nothing else appeared on the screen, Arano's shoulders slumped in despair.

The movement that caught his eye was barely noticeable at first, just an unusual shaking of the underbrush. A large, furry shape emerged, followed by a second, skulking swiftly along the trail behind the doomed jogger.

"There!" exclaimed Arano, rising from his chair. "Freeze and enhance!" Videre complied, zooming in on the image of the two Disciples as they stalked their prey. "Two Tsimians . . . is that a stun stick the first one is carrying?"

"I'll try to enhance it further," said Videre, frowning. He tried several different means of enlarging the picture, but each enlargement distorted the picture to the point it was unreadable. "I can't do anything else with this equipment. I think we're going to have to submit it to the lab. They should be able to enhance it enough to allow us to see their faces clearly."

"What's this?" asked Cono curiously.

"Video from the latest Disciples killing," replied Arano without taking his eyes off the screen. "We're fairly certain these two individuals are our killers." He briefly described what had transpired at the lake, resulting in the finding of the video. Cono stroked his beak as he nodded in understanding, his shaggy, sharply raised eyebrows showing he was very impressed by the turn of events.

"We're hoping," Arano continued, "this may be the key to solving the murders. As soon as this is processed by our lab, we can"

He was interrupted by the piercing wail of the general alert siren, broadcast over the building's public address system. "Attention, all Avengers personnel. Report to the mission briefing room in ten minutes for deployment orders. This is not a drill."

Arano drooped his head in defeat, sighed, and looked at his teammates. "Videre, I need you to make arrangements to get this video to the lab. Make sure we have a backup copy saved in our computer before that video leaves your sight. When you're finished, catch up with us in the briefing room. Cono, since you've been granted security clearance for these matters, you can accompany us to the meeting if you wish. I'm not sure what has happened, and with our ships still out for repairs I don't know how much help we can be."

The team filed out into the hallway, Arano and Alyna trailing along behind the other Avengers, watching as Cono and Cadron conversed quietly on their way to the briefing. Arano walked in icy silence, repeatedly clenching and releasing his fists, the frustration inside him so thick he felt he could cut it with a knife. He felt a light squeeze on his hand and glanced over to see Alyna smiling at him. "Cheer up, Captain," she told him. "It's just a delay. We're on the verge of cracking this one wide open."

Arano took a deep breath, letting it out slowly. "You're right," he acknowledged. "It seems events have conspired against us lately. Every time we start to make progress, some great crisis rears its ugly head, and Team 5 has to answer the call."

They turned another corner and entered the Avengers Briefing Room. Arano's team took their customary seats to await the briefing, and were joined shortly by Videre Genoa.

Arano glanced impatiently about the room. The teams were all assembled and awaiting the arrival of the command staff. The seats for the Avengers of the various teams were arranged in a concentric semi-circular pattern, with each row of seats offset at a slightly higher level than the row before it, allowing all present to have an uninterrupted view of whatever presentation was made.

The commotion in the room quieted down, and Arano saw that two Human officers, Commander Mendarle and General Tamor, had entered. The rest of the Avengers command staff took their places.

Commander Mendarle held up his hand for silence and stepped up to the podium. "The Bromidian faction Rising Sun has crossed the line, and the time has come for us to eliminate them. Let me first fill you in on recent developments, and then I will explain the actions we've planned.

"In recent times, President Bistre has been the greatest ally the military has in the Coalition government. He has tried for years to get permission from the Coalition High Council to raid Rising Sun's headquarters at Solarian, but the Council has remained squeamish about the idea. We've been able to conduct retaliatory attacks in rare instances, but nothing else.

"Just two hours ago, as the USCS Diplomatic was enroute to the Leguin system from Immok, it was pulled from its artificial wormhole by a picket line of Thief Class Cruisers, and it was boarded. The President and several members of the general staff were abducted. We have confirmation from the crew of the Diplomatic that Rising Sun operatives were responsible." He paused, looking grimly out over the silent warriors sitting speechless before him. "It appears the Rising Sun ships were escaping to the Karlac system, but we can't get any further confirmation from Diplomatic's crew. Before the Bromidians left the ship, they disabled the Diplomatic's scanners and inertial stabilizers. The crew estimates it'll take them the better part of three weeks to get the ship stopped. Because of that, they were unable to track the Bromidian ship." He paused again and turned to consult with General Tamor.

Cono leaned close to Arano and whispered, "I didn't understand all that about the inertial stabilizers. I was never much of a physics student."

"How about an analogy, then?" replied Arano, his politeness belying his true feelings about Cono. "Picture being in a ground transport that has to stop suddenly. Even though you may have only been traveling at forty, maybe fifty kilometers per hour, you'd still be thrown toward the front of the vehicle with a tremendous amount of force. Now, picture a starship traveling at over 40,000 kilometers per second. Imagine the kind of force that would be involved if you attempted to slow or even turn the ship. The inertial stabilizers eliminate the forces of inertia, allowing ships to make radical changes in velocity without affecting the ship or its crew. The only problem is the stabilizer can't anticipate the effects of impacts from beam weapons and torpedoes, so a ship in combat tends to get tossed around a bit." Cono nodded in acknowledgment as Commander Mendarle stepped back to the podium.

"Each of your teams will have a separate assignment. The High Council, already in session at the time of this attack, has given us the approval to wipe out Rising Sun, using any means necessary. The Grand High Councilor was violently opposed to the idea, but for once he didn't get his way. The High Council military committee approved a motion to declare war on Rising Sun, and the full High Council followed suit. Our first priority shall be to locate and rescue the President and the missing members of the general staff. Most of you will be assigned various reconnaissance missions to that end. Two of the teams, 5 and 12, have assault fighters in repair. Those teams will be assigned to Task Force Blue, which is presently enroute to a rally point in the Earth system. You'll each be assigned a standard fighter craft and will provide fighter escort for the task force." Several audible groans accompanied the announcement as the battle hardened veterans expressed some displeasure at the idea. The commander continued, running down the list of assignments for the various teams as they began the struggle to rescue the President.

Alyna returned to the team meeting room, a scowl

creasing her perfect features. "When it rains, it pours . . . no pun intended," she quipped.

"Now what?" groaned Arano in exasperation.

"We've been assigned to the new prototype Firestorm class fighters. Firestorms are the only single-pilot fighters with shields strong enough to survive a direct hit from a torpedo. They're only slightly larger than standard Stingray class fighters, but they've been outfitted with Rift Drives."

"Uh oh," said Videre wryly.

"Team 12 was taken to the Earth system by transport because there were fighters available for them on one of the assault carriers," continued Alyna. "We have to fly our own fighters to the system."

"That promises to be moderately uncomfortable," noted Videre with a chuckle.

"I have to admit, I'm impressed with their new engines," continued Alyna. "Sure, Rift Drives on smaller ships tend to cool down pretty quickly, but these engines can make three back-to-back jumps without a cool-down period. The Phoenix Class Frigate was previously the owner of the engines with the lowest heat ratio, and it still takes a Phoenix nearly two hours to be ready for a second jump.

"We can't leave for several hours. There's a severe storm system moving through, and no fighters are allowed to take off until the storm passes. In fact, the storm is strong enough that power and computer networks are going off-line all over the city. Looks like we're going to be late for the party."

The door opened and a courier entered, displaying papers showing he was to take the video of the

Disciples crime scene to the lab for processing. Arano read the man's credentials, grunted in acknowledgment, and picked up the disk containing the video. After a moment's consideration, he moved to a computer panel, went through the ritualistic security clearance process, finishing with the retina identification, and inserted the disk. His thoughts were still on the mission, but he couldn't help think about the Disciples case. Somewhere on this tape was the answer they'd sought for two years, and now he had to wait to see it. He wanted to howl in frustration. After the computer made another backup copy of the video, Arano handed the original disk to the courier, who saluted smartly and left.

After lunch, Arano's team again assembled in their meeting room to discuss the Disciples video while they waited for the weather to clear. "I don't think these Tsimians acted alone," Cadron offered.

"I agree," said Pelos. The big Tsimian was studying photos taken of different Disciples victims, absently toying with the lucky tollep's tooth he wore on a thin, non-descript chain about his neck. "Tsimians don't typically have the stealth or the subtlety to carry out this sort of operation alone. The victims are obviously stalked for some time prior to the attack, probably for several days, if not weeks. I don't know of many Tsimians who could pull that off."

"We have several pieces of the puzzle on the table," said Arano with a sweep of his hand. "Cadron, while we're gone, why don't you see if you can find some sort of method to this madness."

"I believe I can offer you the basic scenario now, after seeing that video," answered Cadron confidently. "Someone, probably not our Tsimian movie stars, selects the victims. If the intended victim is a Human, someone verifies the victim is not a Padian. The victim is stalked for several days or even a few weeks, establishing patterns of behavior such as regular appointments, routes taken to and from work, the hours they keep, and so on. It seems that if the victim is a member of a health club, the attack occurs on the way home after a workout."

"When the victim is tired and won't be able to fight back as effectively," added Lain.

"Exactly," continued Cadron. "After studying the victim's habits, the three perpetrators get together and decide on a time and place for the attack. Since the attacks are pulled off so efficiently, there are probably lots of preparations made, including multiple getaway vehicles, rehearsals of the attack, and military-style contingency planning. They stalk the victim, make certain no one else is around by using a motion tracker of some kind, and attack. They stun the victim with the stun rod, tie the victim down, and conduct their ritual."

"I'm impressed," admitted Cono grudgingly, eyes opening wide. "I have to admit, I believe your plates are too full, what with trying to solve these murders while conducting counter-intelligence assignments and other typical Avengers missions. Despite all the obligations and distractions, you seem to be making progress. I guess I'm going to have to eat my words, but I think a large part of your success is due to Cadron. I'm seeing my opinion about the use of civilian consultants change. I might even put in a good word for you."

"Message from the fleet commander," interrupted Kish. "There's a break in the weather coming, and we can launch in thirty minutes."

Pelos gave Kish a playful shove. "There, you see?" he asked. "The Tsimian gods of war are smiling upon us."

Kish gave a friendly laugh, shaking her head. "Yes, Pelos, I'm sure they are." She smiled sarcastically. "You might make a believer of me yet."

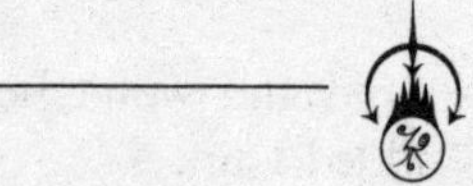

Arano sat in the confining cockpit of the new Firestorm class fighter, waiting impatiently as his ship hurtled through the wormhole. His thoughts leapt from one topic to another, and he realized he had a lot to think about. The upcoming mission loomed largest in his mind. While all Avengers trained regularly in ship-to-ship combat, he still preferred their standard Assault Class Fighters rather than the smaller single pilot ships. He also mulled over the new data on the Disciples cases. He had wanted to take a copy of the video to his house, but their departure had come sooner than expected. He made a mental note to do it immediately upon his return.

And then there was Alyna and his unexpected feelings for her. The feelings were obviously mutual, but he didn't know what to do about it. He had too many other obligations to let personal matters interfere with his duties. He shook his head and sighed, shifting his weight to make himself more comfortable.

He started when the warning beep from the computer indicated his flight was nearly at an end. "Prepare to exit the wormhole . . . oh, jeez," laughed Arano, remembering he was alone. "Now I know I'm losing it. I'm talking to myself." He waited, and at the computer's prompting touched a control and exited the wormhole, the other five Firestorm fighters emerging in perfect formation. They all checked in by radio, and Arano led the way to the rendezvous point.

It wasn't long before he realized something was wrong. By now, the fleet should have contacted him. He opened his hailing frequencies and announced, "This is Captain Lakeland calling Task Force Blue. Do you copy?" He was greeted by an ominous silence, and he frowned at the implications. "This is Captain Lakeland calling Task Force Blue. Do you copy?"

"I'm conducting a scan of the area," announced Alyna. "The task force isn't where they are supposed to be. They may have left early. When we get closer, I can conduct a more thorough scan."

"Right," said Arano. He pressed a few buttons, opening a subspace channel to fleet headquarters. "Captain Lakeland calling Fleet Headquarters."

"Sergeant Anas of Fleet Headquarters, go ahead," came the reply.

"Avengers Team 5 has arrived at the rendezvous point, but Task Force Blue isn't here. Were they called away?"

"Give me a moment to verify." A few anxious moments ticked by before the answer came. "Negative.

Task Force Blue is still at the rendezvous point. They reported a group of ships emerging from a wormhole about four hours ago, and we've had no contact with them since. Admiral Absot says you're to investigate and fill us in ASAP. Relief forces are already enroute."

"Roger, out." He closed the channel and reopened communications with his team. "You all have the exact coordinates of the rendezvous point. Let's split up into our two squads, get a thorough sensor sweep on the way in, and meet at those coordinates. Everyone get a calculation for the jump to Tellen Station in the Eden system and have your computer recalculate every 30 seconds. If we get into trouble, I want everyone to jump out on my mark. Alyna, take your squad on a heading of 217 mark 80. I'll see you in a few." The squads separated, heading on different trajectories to their established meeting point.

"Viper," announced a troubled Lain, "I'm conducting a chromatographic vapor scan of the area, and it indicates traces of nebula emissions on some of the space debris."

"That doesn't make sense," responded Arano. "There are no nebulae for thousands of light years."

"I'm getting it, too," Videre chimed in. "I'm also picking up traces of Elerium."

Which is used in torpedoes, Arano thought, certain now something had happened to the fleet. "This is starting to look worse and worse."

"Alyna to Viper."

"Go ahead," he responded.

"I've found the fleet," she told him, "or what's left of it. I've been able to identify the remains of the Command Battle Cruiser, a Thor Class Cruiser, a battleship, and several frigates. The rest of the mess appears to be the remnants of fighters."

Arano's blood went cold. "Any sign of Firestorm Class Fighters?"

"I'll check," she replied. A few minutes later, Arano got the answer he feared.

"I've located enough debris for several Firestorm Class Fighters. It looks like the task force has been destroyed, and Avengers Team 12 with it."

CHAPTER SIX

ARANO'S FIGHTER DRIFTED THROUGH THE DEBRIS field while he scanned for lifesigns. He had contacted Fleet Headquarters and informed them of the incident, and a recovery team was on the way to examine the wreckage. So far, not a single survivor had been located. The wreckage of several lifepods gave mute evidence to the fact no witnesses were to be left behind.

Since the task force was unable to send a signal indicating they were under attack, the invading fleet must have immediately jammed radio and subspace transmissions. Of course, that meant the raiders knew Task Force Blue would be waiting, making it a deliberate ambush. The circumstances indicated, once more, the Coalition had been betrayed from within. This was to have been a secret mission for the Coalition fleet.

A warning beep sounded on Arano's console. "Heads up," he announced. "We've got company. Ships are coming out of a wormhole. Looks like six light fighters. Alyna, your squad is closer. Can you get a make on them?"

"Getting it now," she replied. "Hang on . . . got

it. Shields up! It's a Rising Sun fighter wing!"

"Form up, standard battle formations. Let's do this by the numbers. With the six of us, we can handle it. Accelerate to attack speed and move in." Their endless hours of training took over, and the two squads moved in with practiced skill. Three enemy fighters disappeared in balls of flame on their first pass, and they swung about to make another charge. Lain's fighter had taken a few hits, but his shields seemed to be holding up.

"Watch it," exclaimed Videre, "there's an Asmodeus Class Battle Cruiser jumping in. It appears to be Rising Sun also. We're going to have to get out of here in a hurry!"

"We can't jump out without deactivating our shields first. We have to finish these fighters off and make a run for it," ordered Arano. He checked his fighter's temperature controls, noting the engines had cooled sufficiently for another jump just as Alyna had said they would. "Listen up: go to Formation Two, and let's end this as quickly as we can."

The squads rejoined and split into three groups of two ships, each group diving in a different direction as the enemy fighters milled about in confusion. Arano swung in behind an enemy fighter and initiated his missile lock sequence. He inhaled sharply when the computer was unable to get a lock.

"I've got a secondary weapons system failure," Arano announced. "Can't get missile lock. I'm switching to guns . . . computer is tracking fine on the plasma battery. Moving in."

"My shields are malfunctioning," Alyna announced.

"Kish, stay on my wing and watch my six!"

The Rising Sun warship continued to close the distance, getting dangerously close to the floundering Avenger ships. Arano accelerated, drawing closer to a fleeing enemy fighter. He poured murderous plasma fire on the hapless ship until it exploded in a brilliant flash of flame. The other two fighters tried to close in on Alyna's wing from behind, but the more agile Firestorm fighters outmaneuvered them, bringing their plasma weapons to bear and ending the skirmish.

Only Videre's ship had functional shield systems, and none of the ships were able to secure a missile lock, even on the ponderously slow battleship. As one, the Avengers turned and fled from the large capital ship. On Arano's signal, Videre deactivated his shields and they made the jump to the safety of the Tellen Space Station in the nearby Eden system.

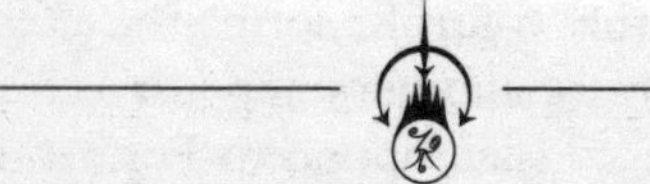

Avengers Team 5 sat before the subspace video communicator screen in the debriefing room at Tellen Station. Arano noted with a grimace the accommodations weren't as comfortable as they were back on Immok. The chairs his team used were unpadded metal stools, for one thing, and instead of a regular meal his team was finishing up a dinner of field rations. The soundproofing in the walls was not as effective, and the low hum of the life support system was noticeably louder.

Having given their reports on the incident in the Earth system, they were answering questions from the Coalition Fleet Commanders. "Lieutenant Marnian, you indicated you believe your team was set up by someone who gave intelligence information to Rising Sun operatives. We would agree with you where the task force is concerned. The fact very few Bromidian ships were destroyed indicates they knew the strength of the fleet they were moving against and prepared themselves accordingly. What was it that made you believe your team was set up as well?"

"We had been in the system barely long enough to make our sensor sweep when the Bromidians attacked, sir," replied Pelos respectfully. "There's no way they could've had enough time to pick us up on long range scanners and send ships against us. Also, they jumped in practically on top of us. The fighters hit us first, and about a minute later the battleship jumped in. I think the fighters were supposed to engage us, allowing time for the battleship to finish us off. They knew we were coming, and they knew exactly when we were going to be there. Since we didn't leave at our scheduled time, I believe someone on Immok 2 told them we were coming in."

"What I can't understand," complained Alyna, "is why they would be concerned about six fighters coming into the system. We obviously posed no threat to capital ships. The only thing that comes to mind is there's something in the system they didn't want us to scan."

"We have our analysts going over every piece of the data you sent us. If anything in there turns out to be important we'll let you know. Lieutenant Waukee, you inspected the fighters upon your return. What is your opinion for the cause of the equipment failures you experienced?"

"Unknown cause, sir," answered Kish, her leathery skinned face wrinkling in concentration. "I went over those ships carefully, but I couldn't find anything wrong with them. In fact, they worked fine once we reached the Eden system. I also can't explain why Lieutenant Genoa's shields continued to function normally, while the rest of our shields failed."

"I'd like to put an idea on the table," said Videre. "Suppose the task force experienced the same problems. Wouldn't that explain why they were destroyed so handily?"

The admiral and his staff looked at each other in concern as thoughts of the scenario played out in their minds. "Could an anomaly in the Earth system have caused your failures?"

"Doubtful, since no one has reported anything like that before," replied Arano. "But if it was an anomaly that would affect both fleets, why would Rising Sun jeopardize their fleet by jumping in to combat for a second time?"

"I think this will take some considerable time to sort out. Captain Lakeland, you're to return with your team to Immok 5, and we'll assign you a new mission. Command, out."

A few hours later, Arano settled into a bunk in the crew's quarters of the USCS Wilman, a troop transport. Although the lighting was at a minimum, he could easily pick out the still forms of his sleeping teammates; they were the only ones in the squad bay.

He tried to grab a short nap during the return trip, but sleep wouldn't come. His thoughts randomly flitted from problem to problem. Who had betrayed his team to the Bromidians? What really happened to Task Force Blue, and how large was Rising Sun's fleet? Why had so many systems failed on the new fighters, only to function normally again after leaving the battle? And finally, what would be found on the video from the Disciples crime scene? He dwelled on the last question for a few minutes, until his thoughts finally scattered and sleep grudgingly took him.

Cono entered the Team 5 planning room, and Arano inwardly groaned. He looked forward to making headway with the results of the Disciples murder video, but it would be hard to accomplish anything with the Grand High Councilor's aide asking perpetual questions. Somehow, he managed to keep his face neutral, hiding his irritation.

"Captain Lakeland, I want you to know we're doing everything in our power to find the security leak. Grand High Councilor Tient has ordered Midnight Sun to flush out the traitor. Commander Mendarle will be contacting you soon to give you the details we've turned up so far."

Arano grunted in response. Seeing the perplexed look on Cadron's face, he explained. "Midnight Sun is the Grand High Councilor's secret police force."

"Please," protested Cono, shoulders slumping and a pained look on his face. "That makes them sound like they sneak through cities at night, abducting people from their beds. Midnight Sun is a counter-intelligence group the Grand High Councilor formed to combat the efforts of the spies set against us by Rising Sun and Event Horizon."

"And spies from the Bromidian High Command," added Alyna.

"And anyone who tries to dig up dirt on the Grand High Councilor," added Pelos, without looking up from his work.

"I see," said Cono slowly. "I've a few things I want to check on. I'll be back later this afternoon." He pulled out a notepad, checked off some items of interest, and left the room.

"At any rate," said Arano, reaching for the controls to the Comm, "I wish them luck. Whoever is sending Rising Sun that information is costing lives." He pressed a few buttons and contacted the crime lab. "Thom, old buddy, how have you been?"

"Not too, bad," came the reply. "What's new with you? Anything on the Disciples I can help you with?"

"Ha, ha," muttered Arano. "What did you find on that video?"

"What video?"

Suddenly the room seemed very cold. "The video I sent to you yesterday to process for enlargement and clarification."

Thom frowned, checking his records. "Nope, we never got it. You sure it was sent?"

"I sent it yesterday. It showed two Tsimians stalking the latest victim. We hoped you could blow it up to give us a clear view of their faces. I'll send you a copy later today. In fact, I'll bring it myself." He turned off the Comm and stood unmoving for a few seconds, chewing on his lip, before he turned to Lain. "Can you call up our copy of that video? I'll need it on a disk again."

Lain Baxter worked at his computer briefly, reptilian Kamling features suddenly scowling in anger. "Something is wrong, Captain," he growled. "Most of the data on this computer is either corrupted, missing, or destroyed. I can't find the video anywhere."

Just then the Comm beeped, and Arano answered. "Captain Lakeland, this is Commander Mendarle. We've had a security breach. I need you in my office right away."

"On my way," Arano said quietly, anger causing his voice to tremble. He slammed his fist on the Comm, scattering several datapads.

He started toward the door but turned back to Lain. "Keep working at it, and see what you can come up with. I'll be back shortly." He moved woodenly through the door, heading to his destination with no particular sense of purpose. All he felt was rage, white-hot rage as he contemplated yet another betrayal. Someone had betrayed the Coalition task force at the Earth system, sending an entire task force to its doom. Someone else had intercepted the only piece of evidence he had in the Disciples case, pushing the investigation back to square one. And now, according to the Commander, there was another problem.

All kinds of crazy ideas ran through Arano's head as he entered Commander Mendarle's office. He scarcely noticed the opulent atmosphere of the Commander's outer office, which served to house his aides and assistants. He had long since given up wondering what uses a warrior like Commander Mendarle could find in such frivolity. The plush white carpet, the elaborate artwork hanging on the walls, the ornate sculptures on the shelves, all reeked of a vanity and a materialistic attitude that seemed out of place with a veteran combat pilot.

The Corporal behind the desk just inside the door motioned for Arano to enter the Commander's private meeting area, and Arano entered without knocking.

"Ah, Captain Lakeland, thanks for coming so quickly. All the other Avengers teams are out on assignments with the fleet, so this is going to be your project and yours alone. I know you already have enough going to keep you busy for a year, but I have no one left." He sighed, shook his head sadly and searched through the pile of papers on his desk. "Someone planted a virus in our computer system. It wiped out the data storage components in about half the computers in Coalition Headquarters. The vital data can be retrieved from archives, but it'll take time. What we need to find out is who did this and why. We also need to know if classified information was compromised while they had access to the system."

"I think the answer to your last question has already been found," Arano replied testily. "The fact there was an ambush in the Earth System, destroying an entire task force, points to a rather glaring possibility of espionage, wouldn't you say?"

Commander Mendarle's eyes took on a pained look. "My God, I hadn't thought of that. I've been so tied up with this mess here that I didn't . . . wait here a minute." He stuck his head through the door and gave instructions to the Corporal sitting dutifully outside the door. "He'll notify the High Command for me, and they can decide where this goes from here. Captain, I want you to make this a top priority. Whoever did this must be caught immediately!"

"Yes, sir," replied Arano. He saluted, turned, and left the room. As he went out, he glanced back into the Commander's private meeting room and considered telling him about the loss of the video from the Disciples crime scene. He changed his mind when he caught a glimpse of the Commander, face buried in his hands, slowly shaking his head in despair. The Commander has enough to worry about, thought Arano. He closed the door behind him and wordlessly left, pausing long enough to send a quick message to his team to explain what had happened.

Arano headed to the offices where the agents in charge of internal security were housed, seeking out Dar Noil. If the Avengers' meeting rooms were considered full of computers, then Dar's work area could only be described as a technological wonder. Computers of vastly different sizes, shapes, and purposes sprawled throughout the office, with walking paths randomly left vacant to allow the security agents to move around. After asking for directions, he finally spied Noil standing next to a water cooler.

"Dar," he said as they shook hands, "I need your help. You're aware someone planted a virus in our computer system." Dar nodded and took a long drink of water. "You'll be assigned to me for this. Everything we do here will be kept in the strictest confidence. Your job is to track down this virus for me. I need to know when the virus was introduced, what else was done, and who did it. Make this priority one for you. We need to stop the leak before any more damage is done."

Dar chewed on his lip. "I'm on it," he answered, rubbing his eyes as he turned back to his computer. "I'll notify you in person when there's a breakthrough."

"Thanks," replied Arano. "Whoever did this has already cost us a lot of lives. Let's squash the problem before anyone else has to die."

"Anyone innocent, anyway," Dar said in response.

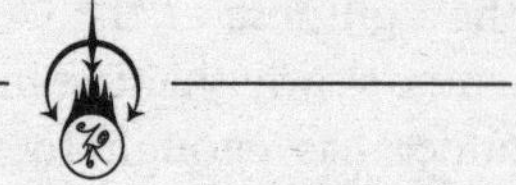

Arano returned to his own planning room and immediately noticed the broad grin on Videre's face, the feline muzzle baring long teeth in a soundless laugh. "All right, Lieutenant," Arano sighed, "out with it."

Barely restraining his laughter, Videre intoned, "Dead man walking! Dead man walking!"

"What's that all about?" asked Arano, dropping his hands to his sides in exasperation.

"You're dead," replied Videre, laughing openly now. "The virus did a few other dirty deeds while it was out destroying data. Several active Avengers, including you, have been classified as dead. I imagine your aunt will be getting a nice check here in a few days. I wish you luck on your resurrection, but if I were you I wouldn't get my hopes up for a speedy recovery. A buddy of mine from Avengers school had this done to him once, after he broke off a relationship with a girl who worked in personnel. Women can be vindictive, can't they?"

"You're walking on thin ice, Videre," warned Alyna.

"And getting off the subject," added Lain, rubbing the line of reptilian bumps along his forehead.

"Anyway," Videre continued, "it took my buddy six months to get the whole mess cleared up. In the meantime, he wasn't getting paid. It nearly bankrupted him."

"Wait a minute," said Arano. "How long has my status been this way?"

Lain checked his computer before responding. "Since late last night, shortly after midnight."

"But I just accessed the secure computer system this morning. How could it let me in if I'm dead?"

"I'll have to look into it, but with the bureaucracy being what it is, I imagine they're pretty slow to close out someone's security access after their death. How is a dead person going to be a security threat?"

"That's true," conceded Arano. He sighed. "That's one more project for me . . . convincing the bureaucracy I'm only dead in the computer system."

Videre looked straight-faced at Arano, the mirth hiding just beneath the surface. "Arano, you give whole new meaning to the words 'computer terminal'."

Kish suddenly snapped her leathery fingers, coming up out of her seat. "Lain, what was the exact time the computer killed Arano?"

"I'll check," chuckled Lain. "Here it is. Five minutes after midnight." He tried vainly for a few moments to maintain a straight face, then burst out laughing. "Wow, this looks personal. It says here under cause of death you choked to death on your pride."

There were a few chuckles from the room, and

even Arano had to join in. He appreciated a good joke when he saw one, and in his job having a dark sense of humor was almost a necessity for maintaining sanity. But their current situation was no laughing matter. Whoever was responsible for this act of treachery would pay dearly, Arano promised himself.

Kish turned back to her computer screen. "Give me a printout of the order, including the time of execution." Seeing Videre burst out laughing once more, she said, "Sorry, Arano. Poor choice of words, I guess. I meant I needed to know when the order was executed. I need the time Arano's status was officially changed. That'll give us an idea of where to start our search for the insertion of the virus."

Videre was still laughing so hard tears stained his fur-lined face, and even Arano was laughing again. He returned to his desk and tried to regain his composure.

"Copy Dar Noil on that information," said Arano. "He's our contact person in security." Seeing Videre trying without much success to stifle a laugh, Arano sighed and said, "Okay, Videre. Let's have it. I know you have something else to say."

"Not really," said Videre without the slightest trace of a grin. "I'm just dying to see how you're going to get out of this one."

Later that evening, Arano's team gathered at a local bar for dinner. The flavor of the barely adequate but satisfying food was masked by the thick pallor of smoke hanging in the air. Arano and his friends enjoyed the bar, however, because it was never overly crowded and the music played at tolerable volume levels, so no one had to shout to be heard. The natural wood tables and chairs added a homey ambiance.

After dinner they lingered at their table, discussing unimportant matters and trying to forget the troubles facing them. It was another favorite pastime of Arano's team, and he knew it was a great stress reliever.

Arano noticed their waitress was conspicuously absent, so he excused himself and strolled through the smoky room to the bar to order a round of drinks. As he stood waiting, a tall Human with a wicked scar on his right cheek turned to face him. "I don't want you standing that close to me," he warned.

Arano ignored him, waiting patiently for the bartender. The man gave Arano a sharp push. "I said I don't want you standing there. In fact, I don't want you in this bar at all."

Although he was not normally a belligerent man, the frustration of recent events had shortened Arano's patience considerably. "Any time you feel man enough to try," he stated in a voice as cold as death, not even looking at his antagonist.

The man was briefly taken aback by Arano's demeanor, but turned to the two men seated beside him. All three gathered around Arano. "You're about to get a lesson in manners," the first man told him. Arano's friends started to get up, but he waved them back.

"I'm just trying to get a drink," Arano said coldly. "It would be in your best interest to leave me alone."

"Here's the deal," the first man told him. "The patch

on your sleeve tells me you're Padian. You ignorant savages have no business here. Why don't you go home before we turn the Bromidians loose on you again?"

Arano knew the fight was unavoidable, and didn't warn his assailant before he struck. He spun around, the bottle in his right hand catching one of the men in the left temple; his eyes glazed over, and he collapsed in a twitching heap. The first man swung a punch at Arano, who smoothly caught the arm and twisted it against the joint. There was a pair of satisfying cracking sounds, and the man dropped to the floor, howling in pain and clutching his injured arm.

The third assailant pulled a knife from inside his coat and waved it menacingly. Arano advanced on him, seemingly heedless of the weapon. As soon as Arano was within reach, the man struck, but Arano was quicker. He blocked the knife aside and rammed his knee into the pit of his foe's stomach, eliciting a grunt of pain. Grabbing him by the hair, Arano slammed his face into a nearby table, then kicked him solidly in the ribs.

Arano returned to his first assailant, rolled him over and looked threateningly into the man's eyes. "Next time you mess with a Padian, you might want to make sure who you're dealing with first," Arano told him. Satisfied, he returned to his table and calmly took his seat. He had to laugh at his friends' smiles, and knew the wisecracks were coming.

"Not bad," commented Videre dryly, "for a dead man." They all burst into laughter again, and Lain ordered a round of drinks when the waitress finally made her appearance. Alyna's laughter faded quickly, and she leaned close Arano, concern mirrored in her eyes.

"Arano," she asked him seriously, "how bad is this problem for your people? Are Padians treated this badly everywhere you go?"

Arano sighed and shook his head. "No, most of the time, we have no problem. But it seems no matter where you go, you'll find idiocy. There are certain parts of the population who have preconceived notions about us, thinking we're all just a bunch of 'ignorant savages'. For that reason, most Padians tend to be fairly secretive about their heritage, preferring to pass off as Humans to avoid hassles. Personally, I like to consider what I just did to be an education for these gentlemen. I'm always willing to help educate those who need it."

"You'd think they'd at least appreciate the fact you're serving in the USC military, protecting their rights."

"I'd expect to find respect for the military less than I'd expect a Padian to be president. There are few civilians who appreciate anything we do for them. That's not why I'm here. A little appreciation would be nice, but I'm here to see to it no other system has to suffer the same fate as Leguin."

"I still think it isn't fair," Alyna objected. "Speaking of things unfair, Viper, you never told me how you came by your nickname."

"I'll leave that for another time," he replied. "I'm not here to talk business tonight. Who's up for a game of darts?"

The evening continued, Arano's team finally enjoying a night of relaxation after so many days of endless tension. The drinks flowed, and one by one his teammates filtered out toward home. Finally, it was just Arano, Alyna, and Lain, lingering over their drinks. They laughed, reminiscing over past cookouts at Arano's house and the inevitable legendary incidents associated with them.

"I think that was the night Videre got really drunk," laughed Lain, "and I gave him a ride home. I let him off right in front of his house, and he walked behind me, crossed the street, and started through someone else's yard. I was about to say something, but he stopped, looked around, and said, 'Wait, this isn't my house'." All three erupted into another fit of laughter.

Arano, wiped his tear-damp eyes. "I think we're going to regret this tomorrow," he chuckled. "Oh well. Better enjoy it while we can. Where's that waitress?"

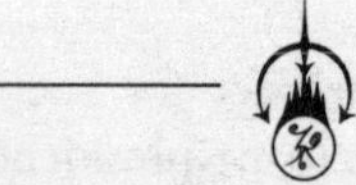

Arano awoke to a darkened room, wondering how long he'd been home. Judging by his headache and the way the room was spinning, he concluded his earlier supposition was correct: he was going to regret this in the morning. He reached for his watch to check the time, but found a solid wall instead of the nightstand he'd anticipated. The room spun with a feverish intensity as confusion settled over him. Not only was he not in his own house, but he suddenly realized he was naked. He almost started laughing at his predicament, but caught sight of the still form lying silently next to him. Even in the near total darkness, he recognized

Alyna's face silhouetted against the pillowcase. As she lay sleeping, his heart leapt into his throat and memories flooded his mind from the passionate night they'd spent together. He lay back down, wrapped his arm around her, and drifted off to sleep.

Arano arrived at Coalition Military Headquarters early the next day; surprisingly, Lain was already there. "You're here awfully early," noted Arano as he sipped his cup of tea.

"I thought I'd get to work early and try to track down this computer virus problem. How do you feel?"

"I have a five-alarm hangover going. How about you?"

"I feel great. I took an herbal hangover remedy last night with lots of water. It's like I never drank at all." Lain seemed to remember something, and peered down the hallway.

"She's still in bed," answered Arano shortly. "Can we keep what happened just between us? I'd rather not have word of this get out." Lain nodded reassuringly, then returned to his computer.

"You've been in here for a while," said Arano, changing the subject. "What do you have so far?"

"I have the time the virus became active down to a thirty minute window. During that time, all entries by all infected computers were erased. Unfortunately, that doesn't necessarily mean this was when the virus was introduced to the system. If it was operating on a time delay, it might have been inserted days, weeks, even months before it became active. Oh, by the way-there's a message for you from Commander Mendarle. It's on the console by the door."

Arano crossed the room and retrieved the message, quickly reading over its contents. He tossed it negligently on the table and sneered in contempt. "You might as well quit while you're ahead, Lain," Arano told him. "The case has been reassigned due to the size of our workload."

"Actually, that might not be all bad," Lain said, organizing a pile of printouts. "We had a pretty full plate. Maybe now we can concentrate on this Disciples case. We might even get a serious assignment in the war."

"That's true," conceded Arano, "but they've reassigned the case to Midnight Sun. They're as likely to find a scapegoat as they are to try and actually solve the case." Lain nodded in agreement, shutting down the screen he was working on.

"Let's go get some breakfast," Lain suggested.

"I don't think I could even handle the sight of food right now, let alone the smell." Arano shuddered. "My stomach's still a little delicate after last night's festivities. I'll see you back here when you're done."

It was shortly after noon and Arano and his companions had just returned from a brief lunch. "The most likely scenario," theorized Cadron, "is the traitor who betrayed us on a few occasions is also the one who planted the virus that nearly wiped out the entire computer system. The question is whether it was intended as general sabotage, or if there was a specific target in mind."

"I think they had specific data in mind when they struck," mused Videre, running a thoughtful finger along his fur-lined jaw. "Wiping out simply the data they wanted to eliminate would enable us to focus our investigation. Wiping out as much data as they did means we can't tell with any degree of certainty what they were after. Some of it, such as intelligence reports, can eventually be recovered by backtracking through our agent contacts. Other items, like our copy of the Disciples tape, are irreplaceable."

"What do you mean?" asked Cadron. "What happened to the original?"

"Oh, that's right," remembered Arano, "you were gone yesterday. We sent the original tape over to the lab to be enlarged and clarified. The courier never made it, and the tape is missing and presumed destroyed. More than likely, the courier was murdered."

"Wait a minute," said Alyna excitedly. "We make this remarkable discovery, make a copy here, and send the original to the lab to be analyzed. Then, within a very short time, the tape disappears, the courier is probably murdered, and the virus attacks our databanks, destroying copies we might have made. Does this seem more than a little coincidental to anyone?"

"All right, let's look into it," agreed Arano, pulse quickening and a boyish grin crossing his face. "Alyna, I want your squad to start talking to people. I want a list compiled of everyone who knew about the tape, from the time we found it until the time it disappeared."

"Also," added Kish, "we ought to keep separate lists of those who knew we were checking tapes from the crime scene and those who knew we actually saw the murderers. It's very likely we can backtrack to the leak."

"And that leak might be the person who's telling the Disciples who is Padian and who is Human," remarked Cadron.

"Okay," said Arano, "why don't you compile that list and give my squad the names as you find them. We can check into their movements over the past few days and see what kind of security clearances they have."

"Your team will have to work without you," Lain interrupted. "Major Alstor is on subspace radio for you, and he has that 'I've some dirty work for Arano' tone in his voice."

Arano chuckled. "Put him through." The display screen flickered briefly and Major Alstor appeared, a grave look on his face. "What's going on, sir?"

"Relax, Viper," said the Major. "I'm alone. Here's the scoop. The Bromidians are taking advantage of our situation with Rising Sun. They have invaded the Tectos System."

There were several audible gasps from around the room, and Arano slammed a datapad on the table.

"They invaded in their usual fashion, brutally crushing all opposition and murdering all the leaders. They're now in complete control of the system. The Bromidian government claims they're simply recapturing a system that belonged to them before the war.

"The High Council has their military committee meeting shortly to discuss the invasion. Since you're such a forceful public speaker, I want you to talk to them about Bromidian history and try to convince them the Bromidians are a serious threat to the Coalition. The Military High Command wants to declare war on the Broms, and we have the support of several on the High Council. The problem is that before the High Council can vote on a declaration of war, it either has to be recommended by the President, or be passed as a resolution by the military committee. Since the President has been abducted and the Grand High Councilor all but owns the military committee." he trailed off meaningfully.

Arano sighed. "Okay, Laron, I'll see what I can do. If I find anything out I'll let you know." He motioned for Lain to end the transmission and turned to Pelos. "Can you get me an outline of the history of the Bromidians since the early twentieth century?"

Pelos nodded, pulled one of his personal datapads from his pack, and accessed his historical archives. "I've got everything you'll need right here," he informed Arano. "I can have it ready for you in under an hour."

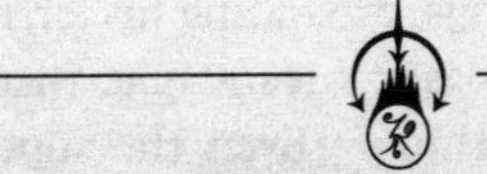

Arano entered the chambers where the military committee had gathered, and was motioned to a podium at one end of a long table. He walked in a crisp, military manner to his appointed position, noticing the curious looks from the bureaucrats gathered in emergency session to discuss the ongoing problems with the Bromidian Empire. Glasses of water lined the table, the dark ceramic cups standing out in stark relief against the white background of the numerous reports that had been presented to the commission.

After introducing himself, Arano got down to business. "As you're aware, the Bromidians have invaded the neutral system of Tectos. While this system is neither a member nor a protectorate of the Coalition, the event is still a cause for alarm, and the military High Command wishes to express the desire to liberate the system from Bromidian control. We have to show them that even while we're at war with Rising Sun, such acts of brutality will be dealt with harshly and swiftly. Some might argue that since this system isn't part of the Coalition, what has happened there is none of our business, and we should not get involved. They might tell you we can't be the police force for the entire galaxy. Let me tell you a little history of the Bromidian Empire.

"Chronologically, the Bromidians developed along lines pretty similar to Humans. In the year 1921 a fascist regime, led by the infamous Zorlyn Gorst, invaded several nearby countries. Every year, Gorst's forces overran more sovereign nations, expanding his territory and building his industrial base. Meanwhile, that world's other countries did nothing. Even the superpowers were inactive. 'They won't invade our country,' they said. 'It's not our problem,' they said. One country at a time, however, learned of its mistake when Zorlyn Gorst's forces became their problem. By the time the planet's leaders realized Gorst had global aspirations, it was too late. By 1932 Gorst owned over 85% of the planet. However, he met stiff resistance from two allied republics, and actually began losing ground.

"It was at that point Gorst's scientists developed the atomic bomb. One of the republics had actually developed it two years earlier but had decided against using the weapon of mass destruction, thinking it immoral. Gorst proved he had no such compunctions by using the atomic bomb mercilessly, attacking two targets in each country, each day, until they surrendered. The unified nation of their entire world was renamed Vagorst, which loosely translates to 'Gorst's world'.

"Since then, it has been ruled by Gorst and his descendants. Each emperor gets five wives, and fathers several children with each. When the time comes to pick a successor, every child is tested extensively. The most intelligent, talented, and ruthless of the offspring is selected to become the next emperor, while the others form a cabinet of sorts. There are also a number of fatalities among the children; murder is encouraged as a means of besting the competition.

"The Bromidians developed space travel in 1952 and Rift Drives in 2051. The first two races they encountered were exterminated in a genocidal frenzy. The next race they met, the primitive Latyrians, was enslaved. This provides an interesting insight into the Bromidian mind and a contrast between them and the Humans. The Humans met the Padians and found them to be very similar, physiologically speaking, although far behind in technology. The Humans responded by befriending the Padians. In contrast, the Bromidians located the Latyrians, who were similar to the Bromidians, although behind them technologically. The Bromidians responded by brutally conquering them.

"Emperor Gorst VIII was on the throne when the Humans were first encountered by the Bromidians in 2099. The decision was made to exterminate the Humans, leading to the Bromidian Empire's defeat of 2104 at Vagorst, or Rystoria 2 as we call it. Relations with the Coalition were then established, and by 2140 this relationship had been normalized. However, the Bromidians rebuilt their military in secret, in direct violation of the Treaty of Rystoria, which put strict limits on the size of their military.

"Additionally, they've invaded five systems in the last seven years, also a violation of the Treaty. The Bromidian Emperor has made it plain his people will only honor the Treaty of Rystoria for as long as it's convenient to them. They suffered a humiliating defeat at the hands of the Coalition in 2104. That was over 100 years ago, but a militaristic society such as theirs never forgets such an insult. I can assure you they have plans to amend that situation, and the time for their revenge is at hand.

"They're maneuvering into position now, and we're certain there's manipulation going on behind the scenes. We won't be aware of their plots until it's too late. These forays into neutral systems are just a part of their overall plans to destroy the Coalition. They need those systems to launch attacks on our strongholds, because they don't have direct control over any systems close enough to our space to begin an offensive with secure supply lines. If they take over many more systems, they'll be able to invade Coalition territory without fear of us sneaking in behind them and attacking their unguarded rear areas. We must act quickly and move to block them before it's too late."

An older Tompiste councilor shuffled some papers and looked uncomfortable. "Can you clarify this for us, Captain Lakeland?" he asked, ignoring the scowl from Grand High Councilor Tient. "Why not just attack our main systems, such as Immok, and finish us off right away, rather than utilize such a piecemeal approach?"

"There are several reasons. Warfare in space isn't much different from warfare on land, except there's a three-dimensional battlefield. You never leave an enemy stronghold behind you, and you have to watch your supply lines. If they came and attacked Immok, our defenses could hold them off for weeks. Meanwhile, part of our fleet could begin attacking their outer systems. Besides, from their current front lines, they can't reach our prime systems in a single jump. They need to secure systems on our borders, and once they've accomplished that and finish their new supply depots, they'll turn their attention to the heart of the Coalition. Also, keep in mind there's no possible radio contact with ships in a wormhole, so if they sent a fleet on a long jump, we could maneuver a small strike force behind them and destroy their supply lines.

"They'd also have to worry about us setting up a picket line with Thief Class Cruisers, putting up a neutrino field to pull them out of their wormholes. We could destroy them while their shields and weapons systems were still powered down. No, they intend to continue taking one system at a time until they're poised to attack primary Coalition targets."

Grand High Councilor Balor Tient looked up from his notes. "Captain Lakeland, what makes you so certain the Bromidians have aspirations of invading our space?"

Arano resisted the urge to jump up and strangle the pompous, arrogant Human bureaucrat seated across from him. "Aren't the activities of Rising Sun proof enough?"

"We have no proof of any connection between Rising Sun and the Bromidian government," argued the Grand High Councilor.

Arano shook his head sadly. "I see now what I'm up against. This committee won't move against the Bromidians, regardless of what I present to you. I've said all I can. Do you have any further questions for me? I have real work to do."

Balor's nostrils flared at the insult. "That will be all, Captain," he said coldly.

CHAPTER SEVEN

ARANO LOOKED UP FROM THE DATAPAD HE WAS reading at his desk, and smiled nervously at Alyna when she entered. She returned a comfortable smile. "I spoke with Captain Pana on Team 4. He said they've compiled a list of the recent military secrets that have been compromised and the people who had access to the information. It looks like the leak is either coming from Military High Command or the Coalition Security Council."

Arano strummed his fingers on the table. "Or both," he theorized. "I don't want to lock myself into the idea only one person is involved in this."

"Probably a good plan," said a voice from the doorway. Arano turned, already recognizing Captain Lon Pana by the sound of his voice. He knew without asking Lon had some just-discovered information for him, more than likely relating to either the Disciples or the recent security problems at Headquarters. Lon was captain of Avengers Team 4, and any time he dropped by Team 5's office unannounced, the visit was typically followed by some sort of dangerous mission. Arano found himself hoping it would be the case today. The night he'd spent with Alyna had left him in a state of mental turmoil, and Arano welcomed anything to divert his attention from his personal issues.

"I have some information for you, Arano."

"What's up?"

"My team managed to gather a bit of intelligence from Rising Sun. We intercepted a signal to one of their field operatives. It seems he's supposed to meet with a certain spy who holds a sensitive position here within the Coalition. They have scheduled a meeting for tomorrow evening in the Karlac System. I'll give you the details later. My team leaves in the morning for a mission, so we can't go to Karlac. I thought you might be interested in paying our traitor a little visit."

"You thought correctly, my friend," said Arano, rising to his feet with a grin. "I owe this traitor many times over."

"Remember," said Captain Pana, holding up a cautionary hand. "We need the traitor alive to obtain proof of the cooperation between Rising Sun and the Bromidian High Command."

"That's true, Lon," agreed Alyna. "The Council won't act until it's too late. I'd say we have only a few months left before the Bromidians take some fairly drastic actions, and we need to be ready."

"This will be tricky," Lon told them. "The locals on Karlac 3 are suspicious of the USC military. If you go in, you'll need to be in civilian clothes and use a civilian ship. The clothes won't be a problem, but you won't be able to get a ship without a requisition. Since a requisition would have to include your destination, the request by itself would probably alert our spy that we're on to him."

Arano grinned. "Who've you told about this?"

"Just you," Lon answered. His eyes narrowed as he gave Arano a long look. "What are you planning?" Arano's grin grew vicious.

"Oh, God help us," groaned Alyna. "He wants to take the Eclipse."

"It would be perfect," laughed Arano. "In order to avoid problems with the outer systems, I registered her under the name of one of my aunt's friends. There's no way anyone could link her to me or the Coalition."

"Would our spy know the ship by sight?" wondered Lon.

"I don't think so," said Alyna. "And besides, he's probably not going to be sitting at the spaceport watching every ship arrive. I'd say the only hitch in this crazy scheme is getting the Eclipse to make it there and back without engine troubles."

"Ha, ha," laughed Arano sarcastically, and rolled his eyes. "I bypassed the dealer and paid for the repairs myself this time, having someone I trust fix her instead. She ran just fine on the return trip from Leguin 4." He paused, pretending his next thought had just occurred to him. "Of course, it'd be a damn shame if something happened to her and the Coalition had to buy me a new ship."

Arano leaned back in the pilot's chair of the Eclipse. He checked the time on the flight computer and saw there was still over an hour before he'd need to exit the wormhole. Relaxing, he mulled over the plan one more time.

Only he, Alyna, and Videre had come on the mission. The others had stayed behind to maintain the fiction of business as usual at the Avengers' office in the Coalition Headquarters facility, since technically the mission didn't exist. Arano and his friends would touchdown at the spaceport in the rowdy town of Lenta where they'd meet with a civilian operative working with Captain Pana's team. Known only as Storm, he was familiar with the Rising Sun contact who was to meet with the Coalition spy. Once the contact was located, he should unwittingly lead Arano and his friends right to the spy. Both subjects would then be apprehended and taken back to the Eclipse. They'd be immediately returned to Immok for interrogation and, eventually, a trial.

Arano had briefly toyed with the idea of executing both spies right on the spot. He had the right under Coalition law, since the Coalition had issued an official declaration of war against Rising Sun. Further consideration of the idea had changed his mind, however. The information the spies could provide was simply too valuable.

Arano considered the terrain on Karlac 3. The planet was an anomaly in itself, producing a unique ecosystem. Karlac 3's rotation period and revolution period were equal, so the same side of the planet always faced the Karlac star. The area of Karlac 3 with the most direct sun exposure was a burning desert, with temperatures at its center point exceeding 150 degrees. The varying climates moved out from that center in nearly concentric circles: a savanna region, an area of jungle, and a subtropical region complete with swamps, followed by the standard temperate and steppe zones, and on out to arctic. Temperatures on the far side of the planet were an unbearable 100 degrees below zero.

Lenta was located in the desert ring, about 50 kilometers from what was generally considered to be the start of the savanna. The average temperature was around 110 degrees, and there was some scrubby plant life. What bothered Arano was the mission would have to take place during daylight hours. There was no choice, since it was always daylight on this side of Karlac 3.

If something should go wrong, and they were unable to leave on the Eclipse, they had a contingency plan. About 100 kilometers from Lenta was a small Coalition outpost which would be their alternate route to safety. Since the Karlac system was only a Coalition protectorate and not a full member it wasn't a very large Coalition base, but it would at least provide some measure of safety and a means to return to Immok.

Arano smiled to himself, thinking grimly that at least this time their mission wouldn't be compromised by the spy inside Coalition Headquarters; no one else knew of the trip. He propped his feet on the empty copilot's chair, and had just closed his eyes for a brief nap when Alyna entered the cockpit.

"Videre's sleeping," she said in answer to his unasked question. Arano nodded awkwardly, turned to the controls of the Eclipse and ran some unnecessary diagnostics. Alyna scrutinized him for a few silent moments, then said, "Do I make you uncomfortable?"

Arano sighed. "Only when we're alone."

"Look," Alyna replied, "I'm sorry about what happened. Going home together from a bar like we did was probably not the best way to start off a relationship. I thought we agreed to put that behind us."

"We did, and I have," Arano replied as he turned to face her. "Lain is the only other person who knows about it, and he promised not to say anything."

"That's not what I meant. If I didn't know better, I'd say you've been going out of your way not to be alone with me ever since."

Arano pursed his lips tightly for a few moments, reflecting on her words. "How about this? When we get back, if they give us an evening to ourselves, we'll go out to dinner, just the two of us."

Alyna looked at him, the expression in her eyes a mystery. "It's a start," she noted. She leaned forward and gave him a quick kiss on the cheek. "I'm going to grab some sleep. You might want to do the same." Arano watched her go, his feelings and desires in a state of utter turmoil.

He was undeniably attracted to Alyna, he had to admit. And the thought of eventually making their relationship a more permanent arrangement wasn't unpleasant. He shook his head, knowing such possibilities were far into the future. He had too much to do with the Coalition's fight against Rising Sun, and he knew he couldn't allow himself to be distracted by personal pursuits. Duty first, always. Leaning back in his chair, he let his tired eyes close.

It seemed he had just fallen asleep when the

computer warned him the Eclipse had reached its destination. He eased the ship out of the wormhole and set a course for Karlac 3. A short while later they entered the planet's atmosphere with a bump, and were given permission from the Lenta Spaceport Authority to land. Arano, Alyna, and Videre, dressed in the rough cloaks of common outer system space travelers, exited the Eclipse.

They were immediately assailed by the blindingly bright sun and blistering temperatures. The burning air seemed to sear their lungs. Arano shook his head, wondering why anyone would want to call such a desolate wasteland home. Their booted feet raised clouds of dust from the rocky, unpaved streets as they strolled casually to their destination.

Following instructions provided by Captain Pana, they proceeded to a local restaurant and ordered lunch. The clientele lounged about, casting disinterested glances around the diner's dusty interior. The room was dimly lighted, presumably, in Arano's opinion, to disguise the actual level of unseemliness the proprietor had allowed the establishment to fall into. Arano and his friends relaxed in the cooler indoor climate, waiting for the man they knew only as Storm.

After a short wait their food arrived, and they ate anxiously while they awaited Storm's arrival. The fare was edible, but Arano found himself hard-pressed to deliver a more forceful compliment than that. He sipped his tepid water and kept a watchful eye on the crowd. He'd been provided with a description of Storm's features as well as the type of clothing he'd be wearing, and glanced at his watch to see it was time for their rendezvous. He paid for the meal, and they returned to the savage heat outside.

A tall, thin Human dressed in a hooded cloak approached them, motioning surreptitiously for them to follow. As he passed, he mumbled, "I hear there's a storm coming. Better take cover." So saying, he entered a crowded bar across the street.

Arano and his friends followed him inside, surprised at how busy the place was. At the stranger's suggestion, they seated themselves around a table in a dark corner. If their choice of eateries was dirty, then this bar could only be called a pigpen. A waitress stopped at their table and tried to wipe the dust and grime away, but most of it just settled stubbornly back into place. She took their order and disappeared into the bar's interior.

"This place is awfully crowded for the middle of the day, isn't it?" asked Arano, breaking the ice.

The stranger snorted. "Are you kidding? It's nearly midnight here. You're forgetting it never gets dark on this side of Karlac 3. And the crowd is perfect. The noise they're making will keep others from overhearing what we have to say.

"I'm Storm. Pana said you want to watch the meeting between the Rising Sun agent and the Coalition spy. I'm not going to compromise my cover here, so this is the way it's going to happen.

"In about an hour, the Rising Sun agent will enter the bar. I will point him out to you, and then you're on your own. This is a good table since it's in a corner, so stay here. You won't need to get close enough to hear them; you can wait for the Coalition spy to leave the bar and grab him outside.

"Remember, the Rising Sun agent has a lot of friends around here, so be wary of him. And a bit of advice: If you want to blend in, you need to relax a little. You guys have been walking around here looking so tense I can't believe no one has accused you of being cops. Trust me, you don't want that accusation here. The locals tend to kill first and confirm later. Stay sharp, but relax."

Storm broke off briefly when the waitress returned with a round of drinks, and he continued to give the Avengers information about local customs, helping them to remain anonymous. Finally, he motioned to a gray-skinned Tompiste who had just entered the bar, calmly moving to an empty table.

"That's the Rising Sun agent," Storm told them. "You're on your own. Good luck." Pulling up his hood, Storm left their table and exited the bar.

"A Tompiste?" wondered Videre. "That's a surprise."

"We should have expected someone besides a Bromidian," commented Alyna. "Other races can move around easier and not attract as much attention. We already knew they have spies among all the races."

"Let's keep a close eye on him," decided Arano, "but without attracting his attention."

"Here," said Alyna, sliding her chair between Arano and the Tompiste agent. "Just keep talking to me, and you can watch him the whole time. From that distance, he won't be able to see where your eyes are looking."

Arano complied, marveling at the simplicity of her idea. In this manner, he kept an eye on their target for perhaps an hour. The Tompiste seemed at home in the filthy environment of the establishment, seeming not to notice the stench in the air or the filth on the table. A few patrons came and went, but for the most part the patronage was static.

Finally, the trio's patience was rewarded when a tall figure approached the agent, hood drawn up, features hidden. Judging by the height and stature, Arano knew the newcomer was not a Tompiste. Unfortunately, since he was unable to get a look at the face or even the hands of the Coalition spy, he couldn't be certain of the race, let alone make an identification. The two figures had a heated exchange, and the spy gave the Tompiste a data disk before standing up. The spy stood to leave but sat back down and conferred again with the shadowy Tompiste companion. Suddenly, Arano's danger sense warned him he was in extreme peril.

"What is it?" asked Alyna.

"I don't know," responded Arano, scanning the crowd for trouble. "Danger sense is kicking in. I think we've been compromised. Let's start toward the door and keep an eye on our spy. We'll want to grab him outside anyway."

They stood up and slowly made their way toward the exit. Every nerve in Arano's body screamed at him to run, but he maintained calm. Running would only draw unwanted attention and eliminate any chance of catching the spy. His skin began to crawl, and he felt as if every eye in the place was on him and his friends.

Suddenly, there was a cry from the corner. Moving excitedly in their direction and gesturing wildly, the

Tompiste yelled, "Coalition agents! Get them!" An angry mutter from the crowd quickly turned to a roar as the intoxicated patrons clambered to their feet in anticipation of the fight.

The Avengers lunged toward the door, but found their way blocked by a cudgel-wielding ruffian. Videre seized the surprised Kamling by his rough tunic, lifted him off the ground, and threw him through a large window. The three embattled soldiers scrambled through behind him and dashed off down the street, a mob snapping at their heels.

"Everyone all right?" gasped Arano as they sprinted around a corner. Seeing the nods from his companions, he concentrated on making his way back to the Eclipse. A shot from a laser pistol hummed past his head, close enough to shower his face with the shattered fragments of an exploding brick. Arano dove around the corner of the nearby building, rolled and came to his feet, his own pistol in hand. Videre and Alyna took cover behind a nearby vehicle, but were pinned down by laser fire coming from three members of the encroaching mob. Arano returned fire, felling the lead members of the crowd as they pressed toward his position.

"Fighting withdrawal," he ordered tersely. Under his covering fire, Videre retreated to a recessed doorway across the street, where he also returned fire. Alyna followed suit, falling back to another position of cover to lay down suppressing fire for Arano.

In this manner they leapfrogged the short distance back to the spaceport, finally catching sight of their ship. At Arano's signal, all three broke into a sprint, pounding up the ramp to the safety of the Eclipse. Arano fired up the engines, which for once started without a protest. While Arano worked anxiously to get the engines ready for takeoff, Videre charged up the weapons and shields. The Eclipse's hull rattled as the remaining assailants fired on the ship. Finally, the shields and weapons hummed to life, allowing Videre to suppress the incoming fire with the ship's main guns.

"Hang on," warned Arano. "We're going!" He touched the Eclipse's controls and the ship lifted gracefully from the landing pad, soaring away from the dangers of the city of Lenta and out over an enormous sea of sand dunes. The ship shuddered several times as Arano continued to try to gain altitude, but his efforts seemed to be in vain. They continued to race at breakneck speed away from the dangers of the spaceport, but the ship was unable to climb higher. Futilely, Arano swore at his control panel and scanned his systems for the trouble.

"Arano," Alyna joked weakly, "not to be a backseat pilot, but don't you think we had better get a little more altitude? It's hard to break out of the gravity well from a mile above the planet's surface."

"I'm trying." Arano frowned in frustration. "Before our shields went online someone out there got in a lucky shot. I don't think we're going to make it in the Eclipse. We'll have to try to make it to the Coalition base for repairs. Setting a new course."

The ship shuddered violently for a few moments before settling into its new course. "Engine number one is overheating," warned Alyna. "It's in danger of overload."

"Damn!" swore Arano. "Engine two is damaged, too. If I shut down engine one, the best I can manage is a controlled landing."

"You'd better do it, then," said Alyna. "It could go anytime now."

The three held on tightly as the critically damaged ship bucked and shook its way toward the ground. Arano checked the terrain below and saw they'd managed to fly past the sand dunes and were over a fairly rocky tract of land. Selecting a more or less level area free of large boulders, he eased the Eclipse down to the planet's surface. A violent blow rocked the ship when it touched the ground, sliding forward for several seconds before lurching to a stop.

Kish entered her apartment, changed out of her uniform, and fixed her dinner. Then she turned on some music and sat back to relax for a quiet evening alone. After about an hour of her wordless reverie, she decided to catch up on the day's current events. She turned on her televiewer, leaned back in her chair, and put her feet up. She took a quick sip of coffee, her favorite Human drink, and tuned to the news. Eventually, she found herself dozing.

A light tapping on her window startled her into full alertness. Extinguishing the light, she moved cautiously to the window. She peeked through the curtains and saw a very frightened Cadron Stenat motioning hurriedly for her to open the window. Kish complied, and Cadron scrambled frantically through the opening. He collapsed exhausted into a nearby chair, and Kish brought him a glass of water after securing the window and closing the curtains. Cadron drank gratefully, then looked up at Kish.

"Okay," Kish said slowly, "start at the beginning. What happened?"

"I've been chased for the last fifteen minutes by a rather nasty-looking Kamling with a bad disposition," he commented dryly. "I think he was after this." He held up a data disk that had been concealed in his lightweight jacket.

Kish took the disk, looking it over carefully before handing it back. "It looks intact. What's on it?"

Cadron managed a smile. "Oh, not much. Just a copy of the missing video from the latest Disciples killing."

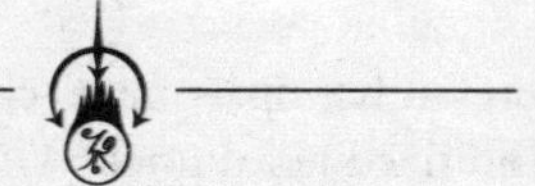

Arano peered intently at the regional map of Karlac 3. "There," Videre said, pointing to a position on the map dominated by a hilly savanna. "When we flew in, I saw a settlement. It's not on the map, so we should be able to escape notice."

"Okay," nodded Arano in agreement. "Here's the plan. We make for the settlement first, replenish our supplies and change direction toward the Coalition outpost. If that spy sets anyone on our trail, they'll concentrate on the area between the outpost and our present location. This track ought to carry us far enough east of their search that we can bypass them. When we leave, I'll set the ship's Rift Drives to self-destruct in one hour, eliminating any chance they might get something useful from the Eclipse."

Mentally, Arano reviewed what he knew about desert survival. Under other circumstances, his best bet for survival was to stay put and wait on a rescue, but the only ones likely to come looking for them wanted to kill them, so they had to keep moving. *We will drink as much water as we can before we leave the ship,* he thought, *and we'll also carry as much water with us as we're able.* The body is better at rationing water than the mind, so they wouldn't try to save water. When people wait until they're thirsty before drinking, it's too late. Videre's Gatoan physiology made him more resistant to the conditions; Gatoans can go longer without water, and the fur covering their bodies helps to protect them from the sun while keeping water in their bodies longer.

Arano didn't bother carrying much food. The body required water for digestion. The supplemental nutrition pills they carried would help them maintain energy and provide them with salt and other essential nutrients.

Snakes they encountered would likely be poisonous, and without antidotes they would have to use extreme caution. They would have to be especially careful when they entered the savanna, as there were several breeds of large predatory cats living there, although his projectile rifle should fend off the cats. The noise would scare them, and as an added benefit their enemies couldn't pick up the rifle on their scanners like they could a laser rifle. If they encountered hostiles, they would use their laser weapons. Enemies would likely be firing lasers anyway, so the spy's handymen would have the Avengers on their scanners, regardless.

"All right," he told them, standing up. "Let's gather our gear and get a move on. Remember, keep as much of your skin covered as you can, and that includes wearing a hat. It'll keep the moisture in your body a little longer."

The soldiers gathered water and other supplies from the small craft and carried out their final preparations. Arano initiated the self-destruct sequence in the engines, and they moved out into the oven-like heat. The sun pounded down on Arano like a sledgehammer, and there was no shade to provide even a few moments' relief from the relentless heat.

Small rocks dislodged and slid away underfoot as he trudged along with his companions. Arano passed the time by alternating between watching the ground at his feet and watching the high hilltop that was their first destination, plainly visible in the distance although it was still over 10 kilometers distant. He closed all thoughts of his current circumstances from his mind and concentrated on putting one foot in front of the other.

Kish stared incredulously at Cadron, a desperate hope dawning in her eyes. "Say that again?"

"It occurred to me this afternoon," Cadron explained, taking another nervous gulp of water as he glanced out the window. "When I was assigned to your team, I persuaded a friend of mine to set up a link between our team computer at Headquarters and my computer at home. He set it up so the computer would automatically download the day's information once I got home and activated the link. Since the link was temporarily knocked out by the storm that evening, my computer was protected when the virus struck. I went home early today and was browsing through some of our notes on the Disciples when it occurred to me there might be an undamaged copy of the tape on my computer. Sure enough, I found it, right there all along."

"Cadron, I could kiss you!"

"Umm, anyway," Cadron continued, "I sent a copy of the tape to our Headquarters computer. I was going to contact you so we could take the tape to Arano's friend Thom, over in the crime lab. Someone must've been monitoring, because less than 30 minutes later I had company."

"How did you get away?" asked Kish.

"I was on my way over here with the tape, and I had just walked out my front door when this Kamling came after me with a knife, right in front of my house. He chased me, and when he tripped over some landscaping I managed to get into my groundcar. Since your house was closest, I jumped out of the car at a corner a few blocks from here and let it keep going. I don't know if I lost him or not, but at least I made it here."

Kish nodded speculatively, running several possible courses of action through her mind. "Hang on a minute," she told Cadron, reaching for her handheld Comm. She activated the link, contacting Pelos. After a few moments, the familiar Tsimian voice came across the Comm.

"Lieutenant Marnian," he announced.

"Pelos, this is Kish. Did I leave my dress uniform hat over at your place the other day? I can't find it here, and it's not at the cleaner's."

Pelos gave a heavy sigh. "I must've told you five times already this year that if you don't start putting things away, you're going to lose them. Why do you need it?"

"Just for an old religious ceremony. They're going to kill me if I don't find it. I guess I'd better get looking. See you in a few hours." She closed the link and handed the Comm to Cadron, then motioned for Cadron to follow her. She entered a spare room she used for storing equipment and gathered a few items.

"So what do we do now?" asked Cadron nervously, obviously put off by Kish's seeming inattention to the matter at hand.

"I'm going to grab a few things we need, and then we'll meet Pelos in about ten minutes. He and I are your bodyguards until we get this whole mess straightened out."

"But how.?"

"Oh," laughed Kish, "I'm sorry. You don't know about when one of us is in trouble, and it's likely our conversations are being monitored, we have a few duress codes we can use for help. Anything referring to the dress uniform is considered a duress code, especially since you'd just about have to point a gun at us to get us to wear one. When he mentioned telling me something five times, that was a code for our fifth meeting place. Telling him that I'd see him in a few hours meant I'd be heading there immediately. I don't know if he picked up on the rest of it, but I told him about an old religious ceremony, a vague reference to the Disciples. He knows I'm not going to be involved in a religious ceremony, so I'm sure he understood.

"I also said they'd kill me if I lost my hat, which I'm certain he took to mean that this is a life-threatening situation." Kish strapped on her equipment belt, placed her laser pistol in its holster, and attached a spare Comm to the belt. "Keep the Comm I gave you, and take this." She handed Cadron another, smaller laser pistol. "I usually carry this as a backup weapon, but if we have problems you may need it. I'm going to make a couple of copies of that data disk, and then we're out of here."

It was impossible to tell how long they'd been walking. Distances were deceiving in this flat, barren land, and with the sun overhead constantly the passage of time was obscure. Arano looked down and saw his clothes were still dry. His sweat evaporated as soon as it touched his skin, giving the appearance he wasn't sweating at all. Only the white streaks of salt staining his clothes and those of his companions gave mute evidence of the ravages the land inflicted upon their bodies. He took another long drink from one of his canteens and squinted into the distance, trying to make out details of their destination.

The ship's engines had detonated about 30 minutes earlier, giving Arano a rough estimate of their location based on their walking speed and the length of the ship's self-destruct countdown. By his calculations they should soon enter the savanna where they would hopefully be able to replenish their dwindling water supply.

About thirty minutes later, Arano called a halt for a much-needed rest. He noticed with some satisfaction the scrubby plants populating the area were becoming larger and less sparse, leading him to believe they were in fact entering the savanna. He propped his feet up on a nearby rock, hoping to cool them down and reduce the chance of blistering.

After a ten-minute break, they began moving again. They'd gone about a kilometer further when Arano got a vague warning from his danger sense. Videre suddenly froze in place, motioning the others to do the same. At Videre's hand signal, they slowly knelt and gathered close for a whispered conference.

"Over there," Videre told them, "in that brush field. I saw something that looked like a luad."

"A luad?" Arano asked.

"A predator on my homeworld. It looks like a cat, only much larger and without the happy purring. If it was anything like a luad, I can guarantee you it has our scent. We're upwind from it."

Arano couldn't see anything, but he'd learned to trust Videre's sharp vision. "Can we sneak past it?" he asked.

Videre shook his head. "It'd be too risky. Even

from this distance, it can probably hear us whispering. If we backtrack and give it a wide berth, it will probably leave us alone."

Arano grimaced at the loss of time and effort, but knew there was no other option without a direct confrontation. "Okay, let's go then," Arano sighed.

They cautiously retraced their steps, swinging out in a wide arc to avoid the beast's territory. Videre indicated it didn't move from its place of concealment, but merely watched them leave. About 15 minutes later, satisfied they were safely away from the predator's territory, they again swung southward.

As they topped a small rise, they were surprised to see a modest oasis to the west. They were anxious to replenish their nearly non-existent water supply, and pushed forward eagerly. The Avengers reached the water hole and set down their packs, but Arano shook his head in disappointment, shouldering his equipment once again.

"We'd better not drink it," he warned them. "There isn't any wildlife here. If this were a good supply of fresh water, there'd be signs of use all over it. Since we don't have a test kit, we'd better move on." Arano's teammates cast longing looks at the pool as they stood to leave. They consumed the last of their water with chagrin, secured their equipment, and renewed their seemingly endless trek through the broken landscape. The paltry amount of water Arano had left did nothing to assuage his thirst, and licked his dry, chapped lips as he bent under the unyielding sun.

After another grueling kilometer walking across terrain gradually becoming flatter, Arano's sharp hunter's eye spotted a well-used game trail crossing the path ahead of them. He motioned for his companions to wait for him, then moved briskly down the path. A few minutes later, he found what he was looking for: a fresh water spring bubbling noisily up through the limestone to begin its lonely trek southward in a narrow stream. Repressing the intense urge to drink immediately, he returned to his companions and brought them back to the spring.

Arano knelt, gulping the deliciously cold water. The other three Avengers drank wordlessly, filled their empty containers, and sat back to rest. Almost as an afterthought, Arano dunked his head in the chilling waters, and his body trembled with relief from the scorching heat.

"How did you know which way to go on that game trail?" asked Videre. "You could just as easily have gone left instead of right and not found this."

"Lucky guess," chuckled Arano. "There were tracks leading in both directions, so I had to trust to my luck."

"When do you want to start moving again?" asked Alyna.

"Let's wait an hour or so," answered Arano, rubbing at the stubble on his chin thoughtfully. "We need a rest, and we can get another drink before we move on."

Kish peered carefully from her place of concealment in a row of bushes, scanning carefully for signs of danger. The grassy field between rows of buildings appeared to be empty, and she decided to attempt to cross to the cover of the warehouses waiting silently in the distance. She nodded to Cadron, gesturing with a narrow, leathery finger, and they moved cautiously from their cover, nervously crossing the open ground to their north. Kish had decided use of ground transportation would be foolhardy, and was foregoing speed to rely instead upon stealth. She found herself wishing fervently Arano was with them; his uncanny ability to sense danger would be invaluable. They crept up to the southern face of a warehouse and circled around to the East.

"Stay close to the building to minimize your silhouette, but don't touch it," whispered Kish tersely. "If you make contact with the building, your clothing will scrape and give us away." Seeing Cadron nod nervously in response, she moved on.

As they moved around the corner, the large, reptilian form of a Kamling hurtled in their direction, knocking Kish to the ground and sending the breath whooshing from her lungs. As she struggled to regain her feet, she saw a second form attack Cadron. Kish's hand reflexively snapped her weapon free, but her assailant knocked it away as soon as the pistol had cleared its holster. She delivered a blow to the Kamling's sensitive armpit area, momentarily stunning him, and she took advantage of the respite, scrambling away and regaining her feet.

She sized up her opponent, judging by his stance that he was a decent rough and tumble fighter, but believed the intricacies of martial arts hand-fighting would be lost on him. She took up her fighting stance, leaning slightly forward to give the Kamling the illusion she was closer than she really was. He pulled a knife from his belt, weaving it threateningly in front of him, and swung the blade at Kish in a tight arc. She smoothly blocked the attack, delivering a blow with the edge of her hand to the Kamling's throat and driving him forcibly to the ground.

As she wrenched the knife free from her assailant's hand, she glanced up and saw Cadron had lost his fight with the other Kamling who had a knife to Cadron's throat. Seizing her newly acquired blade in both hands, Kish jammed the blade home deep inside her foe's neck, angling upward where the blade found the Kamling's brain. With a short, gurgling scream, the Kamling ceased his struggles.

Kish turned and faced the other opponent, who looked at her with a sneering smile. "Where's the disk?" he hissed.

"Disk?" asked Kish dangerously, taking a step forward. "What disk?"

"Don't get cute with me," the other warned. "Give it to me or he dies." To emphasize his point, the Kamling slid his knife lightly across Cadron's throat, drawing a line of blood.

"Looks like we're at a standoff, then," noted Kish calmly. She was trying to put on a brave front, hoping to bluff her way out of the situation. The fight with the other Kamling had nearly exhausted her, and she was just getting her wind back. Her gray skin was turning darker with anger, and she could feel her pulse pounding in her chest. "You saw what I did to your friend here. He underestimated me because of my size. I don't think you want to make the same mistake." She edged slowly toward her discarded pistol, trying to disguise her maneuver with conversation. "How did you find us?" she asked.

"You've been followed since you left your house. This just happened to be the best ambush point I could find. Give me the disk."

"What good would that do you?" asked Kish, moving still closer to her discarded weapon. "What if we made copies?"

"First things first," laughed the Kamling. "First I get the disk, then I kill your friend if you don't tell me where to find the copies."

"Sounds like you have it all worked out, except for one small detail," commented Kish as she moved to within an arm's reach of her pistol. With a fluid dive, she seized her weapon and rolled to her feet. "You brought a knife to a gunfight."

"Drop the gun, or I'll kill"

The Kamling's threat broke off abruptly when Kish fired, striking the assailant between the eyes. Without a murmur of protest, he fell limply to the ground. Cadron fell to one knee, gasping for air and holding his hand to the bleeding wound left by the Kamling's knife. Kish rushed to his side, and he assured her that he was all right. Without another word, she pulled him to his feet and they moved out as swiftly as stealth allowed, her actions conveying to Cadron louder than words she believed other threats might be about.

CHAPTER EIGHT

ARANO BREATHED AN AUDIBLE SIGH OF RELIEF when their next checkpoint, the tiny, unnamed settlement, came into view. The buildings appeared to have been put together in a haphazard manner, speaking volumes about the work ethics of the residents. As had been the case in the city of Lenta, the streets were unpaved, but with the higher levels of precipitation here, the roads and buildings weren't quite as dusty.

Arano called a halt and studied the inhabitants from a safe distance, trying to decide the most favorable plan of action. They needed supplies, and a transport if they could get one, and this was their only chance of finding either. He absently scratched the back of his neck and considered the alternatives.

The settlement appeared to be a mining camp, established by some local company mining the nearby hills. The lack of uniformed policemen indicated the inhabitants probably policed themselves, which meant things could get rowdy. There was a noticeable lack of female inhabitants, which added to Arano's concerns; would Alyna be allowed to pass through the town without trouble? Using a small spotter's scope, he noted the locations of such important features as a little store where they might be able to purchase supplies, and a tavern, where they might find transportation for rent. The three Avengers held a brief whispered conference and cautiously descended into town.

As Arano led his two companions along the narrow main road, he kept a wary eye on the locals who passed. He knew his danger sense would alert him to imminent danger, but catching a look or two might give greater advanced notice of an assault, and might even deter one. They first stopped in at the store, and Arano used a portion of his supply of Coalition currency to purchase non-perishable foods and other necessities. He spoke briefly with the proprietor, a friendly Tompiste named Eruto whose gray, leathery skin was so light colored it was closer to an off-white hue.

"Thanks for coming in," concluded Eruto, shaking hands with Arano as the latter turned to leave. "We don't get many outsiders here. Is there anything else I can do for you?"

"Yes, as a matter of fact, there is," replied Arano. "We're looking for transportation to the nearest spaceport. Do you think anyone around here might be able to accommodate us?"

"Hmmm," Eruto wondered out loud, almond-shaped eyes narrowing in thought. "You might try Inruss over at the bar across the street. He's an old Gatoan with an ugly-looking scar from his right ear to his nose. He doesn't actually drink, but he loves to sit in the bar and talk the day away. He has a large groundcar he uses to haul freight, which should be able to get you where you're going. For a price, anyway . . .

"One other thing about that bar. The customers inside are a very rough crowd. Your lady friend might want to consider either waiting here or waiting outside. She's likely to receive a few 'offers' if she goes in."

"Thanks for the warning, friend," replied Arano with a disarming grin. "We'll be extra cautious."

Arano headed for the door, motioning with a jerk of his head for his companions to follow. They shouldered their now-heavy packs and returned to the inferno constantly baking the sunward side of the planet. Fortunately, Arano thought, the air was noticeably less scorching than it had been back in Lenta.

Arano squinted into the suddenly bright light, took a moment to spot their next destination, and boldly crossed the street, entering the establishment without hesitation. They seated themselves at an empty table and motioned for the waitress. In contrast to the businesses in Lenta, Arano noticed, this bar was meticulously neat, free of the dust and dirt that had necessarily plagued the buildings in the desert city where the Eclipse had met its demise. As Videre placed his lunch order, a rather shabby looking Human sauntered up behind Alyna, placing a familiar hand on her shoulder.

"Hey, honey," he slurred drunkenly, "let's you and me head out the back door of this dump." He slid his hand suggestively off her shoulder and down the front of her tunic. Alyna smiled innocently, seized his hand and spun quickly to her feet. She twisted the hand, ignoring the howls of protests from its owner. With deliberate, inexorable pressure, she forced the man to his knees. With one swift move, she dragged his arm forward and brought her knee up sharply, striking a stunning blow across his chin and knocking him several feet backward. He crawled awkwardly to his feet and staggered back to his table, ignoring the catcalls from his companions. Arano noted with some satisfaction, however, the obvious respect in their eyes for Alyna, even fear. With a little more coaxing, there would be no repeat performance.

As the din in the smoky room returned to normal, Videre leaned closer to Arano. "I think I see Inruss over there across the room. It'd probably be best if I talked to him alone first, Gatoan to Gatoan."

Arano nodded, and watched Videre move cautiously through the room and take a seat next to a rather rough looking Gatoan, dressed in sand-blasted work clothes. Arano chatted with Alyna to pass the time, all the while keeping a wary eye on the patrons around him. A few minutes later, Videre returned to their table to report he had struck a deal with Inruss, and they would leave within the hour. Inruss was already on his way to prep his transport. The Avengers chatted quietly until their food arrived, and had a rather tense meal.

"All right," announced Arano when they stood up to leave, "you two head for the door. I'm going to go talk with Alyna's suitor and his friends just to make sure they don't try and start more trouble." Arano strode casually to the others' table, deliberately selecting the rough-looking man who had confronted Alyna.

"No hard feelings, guys," he told them in a disarming tone. He tossed a small jingling coin purse on the table. “That ought to be enough to buy you each a few drinks. Enjoy, gentlemen.”

He turned and, without waiting for a response, left the bar. He joined Alyna and Videre in the searing heat, and they followed the directions given to them by Inruss.

“Why did you do that?” asked Videre.

“I could see in their eyes they were afraid to challenge us, but one of them was nursing his injured pride. He would probably have felt compelled to try something to massage his damaged ego. This way, he had a face-saving alternative to violence.”

“A fight avoided is a fight won,” agreed Alyna, quoting the old adage.

They turned down a side street and entered the open garage where Inruss had finished loading a few supplies onboard his transport. He waved them on up, and they climbed aboard without a word. Then he eased the transport out into the street and made his way toward the spaceport at the nearby United Systems Coalition base.

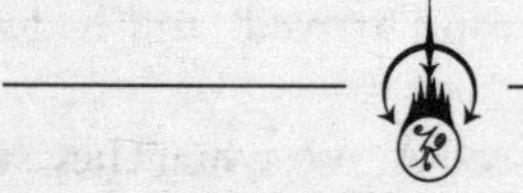

Kish motioned wordlessly to Cadron, and the two moved on careful feet through an alley behind a row of empty buildings. Kish's senses were on alert, and she studied every sound in the night air. They moved slowly now, following the earlier attack, but the alternative meant the risk of stumbling blindly into another ambush. They were still about a half-kilometer from their rendezvous point with Pelos, and were already running late. She resisted the urge to move more swiftly and concentrated on watching her surroundings. The key to their survival for the next few minutes was staying alert and ignoring nothing.

Although the bureaucracy in Immok was fairly particular about proper lighting in most areas of the city, this district was noticeably lacking. Just as well, thought Kish; she preferred to move about unseen. Whoever controlled the light controlled the advantage, and as long as she and her charge stuck to the darkness, they could hold that advantage.

The sound of plastic scraping on stone brought her up short, and she motioned for Cadron to stop. She lowered herself into a crouch, and Cadron followed suit. She edged over to him, putting a gray-skinned finger to her lips for silence. In a voice that was scarcely a whisper, she said, "There's someone ahead, hiding along the right side of the alley. They might not be after us, but I'm not going to risk this on a 'might be'. Let's back up slowly, take that alley to the south of us, and go around. It'll cost us some time, but it's better than fighting." Cadron nodded in agreement, and they backed down the alley toward their detour.

There was no time or need for stealth when, minutes later, laser fire erupted against the building next to Kish. She dove for cover behind a garbage dumpster, and Cadron took shelter in a recessed doorway. They were under fire from opposite ends of the alley, the interlocking fields of fire making it impossible for Kish to lean out and take an aimed shot. She knew they were in a desperately dangerous situation; only a radical solution might extricate them. Looking down at her belt, she seized her two smoke grenades.

"Cadron!" she shouted. "I'm going to pop smoke grenades to our right and left. When I do, I want you to follow me out. I'll do what I can to take out whoever is firing at us from the east end of the alley when we charge them. But whatever you do, don't stop running. The time for stealth is over. You have to get to Pelos with that tape. No matter what happens to me, don't look back or this'll all be for naught!"

Without giving him time to argue, she activated the two grenades, throwing them in opposite directions and filling the alley with a dense smoke screen. She fired a few shots in the direction of the assailant on her right, then bolted left, firing madly with her pistol, Cadron hot on her heels. Return fire, she didn't know from which direction, struck her a glancing blow on her left arm, but she continued her charge.

Suddenly, the fire coming from her front ceased, the silence eerily offset by the continuing fire from behind. From out of the smoke, the familiar Tsimian voice of Pelos called to her.

"Kish! Over here!" She saw his bestial form outlined in the smoke, and slowed to a crouching walk. She caught her breath as she and Cadron moved to Pelos' side behind the protective cover of an abandoned truck. She was about to ask if there was any other help in the area when Lain's reptilian silhouette emerged from the darkness, laser rifle in hand.

"There was someone firing at you from this end of the alley, but I took him out," he informed them. "Fall back to the transport, and I'll cover for you." Without waiting for a response, he took up a defensive position behind a stone staircase, rifle pointed back down the alley, and provided suppressive fire while his teammates fell back to the transport.

Pelos ran to the fallen body of the man who had fired at them, another Kamling. He roughly searched the body, tossed it over his shoulder, and hauled it to the waiting transport, then returned and secured the fallen Kamling's gear. Once his companions were safe, Lain retreated and joined them in the transport. Lights extinguished, they sped off into the night.

Arano stared incredulously at the soldier guarding the gate to the United Systems Coalition compound, a tall thin Human with short blond hair named Corporal Dentas. "What do you mean, I'm under arrest?"

"Impersonating an officer in the USC military is a serious offense. The officer you're claiming to be, Captain Arano Lakeland, died recently. You'll have to come with me." He turned to regard Arano's companions. "And who are you supposed to be?"

Videre was nearly incapacitated with laughter at Arano's plight, and Alyna was forced to answer. "I'm Captain Alyna Marquat, and this is Lieutenant Videre Genoa. We're all assigned to Avengers Team 5. If you take us to a computer terminal, we can perform a retina scan to verify our identity. We were on a covert mission, and we brought no identification with us. Captain Lakeland was mistakenly declared dead during the recent virus attack on the Headquarters computer system at Immok City."

The guard looked slightly less sure of himself. "I heard something about that. Okay, here's what we're going to do. You'll all surrender your weapons, and we'll escort you to the detention center. We have a secure computer system there, and we should be able to verify your claims." He motioned for a few nearby soldiers to come forward. Arano and his companions handed over their weapons and submitted to a search of their persons before they were formed up and marched to the detention building.

The base itself, while relatively small as Coalition bases went, was well-equipped and laid out in a predictable military fashion. As was always the case, the detention area was located in the center of the camp. They marched obediently ahead, passing row after row of orderly buildings and the occasional curious onlooker who was, no doubt, wondering what riff-raff had been brought in this time.

Corporal Dentas radioed ahead to the detention area to inform his commanders of the situation. A lieutenant, a rather overweight and balding Human apparently in his late thirties, met them at the doors and escorted the group to an interrogation room. At the lieutenant's imperious gesture, the three Avengers seated themselves behind a plain wooden table, the room's only furniture.

"I'm Lieutenant Hemfil," he said with a sneer. "You claim to be members of USC Avengers Team 5. Is that correct?" Arano nodded in agreement, not trusting himself to speak. "I don't see the need for a retina scan. You're obviously lying. I checked in the computer, and I even called a personal friend of mine who is on the staff of Grand High Councilor Balor Tient himself. In fact, he's one of the Grand High Councilor's closest military advisors. He assures me that Team 5 is still on Immok, having spoken with one of the team members to verify it."

"Look, Lieutenant," growled Arano dangerously, slapping his hand on the table. "I'm who I say I am. I understand your distrust, but this is getting us nowhere. Give us the retina scan so we can get out of here."

"I will do no such thing," replied the lieutenant with a sneer. "It's obvious from the way you're dressed you're just locals out for a cheap thrill. I think we'll simply turn you over to what passes around here for a local police force. They can deal with you as they please. If you come back, things won't go well for you."

At that moment the door opened to admit a wizened-looking Tsimian officer. The lieutenant immediately snapped to attention, and the condescending tone he had taken with Arano quickly changed to a sniveling, obsequious whine. "General Tralak, sir! I'm sorry they bothered you. I told Sergeant Beeson there would be no need to disturb you, but he seems to have taken matters into his own hands."

The general stared at the lieutenant with a dark, disapproving scowl. Arano suppressed a grin when he realized the general likely thought of the lieutenant as little more than a fawning bootlicker. "Did it ever occur to you to try the retina identification, as per standard procedure?"

Lieutenant Hemfil stared at the general, jaw dropping wide open. "B-b-but sir, I-I-I thought"

"You aren't paid to think!" roared the general, thrusting a clawed finger at the cringing junior officer. "We're at war, and you'll follow military procedures I've laid out to the letter! Do you understand?" The lieutenant could not answer, other than to nod fearfully. "What if they turned out to be known spies or saboteurs? What if they were wanted criminals? A retina scan would have identified them immediately. In this case, however, the scan would've revealed they were telling the truth."

The general turned to face the Avengers, and his manner eased; a slow smile appearing on his weather-beaten face. "Lieutenant Genoa, I haven't seen you since your graduation from Avengers school. How is your mother doing?"

"Just fine, Sir," Videre replied, winking at his open-mouthed companions. "I'll tell her you asked about her."

"Why don't you three come back to my quarters? I'll have the evening meal brought in, Videre and I can talk about old times, and within a couple of hours I'll have you on your way back to Immok."

Kish winced as Pelos examined her injured arm. "It's not bad," he told her. "It just grazed you. A quick bandage and you'll be okay. So, what was this all about?"

"Cadron showed up at my house with a copy of the missing Disciples murder video. He had company with him, and they played for keeps."

"You have a copy of the video?" asked Lain excitedly.

Cadron nodded solemnly, retrieved the disk from his pocket and handed it to Lain. Kish went on to explain all that had befallen her and Cadron since leaving her house. "This confirms someone at Coalition Headquarters is a spy," she concluded with her hands out wide in disgust. "Cadron was attacked within 30 minutes of sending the video to our computer."

"I also contacted someone in Dar Noil's office," Cadron noted thoughtfully. "One of Captain Lakeland's instructions was that Noil should be copied in on all developments."

Kish pondered these events slowly, not wanting to miss anything in her assessment. Obviously, the likelihood of someone monitoring Cadron's actual transmission of the video was very low, so the most probable source of the information leak had to be Dar Noil's office, and was more than likely someone working the late shifts who'd noticed the incoming transmission. "We need to find the names of everyone who heard about the message you left for Noil. One of them set these Kamlings after you. That's a mystery in itself: Why were all the attackers Kamlings? We're fairly certain from the video the murderers are Tsimians."

"When we get back to Coalition Headquarters," commented Pelos, "we can run a retina scan on this Kamling and see if he has a criminal record, or if he has any connections to one of the major anti-Coalition groups. I can't find any identification on him. All he had was a knife and a pistol hidden in his clothing; no money, no papers, nothing. This doesn't make any sense at all."

Fifteen minutes later, they pulled into the parking

garage at Coalition Headquarters, parking close to a little-used entrance. Moving with an intensity that demonstrated the seriousness of their task, they stepped out of their vehicle, each Avenger scanning the surroundings to make certain the group was safe. A whispered conference told Pelos they were alone, and they turned to their burden.

They wrapped their dead Kamling in an old equipment tarp and unceremoniously hauled him inside. Kish opened a supply closet, retrieving a wheeled cart. Lain casually dumped the body onto the cart, and they hastily pushed their burden to the Team 5 meeting room.

"Give me a minute to crack into the identification system," Lain said, accessing his computer terminal while Pelos stood guard at the door, weapon drawn. After a few moments, Lain announced he was ready. With Kish's assistance, he lifted the Kamling to the retina scanning station. Kish pried open the Kamling's eyes, and Lain activated the system.

The computer hummed to life, announcing, "Scan successful, processing now. Please wait."

Cadron, tapping a narrow finger to his lips, looked curiously at the computer as Kish and Lain rolled the body back up into the tarp. "Will this retina scan still work after death?" he wondered out loud. "With the lack of blood flow, plus the trauma that caused the death, I'd think it would be impossible."

"It'll still work," Lain assured him. "The police identify bodies like this all the time. I simply hacked into their system. The Coalition Police have an enormous database, and they have access to the files that

Coalition Security keeps on suspected enemies. I can almost guarantee you we'll find something. In fact," he paused, turning back to the computer screen, "here it is. His name was Len Sedom, Kamling male, 32 years of age. He has a history of violent offenses and oh, this is interesting. It seems our Kamling friend here was an active member of Event Horizon!"

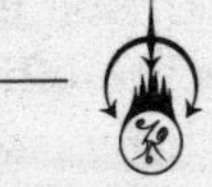

Arano squirmed impatiently in his seat as the military transport slowed to a stop outside the Coalition Headquarters building. He knew something momentous had occurred while he was gone, but the message from Lain had been vague; deliberately vague, if he knew his friend. Arano gathered the event was probably related to the Disciples case, and he bit his lip with impatience while he waited to get inside.

Finally he disembarked and entered the building, flanked by Videre and Alyna, and strode purposefully through the sprawling structure, eventually arriving at his team's meeting room. He tried the door, but it was locked from the inside, and he exchanged a curious look with his companions, shrugged, and knocked on the door.

The door opened a crack, and he saw Pelos' alert face peering through the crack, the big Tsimian's bestial features furrowed in suspicion until he saw Arano. The door opened wider, allowing Arano and his teammates to enter. He was surprised to see Pelos step close the door and lock it, pistol in hand.

"My, aren't we nervous," he remarked. "All right,

Lain, what's going on here?"

Lain allowed himself a tight grin. "Our esteemed colleague, Cadron, located a copy of the Disciples video on the computer at his house. It wasn't affected by the virus because the storm had knocked out his network connection." Lain briefly described the previous evening's events. "At any rate, we personally escorted the video to Dar Noil for processing. I assigned three military police officers to guard him. They were already guarding top secret sections of the Avengers' HQ, so they ought to be trustworthy."

"Why isn't Thom working on it?" asked Arano. "He's the video expert."

Lain sighed and shook his head. "Apparently, the time for subtlety is past. The spies didn't even try to make this one look like an accident or a disappearance. He was found murdered in his house this morning. Probably after they realized we'd escaped their attempts to recover the tape, they decided to prevent us from enhancing it. Dar is good, but nowhere near as talented as Thom was. We'll have to see what he can turn up. So, you ran into a few difficulties also, I understand?"

Arano slowly nodded, his mind elsewhere as the news of Thom's death soaked in. He described the series of mishaps they'd encountered while trying to arrest the spy in the Karlac system, resulting in the crash and ultimate destruction of the Eclipse. He paused at that point while the three members of his team who weren't present on the Karlac mission laughed themselves into hysterics.

"How ironic," said Videre, laughing so hard he had trouble catching his breath. "You finally got that hunk of junk running, and you ended up wrecking it."

"Is the Coalition going to buy you a new ship?" wondered Kish.

"I was told to submit the paperwork through the proper channels," complained Arano. "With the way the Coalition bureaucracy works, I'll be retired before they even get around to having a hearing about it."

"Oh, ye of little faith." Alyna said with a mysterious smile. "You simply need to have the proper angle when attacking these little problems."

"Little?" Arano replied, his eyebrows arching. "We weren't on an official mission out there, if you'll recall."

"That's true, Viper," Videre chimed in. "Not to mention the fact you're still dead."

"Exactly," complained Arano.

"Just wait," Alyna said with a knowing smile. "I called in some favors for you. We'll see what happens."

Arano returned to his story, ending with their trip to the Coalition outpost and their difficulties there. His mind raced, once again mulling over the prospect the betrayal by someone he trusted had cost him the life of someone close to him, this time his longtime friend, Thom. He finished his recap by saying he'd contacted someone in personnel and they were working on correcting the rumors of his demise in the Coalition computer system. He admitted, following more good-natured ribbing by Videre, that the prognosis for his immediate resurrection was not good.

He was about to turn the discussion to the team's current status when there was a knock at the door, and Dar Noil entered. He crossed the room, tossed the data disk containing the Disciples murder video on a table, and flopped into a nearby chair, his eyes swollen with exhaustion and fatigue.

"Sorry, Captain Lakeland," he said, shaking his head, "I just can't do very much with this video. The original image might have been more readily manipulated, but we're talking about a copy of a copy of a copy, from an older camera with low resolution. Can you bring the video up on the screen?"

Kish responded by inserting the disk into her computer monitor and activating the screen. The critical few moments of the video played, showing the two Tsimians stalking their prey as they passed in front of the camera's viewing area. After a pause, the video played again, enhanced this time for a much closer view. Alyna pointed at a blurry object carried in the hand of one of the Tsimians. "I think we were right," she said, tapping a finger on her lips thoughtfully. "That definitely looks like a stun stick."

"I thought the same thing myself," commented Dar thoughtfully, tapping his fingers on the table. "The stun stick is the only part of the enhanced video that has given us any information we didn't already know, and even that was something we already suspected. I'm afraid this might be a dead end. Captain Lakeland, did you want me to try anything else with the video?"

Arano stared at the screen for a few moments, running several options through his head. "Negative," he responded. "Why don't you continue running down leads on who had access to the information on our mission to the Codian system. Right now, the spy who betrayed us is more dangerous to the Coalition than the Disciples are, so we need to plug that leak as soon as possible."

Dar nodded. "What will your team be handling?" he inquired.

"One squad will check on some leads concerning the intelligence leak coming from the upper levels of the Coalition government, the other will be checking with Captain Pana. He said he had some information on the betrayal at the Earth system. Cadron will be here going over the Disciples information again, and I assume Cono will be standing around asking questions."

He looked at Dar a bit more closely. "Dar, your eyes look terrible. Are you allergic to something?"

Dar laughed, shaking his head. "I've been spending too much time with computers lately. If I stare at a viewscreen for too long, my eyes start to look like this."

"Looks painful to me," said Arano, smiling. "Oh, well. Back to work, I guess."

"Good luck," commented Dar as he left. "I'll let you know if I find anything."

Arano grunted and turned back to the computer screen, his mind wandering as his eyes watched the endlessly repeating video sequence from the last known attack by the Disciples of Zhulac. There was something oddly familiar about all the cases he was handling, and he couldn't shake the feeling something fairly important was right in front of him, if only he could recognize it. He barely noticed the sound of the door opening when Cadron entered, followed closely by Lon Pana. Clearing his head of the fog engulfing it, he turned to face the newcomers.

"Tell me you have something important," he implored them with his eyes open wide.

Cadron smiled, stretching the leathery gray skin of his face as far as he could. "Do you want the good news, or the really good news?" he asked with a laugh.

"All right," chuckled Arano, "I can see you've been talking to Videre again."

Videre put on the most innocent expression his feline features could construct. "Would I do that, your Captain-ness?"

"First," continued Cadron, "your new ship is here. Second, we have"

"My new what?" asked an astounded Arano, mouth agape.

"Ship," replied Cadron calmly. "It flies around out in space. I believe it was ordered to replace the Eclipse."

Arano could only stare in open-mouthed astonishment, unable even to mutter something inarticulate. "Like I said," Alyna gloated, "you just have to have the right angle to fix these little problems."

Lon offered an evil grin. "It cost quite a bit of money, but we managed to divert the cost through the Grand High Councilor's office. The beauty of it is, it was all done perfectly legally. The office in charge of the war automatically incurs these types of charges. Since the President is missing, and the grand High Councilor is in charge, his office gets the bill.

"I hope you don't mind if the new ship is a little bigger than your last. She's a Raptor Class Frigate, equipped with experimental weapons, shields, and engine designs. She's actually much more maneuverable than your old ship, on a par with your Assault Class Fighters, and heavily armed. There's a forward mounted Disruptor Beam, two top- and bottom-mounted plasma cannons, two torpedo launchers, and a brand new targeting computer to help you get the job done quickly."

"Wait a minute," interrupted Arano, "how did they get a Disruptor Cannon on a frigate? They take up too much space to be effectively used in a ship that size."

"You weren't listening," corrected Captain Pana. "I said Disruptor Beam, not cannon. It's a new weapon design, not as powerful as the cannon, but smaller and more versatile. I can tell you all about it on the way to the Branton system."

"That went by a little quick," complained Videre, eyes narrowed in suspicion. "Why are we going to the Branton system?"

Captain Pana held up a data disk. "The orders are from Major Alstor. This was the 'really good news' Cadron was talking about. We've been following leads, trying to find the source of the security breach on your rendezvous at the Earth system. Today, my team found the man who transmitted the information to the Rising Sun operatives. We're not sure how he was able to obtain the information, but I'm sure you'll be able to talk some answers out of him.

"He's currently operating an underwater casino on Branton 3. We've arranged lodgings for all of you onboard the casino. Videre, Kish, Lain, and Pelos are all listed as college professors on vacation. As for you, Arano, we booked you and Alyna in the honeymoon suite. Your mission . . ."

"You did WHAT?" Arano protested, half rising as Videre leaned back his chair, howling with laughter.

Captain Pana smiled. "I hope you don't mind, but Major Alstor's the one who issued the orders, after all. I'm just the message boy. You two were married yesterday, and you're taking your honeymoon on the casino."

"And just how, pray tell, do we get on the casino?" growled Arano, trying his best to maintain a scowl as Videre hummed wedding tunes while the rest of his teammates laughed, enjoying the joke at his expense.

"We're flying into the system on your new frigate as a test flight. We will rendezvous with the orbiting space station where you'll board a freighter which will take you to the floating city of Andorin."

"Floating?" giggled Lain, wiping tears of laughter from his narrow, reptilian eyes.

"The entire planet is covered with water," replied Captain Pana. "Other than the polar ice caps, there's no solid ground to walk on. It produces some fairly violent weather at times, but the temperatures stay pretty stable. At any rate, there's a submarine they use to shuttle tourists between Andorin and the casino. After you arrive, capture your target and get to the surface as soon as possible. I'll fly your frigate down to pick you up."

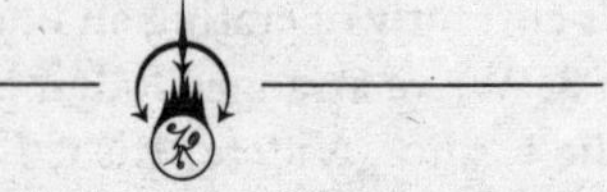

Arano and his team sat in the ready room of his new frigate, which, in a brief ceremony, he'd dubbed the Intrepid. The computerized control panels still had a slight sheen to them, evidence they'd seen very little use. The air was permeated by the sweet smell of new plastic and paint, a pleasant alternative to the normally stale odors found on older starships. It would take some getting used to, but Arano knew he'd find this ship to be a more than sufficient replacement for the Eclipse.

Captain Pana was present as an advisor, as was Cadron, while Captain Pana's team manned the various stations around the ship. It'd take them another four hours to arrive at their destination, and while the plans for this mission were complete, Cadron and Captain Pana had provided copious amounts of data that needed to be analyzed. The information had been separated into two primary topics: the Disciples killings, and the recent series of security breaches. Since there'd been recent breaches of the Disciples information, the two topics had a small area of overlap.

"I've been running a lot of numbers," said Cadron. "I've compiled lists of all personnel who accessed information about each security leak we've had, including the Disciples case, the missions to Codian 3 and the Earth system, the discovery of the Disciples tape, and other missions and intelligence information your teams weren't a part of. Combining the names from these cases produced a list of about 200 people."

Arano scowled at the announcement, looking up at the ceiling in resignation. "This is ridiculous. Have you ever heard the old saying, 'three people can keep a secret only if two of them are dead'? How can so many people have such easy access to such sensitive information?"

"I agree," said Cadron plainly, his almond-shaped

eyes narrowing into his leathery face. "My next step was to see how many people accessed all of this information. There were none. In fact, nobody accessed more than four sets of the compromised intelligence data, and I had included fifteen incidents.

"The next thing I did was compile a list of people who'd accessed more than one set of the data, but the list was still over seventy people, too large a number to be significant. Besides, since we're probably dealing with multiple leaks here, the spies undoubtedly had access to three or more sets of data apiece, because the fewer the people involved, the easier to keep it quiet. When I compiled a list of those who had accessed three or more sets of data, my list was down to twenty. I haven't been able to do anything else with the list since then.

"A few of the names could probably be eliminated right away. Eight I know of are deceased, and a few others didn't access the information deeply enough to compromise any missions. That leaves only nine names on the list, but even if they were all spies, they couldn't have pulled this off alone."

"What makes you say that?" asked Alyna, leaning forward, her eyes alight with curiosity.

"Because there were a few areas that were compromised none of them hit. I suppose it's possible some of the deceased were involved, and either they died accidentally or they were murdered after they'd outlived their usefulness. Out of two hundred people who had accessed the information, having eight of them dead seems like a high number, so I tried to look into these peoples' backgrounds as well. The problem is I can't access the information about how and when they died. That information is classified, and only people from the Bureau of Personnel can get it."

"Bureaucracy at its finest," said Arano, folding his arms across his chest and glaring at the table. "Now, about the Kamlings who attacked Kish and Cadron. We know at least one of them was a member of Event Horizon. Since that group tends to stick to its own, I'd say we can safely assume all the attackers were from Event Horizon. Lon, your thoughts on this?"

Lon Pana leaned back in his chair, stretching his legs in front him. "I suppose it's entirely possible for Event Horizon to be behind this whole Disciples mess. We know them to be terrorists, and they will do anything to disrupt the Coalition, including murdering innocent civilians. Of course, if this is the case, and they also turn out to be responsible for any of the security breaches, they've somehow managed to infiltrate someone into our highest levels of security."

"How about the transmission we intercepted from the Branton system," interrupted Kish. "What have we learned from that?"

"My area," noted Pelos shortly, setting down one datapad and retrieving another. "I've been going over this transmission with Lain. The Coalition cryptologists managed to decode enough of it to get the gist of the message and to find out who it was from. Lain and I have decoded most of the rest of the message. The spy is Ollem Nanon, a Human who operates one of Branton 3's underwater gambling casinos. He also has a history of multiple arrests, mainly for smuggling. He doesn't appear to have any ties to known terrorist groups, but a mercenary like him will deal with anyone if the price is right.

"From what we can tell, an unnamed spy back in the Immok system shipped him a data disk, smuggled inside a routine shipment to the Branton system. It contained the arrival time at the Earth system for Task Force Blue, as well as a complete list of the ships attached to the task force. Whoever attacked the task force knew who was coming and knew when they were going to get there. The task force didn't have a prayer. On an interesting side note, while perusing Ollem's file I learned he's a major stockholder in the Biomek company."

"Interesting how a company with secret ties to Balor Tient is popping up," mused Arano thoughtfully. Seeing the perplexed look on Lon's face, he explained that Biomek had paid large sums of cash to the Grand High Councilor for information on interspecies live-organ transplant techniques.

The communications officer, one of Lon's team members, caught their attention. "We've just dropped out of the wormhole," he informed them. "I'm receiving a distress call from the Selpan system. We had a large patrol on maneuvers in the system, and they are under attack by a Rising Sun Fleet. According to the message, the battle was going well until a Rising Sun battle cruiser jumped in. Soon after, while concentrating their attention on a few wounded cruisers, our smaller ships lost their shields. Some are reporting problems getting torpedo locks on their targets. Our remaining ships are preparing to retreat. They won't be able to activate their Rift Drives for another thirty minutes while they wait for their engines to cool. The fleet commander is trying to regroup now."

Arano stared absently at a datapad for a few moments. "Obviously," he thought out loud, "This isn't an anomaly associated with something at the Earth System. This has something to do with Rising Sun."

"If I recall correctly," said Kish, her near-perfect memory causing Videre to groan and drop his fur-covered head into his hands in mock disgust, "we had problems with our shields and torpedoes immediately following the arrival of a Rising Sun capital ship, the same as this patrol did. It has to be significant."

"Definitely," agreed Cadron. "Wait, suppose someone accessed information about our shields and weapons technology. Would they be able to have used that information to, in some way, cause these malfunctions?"

"How about a virus?" suggested Lain. "They could very easily have hidden a virus in the computer systems of our ships that would instruct them to lower their shields and shut down the weapons targeting computers on the arrival of Rising Sun ships."

He paused, and another idea occurred to him. "It could've happened the night someone accessed the computers and killed Arano in the system. We know there was other mischief done that night, and we have no way to track it down. A virus implanted into the starport's computer system would've infected the entire fleet in a matter of hours."

Captain Pana nodded in agreement. "Okay, we need someone looking into this." He turned to his communications officer. "Send a message to Headquarters. Tell them to start searching through the computer systems of all the ships in the port at Immok, as well as the main starport computer there. We need to find out if there's a virus, and if so, isolate and eradicate it."

"Acknowledged," came the reply. "Beginning docking procedures with the starbase orbiting Branton 3."

CHAPTER NINE

HAND-IN-HAND, ARANO AND ALYNA WALKED GRATEfully into the honeymoon suite in the Praymar Casino, quite possibly the most opulent casino in the entire quadrant. Their luggage was already in the room, carried in by some unnamed porter. Arano flopped onto a well-cushioned sofa, exhaustion etched in his face, watching passively as Alyna unpacked her bags. He looked around, wondering how much a room like this cost. The enormous bed with the plush comforter, the chairs that seemed to swallow you in softness, the ornate furnishings lining the walls, and the almost priceless bottle of Tsimian wine lent an atmosphere of unrestrained luxury to the suite.

Mentally counting back, he decided it'd been nearly 24 hours since he had slept. Upon return from his unsuccessful mission in the Karlac system, he and his team had immediately flown in the Intrepid to the Branton system, a flight of nearly nineteen hours, during which time he'd only been able to grab a brief nap. After docking with an orbiting space station, they'd boarded a shuttle flight to the city of Andorin. From there, they were shuffled around like papers on a businessman's desk, finally boarding a submarine for the two-hour trip to the casino.

Arano's thoughts turned to the other members of his team. His four lieutenants were posing as simple tourists, just a small group of college professors on a vacation. Kish's photographic memory made her a cinch to win big in certain card games, and Ollem Nanon had a reputation for wanting to hobnob with the big gamblers. The idea was to lure him out and draw him into their trust. It would then be a simple matter to bring him to a location where he could be removed from the casino and taken to Immok for questioning. Arano and Alyna would remain separate from the others in order to surreptitiously watch the whole operation, try to spot Ollem's bodyguards, and act as a safety net for the rest of the team. Glancing over at his roommate, his new "wife", Arano couldn't help thinking he'd gotten the best part of that bargain.

"You look exhausted," she noted, as if reading his mind. "I'm going to take a shower. Why don't you try to get some sleep? I'll join you shortly. We still have several hours before we need to meet with the others."

Arano agreed with a slow nod, somehow gathered the energy to stand, and headed toward the couch. "Don't let me sleep too long," he mumbled as he spread a light blanket over the cushions.

"Hold on," she told him in exasperation. "What if room service comes barging in? We have to maintain our cover. We both sleep in the bed."

"You're right," he agreed. "I just didn't want to appear presumptuous." Moving over to the enormous bed, he slid easily under the blankets and tried to relax.

But he was so exhausted it seemed sleep just wouldn't come. Finally, as his eyes grew heavy, he rolled over and saw the architect had apparently forgotten to place walls around the shower area, probably in an attempt to add intimacy to the honeymoon suite's atmosphere. He stared blankly at Alyna's silhouette, also noticing the shower had only a thin set of sheer curtains around it, leaving little to the imagination. He closed his eyes as sleep finally, mercifully, took him, painful memories of times past running through his head.

Later, having rested and refreshed themselves, Arano and Alyna went downstairs to their prearranged meeting with the rest of the team. Arano couldn't help wonder about the Coalition patrol and its fight with the Rising Sun fleet in the Selpan System, but trying to contact the Coalition from here risked blowing his team's cover. They stepped out of an elevator and strolled casually through the gaming area, gawking like tourists while they searched for their friends. The likeness of a Human face, presumably Ollem Nanon, was present on the curtains, carpeting, and on every beverage glass Arano could see. Gaming machines were packed in tightly, the designer obviously trying to push the maximum profit out of the space available. At nearly every machine, people of the various races were gathered, trying their luck with games of chance although the odds were stacked against them.

Arano felt a casual squeeze of his hand and glanced in the direction of Alyna's gaze. He saw Kish sitting at a card table, an enormous pile of chips in front of her, with Videre and Pelos to one side and Lain to the other. Catching Lain's eye, Arano acknowledged his presence. He sat at a nearby slot machine and began playing while Alyna stood behind him, arms around his neck. From their vantage point they could see and hear everything at Kish's table.

"Players," announced the dealer, "the new game is Tai Si Poker. Antes, please." While the four players tossed their playing chips onto the center of the table, the dealer passed out cards. As the hand progressed, Kish made what seemed to be reckless bets, but Arano knew better. With Kish's photographic memory and skills at mathematics, she was constantly recalculating the odds, allowing her to place strategic wagers. Since most of the cards in a game of Tai Si Poker are dealt face up, it was a simple matter for Kish to dominate the other players.

"The call is to the lady Tompiste," noted the dealer.

Without hesitation, Kish tossed another handful of chips into the growing pot. "Double," she announced.

The other players were visibly shaken, and one immediately turned his cards over on the table. "Out," he announced. The player to his left looked uncomfortable, but followed suit, throwing his cards into the discard pile in disgust.

The remaining player, however, an unreadable look on his face, matched Kish's bet. He stared at his cards a few moments longer, then announced, "Up," adding yet more game chips to the pot. Kish immediately matched the bet, and the dealer dealt out the final cards. Two small bets later, they both turned over their few face-down cards, and the dealer announced Kish the winner. He pushed the chips in front of Kish, adding to the already towering collection she had amassed.

Arano and Alyna continued moving from machine to machine, not wanting to draw attention to themselves, but staying near Kish's table. A few hours and several opponents later, an outlandishly dressed Human came up behind Kish, his eyes intent on the game. He grinned as Kish counted out another large bet, sliding it to the center of the table. "Block," she announced. The hand finished quickly, and Kish was again the winner. A tall Tsimian, his beak clicking in anger, got up from the table and, gathering what few chips he had left, stormed away amidst a flurry of curses. The Human behind Kish moved to the empty seat.

"Mind if I join you?" he asked.

The other players silently approved, nodding at the vacated chair. Arano, who watched as Alyna fed coins into a gaming machine that occasionally gave her one back, noted the two Gatoans lurking unobtrusively several feet away, to either side of the Human. Leaning toward Alyna as if to kiss his new bride, he whispered to her he suspected Ollem Nanon had taken the bait, and described the two possible bodyguards. Catching her barely perceptible nod, he turned so that, while appearing to be watching Alyna, he could keep an eye on the bodyguards. He glanced back at the card game and saw Kish and the newcomer had already run the bet up high enough to force the other three players out of the game. Kish raised the bet yet higher;

undaunted, her opponent matched her bet without an apparent thought.

Kish received her final card and stated, "Intervene." She paid a few extra chips into the pot, and the dealer dealt the contingency cards to the two embattled players.

The newcomer flipped over his face-down cards with a grin. "I've got you this time," he proclaimed. "There's almost no way you can beat this hand."

"The gentleman has a 'whole scan'," announced the dealer, drawing murmurs of approval and some scattered applause from the large crowd that had gathered behind their table. Kish sat unmoving for a few moments before slowly turning over her cards.

The people closest to the table gasped, and even the dealer froze in shock for a moment. "The lady has a 'Grand Star', winning the hand." The crowd erupted in cheers, some even pushing forward to pat Kish on the back, a few of the more superstitious ones perhaps hoping some of her luck would rub off on them. As the din died down and Kish drew in her winnings, her final opponent laughed, shook his head and held out his hand.

"Nanon's my name," he told her. "Ollem Nanon. I'm the owner of this facility. Care to join me for dinner? I'm buying, of course. I like to entertain the high-stakes gamblers who come through here. It's becoming a tradition, you know. Your friends are welcome to join us."

"My name is Arba Walker," Kish told him, "and we'd love to join you." She signaled for the dealer to give her a marker for her chips, and a few moments later they crossed the spacious gaming area and entered the restaurant. Although not large, the restaurant was as ostentatious as the rest of the facility, with unnecessary amounts of money poured into decorations not many people even noticed.

Since Ollem escorted them, they were treated as VIPs and given priority seating. Arano and Alyna entered the restaurant several minutes later and were lucky enough to get a seat near Kish's table. Videre was just finishing a bawdy joke, and the punchline brought raucous laughter from the others.

"So, Arba," Ollem stated casually, "you were saying you are professors at Immok University. What is your specialty?"

"I'm a math professor," Kish said carefully. "Not a real fascinating conversational topic, but it keeps me busy."

"What about your friends?"

"I teach computer classes," said Videre. "I concentrate mainly on networks, security, that sort of thing. On the side, I like to tinker with gadgets. Small useful toys just absolutely fascinate me."

"And I teach history," added Pelos. "I stay mostly within the bounds of military history. In fact, I teach a class that consists solely of the events surrounding the Human-Bromidian War."

"Military history, huh?" queried Ollem in an offhand manner. "Do you know much Padian history?"

"Some," replied Pelos cautiously, eyes narrowing. "What did you have in mind?"

"I've always been curious about the race in general, but especially about the effects their sudden technological advance during the War had on their society."

"Not much," interrupted Videre, speaking slightly louder to ensure Arano could hear him. "They're all still a bunch of ignorant savages." Arano nearly choked on his water, and Alyna had to wipe her mouth with her napkin to cover her broad grin.

Unabashed, Ollem continued. "More importantly, what do you know about the Daxia? I've heard stories, but you know the old saying: 'Believe half of what you see, and none of what you hear.' I have to believe the stories I've heard are exaggerated, but I'd like confirmation. I've been thinking of acquiring a few . . . artifacts from their homeworld, and I want to know what I'll be up against if they take offense."

Pelos cast a surreptitious glance in Arano's direction, seeking guidance. Arano briefly considered the situation, then gave a barely perceptible nod. Following the occupation by Rising Sun forces, the information on the Daxia wasn't held in secret anymore, so if Ollem was really interested he could get the information elsewhere. Best to give him what he could easily obtain anyway and possibly gain his trust in the process.

"Let me start with a brief overview of modern Padian history," Pelos said professionally. Videre groaned, muttered something into his empty glass, and ordered another drink from the waiter, to Ollem's obvious amusement. "The history of the Padians prior to 2083 is largely unimportant to the galaxy as a whole. Their homeworld on Leguin 4 has only one inhabitable land mass, so their society is fairly monolithic due to the lack of isolation.

"Their government has always had a clan-based structure, with one individual from each clan serving both as clan leader and as a member of the ruling council. Since they were united under a common government, they've avoided large-scale wars between groups of clans. The ruling council has always been able to keep the clans from getting involved in other clans' conflicts.

"Despite being largely considered to be 'ignorant savages,'" Pelos said with a withering look at Videre, "they've actually developed their technologies at a faster rate than most civilizations, mainly due to the personal freedoms granted by their government. They'd begun to industrialize when the Humans came. Soon there was a blending of the two civilizations; technology was obtained on the black market, there were marriages between Humans and Padians, and so on. Commerce between the two became extensive, although the Humans steadfastly refused to give the Padians the secrets of space travel. Even those operating on the black market wouldn't give space-related technologies to the Padians, for fear of retribution.

"In 2099, when the Humans began having problems with the Bromidians, commerce between Humans and Padians started to fall off. In 2103, the clan council met, and they drafted a letter to the Humans volunteering the Padian military to assist in ground conflicts. At first, the Humans were reluctant, but following the formation of the Coalition it was decided to bring the Padians onboard. For several months, Human soldiers trained the Padian military units in the tactics and weapons they would be using, while Human scientists introduced the technologies so desperately desired by the Padian people.

"The Padians have been generally accepted as members of the Coalition. Daxia who've completed their terms of service on Leguin 4 are in especially high demand throughout the Coalition in positions as consultants and bodyguards. No outsiders have ever been accepted to the Daxia training at Whelen Academy, and it's doubtful it will ever occur.

"Whelen Academy is run by a master named Axial, in honor of Axial Whelen, who established the Academy over 1500 years ago. Graduates are called 'Daxia', which means 'Disciple of Axial', and instructors are called 'Ma-Daxia'. Students are selected young in life, based upon early signs of strength, speed, and intelligence. They begin the school at the age of eight, spending a total of ten years at the Academy. Following their graduation, they work for the Ruling Council for four years, primarily as spies and assassins. After that term is up, some are asked to continue working for the Ruling Council, but most return to their clans and continue their intelligence careers at home."

Ollem was listening intently. "What kind of training do they put the students through to get the tremendous reputation they have?"

"Obviously, Padians have a natural ability to be aware of their surroundings, knowing ahead of time when they're in some sort of danger. They hone this ability to a razor's edge at the Academy. Starting at age 12, the Ma-Daxia stalk the students as they move about the campus. If they catch a student unaware, they deliver a fierce beating. Due to the extensive martial arts training the Ma-Daxia have been through, they know how to inflict pain without causing serious injuries, and they use the knowledge as a teaching aide. These frequent attacks sharpen the students' danger sense as well as their fighting abilities.

"To improve their stealth abilities, in their last year students are forced to 'bell-up'; that is, every night they must attempt to cross the campus unnoticed while wearing bells tied at every major joint and around their heads. It doesn't take many attacks by the Ma-Daxia to teach the students to glide more smoothly, reducing their movements. This is why they are so adept at moving around unseen.

"The Academy has a varied curriculum, which goes beyond the study of fighting. They learn about religion and history, both Padian and galactic. They study the psychology of all the known races, although information on Bromidian psychology is limited. Their fighting studies involve hand-to-hand fighting, armed combat involving hand-held weapons, both blunt and edged, archery, projectile weapons, and most recently, the powered weapons employed by the Coalition."

"Impressive," admitted Ollem. "You have a remarkable understanding of the Padian people. I'm surprised they're that open with their information, especially about their secret society."

Pelos smiled. "They weren't, up until the time of the Rising Sun occupation of Leguin 4. A Daxia discovered the leader of the Waya Plains Clan was selling information to Rising Sun; information about Padians in general, but especially about the Whelen Academy. As it turned out, he gave away the names of all the active Daxia, as well as the names of clan leaders and their families. As soon as the Ruling Council discovered it, they sent a Daxia in to silence him. Fearing for his life, the clan leader erected a perimeter around his house extending out 1200 meters in all directions. The Daxia assassin sat on a hilltop a few hundred meters outside the wall and killed him with a projectile rifle. The shot was estimated at 1500 meters."

"That's quite a shot." Ollem said, his eyebrows raised.

"Too late, though," said Pelos. "The damage had been done before the Council was even aware of his activities. Less than three months after the assassination, Rising Sun forces invaded Leguin 4. They used the information provided by their spy to eliminate all the leaders in order to prevent the formation of an opposition group. They also tried to eliminate as many of the Daxia as they could, but weren't very successful there. Apparently, either the spy didn't impress upon them the extent of the Daxias' abilities, or the Bromidians didn't believe him. Either way, most of the Daxia escaped. With some help from a detachment of Coalition troops, they managed to drive all the Rising Sun troops off the planet."

"I've heard that part," admitted Ollem with a scowl. "Avengers. As much as I despise them, you couldn't ask for better help. They would've had to send in several divisions of regular troops to drive the Bromidians out, and risked an interplanetary incident in the process. They got the job done quietly and cheaply."

"I'm surprised they didn't send in regular troops," complained Kish grumpily. "You know how the Coalition likes to flex its muscles."

Ollem chuckled at this last remark. "Walk with me," he commanded. When they were alone, he said, "I like you, but I have a confession to make. Before I invited you to dinner, I checked our guest log to find out who you were, and then I did some checking on you. It seems your office at the university is in the same building as the artifacts warehouse."

"Tell me about it," griped Kish. "Do you know how many pockets you have to line among the Campus Committee members before you can get a good office? The bribes there are atrocious."

Ollem leaned forward, his voice dropping to a conspiratorial whisper. "What if I could help you with those bribes? A few well placed donations in your name would certainly go a long way toward getting you a room with a view."

Kish smiled. "I might be interested. What did you have in mind?"

"There are a few items of interest in the artifacts warehouse I'd like to take possession of. I have buyers already lined up for several of them, but I need help obtaining them. What I'll need you to do is remove the items from the warehouse and bring them to a collection point, where you'll meet with my contact for Immok City. He'll see to it the items are properly shipped to me. Upon successful receipt of the items, the proper donations will be made."

Kish pretended to consider the matter, her thin, leathery lips pursed in concentration. "I suppose it'll depend on the amount of money you're talking about, and which items. Not that I care what disappears from the warehouse, but some items are more closely guarded than others and require more effort and risk to obtain."

"I'll tell you what," conceded Ollem. "We have a lot to discuss. Here is a security card that'll gain you access to the wing of the casino where my quarters are. It's in the highest level of the facility. Just put that card in the security slot, and you can come on up. I'm in room 100. Stop by tonight around 2200 hours, and we can work out the details. Your security card has also been encoded with a list of some of the items I'm looking for. If your friends would be interested and can be trusted, bring them along."

The two shook hands and separated, Ollem heading back to work and Kish returning to her friends. She sat at the table, verifying Arano and Alyna were still seated within earshot. She placed her napkin back into her lap and resumed her meal.

"He made me a business offer." she told them. "I have a meeting with him tonight to finalize the deal. I'm going to tell him the only way I'll cooperate is if he includes you guys. We just have to keep it quiet from the university."

Videre lifted his glass for a toast. "Here's to silence, and all the money it brings."

Lain drank deeply from his glass of non-alcoholic wine, trying to avoid the problems his Kamling physiology developed when presented with alcohol. "When is the meeting?"

"It's at 2200 hours tonight in his suite on the top floor, room 100. We have to use this access card to get past the security checkpoint."

Pelos leaned forward, looking intently at the card

in Kish's hands. "Looks like a standard Silex security card. I'll put the encryption codes on our datapad, just in case something happens to the original." The big Tsimian took the security card from Kish, connected it to a port on his datapad, and studied the screen intently for a few moments. Finally, he leaned back in his chair, sliding the card back across the table to Kish. "They used a fairly rare encryption on that card. Expensive stuff." He chuckled. "Waste of money, too."

An hour later, Arano closed and locked the door to the honeymoon suite as Alyna made a careful sweep for listening devices. "Can't be too careful," she explained when Arano sighed and shook his head at her extravagant security measures. After she gave the room an "all clear", Arano retrieved his own datapad from their luggage. He tapped gingerly at the controls, gratefully accepting a glass of water from Alyna.

"What, no ice?" he teased. "What kind of wife are you?" She answered him by dumping her glass of water on his head. Laughing, he wiped his face with the towel she had laid out for her bath, and turned back to his datapad.

"This is interesting," he told her shortly. "We have a message from the others. Kish has Ollem ready to buy stolen artifacts from her. That's what their meeting was all about. This looks like the perfect opportunity to grab Ollem and make a run for it. I'm pulling up the schematics for the casino now."

Arano sat on their enormous bed and pulled the needed data from their intelligence files stored in his datapad, making notes as he went. He paused to remove his shirt, still wet from Alyna's retributive strike with the glass of water. Alyna passed the time by taking another shower, to Arano's endless distraction. He began to have a hard time concentrating on his work, eyes constantly stealing glances at the unwalled shower. She finally finished, wrapped herself in a towel and sat next to Arano to see what he had found. As he was about to explain his idea, the datapad indicated an incoming message on the encrypted channel.

He touched a control and the pad's screen activated, Videre's fur-lined face appearing where there had been maps and technical readouts of the casino. Videre looked at Arano, shirtless, and Alyna wrapped in a towel, and he grinned. "Soooo," Videre said slowly, "how are your accommodations?"

Arano's face turned a bright shade of red while he fumbled for a response, but Alyna gave an evil grin. "Luxurious," she replied, running her fingers through her still-damp hair. "I hope you're enjoying your stay."

Arano recovered enough of his composure to form a coherent question. "Okay, what am I supposed to do with this security code you sent me?"

Pelos' bestial face intruded on the small monitor. "If you take one of the cards you use to access your room, you can reprogram it with the datapad and give it the code I sent you. It should get you past all the checkpoints."

Arano picked up the brief notes he'd taken while

studying their intelligence reports on the casino, which outlined his plan for capturing Ollem. As he began his oration, he realized Alyna had used some type of perfumed oil during her shower, and the scent was definitely distracting him. He forced his thoughts back to the matter at hand.

The plan was fairly simple. Kish and the others would keep the appointment at 2200 hours, with all four of them heading in together. While Ollem was distracted by Kish's business proposal, Arano and Alyna would enter the secure area using the stolen security code and overpower any bodyguards stationed outside Ollem's suite. They would enter the room, capture Ollem, and take him up to their planned escape point. Ollem's room was in a tower, protruding from the main body of the casino, thrusting upward to within thirty meters of the surface. At the pinnacle of the tower was an escape pod. They would activate their homing beacon to signal Captain Pana orbiting overhead in the Intrepid, load Ollem into the pod, and head for the surface. Captain Pana would be there to retrieve them before an organized search from the casino could reach them, and they would make their escape.

With the plans finalized, they were ready to terminate the Comm link and make their final preparations. "Well," said Videre, "once we're ready on this end we're going to hit the casino games for a while. Where'll you two be?" Videre gave a knowing wink, smiling broadly. "Or need I ask?"

Alyna murmured, "I'll handle this one." She stood up, stepped out of view of the datapad's screen, removed her towel, and handed it to Arano so Videre could plainly see it. Speaking so Videre could also hear her, she announced, "I don't know about you, but I'm going to finish my bath." Arano closed down the Comm link, taking a secret pleasure in the perplexed look on Videre's face.

Arano and Alyna, arms locked about each other's waists, strolled casually down the walkway connecting the gaming area to the tower where Ollem's suite was located. Made of a crystal clear glass-steel hybrid, its walls had the strength to endure the enormous pressures exerted by the water surrounding it, yet still provide a breathtaking view of the ocean life. The architect had certainly known a thing or two about marine biology, thought Arano, gazing out in admiration. Lights were placed strategically to enable a full view of the ecology around the tunnel. An artificial reef had been built a short distance away, and a myriad of marine life swam excitedly in and out of the underwater flora, while larger predator fish swam about slowly, warily, looking for their next meal. At a wordless agreement, they stopped walking and simply stood admiring the scenery. Lost in the beauty in front of him, Arano was almost able to forget there was a war going on, and a sense of peace came over him.

He glanced over at Alyna, his feelings for her beginning to slip past the mental wall he had erected. Their eyes met, and their lips came silently together. They stood locked in a passionate embrace for a long moment, both content in the feel of the other's body. Then the intercom squelched, the voice calling for some unseen worker to report to a duty area, and Arano pulled away. He chided himself for becoming distracted, reminding himself sternly he was here on a mission.

Arano checked the time when they arrived at their destination, a junction between the main corridors and a restricted security corridor. He verified they'd arrived several minutes ahead of schedule, and they kept a surreptitious eye on the passers-by, watching for security guards. When the time came for them to enter the secure sector, they made a final check of the area before Arano pulled out his altered security card. He placed it against a depression in the wall and waited a few anxious seconds before the door slid open with a barely audible hiss. Arano stepped purposefully through the open doorway, followed closely by Alyna.

They moved silently now, the time for talking past. Both had memorized the course they would follow, as well as their main escape route and two backup escape routes.

A door hissed open behind them, and they whirled to face two startled security guards who stepped into the corridor. "What're you doing here?" the first demanded, reaching for his radio.

"I'm here to see Ollem Nanon. Or rather, she is," Arano told him, nudging Alyna disrespectfully. "Ollem has some odd desires, and she's here to fulfill them. She'll do anything for a price." Picking up on the charade, Alyna gave the guards a seductive look, teasing them with half-parted lips and lowered eyelids.

"He doesn't know I've actually arrived," continued Arano, "and I'd like to sort of keep it that way. His birthday is coming, and she's my present to him. I'd really like to surprise him."

The first guard smiled knowingly. "Sure thing. You have a security card to verify that you're allowed to be back here? Not that I don't believe you, but if Ollem finds out I saw you in here and didn't check you out . . ."

"Here," replied Arano, handing over his altered card. He waited nervously while the guard scanned it, hoping he wouldn't detect the card was a forgery.

The guard handed the card back. "Here you go," he laughed. "Ollem must really like you to give you a card with that level of access. By the way, girl, when you're finished with Ollem, stop by the Officer's Club. If you're half as good as you look like you are, we might be able to work out a deal."

Alyna smiled sensually. "I'm sure we could. Maybe I'll see you there." With feminine grace she whirled about, and she and Arano continued their interrupted journey to their rendezvous at the top of the tower. They stuck to the less-used corridors to minimize their chances of encountering anyone else, finally arriving at a freight elevator in an obscure area of the facility. Again using the security card, Arano was able to gain entrance, and they rode the elevator to the top floor.

Arano stepped out into the open, saw the way was clear and motioned for Alyna to follow. They crept on silent feet down a few more hallways before arriving at a supply closet, their final checkpoint, where they would hide and await a signal from the others that all was ready.

Ollem opened the door to his room, motioning for Kish and her friends to enter. The casino owner seated himself casually, indicating with a wave of his hand the others should sit also. If the rest of the casino was opulent, Ollem's room was nothing short of extreme ostentation. The artwork was in bad taste and did not match the décor of the room, but seemed to be there only to show the owner could afford it. The carpet was made of an expensive silk, harvested from the Tompiste homeworld. Even the liquor cabinet was ornately crafted, filled with obscenely expensive beverages.

Kish rubbed casually at her leathery-skinned face and leaned forward, clasping her hands together. "Thank you for letting us all come up here," she told him.

"How could I refuse?" Ollem smiled pleasantly. "One thing I've learned from all my years in the business is that one should never let an opportunity pass you by.

"My apologies for what may appear to be a lack of trust, but I've had my associates on Immok perform checks on all four of you. You can never be too careful these days. You passed, of course. If you hadn't, you'd be swimming with the fishes." He smiled and laughed as if he'd just told the funniest joke anyone had ever heard, accenting his laugh with several nasal snorts Kish found highly annoying.

"Well, as I promised, here's our offer," said Kish, her bout of feigned laughter subsiding. She pulled out her datapad, called up her business proposition, and in the process activated the signal telling Arano and Alyna they were ready, simultaneously alerting Captain Pana in the Intrepid they would soon be ready for pickup. She handed the pad to Ollem, who accepted it and silently perused the contents. He studied the display for a few anxious moments, face expressionless while he considered Kish's offer. Finally, he smiled and looked up.

"Damn, you are sure of yourself, aren't you? Your prices aren't too far out of line, but I'm surprised you think you can acquire such a quantity of artifacts."

"That's where I come in," interjected Lain. "As a hobby, I construct miniature scale replicas of famous ships and land craft. It won't require much extra effort for me to make life-sized replicas of the artifacts to put in place of the real ones at the museum. We could end up walking out of there with their whole inventory and have no one the wiser."

They continued explaining the details of their planned operation to Ollem, who was suitably impressed with the attention to detail and the ambition the four entrepreneurs displayed. Kish was anxious expecting the arrival of Arano and Alyna at any time. She made a mental note of the location of the Comm in the room, as well as possible places Ollem might have weapons hidden for emergency use. What made the operation easier was Ollem considering himself too important to have his bodyguards close to him; he didn't allow them in the room. In fact, he had such confidence in his security system, there were only two guards posted outside. Kish was fairly certain Arano and Alyna could easily handle those two.

Finally, Ollem broke out a bottle of wine to celebrate the closing of the deal, bragging about how much the wine had cost, and they heard the sound of a scuffle outside the door. Ollem glanced toward the door in surprise, then reached swiftly for his Comm to call for help. Videre reflexively intervened, grabbing the surprised man by his arm and slamming him none too gently against the wall, upsetting the table and spilling the wine.

The door slid open and Arano and Alyna entered, dragging the inert forms of the bodyguards behind them. Arano casually dropped his burden and strode over to Videre who had Ollem pinned against the wall. Ollem's countenance was contorted with anger, his face turning red as he blustered.

"You can't do this!" he shouted. "You think you can rob me and get away with it? Fools! You'll never get out of this facility before"

His tirade was cut off when Videre pushed his forearm sharply against Ollem's throat. Arano stepped up, handing a pair of handcuffs to Videre. "Ollem Nanon, you're under arrest for smuggling, and treason against the Coalition."

Ollem stopped struggling, mouth hanging open in amazement. "Who are you?"

"Captain Arano Lakeland, USC Avengers. Here's the situation. We're going to head out of here, and we're taking you with us. You'll receive a fair trial. If convicted, your assets will be seized and you'll be punished. If not, you'll be free to return. But remember, we're currently at war with Rising Sun, which by Coalition law gives me the authority to execute you right now. If we have to leave without you, I won't leave you alive to continue selling secrets to the other side. Let's move."

The Avengers moved out into the hallway in groups of two, Arano and Videre in the lead, Lain and Pelos in the middle with Ollem, and Alyna bringing up the rear with Kish. They moved with haste, knowing it was only a matter of time before the alarm sounded. They continued down a sub-hallway toward an elevator that would take them to the very top of the tower to an emergency escape pod.

Arano moved like a cat at hunt, smooth and graceful, eyes everywhere. Reaching an intersection, he signaled for the group to stop, and he edged forward. As he was about to peer around the corner, his danger sense kicked in, warning him trouble lay ahead. He dropped lithely into a prone position, peeking around the wall at floor level. Two guards waited from half-concealed positions, preparing to fire on whoever rounded the corner. He slipped back behind cover and used hand-signals to indicate the alarm had apparently been sounded and a problem lay ahead. He drew out a smoke grenade, hoping to use it to screen their movements.

Suddenly, shots rang out from behind them, one shot narrowly missing Alyna as it impacted the wall in a shower of sparks. The rear guard of the Avengers team immediately turned and poured murderous cover fire in that direction as they tried to prevent the guards from obtaining a clear, aimed shot.

Arano tossed his smoke grenade and called for his team to follow. He charged across the intersection of the two hallways, firing randomly into the smoke while he ran. As he had hoped, the two guards stationed there couldn't see the Avengers when they crossed, and were unable to fire on Arano's team effectively. Arano raced on down the hall, leading his teammates to the elevator while Alyna and Kish continued to lay down cover fire to keep the approaching guards at bay.

Arano activated the elevator controls, but they were on a security lockdown. He tried his security card, but to no avail.

"Pelos," he called sharply, "bypass their system!" As Pelos moved to the elevator controls, Arano took over Pelos' firing position. They were taking fire from two directions now and were forced to take cover in recessed doorways. Ollem offered no objection when he was pressed unmercifully against a bulkhead, safe from the guards' shots. Pelos continued to struggle heroically with the controls to the elevator, despite being partially exposed to enemy fire. One shot actually pierced the tail of his shirt, burning through and leaving a trail of smoke as evidence of the close call.

"The elevator is completely shut down!" Pelos shouted over the din. "I'm going to try to release the locking mechanism on the doors so we can access the elevator shaft. We should be able to climb up a maintenance ladder."

"Okay, get on it," yelled Arano, continuing to fire randomly in the direction of their assailants. By now, the guards had extinguished lighting in the corridor except for the area where the embattled Avengers team was holed up. It illuminated the Avengers, but kept them from being able to see the guards. Ollem shouted his defiance, telling them if they gave up he would let them try to swim to the surface from the bottom of the casino. He added as an afterthought that the trip to the surface wouldn't take more than five or ten minutes, if they could hold their breath that long. Videre silenced him with a sharp slap.

A muffled cry came from Alyna when a grenade detonated nearby, a piece of shrapnel piercing her side and drawing a flow of bright red blood. She collapsed senseless to the corridor floor, exposed to enemy fire. Without a second thought, Arano dove on top of her and dragged her back to safety while Kish and Lain covered him. A laser shot struck Arano on the left calf, and he gasped in pain. Just then, with a shout of excitement, Pelos slid the elevator doors open and stepped inside.

"Pelos, you take the point," commanded Arano through clenched teeth. Pelos nodded, moving to the nearby service ladder and starting up the shaft. "Kish, you're next." Without hesitation, Kish darted across the hallway into the elevator shaft and began her climb behind Pelos, pistol in hand. "Videre next, carrying Nanon. If he fights you, kill him." Videre nodded, turned, and punched Ollem in the stomach. When Ollem doubled over, Videre tossed him over his shoulder and climbed the ladder as well. Arano placed the still-unconscious Alyna over his shoulder and darted into the elevator shaft.

"I've got Alyna," he shouted to Lain. "That leaves you to cover our tails. Seal the doors behind you as best you can and follow us up. We'll be waiting at the top."

The elevator shaft had a stale, musty odor, giving the impression the maintenance crews worked in there none too frequently. The rungs of the ladder were covered with a layer of dust, smeared now to a muddy grit by the sweaty hands of Arano's teammates. He had to take extra care in placing his free hand on the rung to make sure he had a firm grip; one slip could mean the end for Alyna.

He looked up and saw Pelos had already climbed the five remaining floors to the top of the shaft and was trying to force the doors open. Kish had taken up a cover position to one side, and was ready to fire on anyone who might be on the other side of the doors.

Arano's thoughts returned to business, and he concentrated on the climb. With one hand on the ladder and the other holding Alyna, he wouldn't be able to fire at anyone, and was totally dependent on his teammates. It was slow going, the strain of climbing with only one hand wearing on him. His wounded calf was also beginning to falter, shooting excruciating pain through his leg. He gritted his teeth and climbed onward, taking some measure of solace in the breathing he felt coming from the inert form draped across his shoulders.

As he reached the limits of his endurance, Arano finally neared the end of his climb. He glanced up and saw Pelos still trying to open the doors at the top of the shaft, while Kish was clinging to some nearby equipment, weapon held at the ready in her free hand. Videre was taking a breather, trying to put more weight on his legs while he held a petrified Ollem Nanon across his shoulders.

Arano hooked an elbow over a rung of the ladder, unwilling to climb any higher until the doors above him were forced open; he didn't want to bunch up his team. He tried to examine Alyna, and noticed with a chill she was still bleeding freely from her side.

"Let's go, Pelos! Get that door open now! I've got to dress her wound, and I can't do it while I'm hanging here!" Pelos grunted an unintelligible reply, continuing his work on the door. Arano felt Alyna's lifeblood running down the front of his shirt, and he wanted to scream in frustration.

"Got it!" came the triumphant shout from Pelos as the doors grudgingly slid open to reveal an open hallway beyond. Pelos nodded to Kish, gave a silent three-count on his fingers, and the two swung into the corridor, facing opposite directions. Arano began his climb anew, the strength in his arms nearly spent. He heard shouts from the open doors, followed by several laser bursts.

Pelos poked his head back into the shaft and waved for the others to come up. Seizing Ollem Nanon by the arm, Pelos hauled him none to gently through the doorway, where the two of them disappeared from Arano's view. Relieved of his own burden, Videre turned to help Arano with his.

Without warning, Arano's injured leg gave way and he lost his footing, barely catching himself with his free hand. Her weight offset by the sudden fall, Alyna slid limply off Arano's shoulder and began tumbling into the darkness. He thrust out a hand, catching her by the arm.

He hung there, dangling by fingers already losing their grip. He knew if he didn't let go of Alyna he'd fall to his death, but he also knew he'd never let her go.

His grip slipped another precious inch as Videre raced down the ladder to his rescue. Finally, with a gasp, Arano lost his handhold entirely, but immediately felt an iron grip latch onto his wrist. Videre was hanging upside-down by his knees, his powerfully built hands holding his teammates, preventing the fatal fall begun just an instant before.

From below, Arano heard Lain hastily climbing up to assist with the rescue. His burden suddenly became lighter as Lain took hold of Alyna. Arano climbed back onto the ladder, shaking his arms to regain some feeling as Videre righted himself on the rungs above.

Once Videre was ready, Arano tied himself to a rung by his belt. He took a few calming breaths, then he reached down for Alyna. He grasped her under the arms and pulled with all his remaining strength. He lifted her as high as he could, and Videre reached down to pull her to safety. Once Videre had the situation in hand, Arano released his ties from the rung and resumed his torturous climb. He reached the doorway and pulled himself through, allowing himself to drop to his hands and knees as he tried to catch his breath. He glanced to his left and saw that Videre was working on Alyna's injury.

"I've got her, Videre," Arano gasped as he pulled himself down the hallway. "I'm too tired to fight right now, so if we meet anyone else up here I want you ready to fire." Videre nodded and took up a defensive position while Arano worked to close the gash on Alyna's side. Lain climbed into the hallway, and finally the team was reassembled. Videre looked to Arano for guidance.

"Videre, Marnian, go on down this corridor and see if that door at the end is the one we're looking for. Lain and Kish will stay here to watch Ollem and provide security for Alyna until I can get this wound closed."

"We're on it," Videre said tersely, and started down the corridor.

Arano almost managed a smile as he thought to himself that when the chips were down, all traces of the joker in Videre vanished and he became all business. He knew with these teammates to help, there was nothing that could stop him. Using a small medical tool he put the final touches on Alyna's wound, and the bleeding tapered off. He removed a hypotube from the medikit, set the proper stimulant dosage and administered it. Alyna shuddered briefly, then her eyelids fluttered and opened. She winced in pain when she pressed her hand to her side.

"Lie still," he told her. "I've got the bleeding stopped, but I've got to seal the wound to keep it from getting infected. We may have to bail out of the lifepod when we get to the surface." He finished working on the wound before administering pain medication. He put all the medical instruments away, then he stroked her hair back from her face. They sat in silence, looking into each other's eyes, Arano smiling reassuringly at her drawn, pale face.

At a signal from Videre indicating the lifepod had been located, Arano looked questioningly at Alyna. "Help me up," she commanded. "If you help me, I can make it." Arano eased her to her feet, and as she leaned on him for support they started slowly down the corridor.

"She's gonna die," laughed Ollem. "She lost too much blood to handle the pressurization in the pod, let alone the pressure changes when you surface. Might as well drop her where she"

But he never finished. Lain swung his laser rifle in a wide arc, the butt of the weapon striking Nanon in the midsection, sending the air rushing from his lungs. Arano nodded his approval and continued his trek to the lifepod and freedom. Despite Alyna's injuries, they easily crossed the length of the open hallway and entered the circular room containing the airlock for the lifepod. Immediately, he knew something was wrong. Videre was swearing and stomping around, and Pelos' face held a scowl as he emerged from the airlock.

"The lifepod is full of water," Pelos announced. "We've just hit a dead end."

"Aren't there regulations about this sort of thing?" asked Alyna weakly. She turned to Ollem Nanon, who had been roughly dumped into a corner. "Don't you have inspectors come around?"

"Oops," he giggled. "I guess those bribes I was paying weren't for nothing. I'm glad to see it was money well-spent."

From down the hallway came the sounds of fresh pursuit. Ollem laughed openly, believing his rescue was at hand. Arano ordered everyone into the airlock, and sealed it behind them after his entire team had entered.

The condition of the equipment in the airlock could only be described as abysmal. Equipment panels stood open, wires hanging uselessly out the openings. The only piece of equipment that seemed to be in serviceable shape was the control panel that operated the air pressure and the floodgate. Arano had no doubt about what needed to be done.

"Here's what we'll do," he said grimly. "Obviously, we can't take the lifepod. We can't go back, either, since the pursuit's closing in on us. We're only a little over 30 meters down from the surface, so we're going to swim for it."

"You're insane!" screamed Ollem, coming to his feet until he saw the threatening look from Lain.

"We have a decent chance at this," Arano said. "Because of the hull strength and shielding of this facility, the air pressure inside is only at one standard atmosphere. Of course, in a lifepod without similar shielding, we would have to pressurize the pod, then surface slowly to avoid decompression sickness. Unfortunately, due to the condition of the lifepod, we're going to have to swim to the surface. That means we'll need to adjust the air we're breathing to match the pressure of the water at this depth, which is about three atmospheres." He motioned to Kish, who intently studied the controls before manipulating the switches.

Arano felt an uncomfortable pressure building in his ears, and had to clear them several times until the pressure leveled off. "There are three air bottles in here. Each holds about a five-minute supply of air at this depth. We're going to flood this chamber, and then we'll head for the surface. Stay together in a circle, and try to avoid becoming separated. The security lights outside the casino will allow us to see sufficiently until we surface. Pass the air bottles around the circle, and try to breathe normally. Whatever you do, don't attempt to hold your breath. As you surface, the air in your lungs will expand, and if you hold your breath your lungs might rupture. Surface slowly, stay calm, and keep exhaling slowly. We can do this. Everyone ready?"

Everyone nodded except Ollem, who violently shook his head and attempted to break away from Lain. Arano nodded to Kish, who touched a final control. From several pipes near the floor, water rushed into the chamber. Everyone gathered into a circle, and for once even Ollem cooperated. Arano gave Alyna's hand a reassuring squeeze while the water crept gradually up their bodies, finally covering them completely as the airlock's latches blew open. A rush of air bubbles erupted into the open sea and an entire wall dropped free to sink into the ocean's depths. The group swam out into the open sea and began the long, agonizingly slow trip to the surface.

Arano took a slow, deep breath from an air bottle and passed it to Lain who gratefully accepted it, placed the mouthpiece to his lips, and inhaled the life-giving air.

Arano felt himself drifting slowly toward the surface, keeping pace with his team. Despite the fact he continually exhaled, the air from his lungs expanded as he rose, giving the illusion of a never-ending supply of air.

Alyna passed him an air bottle which he used and passed on. The slow ascent continued, the six Avengers and their prisoner staying in a tight group as they rose from the depths. Arano maintained a watch on everyone in the group, alert for signs they might be experiencing problems. He knew they hadn't been exposed to the extreme pressures long enough to need decompression stops, but if they rose too quickly they'd be in trouble. To his left, Lain handed an air bottle to Ollem.

Without warning, air bottle in hand, Ollem Nanon kicked savagely away from the group and clawed madly toward the surface. He activated his life vest, which inflated and sent him rocketing upward. Videre started after him, but Arano deftly grabbed him by the arm and restrained him with a shake of his head. With the speed Ollem was rising, he wasn't going to get far.

They resumed their ascent, passing their meager air supply around the circle. Alyna held out an air bottle she'd just used and shook her head, indicating it had no air remaining. The silent climb continued with the end nowhere in sight and a rapidly dwindling air supply.

Finally, they broke through the surface, gasping for air and delighting in the sight of the open skies as they inflated their life vests. The ocean surged about them and wind-driven waves rolled ponderously past.

Arano activated the beacon to bring the Intrepid to their location. He couldn't see Nanon immediately, but knew he was close. The group continued to bob on the waves, awaiting their rescue by Lon, and a few minutes later he heard the roar of ion engines as the Intrepid dropped into view, circling once before lowering to a point just above the water. A ramp lowered into the sea, and the Avengers scrambled aboard, eager to get out of the water.

Arano, the last to board, was halfway up the ramp when he saw Nanon floating about 100 meters away.

He called to the bridge on the ship's Comm, advising them of Nanon's location, and the ship drifted slowly toward the unmoving figure in the water. Arano dove back into the sea and pulled Nanon to the ramp. As he pulled Ollem's inert form into the ship, he noticed the bloody white foam issuing steadily from his nose and mouth, and he knew Nanon was dead. Arano dragged him the rest of the way up the ramp, dropped him to one side, and checked on his team.

CHAPTER TEN

WITH A FAINTLY AUDIBLE BUMP, THE INTREPID docked with the USCS Savior, a medical ship. Despite her protestations, Arano insisted upon transporting Alyna on a stretcher for the trip through the docking port to the medical ship's main sick bay. With Videre carrying the leading end of the stretcher, Arano gave Alyna a reassuring smile as they crossed the narrow confines of the docking port and wound their way to the heart of the hospital frigate. Medical personnel, most of them Tompiste, passed without curiosity as the two Avengers walked on with their burden, finally arriving at the ship's triage room.

Immediately, two aides moved to the stretcher and transferred Alyna to a nearby empty bed. One gave a nod of acknowledgement to Arano, and they wheeled Alyna into the examination room. While Arano and Videre waited nervously in an outer chamber, a Kamling doctor put Alyna through an exhaustive series of tests. The two spent a nervous, impatient hour pacing the floor muttering to themselves, each offering up a silent prayer for their teammate. Arano felt his whole world crumble about him when he realized he could be losing someone dear to him all over again. The ghost of Erlinia Drontas haunted him relentlessly. At last, the big reptilian doctor came out to make her report.

"Her wounds weren't as serious as they appeared," she began with a smile. "The shrapnel passed completely through without hitting anything vital, and although she lost a lot of blood she has come out okay. My aide is finishing up with the Regenerator on that injury.

"The reason she lost consciousness was from the grenade's shock wave. She does have a concussion, which will require some rest. We're generating some blood for her which should bring her energy back up. I'd say she'll be fine in a few days."

"Will she be able to come with us now?" Arano asked hopefully.

"Negative. I want to keep her here for observation. Besides," she added with a wry grin, "I know how you Avengers are. She would be on bed rest until you got into the next system, and then she would be up and running."

Videre managed to look offended, fighting back the broad grin trying to cross his feline muzzle. "Oh, come on, doc! You do us an injustice!"

She laughed. "Well, that's it. You can come in and see her now, but only for a few minutes. I want her to get some sleep."

Together, the three of them entered the sick bay, crossed the open floor and stood at Alyna's bedside. They talked softly to her for a few minutes, and Arano concluded by telling her that while he didn't yet know what their next assignment was, he would be sure to pick her up the moment the medical team gave the okay. Arano squeezed her hand and turned to leave, then stopped. With a look of understanding, tears forming in his own eyes, Videre politely but firmly took the surprised doctor and her aide by the arms and led them from the sickbay.

When Arano emerged wordlessly from the room a few minutes later, he moved immediately to the door and back to his waiting ship, Videre almost having to run to keep up. Arano's head was spinning, and he still had a sinking feeling in his stomach that was part anxiety, part relief, and part wonder at how close he had come to losing one of the most important people in his life. He stopped just outside the docking port and sagged against the wall, face buried in his hands. Videre stopped with him and placed a supportive hand on Arano's shoulder. They stood silently for a few moments before Arano broke the silence.

"Videre, what in the name of the Four Elementals am I doing? She nearly died back there in that casino, and I would've lost her without ever telling her how I feel about her. But every time I get the notion, I start thinking about my duties to the Coalition, and how I can't let anything else take precedence. It's like I've walled away my emotions in some part of my mind and won't let them out."

"Do you think it will be different for you once this war is over?" Videre asked him quietly.

"I don't know," stammered Arano. "Maybe . . ."

Videre took a deep breath, pulled Arano around to face him, and looked him straight in the eyes. "I know how important devotion to duty is to you. It was drilled into you in your Daxia training, and had you not had that kind of devotion to duty I don't believe you could've been successful in your fight against Rising Sun back on Leguin 4. So as a fellow Avenger, I have to say you're doing the right thing. But as one of your closest friends, I need to warn you: Alyna's feelings for you are deep, but she won't wait around for you forever. You two have had a handful of dates, but I can't promise you how much longer 'a few dates' will be good enough. You might want to think about it . . . and think about getting rid of that 'wall'."

Arano nodded silently, and together they turned back to the docking port. His thoughts were in turmoil over his feelings for Alyna. They ran deep, that much was certain. But just how deeply, he couldn't be certain. He didn't want to believe he was in love with her. The Bromidians had murdered the love of his life, and he knew with cold certainty he could never love that way again.

He sighed in silent confusion as they crossed back over to the Intrepid, rejoining their team as their ship separated from the medical vessel. Arano strolled down the corridors , ending up in the Operations Center. He took a seat and updated everyone on Alyna's condition, then rubbed his eyes wearily as his team gave him the latest news.

"It's not good, Viper," said Lon. "According to some sketchy preliminary reports, the patrol at Selpan was ambushed by a weaker force. They were winning until that cruiser jumped in, and then all hell broke loose. Almost all ships smaller than a frigate lost their shields and had trouble getting missile lock. Even their guns malfunctioned. They had to retreat, and lost a few ships in the process. As we said before you went to the casino, it can't be a coincidence. This makes two consecutive encounters where all went well until a Bromidian capital ship appeared."

"Three consecutive encounters, if we accept the premise that this is what happened to Task Force Blue," added Lain.

"At any rate," continued Pana, "the Military High Command is having a brainstorming session to determine what to do about the problem. We have to assume it'll happen again. They're accepting ideas from anyone with an angle on the problem."

"I'll tell you what the problem is," interjected Arano hotly. "We've become too dependent upon technology. We just point the ship in the general direction we want and pull the trigger. The computer does the rest. That's why I insist on teaching dogfighting techniques. You can't use targeting computers or shields in a nebula, so we have to be prepared to fight without our computers anyway.

"In this particular case, we need to arm our fighters with dumbfire torpedoes. Obviously, they don't pack the punch of our newer torps, but you can carry ten times as many as the others, which aren't doing any good anyhow."

"Be careful what you suggest." Videre said dryly, resting his elbows on the table. "We may end up back in Firestorm fighters again."

"About thirty minutes ago, a supply ship dropped out of a wormhole in our vicinity," resumed Lon. "They should be docking with us shortly. Your ship is being equipped with a supply of the new experimental plasma torpedoes. You were chosen because you have the only accessible ship that has torpedo launchers new enough to handle the plasma torps. My team will be leaving on the supply ship, bound for who knows where. I imagine they're going to want you to test those torpedoes on something, so don't get too comfortable."

A beep sounded, and the member of Lon's team serving as navigator spoke over the ship's Comm. "Captain Pana, we're beginning docking procedures with the USCS Triton. We received instructions that both teams are to come aboard the freighter for a meeting via subspace with a military committee from the High Council. Some sort of emergency having to do with the President's whereabouts, it appears."

Fifteen minutes later, Cadron Stenat and both teams were assembled in a crowded cargo bay on the freighter, seated in a semi-circle around a hastily-assembled subspace viewscreen. Although most of the Avengers present were engaged in hushed conversation, Arano sat unmoving, staring first at the blank viewscreen and then at his surroundings, his mind a million miles away. He scarcely noticed the stacks of crates lining the walls, crates more than likely containing the new plasma torpedoes and equipment needed to prepare his ship to fire them.

Moments later, the screen hummed to life and an image of the High Council members appeared. Arano shrugged off his reverie and brought his mind back to the present; he was a soldier once more. Behind the Council, Laron Alstor nodded in acknowledgment, drawing a scarcely concealed grin from Arano.

Laron hated the politics of the bureaucracy as much as Arano, the main reason Laron turned down the promotion to major on two occasions. Now he had to spend his days in close proximity to the politicians and their underlings.

Laron stepped forward and called the meeting to order. "The following information is classified," he began. "Avenger operatives from Team 1 have managed to track the President's whereabouts to a Rising Sun prison camp on a large moon orbiting Synthar 5."

Arano's jaw dropped in surprise at the announcement. He wasn't surprised the Avengers had found the President, but the location itself was shocking. The Synthar system was relatively close to a black hole, and was believed to be uninhabitable. Not only was every planetary body potentially unstable due to the extreme gravitational forces involved with a black hole, but there was another problem. Because black holes consumed objects falling into the depths of their gravitational fields, radiation was emitted in the form of x-rays and gamma rays. The levels of x-ray and gamma ray radiation in the system made life impossible without heavy shielding, therefore it was never deemed worthy of colonization.

"This information was brought to the Military Committee . . . standard procedure." commented Laron, grimacing.

"Standard procedure?" interrupted Lon Pana. "Since when?"

"Since I made it that way," interjected Grand High Councilor Tient. "In the absence of the President, the Committee runs the military, and it was my position that in order to run this war smoothly, we need to be informed. You may continue, Major Alstor."

"At any rate," continued Laron with a sigh, "the Committee decided to use the Grand High Councilor's special unit, Midnight Sun, to effect the rescue of the President. This turned into an unmitigated disaster. The President is still missing, and the entire team of Midnight Sun operatives was either captured or killed."

Arano folded his arms and sat scowling in disapproval. When bureaucrats tried to run military operations, he thought, this was typically the outcome. He did take some small measure of satisfaction, however, in the look of anger that crossed Balor Tient's face when Laron went on to describe the failure of the covert mission. Laron paused as he sent the Midnight Sun team's operation order for the mission, as well as their equipment loadout, across the subspace channel to the waiting Avengers.

"Captain Lakeland," Laron Alstor said, addressing Arano formally, "the Committee has asked me to review this mission and issue recommendations. I insisted you be consulted; you're the best the Coalition has to offer when it comes to small unit tactics."

Arano nodded in acknowledgment of the compliment before he turned to the printout of the specifics on the ill-fated mission. Silence fell over the room for a full fifteen minutes while he read over the report. He felt grateful to have a more worldly problem to deal with, something to take his mind off his situation with Alyna. His battle-hardened military instincts took over, and he was the old Arano Lakeland again, the one who had led the Padian resistance movement and eventually drove away their Rising Sun occupiers. The only hint onlookers had to what he might be thinking was the occasional grunt or wide-eyed, unbelieving stare. He rubbed the stubble on his cheeks and turned back to the viewscreen.

"First," he began with a scornful gesture at the battle plans, "I'd like to know who drew up these plans. There appears to be very little use of intelligence information. It looks like a child playing war games sat down and came up with this over lunch. First of all, the suits your team used to protect them from the radiation were too heavy. This moon is very dense, with gravity half again as strong as the gravity on Immok 2. The team would've been exhausted merely from trying to move. They went in right before dawn, using standard night vision equipment. Not only would their night vision equipment have been inoperative due to the radiation, but they would've had to escape in broad daylight."

"I figured you would assume you could do better," said Balor, curling his lip in a sneer of contempt. "That's why I've already assigned your team to this mission. You'll assault the Rising Sun prison camp, rescue any Midnight Sun operatives still held there, and attempt to locate the President."

Arano leaned back stiffly in his chair and laced his fingers behind his head. "Begging the Grand High Councilor's pardon," he growled, "but my team is still short one soldier. Captain Marquat won't be able to go on a mission for two or three days. Standard procedure calls for no Avengers team to be deployed shorthanded."

"Well, since you're 'the best' we have with small unit tactics, I guess we'll have to see just how good you are. You forget, Captain, I'm in charge, and I make the rules."

Captain Pana snorted in disgust. "And what about my team?" he asked.

"Since your team's assault fighters are going to be out of commission for another week," said Balor with an impudent smile, "you'll be assigned fighter escort duties with Task Force Green. I believe that's all. Report to your duty stations." The screen went blank, and the Avengers teams sat in stunned silence.

After a brief discussion with Captain Pana, Arano led his team back to the Intrepid while Cadron left for Immok with Captain Pana. There was a delay of several hours while the new torpedoes were loaded onto the Intrepid, and in the meantime a group of engineers refitted the new ship's systems to prepare them for the experimental weaponry. After a successful series of tests, the Intrepid separated from the freighter, and Arano's team gathered for a quick meeting on the bridge.

"I don't like this at all," began Arano. "With the politicians in charge, we're in serious trouble. Can't people learn their lessons from history? This is what got the Humans in trouble in the Human-Bromidian War, and we're doing it all over again." He breathed a heavy sigh.

"Okay, Kish," he continued, "you're the ranking member of your team right now, so you're in charge of Squad B. But what I need from you right now is a bit of tinkering." Kish's leathery Tompiste face seemed to light up at the thought. "Can you manage to rebuild our night vision equipment so it will function in the X-ray radiation on Synthar 5?"

Kish thought briefly about the possibilities. "I think it's possible," she said tentatively. "I could definitely increase the shielding on the goggles . . . and I do have an idea I'd like to try. Because of the black hole, ambient light is low in the Synthar system when not in the direct rays of the Synthar star. I'd like to alter the goggles and have them operate off x-rays and gamma rays. It's a different frequency of photons, I know, but I can still adjust the goggles to read those frequencies. Every structure is heavily shielded to reflect x-rays, and anyone outside will be wearing a shielded suit, which also reflects cosmic radiation. Everything outside ought to light up like a beacon if viewed under those wavelengths. I believe the image would actually be better if based on the X-ray and gamma ray wavelengths, as opposed to infrared or the visible spectrum."

Arano nodded in understanding. "Okay," he said, "that'll be your first priority. I'm going to be going over the reconnaissance photos sent back by Midnight Sun before they were caught or killed, and I'll need the rest of you to start reloading the torpedo bays. I want those plasma torpedoes ready to go before we enter the Synthar system."

"Message on subspace from Major Alstor," announced Lain.

"Put it through," ordered Arano. The screen hummed to life, and Laron appeared on the screen.

"Major," acknowledged Arano.

"I'm alone, Viper," replied Laron, seating himself at his desk. "I wanted to fill you in on recent developments. First of all, Tient has announced a new initiative to show we're still friends with the Bromidians, even though we're at war with Rising Sun. He has appointed several Bromidians to sensitive posts within the Coalition government to demonstrate his trust in them." Laron leaned closer to his viewscreen. "Viper, he put a Bromidian into the position of Prelar of Defense."

Arano leaped to his feet in anger. "This is unbelievable! With the likelihood that the Bromidian High Command is behind Rising Sun? Why would he do that?"

"Money, why else," replied Kish. "I'd bet you anything if you dig into his finances, you'll find some unexplained deposits he has received recently. Money is the only thing that motivates the Grand High Councilor."

"That and revenge," warned Laron. "Kish, he's aware you've been digging into his finances. That might explain why he's sending your team in shorthanded on this mission. He wouldn't mind at all if something were to happen to you out there. And Arano, of course you're aware you aren't one of his favorite people either. Watch your back."

"We'd better hurry this mission up, then," mused Videre. "With a Bromidian in charge of the Defense Department, it's only a matter of time before Synthar 5 knows we're coming."

"True," stated Laron. "I have a couple of other

items, but I'll try to be brief. The patrol that was ambushed in the Selpan system managed to escape with most of its ships. The admiral in charge of the fleet recognized what was happening and ordered the retreat quickly. They regrouped and managed to hold off the Rising Sun fleet until their Rift Drives had cooled sufficiently to jump out of the system.

"On a lighter note, we managed to ambush a Rising Sun supply fleet in the Trum system. We destroyed 95% of the fleet, and captured the rest. The downside to the victory is since the task force involved was not in their assigned area of the system, their commanding officer is being reprimanded by the Grand High Councilor. At any rate, our intelligence agents are going over those ships carefully for anything they feel might provide a clue to how Rising Sun keeps managing to shut down our shields.

"The Disciples of Zhulac have struck again"

"What?' Arano interrupted in disbelief. "Laron, it's been barely a week since their last murder. Has this one been verified?"

"Yes, it has, Viper," answered Laron. "This was definitely a Disciples case. They've never struck this quickly before, so I . . . Viper, what is it?"

Videre responded before Arano could answer. "The Disciples have just messed up. There's no way they could've been as thorough in their planning of this murder, which means whatever their motive is, it has become more pressing. If the police don't find a break in the case soon, the Disciples will end up providing it for them. I'll bet you a month's pay that within a week a victim is going to escape a Disciples assault."

"Let's hope so," continued Laron. "The only other item of interest is Event Horizon apparently becoming tired of being out of the limelight. Yesterday, they bombed two bridges, a holo theater, and an outdoor concert. The combined death toll is over 400 people. Curiously, despite the ever-increasing numbers of Bromidians here in Immok City, not one Bromidian was killed in the bombings."

"I'm sure the Bromidian High Command will take some measure of comfort in knowing their spies are safe from terrorist activities," commented Videre.

"Obviously," mused Kish, "Event Horizon is taking advantage of our war with Rising Sun. They know with our stripped-down military forces we're going to have a tough time fighting against Rising Sun and carrying out anti-terrorist activities at the same time, especially with the Bromidian High Command snatching up border systems."

"I agree," said Laron. "We can't pull any more of our forces from the outer systems right now. We barely have enough ships to set up picket lines with our Thief Class Cruisers as it is. If we redeploy any more fleets to another front, Bromidian ships will be able to make jumps through the holes we leave. Without the President to provide the leadership we need, instead of declaring war we just chase Bromidian assaults from system to system. They could string us out from one end of the galaxy to the other."

"Well," said Arano grimly, "that problem may be one we can do something about. We'll see you in a few days."

The computer sounded its warning beep, announcing to the five Avengers onboard the Intrepid the ship was about to leave its artificial wormhole and enter the Synthar system. They all moved automatically to their positions, the hours spent training on their ship's configuration paying off. Arano glanced calmly about the bridge, noticing Lain was pulling double duty in Alyna's absence, covering the Comm and the damage control computer. Videre monitored the ship's systems to ensure the engines, shields, life support, and other vital systems functioned as needed, and ready to reroute power from one system to another if necessary. Kish sat at the controls for the lower plasma cannons, while Pelos was prepared to use the experimental plasma torpedoes. Arano settled in comfortably at the tactical controls to pilot the ship through whatever awaited them, eager to test the new systems his ship carried.

Their plan had the advantage of simplicity. They assumed the Bromidians on Synthar knew the Avengers were coming and preparations had been made for their typically surreptitious assault. The team's answer to the problem was to do the exact opposite: they planned a direct assault on the compound. They would come out of the wormhole fairly close to the planet, orbit Synthar 5 at high speed, and land on the planet's moon near the prison camp. Using overwhelming firepower, they would destroy anything or anyone in their way and raid the prison, looking for the President and any living members of the Midnight

Sun assault team.

Arano announced they were emerging from their Rift Drive jump, touched a few controls, and watched as the swirling colors of the wormhole were replaced by the starscape of the Synthar system. "Shields up, charge all weapons," ordered Arano tersely. "Report."

"Beam weapons online and standing by," replied Kish.

"Plasma Torpedoes ready," said Pelos.

"Damage Control and Comm are both up and running," stated Lain coolly.

"All systems are online," reported Videre. "Shields are operating at 100%, ion engines are online. Scanners are finishing their initial sweep. I'm picking up six fighters, turning and coming our way at 116 mark 52."

"Kish, pick up those fighters with the plasma cannons," commanded Arano. "Pelos, I want to evaluate the plasma torps. Just use them on one of the fighters for now." Arano accelerated to attack speed and veered toward the incoming fighters. From off to his right, he heard Pelos gasp in surprise.

"Viper, I've already got torpedo lock. Our old torpedoes could barely get a lock at half this distance! Firing a torpedo . . ."

Arano watched the front viewscreen as the fluorescent blue torpedo streaked away from the Intrepid on its way to the lead incoming fighter. He glanced down at his tactical screen, amazed with the speed at which the torpedo approached the target. He looked back at his viewscreen in time to see a fighter explode in a silent flash of light, fading into blackness. At a word from Arano, Pelos picked out another fighter, fired a second torpedo, and it quickly went the way of the first. After a third torpedo found its mark, the fighters broke formation, swarming at the Intrepid from different directions.

"I'm switching to the lower plasma cannons," announced Pelos. Kish was already blasting away with the upper plasma cannons, the heavy barrage from the twin mounted beam weapons making short work of a fighter trying to approach from the top of the Intrepid. As Pelos tracked one of the two remaining fighters, Arano veered toward Synthar 5, ready to make a run for the barren planet's moon. Seconds later, the two remaining fighters had been destroyed and the Intrepid was momentarily alone.

"Status," said Arano.

"Shields at 100%. No damage to any of our systems. We hit them so quickly they didn't get many shots off. I . . . wait a minute. Scanners are showing two heavy frigates with a fighter escort heading our way from the far side of the planet. Looks like they knew we were coming. I count eight fighters."

"Stand by," commanded Arano tersely. "Videre, keep a close eye on those shields. I'm picking up traces of nebulatic emissions. Calculate the jump back to the Earth system. If our shields go down, we're going to need to get out of here in a hurry. Marnian, target those heavy frigates with the plasma torps. I'm readying the Disruptor Beam."

"Target acquired," reported Pelos. "Firing now." He fired three torpedoes at the first frigate, then instructed the targeting computer to get a lock on the other ship. While he waited, he pulled the necklace with his Tollep's tooth from under his shirt, leaving it dangling where he could see it. The computer indicated a lock; he fired three more torpedoes and awaited Arano's signal to fire again.

At his station, Arano tracked the new ultra-fast torpedoes to their target and watched the viewscreen in awe as they found their mark on the aft section of the first frigate's hull, near the engines. A brilliant explosion lit the skies above Synthar 5, and the frigate drifted ponderously out of control. The second set of torpedoes found their mark as surely as the first, with only slightly less devastating results.

"I don't believe this!" shouted Arano. "Shields on both frigates are down, and one of them has lost power to weapons and engines. I can't believe three torpedoes did this . . ." He looked back at his display and noticed the fighters were closing to within firing range. He turned to the pilot's controls, accelerating to top speed. "Pelos, get to your plasma cannons. You and Kish have to keep those fighters off us. I'm going after those frigates with the Disruptor Beam. If we can finish them off, we won't have to worry about them on the way out." He looked at another control screen, frowning. "This isn't adding up. We're still picking up nebulatic emissions, but all of our systems are functioning normally."

The team swiftly moved into action. As the Intrepid streaked toward the two nearly helpless frigates, Pelos and Kish fired rapidly at the attacking fighters. The Bromidians were firing as well, and the impact from their weapons rocked the Intrepid. One particularly violent explosion hammered the ship, tossing the embattled Avengers from their stations. Arano regained his seat and checked his scanner.

"There are still five fighters left, and one of them is staying out of range of our beam weapons, firing torpedoes. Pelos, get back to the torpedo station and take him out." Pelos complied, tracking the distant fighter with the torpedo targeting computer. "Videre," called Arano, "how are we looking?"

"This is incredible," said Videre in awe. "Shields are still at 95%"

"That can't be," argued Arano. "Are you sure?"

"I'm positive. I ran a diagnostic on the damage control subsystems, just to be certain. We have superficial hull damage, and all systems are operating normally."

"The distant fighter has been destroyed," announced Pelos. "Returning to the beam weapons station."

The frigate with still-functional engines retreated, falling back to a position on the far side of Synthar 5 where the Bromidians had a small orbital space station. The other ship still drifted helplessly, her crew probably fighting to restore power to the damaged systems. When the Intrepid closed to within firing range, Arano fired the Disruptor Beam, the jagged streak slamming into the frigate. After a second and then a third blast, a corona of energy flashed across the now-doomed ship. It slipped closer to Synthar 5, falling into the planet's gravity well, beginning the long descent into the atmosphere where Arano knew it would eventually perish in a blinding flash of light as it burned up in the thick acidic atmosphere. He looked back at his battle scanner and saw the three remaining fighters retreating, following the frigate to the safety of the armored outpost orbiting the planet.

Arano turned his ship toward the moon of Synthar 5, received the coordinates to the prison from Videre, and chose a course and a landing site. Still traveling at extremely high speeds, Arano guided the Intrepid ever lower, coming within fifty meters of the surface. By following the natural contours of the land, he was able to keep the ship low enough to avoid detection by the scanners mounted at the prison camp. At the speed they traveled, it took only a few minutes to reach their destination.

The Intrepid streaked over the enemy prison, drawing panic fire from defensive installations scattered throughout the area. The heavily shielded buildings were small, the harsh radiation from the black hole making it more feasible to do most of the construction underground where the lead in the soil provided a level of natural shielding. The exceptions to the rule were the weapons towers, built higher to allow the weapons mounted on their tops a greater freedom to traverse the area without the risk of shooting their own buildings.

Arano pitched the ship on her side, allowing both the upper and lower plasma cannons to fire on their targets. Mayhem reigned in the prison camp as violent explosions rocked the guard towers and weapons sites. The ship circled overhead once, then dropped quickly to the ground. Clad in bulky, shielded suits to protect them from the radiation emitted by the black hole, Arano, Videre, and Lain emerged from the ship firing their laser rifles. Kish sealed the ship behind them, raised the shields, and manned her firing station again as Pelos took over at the flight controls. The Intrepid lifted off and circled, Kish providing suppressive fire for her teammates below.

Arano peered at the stark landscape. There was a strange glow about the buildings, and Arano figured it was due to the modifications Kish had made to the night vision goggles. He led his team toward the center of the camp where the prisoners were kept. Or at least, he thought glumly, where they used to be kept, although where they were now was anyone's guess. As they neared the building, Arano felt his movements becoming more strained, his muscles exhausting their strength rapidly in the heavy gravity. He found himself hoping the reports they'd received were correct, and that inside the buildings there were artificial gravity units in place to keep the pull at a more manageable level.

Moments later, they reached the door of the main prison building. One blast from Arano's laser rifle and the door was open. Arano found the feeling of moving from the heavy gravity outside to the weaker gravity inside disconcerting, and nearly fell over when he stepped into the hallway. After his team had sealed the door behind them, the three soldiers peeled back their bulky hoods and started toward the cells where they hoped to find the prisoners. As they eased down the hallway, Arano kept a sharp eye out for the guard station that was supposedly located nearby. Their plans to find the prisoners depended heavily upon the information they found in the computer.

They came to a hallway junction moments later, and Arano spotted the guard station. Only one guard was at the post, his back to the Avengers. Off to the guard's right, Arano saw the computer terminal. He pulled his team back around the corner, drew his knife and motioned toward the guard, indicating to his teammates to wait where they were. As he started back around the corner, the guard's radio squawked. Using the guttural Bromidian language, the guard spoke into the radio briefly, then moved off swiftly down the hall, away from the Avengers.

With a jerk of his head, Arano motioned for his friends to join him. He sprinted to the guard station and took a knee, facing forward. He knew without looking Videre was watching for trouble in the direction they'd come from, and Lain was manipulating the computer, trying to pinpoint the locations of the prisoners.

"Viper," whispered Lain. "I've got it. Go right at the next intersection, third door on the left. There'll be a small squad of guards in the room, and the cells are in the hallway beyond."

"Good job, Lain," Arano told the big Kamling. He rose to his feet and moved off down the hallway. Cautiously, they turned the corner and, following Lain's directions, located their destination.

The soldiers gathered around the door, readied their weapons and nodded to each other. With fluidity acquired through endless hours of training, they stormed the room taking the surprised guards unprepared. Each Avenger knew which sector of the room to cover, and all three immediately fired in earnest. Before the Bromidians brought their weapons to bear, they'd all been put down.

"Clear!" called Arano.

"Clear!" echoed Lain.

"Clear!" confirmed Videre.

They entered the small, sparsely furnished room, ignoring the bodies sprawled grotesquely around the room. Videre stood watch and Lain checked the list of prisoners while Arano searched the guards for the security card to open the prison cells. Arano located the plastic card he needed, and he turned to help Lain, already shaking his head in disgust.

"Sorry, Viper," Lain told him. "I've gone through this list, and the President is definitely not here. In fact, I'm only finding one operative from Midnight Sun. His cell number is 00142. Tsimian male named Polus Vees."

Arano raced off into the dark, narrow sub-hallway at the back of the room. His booted feet echoed hollowly in the metal-lined corridor. He located the room where the missing agent was held and paused to look around, making sure he was alone. He pressed his stolen security card to a control pad and deactivated the lock, which opened with an audible click. He pushed the door open and peered inside.

The cell was structured as an open squad bay, with bunks lining the walls in military precision. There were several occupants in the room, all of them sleeping. He located the only Tsimian prisoner in the cell on a bunk in the far corner.

Arano crossed the room in absolute silence and prodded the bestial form with his rifle butt, his left hand holding the beaked mouth shut to prevent an outcry. When he saw the eyes open in stunned alertness, he pressed a solitary finger to his lips for silence. He silently mouthed the word, "Avengers" and motioned the big Tsimian toward the door. Polus Vees complied, coming to his feet and exiting the cell without a sound.

"Captain Lakeland, with the Avengers," Arano told him once the cell door had been secured. They re-entered the main cellblock control room where Lain continued to study the control station. "This is Lieutenant Baxter, and the Gatoan watching the door for us is Lieutenant Genoa. Where's the rest of your team?"

"Dead," Polus replied coldly. "They systematically executed my entire team, one soldier at a time. They started from the lowest ranking member and worked their way up, hoping to loosen our tongues a bit. No one talked, and the executions proceeded at a quicker pace. I'm all that's left. They told us the President was moved before we left Immok. Someone notified them about our operation, and they were waiting for us."

"Viper," said Lain, looking up from the computer, "I'm finished here. I've got all the data we're going to get, and I've activated our emergency escape plan, just in case. Vees, you'll want to put this on. It will protect you from the X-rays once we get outside." He handed Vees one of the extra suits the team had brought with them.

"Videre, you've got the point'" Arano said. "Lain, you're in the middle with Vees, and I will be the rearguard." He pulled the Comm from his belt and activated the unsecured subspace link to the Intrepid, still circling the area overhead. He preferred to use the secure channel, but the FM frequency wouldn't be able to penetrate the building's shielding. "Kish, do you copy?"

"Kish here, Viper," came the reply. "Go ahead."

"We're on our way out with one guest. What's your status?"

There was a pause, and Arano assumed the always-thorough Tompiste was checking the readouts in front of her. "Shields are at 72%, and the hull is showing minimal damage. We're meeting resistance from mobile ground defense stations and occasional fighters. Still picking up signs of nebulatic emissions, but all systems continue to function normally."

"Right," acknowledged Arano. "See you in a few."

He returned his Comm to its place on his utility belt, and motioned to Videre. The Gatoan peered into the hallway, his powerful but sleek form ghosting from cover and entering the hallway. Lain followed, with Vees a step behind. Arano was the last to leave, and he made sure the door to the room stayed slightly ajar.

They retraced their steps without meeting any resistance, the silence feeling ominous and oppressive. Arano could feel the tension in his body, and took a few deep breaths to try to relax. Thinking he heard a noise behind them, he signaled a halt. The sound wasn't repeated, and they resumed their trek.

When they came to a junction near their entry point, Arano saw Videre stop and go into a crouch, scanning the area in front of him. By the way Videre looked down each connecting corridor, Arano knew Videre hadn't actually seen anything, but there was definitely something making him uneasy. Videre motioned for Arano to come forward, and as Arano moved up, Lain turned and took over rear security. In a whispered conference, Videre explained he was certain he'd heard a quiet voice come from one of the corridors connected to the junction, but he couldn't tell from which. Arano nodded and started forward.

Immediately, his danger sense kicked in and he dove for cover. Just in time, he landed behind the sheltering wall of their hallway as laser fire erupted from corridors to their right and left. Immediately afterward, laser fire opened up from behind them, pinning them down. Without a word, they all jumped behind the meager cover provided by the wall's supporting beams and tried to return fire.

"Videre, use your grenades!" commanded Arano over the din of the fight. "Lain, activate the protocol you installed in their security computer!"

As Videre bounced the powerful grenades in both directions, hoping to get a lucky shot, and Arano continued firing with his pistol, Lain pulled out his datapad and pressed a single control. From deep within the complex, a warning klaxon sounded as the doors to all the prison cells were suddenly flung wide open. Within moments, a throaty yell erupted from the inmates who found themselves with a chance at freedom. The laser fire coming from the Avengers' rear abated when some of their assailants were forced to turn and face the new threat.

But even that proved insufficient to allow the Avengers to fight their way free of the trap slowly collapsing upon them. It was only a matter of time before they would be captured or killed. Arano sorted through several ideas while he tried to come up with a means of escape. Then it hit him. If they couldn't get to the ship, maybe the ship could come to them.

He pulled his Comm out once more. "Kish, this is Viper. We're pinned down, and we can't get out. We need you to make a new door for us. We're along the south wall of the building. My best guess is we're 40 meters east of the entry door."

"Got it," replied Kish. "On our way."

"Helmets on," ordered Arano, and the four hurriedly pulled the soft helmets over their heads to protect them from the radiation they hoped would soon be filling the corridor once the Intrepid opened it to the skies.

Moments later, a tremendous blast and a shower of sparks rocked the hallway as Pelos fired at the building with the Intrepid's lower plasma cannon. A gaping hole opened in the hall, not ten meters from their position. Screams of horror came from the hidden Bromidians at both ends of the corridor, and the crossfire immediately ceased. Arano peered out, saw the new opening, and darted from cover. When he reached the hole, he stepped outside and took up a covering position, the weapon in his hands suddenly weighing down heavily in his arms as the intense gravity took its relentless hold on him once more.

At a sharp command from Arano, Lain sprinted from cover and took up a firing position next to the lowered ramp of the Intrepid. Pelos had returned to the upper plasma cannons and fired madly at the buildings and watch towers around them, trying to confuse any organized pursuit. Vees exited the building next, followed by Videre. Both boarded the Intrepid, and Videre seated himself at his station monitoring the ship's systems. Arano and Lain charged up the ramp, and the ship lifted off before the ramp had even finished retracting. Arano replaced Kish at the flight controls, and Vees was motioned over to the lower plasma cannons. Now that there were six crew members, the ship would be more effective, thought Arano, as Pelos settled in at the controls for the plasma torpedoes.

The ship roared skyward, and the computer chirped a warning beep. Videre turned to his control panel, his dark look showing he clearly didn't like what he saw. Two heavy cruisers, stationed above the moon's atmosphere, were trying to cut off their retreat.

"Heavy cruisers at 351 mark 88," said Videre tersely. "They've already charged their weapons and are targeting us. We're almost within their range. Atmosphere is still too thick for torpedoes, and our beam weapons won't have the range theirs do." He frowned. "They're jamming our scanners; I'm having trouble getting a read on the ships."

Arano's eyebrows furrowed in thought. "It looks like we're going to have to try to outrun them. Keep trying to break through the scanning interference. They might have something else waiting on us out there."

The Intrepid raced ahead at top speed, gradually leaving the planet behind. The two heavy cruisers on an intercept course had the advantage due to their angle of approach, and continued to close the gap. Videre announced they were within range of the superior cannons mounted on the heavy cruisers, and as if on cue a plasma blast rocked the ship, then another. Soon, the

Intrepid was under a constant barrage of plasma beam fire, the ship was tossed about and showers of sparks rained down on the Avengers. The heavy cruisers had moved within range of the Intrepid's plasma cannons, and Kish and Polus Vees both returned fire from their gunning stations.

"Shields are down to 58%," warned Videre. "Rear shield generator is starting to overheat. Also, I'm picking up sensor readings, and I think I'm detecting a neutrino field in the system. They may have a Thief Class cruiser in the area"

"How long until we clear the atmosphere and can use our torpedoes?"

"Ninety seconds."

Arano thought quickly. "Is it possible one of those heavy cruisers is generating the neutrino field?"

"No way," commented Kish immediately. "The equipment that generates a neutrino field is so bulky there's barely enough room for shields, engines, and life support on a Thief class cruiser. Those heavy cruisers out there have extensive weapons systems. I'd guess the Thief Class cruiser is hiding in the shadow of the energy signature of one of the heavy cruisers, and we're just not picking them up because of their jamming signal."

"Shields at 47%," noted Videre. "Rear shield generator is critical."

Arano chewed on his lip briefly, gripping the arms of his chair tightly as a particularly powerful blast rocked the ship. "Set course 180 mark 25," he ordered. "Full power to front shields. Stand by, torpedoes. Videre, set the rear shield generator to standby to let it cool down, but be prepared to switch full power to rear shields on my mark. I'm setting flight controls to manual. Hang on; this is going to get rough."

The Intrepid swung gracefully about and charged its attackers nearly head-on, the ship weaving about on a zigzag course that made it harder for the heavy cruisers' guns to find their mark. Though still some distance away, the maneuver obviously took the Bromidians by surprise, and the two heavy cruisers drifted away from their flanking positions, exposing another ship behind them. Arano confirmed they were within range of his Disruptor Beam and opened fire, a task made even more difficult because he was piloting the ship in its manual mode. An occasional shot from the Disruptor found its mark, sending small halos of energy across parts of their target.

"We're clear of the atmosphere," announced Pelos. "I've got torpedo lock on one of the heavy cruisers."

"Give me three torpedoes at each heavy cruiser," commanded Arano crisply, "then fire at the Thief Class cruiser until you destroy it." He turned to his display, watching as the torpedoes streaked across the vacuum of space to strike with startling impact. Three brilliant explosions lit up the first heavy cruiser, even as three more torpedoes raced toward its sister ship.

But if Arano had hopes the heavy cruisers would be dispatched as easily as the two heavy frigates, those hopes were swiftly dashed. These ships were much larger and, just as their weapons drained the Intrepid's shields more quickly, the larger ships were also able to sustain much more damage. The torpedoes had obviously hurt them, but they were still very much in the fight.

Moments later, Pelos fired on the Thief Class cruiser. Arano fired furiously with the Disruptor beam, no longer trying to hit specific areas of the ships, but trying to keep them off balance, hoping an overload from the Disruptor would succeed where surgical strikes had failed.

"Videre," said Arano, pointing at his teammate, "standby to switch power to rear shields . . . three, two, one . . . Now!" As the Intrepid raced past its attackers, Videre switched power to the rear shields. Vees, his plasma cannon on the side facing the Thief Class cruiser, concentrated his fire on that target, even as another volley of plasma torpedoes struck the now-listing ship.

"Shields took a beating there," announced Videre. "We're at 10%."

"Damn!" swore Arano. "Concentrate all fire on the Thief Class cruiser!"

They opened the distance between themselves and their pursuers, and Arano watched the Bromidian ships swing heavily about to continue the chase. A sudden thought occurred to Arano: according to intelligence reports, Rising Sun had no Thief Class cruisers in their arsenal. He zoomed the visual display in on the ship in question, instantly recognizing the standard Bromidian military markings on her hull.

"Videre, can you raise anyone on subspace? We have to get a message out ASAP! The Thief Class cruiser belongs to the regular Bromidian military. It's the BHCS Nasontic!"

"Negative. Their jamming field is preventing subspace messages from getting through. I've calculated the jump back to the Earth System, waiting for the neutrino field to drop. Shields are at 5%, all systems still operational."

"Only six torpedoes left," Pelos told them. "Firing the last of them."

"Neutrino field still holding," said Arano. "We've got more company coming in. I can't tell how many or where they came from, but there's a large group of fighters inbound, closing fast. Stay sharp."

An intense blast rocked the Intrepid, and the lights dimmed momentarily. The ship righted herself, but warning lights blinked on all systems.

"Shields are gone!" yelled Videre. "Hull integrity dropping!"

But just when it seemed their ship couldn't take any more hits, the last torpedoes struck the Thief Class cruiser. As Arano watched on his viewscreen, several large internal explosions rocked the bulky cruiser and it finally succumbed to the murderous assault of the plasma torpedoes.

"Neutrino field is down," shouted Arano. "We're out of here!" The Rift Drive engines on the Intrepid came to life, and the Avengers disappeared into the wormhole.

CHAPTER ELEVEN

ARANO WALKED DOWN THE RAMP OF HIS SHIP AND boarded the waiting transport for the short ride from Immok City's spaceport to the Coalition Military Headquarters building. He took a long, last look at his ship as the transport rolled away. The Intrepid had proved to be a remarkably durable ship; the repairs had been all but completed during the return trip from the Synthar system.

Their mission to Synthar had been marginally successful based upon its original objectives. They had, after all, brought back the only surviving member of Midnight Sun's team and acquired information that might provide insight into the President's whereabouts. But it was the unplanned outcomes that had produced a windfall of information for the United Systems Coalition.

The first and most obvious bonus had been the spotting of the BHCS Nasontic, a Thief Class Cruiser in the regular Bromidian High Command fleet. Now there could be no denying the collusion between the Bromidian High Command and the attacks by Rising Sun, forcing the USC political leaders to admit the truth of what the military had been telling them for over a year. Arano smiled in spite of himself when he thought of the look on the Grand High Counselor's face when he heard the news.

The other benefit of their mission to the Synthar system had been the overwhelming firepower and destructive capabilities displayed by the new prototype plasma torpedoes. Once the entire fleet was equipped with such weapons, there would be no Bromidian force the USC couldn't handle. Providing, of course, the USC engineers could figure out why the Intrepid didn't experience the systems problems exhibited by other USC ships in recent days while in combat with Bromidian forces.

Polus Vees had been carted off to a debriefing, so Arano led his shorthanded Avengers team back to their planning room. He felt as if he'd been away for months, although in reality it had barely been a week. His team trooped along the familiar halls, Arano nodding in greeting to a few familiar faces along the way. He thought suddenly of Alyna, and wondered once again what had become of her in his absence.

The door to his planning room opened, and he was greeted by an exuberant hug from his missing teammate. Alyna laughed at his surprise, taking him by the hand and pulling him away from the door allowing the rest of the team to enter.

"You . . . I . . ." Arano began, unable to form a coherent thought.

"I'm fine," Alyna laughed, "or at least mostly. I convinced the doctors to put me back on active status this morning. So, tell me, how did things go at Synthar?"

Arano, having recovered his wits, sketched in the details of their last mission. He told of the powerful plasma torpedoes, the Intrepid's performance in combat, the rescue of one Midnight Sun operative, the intelligence they gathered from the prison computers, and the sighting of the Bromidian warship with a Rising Sun task force. While he spoke, Kish moved to her computer station and began sorting through the data she had collected, hoping to find information to help locate the missing President.

"You didn't look at that data while you were in the wormhole?" Alyna asked. "You had the time during your jump to the Earth system, and another 15 hours back here after your cooldown period. What were you doing for thirty hours?"

Kish shook her head. "We knew that upon our return, Avengers Command would download everything in the Intrepid's computers in preparation for our mission debriefing. Somewhere in our chain of command is a security leak, so we didn't want the spy to know what we'd found about the President. I can keep what we learn here away from prying eyes."

"I see," nodded Alyna, a smile spreading across her lips, despite her efforts to conceal it.

Arano sighed. "All right, what did you do?"

"Do? Me? Nothing. I've been recovering from my battle wounds. Oh, I almost forgot. First, I got you resurrected in the Coalition computers, so there's one less thing for you to worry about. Also, that pesky little problem with the Disciples video? Don't worry, I fixed that while you were gone, too." She paused, basking in the stunned silence of her teammates. "It was more luck than anything else. I had dinner at my sister's house last night. After we ate, her twelve-year-old son took me to his hobby room to show off his latest project. It seems my sister took some home videos on their last vacation, but most of the shots were out of focus. The little genius put together a machine from scratch and used it to clear up the tapes.

"I know this isn't standard protocol, but I took a copy of the Disciples video to him, just to see what he could do. Surprisingly, it only took him about 15 minutes to give me a perfect picture of both Tsimians from the video. There are copies on the table over there. I put their photos in the computer this morning, and I'm just waiting on the results. In fact," she said, stepping up to her computer, "it's already done."

She looked the sheet over while her amazed teammates gathered around for a look at the pictures. "The first Tsimian is Renz Hanne. He has a medical degree from Immok University, but never passed the medical certification tests. He has a long record of alleged criminal offenses, but only one arrest and no convictions. He's also listed as an active member of Event Horizon.

"The other is a Tsimian named Pronus." She frowned. "Nothing else, just Pronus. Very little is known about him, other than the fact he's also a member of Event Horizon. He appears to be fairly large in stature, even for a Tsimian."

"I believe I can fill in a few gaps," Pelos cut in. "There's a secret society among Tsimians known as the Kian. They are similar in nature to the Daxia, although their training isn't as intense. Mostly, they concentrate on hand-to-hand fighting. They discard their given names and take on the name of one of the ancient Tsimian demons. Pronus is one of those names. If Event Horizon is responsible for the Disciple killings, it'd probably explain why he was recruited for the murders. Being an excellent melee fighter, he would be useful in subduing their victims."

"That explains his presence," mused Lain, "but why Renz Hanne? Sure, a doctor would be useful if this were a medical procedure, but just about any psychotic nut out there can rip someone's eyes out. Why would you need a doctor?"

"Good question," said Videre, thoughtfully tapping his fingers on the table.

"Is there any information on their current locations?" asked Arano.

"None," Alyna replied, shaking her head. "According to this, they aren't even supposed to be in this system."

Just then, the door to their planning room flew open, and a breathless Cadron Stenat burst into the room. "Come quickly," he gasped. "The police are guarding a Padian down at the main hospital. It seems he just escaped an attack by the Disciples of Zhulac!"

Arano and his team crowded into the room where a team of doctors tended to a young Padian's wounds. The doctors seemed more than a little upset by the group hovering behind them, but there appeared to be little they could do. The murmur of the attending physicians was partially covered by the endless humming and beeping of the various medical computers and scanners lining the walls of the examination area. Several police detectives stood by, ready to ask endless questions of the young man who was the first to survive an attack by the dreaded Disciples of Zhulac. A chart on the treatment table announced him as Nodel Pelen.

Arano gave a start when he saw the name, and pushed his way closer for a better look. He knew Alyna had probably realized something was amiss; she was following him up to the front. When the doctors finished their work and left the room, Arano stood right in front of Nodel Pelen.

The detectives questioned him immediately, seeking information that might lead them to the elusive cult. Nodel described how the assault progressed, pausing now and then to answer clarifying questions asked by the detectives. He had left his fitness club and was walking home, taking his usual route through a nearby park. He was deep in the woods when he realized something was wrong. After his danger sense warned him of trouble, he began to run, already exhausted from his workout and tiring quickly.

Two Tsimians came at him, one armed with what appeared to be a stun stick, and they'd tried to subdue him. He'd fought back, injuring one with a blow to the knee, and then outran his pursuers for over a mile before finding help.

One of the detectives stepped forward, interrupting his narration. "Do you think you'd be able to recognize them?"

Nodel turned to look at the detective when he

asked the question, and momentarily made eye contact with Arano. A flicker of recognition passed between them, and Arano hoped Nodel had caught the warning shake of his head and knowing glance at the detective who had asked the last question.

"No," Nodel told them smoothly. "It all happened so quickly, and my first thought was to escape. One of them will be limping for a while, though." A chuckle broke through the police ranks, and the interview continued. Finally, the detectives filed out of the room, satisfied they had everything the victim could provide. Arano walked over to Nodel, taking his outstretched hand in greeting.

"Do you two know each other?" asked Videre.

"No," answered Arano. "I was about to invite him to come by our offices and take a look at our video of a recent Disciples attack."

Nodel looked at him curiously. "You already have photos of the cult members?"

"Not exactly," lied Arano. "We have a video, but it's too blurry to be useful. We've made several attempts to clear it up, but nothing works. We'd like you to take a look at it and compare it to what you went through. I'm hoping you might be able to provide a little more insight."

"Sure," agreed Nodel. "The doctors gave me something for my bruises and scrapes, so they won't let me leave for another 30 minutes or so. I can meet you somewhere, if you would like."

"I'll leave a couple of my people with you. Consider them your personal escorts. They can bring you to our planning room when you're released. This is

Lieutenant Lain Baxter, and this is Lieutenant Videre Genoa. They'll stay as long as needed."

Nodel nodded. "See you there."

Arano took his seat at his station in the planning room, and the questions began as soon as the door was shut. He knew his teammates would pester him for information about the Padian who'd escaped death at the hands of the Disciples. Not even news the police had located the mutilated corpse that used to be the courier for the original video was enough to sideline the Avengers' curiosity.

"All right, Arano, out with it," said Alyna, a bit tartly. "What's going on here? Where do you know him from?"

"Who, Nodel?" asked Arano innocently. He grinned, seeing the annoyed look on Alyna's face. "He's a Daxia. He and I went through Whelen Academy together and fought side by side during the occupation."

"Why didn't you say anything back there?" asked Alyna.

"There was no need. What was needed was for me to quietly tell him to keep his mouth shut about being able to identify the attackers."

"Do you think he can?" interrupted Pelos.

Arano gave him a withering look. "He's a Daxia. He could tell you the brand name on the pants they were wearing."

"Relletar," came a new voice from the doorway. They all turned to see Nodel Pelen and his Avenger escorts enter the room. "Of course, today's fashion market being what it is, it may have been a cheap imitation of Relletar pants." Arano and Nodel met each other with a rough bear hug.

"I didn't know you'd been assigned to Immok City," complained Arano.

"I haven't been here that long," replied Nodel with a laugh. "The Bureau of Counter-Intelligence thought I might be able to come back here and shed some light on the security leaks they've been having."

"You do realize you're the first Padian to be attacked by the Disciples, don't you?"

"Probably the last, too," agreed Nodel with a smile. "So, introduce me to your friends."

"The two who escorted you are in my squad. The lovely young lady scowling at me from across the planning table is Captain Alyna Marquat, my other squad leader. This is Lieutenant Kish Waukee, and over there's Lieutenant Pelos Marnian." The Avengers nodded in greeting. Arano introduced Cadron Stenat, telling Nodel about Cadron's role on the team, then he explained about the information they had on the two suspected Disciples. Nodel looked at the photos and immediately nodded in confirmation.

"That's them," he said matter-of-factly. "Why didn't you want me to tell the police at the hospital I could identify them?"

"We have to keep it quiet," explained Arano. "The Disciples have eyes and ears in this building. If we let it be known we've identified them, they'd go into hiding. In the meantime, Event Horizon will put new killers in place, pushing us back to square one. We have to proceed carefully. We're finally getting close, and I don't want to blow it."

"What I don't understand," wondered Alyna, "is why you were selected as a victim. No other Padian has ever been chosen."

Nodel laughed. "It's a problem I've been trying to fix for months. Someone changed my status in the computer from Padian to Human. If the Disciples had looked into my background, they would've seen the mistake. My personnel packet shows my status as a Daxia, and only Padians have ever been allowed to go through the training."

"They've been getting sloppy," answered Cadron in explanation. "They used to stalk a victim for weeks at a time, but lately they've been striking more often. We knew it was inevitable someone would end up living through an attack."

"Anyway," said Nodel, "I hope I was able to help you. If I think of anything else, I'll get in touch again." He paused. "Can someone show me where to get some lunch around here?"

Videre laughed. "Your escort should be able to help you out. They're right outside the door, waiting on you."

Seeing the perplexed look on Nodel's face, Alyna explained, "You're the only witness we have, so the police have assigned two officers to be your bodyguards for a while."

Arano and Nodel exchanged an amused look, then started laughing. "Best to just go along with it, Nodel," he told him. "We both know a Daxia doesn't need a bodyguard, but let's humor them. Maybe they will buy your lunch."

"Gee, thanks," replied Nodel with a sarcastic roll of his eyes. He opened the door and stepped into the hallway, trailed immediately by two plainclothes officers. "Okay, gentlemen," Arano heard the Padian's voice as he moved off down the hallway. "Let's eat!"

"Message from Commander Mendarle," announced Kish. "We have an emergency meeting in the General Planning Room in twenty minutes."

Admiral Ronet stepped up to the podium, motioning for silence. Arano glanced casually about the enormous auditorium-like planning room. There were three other Avengers teams present, as well as command officers from nearly every task force in the fleet. The tone this set for the meeting had an ominous feel to it, making Arano feel a bit edgy. The solemnity of the proceedings spoke volumes about the upcoming missions.

"The time for a major assault on Rising Sun has come. Their fleet is preparing for an all-out attack on our base at Subac 2 Prime. They've set up a staging area at Solarian 4, which we believe to be their primary base of operations. We're leaving a minimal force along our picket lines between the Bromidians and us, which will be just enough to make it appear to be business as usual. We've pulled what ships we can from every sector and have formed a task force, code named Task Force Delta. This will be the force that will strike the Rising Sun fleet.

"According to our intelligence reports, Rising

Sun has set a launch time for their assault at just over forty hours from now. We'll hit them in thirty-six hours, before they are fully prepared. That leaves us three hours before we'll have to leave this system to make our time window for our preliminary stop at the Subac system, where we will muster our fleet for the assault. Our fleet will outnumber theirs 4-to-1 in capital ships, and 6-to-1 in fighters.

"I know we've experienced technical problems with our ships' systems when fighting Rising Sun ships. We've determined the most likely cause is some type of a computer virus that instructs our ships to lower their shields and disrupts the combat computers. Our technique to fight this will be twofold. First, we're taking an extreme advantage in numbers. Second, all ships have been equipped with dumbfire torpedoes. What they lack in punch, they make up in sheer strength of numbers. You'll now break up into your respective commands and work out your final plans. Dismissed."

Arano stood and left the general planning room, making his way to where the remaining Avengers teams would gather shortly. He knew the assault was necessary, but the fact did nothing to ease the nagging feeling something wasn't right. He entered the Avengers Mission Briefing Room, hoping he could get some answers.

The other Avengers teams crowded into the smaller planning room, taking their appointed places for the meeting. Commander Daton Mendarle, dressed as sharply as ever in his formal uniform, stepped to the podium and looked around the room.

"We have four complete Avengers teams here; I'm hoping that will be enough. Captain Pana's team, short-handed by two soldiers, will remain here to handle contingencies. Our task in this battle, while small, is significant. All of you will fly your Assault Class Fighters into battle, escorting two light cruisers. We will enter the system approximately ten minutes after the main force has fully engaged the enemy. Since Command believes the large capital ships and space stations are the source of the signal that activates the virus in our computers, we've been assigned to destroy their starbase orbiting Solarian 4. This will ease some of the pressure on the fleet, hopefully saving some lives."

"Excuse me, sir," interrupted Arano. A disruption like this was not permitted in a general military meeting, but the Avengers tended to be less formal when they were alone, and such questions were expected. "Aren't we taking a big gamble, basing a strategy on a theory? We've had our engineers working around the clock, and not one of them has turned up any viruses in our computers."

"I feel the same way, Captain Lakeland," answered Commander Mendarle. "The problem is, with the High Council calling the shots right now, we have to make do with what we have."

"I guess we didn't learn our lesson about politicians running a war during the first war with the Bromidians," noted Videre dryly.

"Lieutenant Genoa," Daton responded coolly. "You have something to add?" Seeing Videre wasn't responding, Daton continued. "In addition to the dumbfire torpedoes, each of your craft will be equipped with one Apocalypse warhead. Wait until the shields on the starbase are down, make a run at the base at top speed, release the warhead and get the hell out of there. Those warheads will do the rest. After the starbase has been destroyed, get out of the system. I don't want to risk losing any of you in random combat. The task force can handle the rest of the battle."

"One more question, sir," added Arano. "Why aren't we taking the new plasma torpedoes? You must've seen my report by now. With those torpedoes, the Intrepid wiped out two Bromidian heavy frigates." He frowned. "For that matter, why are we going in the Assault Class fighters, when the Intrepid didn't see any of the systems malfunctions our other craft have faced? I know she's not truly a military vessel, but we've used civilian craft on missions before."

Daton gave a heavy sigh, eyes dropping to the podium. "The decision on which ships to use was made during a meeting of the High Council's Military Committee. Grand High Councilor Tient and his Military Committee have also made the decision on the torpedoes, deciding those torpedoes are too expensive to justify their purchase." He had to speak louder then, to be heard over the angry rumblings. "In addition, it was the opinion of the committee such a powerful weapon might anger the Bromidian High Command and create an arms race. I guess they received a message to that effect from the Bromidian ambassador."

"But what about the Treaty of Rystoria?" objected Captain Pana. "They can't enter an arms race if their military strength is limited by that treaty."

"I've discussed this and every other answer you can think of with the committee, and I can't say I entirely disagree with them. They feel if we enforce the Treaty of Rystoria at this point, it'd hurt relations with the Bromidians."

"Those relations are going to go south in a hurry when the Bromidians declare war on us," grumbled Lain. "What about the Bromidian Empire ship we saw at the Rising Sun prison base in the Synthar System?"

"Conveniently," said Daton with a sarcastic half-smile, "the Bromidians reported the ship as having been hijacked. That report was issued within 30 minutes of your ship leaving the system. They claim it happened a day before, but they hadn't been notified. The ever-complacent Military Committee bought the story hook, line, and sinker.

"There's nothing we can do about it. The politicians have taken over, so we have to do the best we can with what we've got. I'm as afraid as the rest of you this whole mission is a trap. If we aren't being set up at the Solarian System, then they have another target in mind. The problem is, our intelligence reports aren't wrong. They're massing their fleet at Solarian 4. If they pull out for an invasion of our space, we'll be free to destroy their main base, which would essentially destroy Rising Sun, or at least remove them as a significant threat.

"At any rate, we only have a short time to plan this attack. The captains of the two light cruisers are on their way here, and we need to work together to set our operations order for the assault. Whether it's a trap or not, let's do this thing by the numbers."

About an hour later, a messenger entered the room and whispered briefly to Commander Mendarle. Daton shook his head angrily and motioned for Arano. "You're to take your squad and return to your planning room. Captain Marquee's squad will be going on this mission without you. An agent from the Galactic Bureau of Intelligence has taken an interest in you. You're his until he's done with you."

"What?" raged Arano, throwing a datapad into the corner. "Why? What does GBI need from me? Let them use Pana's team. He's short two Avengers anyway."

Daton glared angrily. "You have your orders, Captain. Now, move out."

Arano stormed from the room, followed closely by Lain and Videre, both showing signs of outrage nearly equal to Arano's. He was still fuming when he burst into his planning room.

Cadron Stenat was there, accessing a computer. A well-dressed Human also waited for them, shuffling through a stack of papers in his notebook. Seeing the look on Arano's face, he smiled disarmingly and rose to his feet.

"I'm Special Agent Imatt Deeps, Galactic Bureau of Intelligence. I want to apologize for having your team split up this way. I wanted both squads, but this was all I was allowed to have."

Arano looked at him curiously, some of the anger draining from his body. "Who has the authority to tell GBI what resources to use?"

"Who else?" replied Imatt with a shake of his head. "Grand High Councilor Tient. This matter concerns your team directly, and I tried to explain to him that

I needed all of you, but he refused to budge. You must've really gotten on his bad side, Captain Lakeland. He detests you with a passion so intense it's almost holy."

"The feeling is mutual," grumbled Arano. He held out his hand in greeting, and Imatt accepted it with a hearty handshake. "You can call me Arano. This is Lieutenant Lain Baxter, and this is Lieutenant Videre Genoa. You've already met our advisor. What can we do for you?"

"Actually," said Imatt pleasantly, "it's what I can do for you. I believe I've found a security leak here in Coalition Military Headquarters. If I'm correct, this will not only be the person responsible for the major breaches of operational security you have experienced, but with the Disciple Killings, as well. I believe I know who has been tapping personnel files to determine which victims are Human and which are Padian."

Arano felt his heart thumping in his chest, the adrenaline pounding in his veins as his excitement built. "How? Who?"

"I was investigating misuse of personnel files. We've seen this sort of thing before . . . usually someone with security access reads a personnel file belonging to a member of the opposite sex. It's mostly harmless, since they are usually trying to determine whether or not their subject is married, but we still discourage abuse of the system like that.

"The reason we're able to track these is a device whose existence is a secret. This is being told in confidence, and you must tell no one else. We have a central location where all computer access is recorded, even if the user makes an effort to cover their steps. We perform random audits of these entries, hoping the number of people we catch during these spot-checks will deter some people from abusing their access. For example, when your team hacked into the police department's arrestee database to identify a corpse later found floating in the river, we saw that, as well."

"Ah, I see," replied Arano with an uncomfortable grin.

"At any rate, we noticed a certain member of a support team had been accessing large numbers of Human and Padian personnel files. What made it unusual was that this person checked members of both genders, and only people in sensitive positions. I attempted to contact some of those people to see if they knew our snoop, or had any recent contact with him."

"Him?" asked Videre. "So you know who it is?"

"Yes, but let me get to that in a moment. At any rate, none of the people I interviewed knew who he was. However, a disproportionate number of the Humans in the group were dead. When I looked further into their deaths, I discovered they were all victims of the Disciples of Zhulac. I looked into your notes on the Disciples, and I found there had been no Padian victims, and the only Human victims were employees of the Coalition who had worked in high security positions. I came to the same conclusion you did: they had someone on the inside identifying Humans as targets and dismissing Padians.

"Then came the virus attack on your headquarters. Despite his best efforts to hide it, I was able to show that the same person who'd accessed those files was the person who launched the virus attack. I believe you might know him. You've worked rather closely with him throughout this investigation."

Arano felt a knot forming in his stomach. His thoughts were running rampant, thinking of all the Avengers support personnel who had assisted in the investigation, and knowing one of them had possibly been working with the Disciples all along.

"Who? Who was it?" he asked in earnest, his fists clenching.

Imatt looked him in the eye. "Dar Noil," he replied.

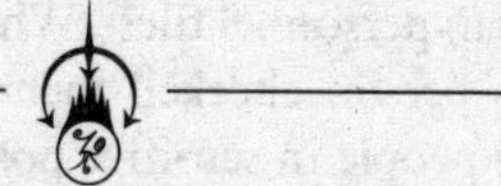

Lon Pana sat in his planning room, frustration lining his face. His team was out of commission for at least a month, which didn't set well with him. On their last mission, his team had entered the Solarian system in secret. They'd landed on a small moon orbiting the system's fifth planet and disabled a long-range listening post put there by Rising Sun forces. However, it had been a trap, and they'd barely managed to escape with their lives. Only a chance ion storm passing through the system had enabled them to escape, but even then they didn't make it out unscathed. Two of the lieutenants on his team were out with serious injuries, effectively grounding his team. When he learned who was responsible for these security breaches

His line of thought was interrupted by the beeping of his Comm. "Pana," he snapped.

"Viper here," came the reply. Lon allowed some of his anger to dissipate upon hearing his friend's voice.

"What's up, Viper?"

"I need you and your team down here on the double. We have an errand for you to run."

"On our way." As he deactivated the Comm, he saw the looks of disbelief on the faces of his three remaining teammates. "In case you didn't catch the sarcastic tone in Viper's voice," he told them, "this is serious. Let's go."

"Dar Noil?" Lon Pana's jaw dropped open in surprise. "I'll kill him!" He started for the door.

"Hold, Captain," ordered Imatt. "If we charge in there and grab him right now, we won't be able to find his compatriots. We're fairly certain he hasn't been operating alone, and we want to catch them all. In addition, he can probably lead us to the two Tsimians who've been committing the murders. We need him alive, and we need him ignorant of the fact we're on to him.

"Here is the situation. I brought with me some special GBI computer equipment. With it, you'll be able to monitor all of his computer access and subspace communications. If he uses a secure FM radio, your task will be more complex. We have a radio here for you; it decodes most of the known Coalition encryptions. The problem is that if he uses an unrecorded encryption on an FM channel, like what you Avengers use, you won't be able to hear him.

"Your mission, then, is this. For the next several days, you're his shadow. Arano wanted the job, but his team has worked too intimately with Noil. You have only had minimal face time with him, and we're counting on him not being able to recognize you. Follow his every move, record his every transmission. We need to know who he's working with and who he's working for. We're counting on you."

"I understand," Lon agreed unhappily.

"Arano, I have a special task in mind for you. A few weeks ago, a member of your team investigated the activities of a company called Transcorp Shipping. We've determined one of their major stockholders was a man named Ollem Nanon. He used an alias, but we've followed the money trail right to his doorstep. Unfortunately, since he's deceased, we can't go interview him.

"However, as I'm sure Lieutenant Marnian told you, the controlling share of the company is in the hands of a conglomerate out of the Selpan System called The Singularity Investment Firm. We've determined this company is a front, used for channeling financial aid to Event Horizon terrorists." He paused, looking around the room for emphasis. "Bear in mind, the majority of Transcorps' shipments originate from within the nebula in the Ervik system. Consequently, their cargo can't be scanned at its departure point. In times past, this would've necessitated a cargo scan upon arrival at their destination, but they've obtained a Writ of Passage from Grand High Councilor Tient, probably as a quid pro quo for campaign donations. This Writ claims their cargo is perishable and should not be delayed in any way, including for scanning when it reaches its endpoint.

"Officials on some of the worlds doing business with Transcorp have visually monitored the unloading of cargo. While most of the cargo does not appear perishable, there's little else going on to raise suspicion. That is, of course, with the exception of the settlements on Navek 6. Navek 6 is a frozen planet, although at the equator the temperature fluctuates above and below the freezing point, allowing for flowing water. The settlements there are mining camps, working to extract Elerium, which they sell to the Coalition. Interestingly, it appears Grand High Councilor Tient owns most of the mining facilities on Navek 6."

The gravity of the situation wasn't lost on Arano. We have to have that Elerium, he thought, because we make our torpedoes for our space fleet from Elerium purchased at Navek 6.

"That explains his position on the new plasma torpedoes," said Videre dryly. "If the Coalition were to stop buying Elerium from Navek 6, he'd lose a fortune."

"At any rate," continued Imatt, "the complication arising from the Transcorp shipments to Navek has to do with numbers. The cargo being unloaded at Navek 6 appears less than what is loaded at their base in the Ervik Nebula. We need to know what they're shipping and what's happening to the missing cargo. Since we now know Transcorp is owned by Event Horizon, we have to assume there's a specific purpose behind these shipments, and we need to know what it is. Since we suspect Event Horizon is behind the Disciple killings, and we know they own Transcorp, there may be a connection in all of this."

"Especially when you throw Ollem Nanon into the mix," agreed Arano. "He was dealing in information, so he might have seen this as a way to capitalize on more stolen information."

"Can't we go to the High Council with the proof Transcorp is owned by Event Horizon and have their assets seized?" asked Lain.

"If the President were here," answered Imatt with a shake of his head, "that'd be the way to go. Our problem is that both Transcorp and Singularity are major contributors to Grand High Councilor Tient. We're fairly certain that's how they got their special Writ in the first place."

The Comm beeped, and Videre turned to activate the link. Alyna's face appeared on the screen, and she gave them a quick smile. "Viper, we're about to make the jump into the wormhole. Our orders haven't changed on this end, so we'll see you when we get back."

"Affirmative," acknowledged Arano. "We'll be busy, too, so good luck to us both. And be careful. All of you."

Alyna gave him an affectionate smile. "You, too. Summerwind, out." As the link closed, Alyna's face disappeared from the video screen. Videre indicated Summerwind had activated her Rift Drives and had disappeared into the wormhole enroute to the coming battle against Rising Sun.

The door to the planning room opened, and Major Laron Alstor entered, dressed in civilian clothes. After introducing Laron to Imatt Deeps, Arano explained the latest developments in the Disciples case, as well as the information brought to them by Imatt. Laron sat stoically while Arano described the many betrayals at the hands of Dar Noil, and only the twitching of Laron's jaw muscles showed the anger he felt.

"So it appears," Arano told him, "Dar was the one who tipped off the Disciples killers about the video courier taking our video to the crime lab, about Cadron finding a copy of the video, and what our latest developments on the case have been. He was also the one who launched the virus that wiped out our copy of the Disciples murder video, along with all the other mischief done to our computers. We owe him, big time."

"I'll second that motion," added Cadron, rubbing at the scar on his throat left by the knife-wielding Kamlings he and Kish had fought with weeks before.

"So, which ship will you take?" asked Laron.

"We're trying to be inconspicuous," answered Videre. "We'll probably be going in the Intrepid. Good thing he doesn't still have the Eclipse. I don't know what I'd do if I had to take another mission in that ship."

Arano chuckled lightly. "The problem, Laron, is we're short on crew. I can fly her alone if need be, but if we run into trouble, I'd prefer at least one more person to make my ship more combat effective."

Laron grinned broadly, and Arano knew what was coming. "That's why I'm coming with you."

Arano actually laughed out loud. "Laron and Viper, together again? Watch out, galaxy. Here comes trouble!"

CHAPTER TWELVE

ALYNA SETTLED INTO HER PILOT'S SEAT IN THE cockpit of the USCS Summerwind, watching the timer as it counted down to her ship's exit from the wormhole. It'd been a relatively long flight; the fleet had first mustered at Subac 2 Prime, the Human homeworld. Actually, half the fleet had been there, the other half meeting at Subac 2, a sister planet sharing the same orbit. It was hoped spreading the fleet out would throw off any Rising Sun spies in the area. Many commanders in the military had objected strenuously to the idea of gathering the fleet in such a populated an area. Unfortunately, the High Council's Military Commission had insisted upon a sendoff from a major population center as a show to the people the government was taking Rising Sun's threat seriously.

The jump from the Subac System to the Solarian System was about fifteen-hours, and it was not a trip Alyna looked forward to. Her edginess was intensified by the prospect of the coming battle. Rising Sun would surely know they were coming and would therefore be ready. She looked around the crew cabin, verifying her team was at their posts. Pelos was ready to charge up the weapons following their exit from the wormhole, and was currently running through a Tsimian battle ritual for good luck. Kish was at her station, ready to raise shields and scan for targets.

The computer beeped its final warning. "Here we go," she announced, bringing the ship out of the wormhole.

"May your gods be with us," Kish stated doubtfully. "I think we're going to need all the help we can get."

The cabin was a buzz of activity as her crew brought all systems on-line. She glanced out the viewport and saw the other six Assault Class fighters flying in a staggered escort formation around the two light cruisers. Her Comm beeped, and Kish opened the link.

"This is Captain Alga of the USCS Vengeance. All teams form up in your wings. Summerwind, since you're alone, we'll hold you in reserve. Stay close to the cruisers and finish off fighters that get past us. If any of us get in serious trouble, you're our cover."

Alyna acknowledged the transmission and guided her ship between and slightly above the two cruisers. Her initial adrenaline rush faded, replaced by the icy calm that came from years of combat experience, and Alyna was able to think clearly. She ran through her final systems checks and made sure all systems were ready. Finally, she checked her scanner. The bulky capital ships traveled at their top speed, less than half the maximum speed of the Avengers' craft. As they drew closer to the fourth planet of the Solarian system, they picked up the expected traces of nebulatic emissions. A few moments later, several warning beeps sounded from the computer.

"Shields are down," confirmed Kish. "It looks like our targeting computers are off-line as well."

"All right," said Alyna, "we expected this. Let's stick to the plan. I hope this works, or we're going to lose a lot of ships."

The main battle was on the far side of Solarian 4; in fact, they'd intentionally come from the far side of the planet to stay away from the fight. The small group of ships made a slight change of direction, bringing the looming battle into view above the horizon of the swiftly approaching planet. Brilliant flashes of multicolor light beams lanced between the distant ships, occasionally marked by soundless explosions as a weapon found its mark. Drawing nearer to the fray, Alyna could see repeated staccato bursts of light from the Coalition ships, a sign they were using "dumbfire" torpedoes. Kish broke the silence with a long-awaited announcement.

"The Solarian starbase will be coming into range in three minutes. Short-range scanners show twenty fighters emerging from the base's fighter ports, and they're headed our way. Time to intercept: thirty seconds."

Captain Alga's voice came over the Comm. "Accelerate to attack speed. Summerwind, hold your position. Let's move!"

Alyna flew the Summerwind higher over the two cruisers, giving their gunners a wider berth for returning fire without endangering friendly craft. She allowed her ship to drift further behind the bigger ships, hiding herself in the sensor shadow of the two cruisers. She resisted the urge to move forward with the other ships, knowing this was more important.

She turned to her teammates, first motioning to Pelos. "Ready weapons!" Seeing him nod in the affirmative, she turned to Kish. "Keep an eye on the scanners, and make sure no one flanks us. We'll stay in position until Rising Sun fighters start slipping past the others. When they make a run on the cruisers, we'll jump them."

The Intrepid slipped out of the wormhole and into the Ervik System, and within a few minutes she had entered the Ervik Nebula. Arano watched through the forward viewport as the ship moved eerily through the shifting clouds. The ephemeral mist was primarily a light purple shade, dotted here and there by sparkles of light. The cloud shifted randomly, as if being blown by some stellar wind, parting when his ship flew through the nebula. Arano could picture the gases swirling in great spirals in his ship's wake. Occasional bursts of electrical discharge ripped through the stunning cloudscape. No matter how many times he came here, Arano was still amazed by the sheer beauty of the nebula. Here was the stuff galaxies were made of. Here, over the next several million years, new stars would be born. The Ervik System itself was only a minute portion of the sprawling nebula, almost half as large as the rest of the explored galaxy combined.

The Ervik System settlements were on the third and fourth planets from the Ervik sun, positioned a relatively short distance inside the nebula. It took nearly an entire day of travel using ion engines to reach the system, since Rift Drives couldn't function inside a nebula. In fact, almost nothing functioned inside the nebula: shields, targeting computers, even subspace communications. To facilitate communication with the remainder of the galaxy, several subspace transponder modules were positioned outside the nebula. These modules converted incoming subspace messages to FM frequencies and rebroadcast them toward the Ervik system. Conversely, the modules received outgoing FM signals from Ervik and rebroadcast them as subspace signals. It was slow going; there was a delay of nearly an hour while the FM signal was in transit between the modules and the Ervik system. In addition, outgoing messages were delayed by another two hours, as the signal had to be cleared of disruptions after traveling through the chaos of the nebula.

The crew of the Intrepid spent the greater part of their transit time in the meeting room at the center of the ship. Once they'd planned their strategy for the upcoming reconnaissance mission, the conversation turned to more mundane matters. Eventually, they rehashed times past, exchanging war stories from long ago. Inevitably, the talk turned to the day Major Alstor had earned the United Systems Coalition's highest honor, the Golden Cross of Valor. Arano was amazed to discover Videre had never heard the story.

"No, Laron." Arano laughed, shaking his head when Laron Alstor began the tale at Videre's request. "I'm not going to let you tell it. You tend to leave out the good parts. I know how to put in all the proper embellishments. The true story was told to me by Commander Mendarle, who was a captain at the time and in charge of Laron's team.

"The year was 2204. A young lieutenant named Laron Alstor had just graduated from Avenger's training, and had been assigned to Team 10, Squad B." Laron's face turned a shade of red; he dropped his head into his hands and groaned in mock despair. "Less than a week later, Team 10 was sent to Niones 4, an Event Horizon stronghold, to rescue five Coalition High Councilors being held there. Event Horizon had hijacked a ship and taken the Councilors prisoner, but they didn't know who they had yet. The Avengers were sent to free the Councilors before Event Horizon caught on.

"The mission started without a hitch. They landed undetected, raided the prison, and found the prisoners. They started back to the ships, encountering no resistance. As they were leaving the compound, one of the Councilors, obviously upset over his treatment, tried to kill an Event Horizon guard. The guard set off an alarm, and suddenly the simple rescue mission turned into a serious survival situation. There was a brief firefight right outside the compound, but the Avengers and their charges managed to escape into the nearby woods.

"For the next hour, they played a game of cat-and-mouse with Event Horizon soldiers. Obviously, if the team had made a straight line for their ship, Event Horizon could have sent out an airship patrol to find and destroy their craft. This necessitated a zig-zag course, which made the trip to safety take much longer. They were about halfway to their ships when their luck ran out.

"By chance, there was a squad of Event Horizon soldiers in the area on a random patrol when the mission was compromised. By listening to radio traffic among their fellow soldiers, they were able to determine the general direction the team was headed, and approximately where they were. They set up an ambush and lay in wait."

"I love it when Arano tells stories," chuckled Videre. "Did you ever think of becoming an author?"

"Anyway," continued Arano, "when the team entered a clearing at the base of a small ridgeline, the trap was sprung. Two Avengers were killed instantly, and Laron was shot in the leg. A projectile round shattered his thighbone and left him unable to walk. Fortunately, the ambushers had launched their attack too soon. The team was still close enough to the trees to duck back into the woods for cover. Laron continued firing, despite his wounds, and helped Commander Mendarle hold their attackers' attention while the other two surviving Avengers flanked them. Soon, those Avengers approached the ambush group from behind and wiped them out to the last man.

"They'd escaped the trap with all the prisoners alive, but two Avengers were dead and Laron was seriously wounded. Additionally, the firefight alerted the other Event Horizon soldiers, bringing more of them into the area. Laron, unable to walk, volunteered to stay behind and perform a delaying action, slowing down the pursuit and allowing the others to escape. They left him most of their grenades, as well as the rifles belonging to the dead Avengers, and proceeded ahead, carrying the bodies of their fallen comrades. Laron took a defensive position in a nearby creek bed and waited.

"To be sure, he was in a very defensible position. The creek bed was deep enough to provide cover, yet was steeply sloped. The latter provided him with a grenade sump; if an Event Horizon soldier threw a grenade into his position, he could simply kick it away down the slope. He lined up all his weapons and waited.

"He didn't have long to wait. He had been in position for only a few minutes when the first soldiers came into view. He allowed them to come in fairly close, and tossed several grenades at them before opening fire with his laser rifle. He fired non-stop; when he didn't have a specific target, he simply fired suppressive fire in their general direction.

"After a vicious firefight, they withdrew. He gathered his remaining weapons and dragged himself further up the slope, moving about 100 meters from his original position. Soon after, a team of enemy soldiers burst from places of concealment, firing wildly into the area Laron had been only minutes before. For a period of several minutes the soldiers milled about uncertainly, as if confused and waiting for orders. It later turned out Laron had killed their commanding officer, and Event Horizon soldiers do not function well without leadership.

"Finally, they started out on the trail of the Avengers once more. Again, Laron conducted a one-man ambush, killing several soldiers and forcing their withdrawal a second time. He retreated up the slope again, dragging himself nearly to the top of the ridgeline. He knew the next fighting position he chose would be his last, because there was nowhere left for him to go.

"This time, there was a much longer lull before the soldiers attacked Laron's vacated defensive position. As before, their efforts were fruitless, and their quarry escaped. Again, they milled about in confusion, waiting for orders. When they finally moved out, Laron was waiting. He had already burned through the power pack on one of the laser rifles and had nearly finished a second. He tossed his last grenades and began firing his rifle. By then, they were coming at him from two sides, and he knew he was trapped. Just when the enemy closed in on him, his team's Assault Class fighters streaked in low overhead, firing into the trees. Laron ignited his smoke grenade to signal his location, and the first fighter came in at treetop level, where they extracted him, while the other fighter continued to harass the enemy soldiers. The team made its escape with the rescued prisoners and the Avengers killed in action. It was Commander Mendarle who recommended Laron for the Golden Cross of Valor, and the five rescued Councilors co-sponsored the effort."

Laron laughed uncomfortably, idly rubbing one hand along the back of his neck. "Viper tells a pretty good story. I wish I'd been there to see it."

"He has to be pretty close to the truth," objected Videre in admiration. "There have only been a handful of Golden Crosses of Valor that weren't awarded posthumously."

"As long as we're trying to embarrass each other,"

said Laron pleasantly, "how about a Viper story?" Seeing Arano shake his head while his teammates nodded enthusiastically, he leaned forward and braced his arms on the table.

"As you all know, Arano was chosen early in life as a prime candidate for Daxia training at Whelen Academy. I'm sure you've all heard that starting at age eight, the students are stalked and ambushed by the instructors, also called Ma-Daxia. The purpose behind the attacks is to teach them to be alert and sharpen their danger sense. A side effect of the attacks is that they become more proficient fighters, as one Ma-Daxia learned, much to his chagrin.

"Arano was 15 at the time. He was crossing the campus on an errand when his danger sense kicked in, warning him of trouble ahead. Instead of avoiding it, he attacked the ambusher. When the fight was over, Arano was only the fifth Daxia student in the history of Whelen Academy to defeat an instructor in combat." Laron glanced over at Arano, noticing the humble Avenger squirming uncomfortably in his seat. With a wicked grin, he continued.

"By the time Arano was 16, the Ma-Daxia would only ambush him if they were in groups of three or more. After Arano defeated a group of three Ma-Daxia, the attacks on him nearly ceased altogether.

"Seeing a need to continue to push his star pupil, Axial, the headmaster of Whelen Academy, made a change in Arano's schedule. Normally, once each day, a Daxia student in his last year at the school had to wear bells while crossing the campus at night. The ambushes by Ma-Daxia are more severe if the student is heard moving around. Axial made Arano 'bell-up' at all times. Within a week, he was moving in total silence once again. In fact, in his last six months at the Academy he stalked the Ma-Daxia. After he put two of them in the infirmary, Axial stepped in and put a stop to it."

"Okay, you win," laughed Arano. "I surrender."

"Wait until Alyna hears this one." Videre grinned. "Or better yet, I could tell her how you came by your nickname"

"Don't you dare," warned Arano.

"What's it worth to you?" asked Videre, pretending to take notes.

"Well," said Laron, changing the subject, "we're almost to the Ervik system. We'd better get back to the present and what we're doing in the near future. Viper, are you sure about this plan of yours?"

"Absolutely. Videre has a story for everything. He'd have made a great salesman. We'll put his verbal talents to good use by letting him do all the fast-talking. We go in pretending to be smugglers and try to arrange a shipment. While the negotiations are ongoing, we can probably arrange a tour of their facility. Once we get a look around, we ought to be able to figure out where we need to go snooping later on."

Laron nodded in satisfaction. "As long as you're confident, I'm satisfied. Of course, if something should go wrong . . ." He trailed off meaningfully, looking down at the laser pistol he was reassembling. He looked back at Arano, a boyish expression on his weathered face. "It's been years since I've been directly involved in a firefight. Those little encounters like you had at the Codian system only serve to whet my appetite. All I ever get to see is the tail end of the battle."

Lain laughed out loud, running his fingers over the bumps on his reptilian scalp. "How many times did I tell you you wouldn't be happy taking that promotion? You have a deep-seated need to be out on the frontlines, not sitting back behind a desk. I have a sneaky suspicion you're going to be hard for us to get rid of when this is over."

"Oh, well." Videre shrugged. "Someone has to keep an eye on Arano."

"As long as you're here, Laron," said Lain, pulling a datapad from his equipment, "perhaps you'd be interested in the information we dug up on Grand High Councilor Balor Tient."

"Great," Laron said with a lopsided grin. "Okay, Lain. What's he up to now?"

"I'm sure you remember our report about Garanth Construction getting the contract to build the new High Council chambers building. We were concerned because their bid was the highest, but they were still chosen to build the new chambers. After we found out Garanth Construction had donated large sums of money to Tient, we dug a little deeper.

"As it turns out, the lowest bid was from a company called Darst Engineering. Tient accused them of tax evasion, and they were forced to withdraw their bid while they defended themselves against the charges, which turned out to be false. Oalco Builders had the next lowest bid, but they had to bow out when their CEO's transport exploded during a flight to the Subac system. Pieran Construction was the other company to make a bid. They actually had the most efficient design, yet were still considerably lower than Garanth. Their angle on the new construction was to tear down some old decrepit buildings they owned and put the new building on the old site. Tient declared their buildings historical landmarks, preventing them from being demolished or even remodeled. Garanth won by default."

Laron shook his head in disgust. "I really wish we could find a High Councilor with the guts to stand up to him. Since he's the Grand High Councilor, we can't take any action against him without the approval of the High Council Judiciary Committee, and they won't move against Tient to save their lives. He probably has some leverage on them."

"Blackmail?" wondered Arano.

"It certainly looks that way."

Arano flexed his fingers. "I have my own way of dealing with his kind."

The panel in front of Alyna continued to flash its urgent warning that the shields system had failed, telling her the Summerwind was left vulnerable to incoming fire. She'd conducted a scan of the two cruisers, showing their shields were no longer functioning. The fighters engaged by the Avengers, however, were another matter. All their systems appeared to be functioning normally. She turned her attention back to the tactical display, watching the battle play out before her.

As expected, the Avengers outgunned their foes despite problems with their craft. Avengers regularly trained in dogfighting techniques, both with and without the aid of targeting computers. In the first two minutes of the skirmish, half the enemy fighters had been destroyed, while only one Avengers ship had been damaged to the point it had to withdraw. Finally, as they'd known would happen, two fighters broke past the attacking Avengers' craft and raced toward the two looming cruisers.

"Two fighters incoming," stated Alyna. "Wait until they've committed to an attack run before we engage them. Pelos, stand by with the plasma cannons. Since our targeting computers are down, I'll engage them at close range. Kish, make sure none of the other fighters slip in behind us."

Alyna held their position for a few moments longer. Soon, the two sleek Rising Sun fighters streaked in close to the cruisers, beam weapons flashing. Alyna deftly maneuvered the Summerwind behind the fighters, and Pelos immediately began firing. Alyna had guided their ship to an angle Pelos wouldn't have to worry about accidentally hitting one of the cruisers with his plasma cannons, and he delivered a murderous barrage. Using the viewscreen as a guide, he walked the plasma cannon fire across the first fighter's path. He blasted away until its shields failed and the fighter exploded in a ball of flame.

Without pausing, Pelos swung his point of aim around, and the second fighter soon went the way of the first. The cruisers hadn't suffered any serious damage, although their shields were down, and the strike force continued toward their target. The last of the fighters had been dispatched, and nothing stood between them and their objective.

Alyna magnified her viewscreen's image of the base and studied the layout. It had been constructed in a standard cylindrical shape, with docking bays and weapons ports scattered at regular intervals around its hull. As the base slowly rotated on its axis, whichever weapons ports faced the incoming ships opened fire, while the ports that spun away from the encroaching fleet fell into frustrated silence. That was always the problem with starbases, Alyna thought grimly. They had impressive armaments, but at best only half the weapons could engage a properly deployed enemy fleet.

While the cruisers laid down a heavy barrage of fire to disable the besieged starbase's shields, the avengers circled the cruisers, trying to draw enemy fire away from the ponderously slow vessels. Two more Assault Class fighters were forced to withdraw from the fight, their systems too damaged to continue. At last the message Alyna had waited for came across the Comm.

"This is the USCS Vengeance. The base's shields are down. All fighters begin your attack run now!"

As if controlled by one pilot, the four remaining Assault Class fighters raced toward the base at top speed. Alyna verified the Apocalypse warhead was prepped and ready to launch and turned her attention to flying the Summerwind. She dodged in random directions, a storm of fire bursting all around her ship while she charged at breakneck speed. When the prearranged signal came across her Comm, she stabilized the ship and launched her warhead. As soon as it was clear, she circled the ship away from the station, trying to get clear before the warheads hit.

She switched her viewscreen to a rear view and watched as the four warheads hit their target in silent succession. With the fourth blast, the starbase listed out of control. The remaining six craft immediately closed in on the dying starbase, blasting away mercilessly until the base's massive hull finally gave way, and a brilliant ball of fire announced the death of the station. Again her Comm beeped, and she heard the triumphant message going out to the fleet.

"This is the captain of the USCS Vengeance. Our objective has been neutralized. All ship's systems should be operational shortly. My strike force is preparing to retreat."

Alyna waited expectantly while she watched her various displays, waiting for all systems to come back online. Her anticipation turned to a sense of dread when her systems showed no change. Her fears were soon expressed in the Comm message she'd feared would come.

"This is Admiral Quinten of the USCS Victorious. Destruction of the starbase has not affected our shield and weapon problems. All craft, formation Delta. Ground strike team, prepare your assault."

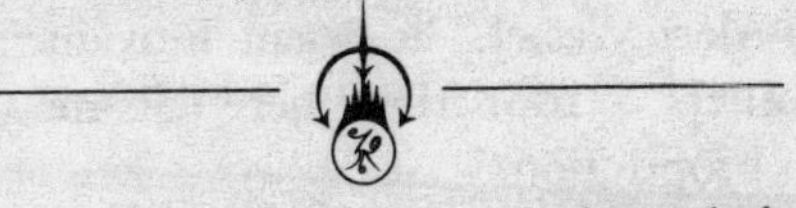

Arano took a swig of his beer and glanced about the bar. Wooden tables and chairs were scattered about the room, and he found them functional, if plain. The room's decor seemed to echo the "good enough"

attitude displayed by the furniture. The walls, while painted, were bare, having none of the wall hangings or sports paraphernalia found in most of the bars back on Immok. A large clock hung on the wall behind the bar and, like most bar clocks, it was a few minutes fast. A couple of waitresses moved disinterestedly through the crowd, serving drinks and taking orders. Several customers were eating dinner, while most simply enjoyed their drinks. A few cast suspicious glances at the newcomers. Arano looked back at his friends, contemplating their next move.

Laron, Videre, and Lain faced him, their faces showing no concern or nervousness. Arano glanced at his watch and realized the time for their meeting had come. Lain had easily set up this interview, telling the Transcorp supervisor Videre owned several freighters and was interested in moving cargo. They'd briefly returned to the Intrepid for a meal, then made the short trip to the bar where the meeting was to be held.

A few minutes later, a balding Human approached their table, two rough-looking Tsimians trailing ominously behind, making no secret of their position as bodyguards. Lain stood, and the two shook hands before seating themselves. The Tsimians remained standing, their arms crossed, trying to look menacing.

"I'm Alern Westel," he began, introducing himself to the others. "Your friend here tells me you have a business proposition."

"Yep," replied Videre nonchalantly, having introduced himself as Ain Sirit. "We've done some shipping for smaller organizations in the central Coalition systems, but the profits just aren't there. Besides, if your shipment originates in the Immok system, the bribes to keep scanners out of your holds are enormous. It's getting to the point it won't be worth your trouble to deal in . . . shall we say, 'less than legitimate' cargo."

"And just what types of cargo do you have access to?" wondered Alern.

"Mostly certain artifacts obtained from the museum at Immok University," Videre replied, building off their cover story from their deception of Ollem Nanon. "We find an occasional pharmaceutical product in our holds, from time to time."

"And what brought you here?"

"That's fairly simple. With the nebula blocking all scanners, cargo shipped from here isn't going to be inspected as closely. Let's be honest, what freighter captain doesn't have a few items in his ship that'd be of serious interest to the port authorities? With my ships leaving from here, I could make a fortune."

"Before we discuss specifics," interrupted Laron, "how about a tour? We certainly can't agree to prices and conditions without knowing what we'll be working with."

Alern Westel laughed out loud. "Your boy here is direct and to the point, isn't he? No matter. I wouldn't expect anyone to make a serious offer without seeing the place first. If you gentlemen are finished with your drinks, we can show you around. Afterward, I'm sure we can arrange some diversions to occupy your time."

With their drinks empty, the group left their seats and headed deeper into the facility. Alern was in the lead, and his Tsimian bodyguards flanked the group and tried to intimidate the guests. They toured the major points of interest with Alern bragging outrageously about the efficiency of the loading crews, the safety inspectors, and other parts of the organization that made the port facility operate smoothly. For a time, they stood and watched as a handful of dockworkers operated their heavy machinery, going about the business of loading a star freighter. The cargo was in containers marked as food supplies, and the ship was clearly marked as belonging to Transcorp.

Alern explained that while they did sub-contract some of their business to freighters outside the company, they kept the truly important business "within the family." While he was more than happy to show the facility and its procedures, Alern steadfastly refused to allow them access to the cargo being loaded on the ships. He explained that entry to the area where the cargo was stored or loaded required a security clearance within the company.

They concluded their tour back at the same bar. As a goodwill gesture, Alern told the bartender the group was to have all the food and drink they wanted free of charge, and said the facility should make available any other forms of "entertainment" the group desired.

They made a show of enjoying the hospitality, and even had dinner before they excused themselves and returned to their ship. A courier awaited their arrival, and presented each of them with a package, explaining they were gifts from Alern Westel in token of his appreciation for their offer of service; inside the boxes they found military-style watches. They thanked the courier, put the watches on to show their gratitude, and entered the Intrepid. Once inside, they immediately scanned all four watches and the entire ship for tracking devices and listening devices but found none. Satisfied they could speak freely, they gathered in the meeting room to discuss their next move.

"They make no secret of the fact there's some major smuggling going on here," began Videre. "They just don't want us to know what they're smuggling."

"Let's think about their destination," said Lain thoughtfully. "They are leaving the nebula and proceeding directly to Navek 6. What could they be smuggling into a frozen mining colony?"

"What if their destination is in the asteroid belt?" wondered Arano. "I recall hearing from Pelos that the Transcorp freighters are flying along a trajectory in the Navek system bringing them in proximity to the Navek Asteroid Belt. They must be traveling close to the asteroid field for a reason."

"Are there any known settlements on any of the larger asteroids?" asked Videre. "Maybe they are smuggling something to a small settlement."

"No," answered Lain, shaking his head. "There are no listed settlements in the Navek system other than Navek 6. Of course, it's possible there might be an unlicensed settlement, or maybe even pirates. If so, they might be selling them supplies."

"There's only one way to find out," Arano said grimly. "I'm going to have to find out what's in those cargo containers. And I think I know how to do it . . ."

Alyna slammed her fist on the armrest of her chair

and watched the tactical display, sitting in helpless frustration as the main battle played out before her. The Coalition fleet's battle plan had depended on the destruction of Rising Sun's starbase restoring their systems and allowing them to easily win the battle. It hadn't happened. In fact, the Coalition ships experienced the worst system problems to date. Only the Command Class Battleships had functional shields, and all Coalition ships smaller than a heavy cruiser had targeting computer problems. Only the superior skills of the Coalition fighter pilots and their vastly superior numbers kept the battle from becoming a total rout. As it was, although the Coalition inflicted serious damage on Rising Sun's fleet, they took heavy casualties themselves.

The remaining Avengers had taken in the situation and volunteered their assistance, despite orders to stay clear of the general melee. At the suggestion of the ground forces commander, the four Assault Class fighters escorted the transports carrying the ground troops toward their objective. In minutes, the troops were deployed on Solarian 4 while the Avengers circled protectively overhead. Once the troops had deployed their anti-aircraft weaponry, the Avengers scattered and searched out the various planetary defense installations. Kish indicated to Alyna the location of the nearest facility, and she adjusted their course to an attack vector for the target.

She continued to monitor the battle fleet's Comm channel, listening as ship after ship described heavy damage. Without their protective shields, and deprived of the offensive capabilities of their targeting computers, the fleet was vulnerable even to the outdated weaponry employed by Rising Sun's forces. She cleared her thoughts and concentrated on the task at hand. Taking out a few of these planetary defense installations should help alleviate some of the pressure on the fleet, saving Coalition lives.

The USCS Summerwind streaked low across the landscape, staying just above treetop level as they approached their first target. Anti-aircraft defenses immediately opened fire on their approach, but the emplacements were widespread, and staying low to the ground Alyna was easily able to avoid them.

When the installation came into view, she stabilized their flight and Pelos automatically opened fire with the plasma cannons. After their first pass, the installation's main guns were smoking. After the second pass, fires raged in several areas of the Rising Sun base. On their third pass, Pelos hit the main capacitors, causing a major feedback in their power system. As Alyna swung her ship around for another pass, the entire site disappeared behind a gigantic explosion, an enormous ball of fire expanding and reaching for the skies.

In this manner, the four Avenger Assault Class fighters destroyed installation after installation, all the while monitoring the location of the ground forces to avoid a friendly fire incident. Despite their efforts, however, the situation was becoming desperate for the main fleet. Their losses were unacceptable, and it was clear from their transmissions the fleet commanders were seriously thinking of pulling out of the fight. It was obvious that unless something changed, and soon, the Coalition fleet could suffer a humiliating defeat.

Just then, Kish snapped her fingers and held up a gray-skinned hand for silence, listening intently to one of the Comm channels at her station. "One of our armored brigades is reporting contact with a major command and control center. They are meeting heavy resistance and are requesting assistance."

Alyna sat up straighter, her eyes intent. "Let's go," she said simply.

CHAPTER THIRTEEN

ARANO STAGGERED IN AN APPARENT DRUNKEN STUpor down the ramp, leaving his teammates aboard the Intrepid. Not surprisingly, two of the omnipresent Tsimian guards immediately intercepted him. "Where do you think you're going?" growled the first.

Arano swayed as he looked up at the tall, hook-beaked figure standing before him. "Back to the bar. Alern said there were women to be had there, and I intend to have them."

The guard thought about that for a moment, eyes narrowing, almost looking as if he were trying to find something wrong with Arano's plan. Finally, he shrugged. "Go ahead. Mind you don't go anywhere else, though. I'd hate for something to happen to you while you're our guest." He gave Arano a direct look that could only be taken as a threat.

Arano nodded with a foolish grin on his face, saluted the grumbling guard, and staggered off toward the bar. After walking a short distance, he stopped for a moment, pretending to adjust a strap on his shoe. As he did so, he glanced back the way he'd come, spotting the guards trailing loosely behind him. The guards were Kamlings, though, which meant Videre had been right: the two guards based at the Intrepid wouldn't leave their post.

He entered the tavern, emptying as the patrons finally had their fill of drink. Over in one corner, a waitress cleaned up a mess of spilled drinks while a pair of drunken Human patrons looked on, laughing. The room reeked of stale sweat and beer, the odor nearly turning Arano's stomach. The interior of the bar was poorly lit, probably less for reasons of atmosphere than because the owner was trying to save money. Arano sauntered up to the bar, waving rudely at the bartender, who nonetheless politely asked what Arano wanted.

"Alern said there were women here," Arano slurred. "I don't see them anywhere."

"Upstairs," mumbled the bartender. "Alern told me he's buying whatever you want, but you can still tip the girls. And remember, one shout from a girl will bring the bodyguards, and they deal rather harshly with anyone who harms one of the ladies here."

"Gotcha," smiled Arano grandly, striding up the narrow staircase. He selected a room with an open door and stuck his head inside. A scantily clad Human sat inside, a bored look on her face.

Seeing Arano, she forced a smile. "Come in, honey," she said pleasantly. "Don't be shy."

Arano entered the sparsely furnished room and closed the door behind him. As he moved toward the bed, he noticed the worn flooring and aging furniture, signs the keeper of the place was less than concerned with the maintenance of his rooms. Small wonder, thought Arano, when your clientele wasn't there to critique the decorations. He sat down on the bed next to her, and she reached for him seductively.

"Wait," he said, holding his hands up between them. "I need your services, but not in the way you're thinking. Is there a back way out of this room?"

She gave him a direct look, crossing her arms in defiance, a move that made her look even tinier.

Arano sighed. "Okay, if I pay you double your normal fee, will you help me?"

She chewed on her lip, considering the offer. "I take it you're being followed, and you have something you want to do without an audience?"

Arano laughed softly. "You're very perceptive."

"Okay. For triple my fee I'll show you the back door, and I'll even make so much noise in here your unwanted following will have no doubt you're in here having the time of your life."

"Done," agreed Arano. He paid her what she wanted, and followed her to a corner. She stepped lightly to an old, worn-looking dresser, opened the top drawer, reached a slender arm inside, and triggered a hidden release. The dresser swung silently open to reveal a hidden passage. At Arano's prompting, she gave him directions to the facility's main command center. He thanked her, then surprised her with a quick kiss on the cheek.

"That will cost you extra next time," she laughed. "By the way, when this business of yours is done, if you have a little spare time . . ." She trailed off suggestively, then opened her shirt wide, displaying what she had to offer. Arano gave her pale, naked skin his best appreciative look, waved to her, and headed down the passage. She closed the dresser behind him, and as he moved away he heard her bouncing on the bed, moaning in apparent ecstasy.

He followed her directions for the next several minutes, but when he neared the command center he took a detour. He hadn't entrusted her with his actual destination, but he knew how to get to the loading docks. After several minutes, they finally came into view.

Despite the importance of the area, lighting was sparse, creating an eerie setting. The streets were littered with debris, and even the walls of the buildings were covered with a layer of filth. The smell of Rift Drive engine lubricants was thick in the air, almost to the point of being cloying. There were no workers present, as the process of loading the ship had stopped for the evening. He saw a number of freighters lined up, all either awaiting the loading of their cargoes or the return of their crews, or both. There were a number of pieces of heavy equipment and personnel transports scattered around, and Arano was confident he could use them as cover and enter the area unseen.

He slipped into the shadows, moving more slowly as stealth became of the utmost importance. Two guards walked along a darkened roadway, passing within ten feet of Arano without knowing he was there. He crossed the road, moving closer to the moored space freighters. He felt no particular sense of urgency and bided his time in the darkened shadow of a warehouse. For several minutes he watched the guards, noticing their indifferent attitude to their task. Satisfied the guards posed no serious threat, he studied his surroundings.

The buildings in that area of the port showed signs of wear. Part of that, he surmised, was from the elements. There was a peculiar gas in the atmosphere that, while harmless to life forms, protected the planet's inhabitants from the gases of the nebula. As a side effect, the daytime sky was a constant gray color, and severe storms sprang up regularly and without warning.

Arano's eyes searched from building to building, looking for signs of security systems. Mounted at irregular intervals among the crumbling mortar of several buildings were security cameras, but he was fairly certain he could bypass them without too much effort.

Finally, he started forward, slipping from one place of concealment to another, making no sound as he went. Another pair of guards walked past him, their voices low in whispered conversation. He slipped in behind them, followed them a short distance, and darted across a narrow walkway to a darkened freighter.

Arano glanced down the side of the ship and spotted the Transcorp logo plainly visible on her port side. He pressed his lips together in thought and made his decision. Staying close to the ship for concealment, he circled around the port side until he came to the entry hatch. The entry was open, the crew probably out enjoying a night of carousing. With a quick look around, Arano crept onboard the freighter.

As he moved down the entry corridor and through the ship, he was struck by the fact the crew didn't spend a lot of time in maintenance or cleaning. In the rooms with open doorways, he saw meeting rooms with scattered papers on the desks and floor, crew quarters with unmade bunks and scattered clothing, and a general disarray that spoke volumes about the ship's captain. He grinned to himself thinking of Pelos' reaction; the Tsimian Avenger had been a stockholder in this company at one time.

After about five minutes of searching the ship, Arano found the hold, already loaded with the cargo waiting to be taken to the Navek system. Containers of varying sizes and shapes were stacked in orderly rows throughout the bay. Again, Arano paused in the shadows, something appearing amiss to his senses. His danger sense hadn't warned him yet, but another corner of his mind whispered warnings. He didn't believe the ship was completely abandoned, even in a friendly port such as this. If anyone was still onboard as a guard, this would be a good place to find them.

Arano stayed immobile for several minutes before the guard came into view. He staggered and the reason for his swaying gait was made apparent by the nearly empty bottle in his hand. He sat down on a nearby crate and took another long pull. Sitting quietly for a few moments, he finished off the bottle, and settled back against the stack of cargo. Within moments, he was fast asleep.

Convinced the area was safe, Arano moved forward once more. He selected a container at random, its manifest indicating there was food inside. A check of the container's contents verified it and he moved on. After searching a number of containers, he had found a few stockpiles of illegal contraband, but nothing else. He made a mental note to report it to the Galactic Bureau of Intelligence upon his return. The resulting investigation would likely shut the shipping company down. But still, something about the whole situation told him there was more than what he had seen. He moved deeper into the cargo hold.

Finally, he found what he was looking for. In the center of the hold, far from prying eyes, he found several unmarked containers. He checked his surroundings one more time, pulled out his knife, and went to work on the closures. In a short time he freed the lid and looked inside expectantly.

The container held row after row of fragmentary hand grenades, all United Systems Coalition issue. His heart thudding in his chest, Arano checked several of the other unmarked containers, finding artillery rounds and hand-held laser weapons. There was even one containing warheads for ship-to-ship missiles. There were enough munitions to outfit a small army. Arano thought fast, knowing he couldn't stay much longer, but still had to do something. He found himself sweating freely as he mentally ran through his options.

He tried to puzzle out what was going on. He knew nearly all of the Transcorp freighters leaving the Ervik system were bound for the Navek system. Obviously, since they didn't detour from their flight pattern and came back empty, the entire cargo was bound for a location in the Navek system. His first thought was that they met other smugglers in the Navek system and transfer the weapons and other contraband to the smuggler's vessel before continuing to their destination at Navek 6. But that just didn't sit right with Arano. Why would they delay with an extra stop, when the smugglers could just as easily pick up the illegal cargo in the Ervik system?

Likely, he thought, the contraband was being dropped off at a storage site in the Navek system. It couldn't be on Navek 6, because officials there wouldn't tolerate side trips, and while they didn't scan a high number of cargo containers, they'd eventually scan one of the contraband containers, just by the law of averages. It had to be something else.

Once again, Arano remembered what he and Pelos had discussed so long ago: Transcorp freighters entering the Navek system traveled along a flat trajectory in the same geometric plane as the planetary orbits, flying dangerously close to the Navek asteroid belt. There must be a weapons depot there! But why store them in such a dangerous area? It wouldn't be done unless there was a tactical advantage. And there was only one thing in the Navek system worth fighting over: the Elerium needed for the construction of torpedoes for the Coalition space fleet.

Now that he suspected an extremely dangerous scenario, he decided to move swiftly. He returned to the containers of grenades and placed a few in his pockets while holding onto three of them. These he placed on the ground and accessed the primer mechanisms. He set them to their maximum sixty-minute delay, placing one in each grenade container and one in the torpedo warhead container. That accomplished, he sprinted out of the room, laser pistol in hand. He still had over an hour before dawn, but he had no intention of being on the streets that long.

It took him the better part of twenty minutes to retrace his steps to the bar. He moved with greater haste but was still forced to hide from several patrols. He re-entered the bar through the hidden doorway and made his way back to the entrance to "his" room. He knocked timidly on the door, surprised to feel his face flush with embarrassment. A few moments later the dresser swung silently open.

"It's about time," greeted the smiling young lady. "I was starting to get pretty creative in here."

Arano retrieved more money from his pocket and handed it to her with a smile. "For your trouble," he told her, "and for the kiss."

She looked at the money in her hands, tears suddenly in her eyes, and gave him an impulsive hug. "You come back soon," she told him when he turned to leave.

Arano paused as an idea came to him. Since leaving the Transcorp freighter, he had puzzled over the problem of getting a message to the Coalition about the weapons shipments. He couldn't use a subspace radio while still inside the nebula, and there was the possibility they wouldn't escape the system to send a message from open space. As he reached for the door, however, the answer came to him.

He pulled out his datapad and typed a coded message into it. Using a secure FM frequency, just as his team had used during their mission on Ollem Nanon's underwater casino, Arano sent the message out, knowing in the matter of an hour or so the signal would be received by one of the subspace transponders located outside the nebula. It would be another two hours before the cleaned-up signal would be rebroadcast on subspace and received by Alyna's datapad. She could decode it and pass it on from there.

Arano gathered himself, put his mindset back into that of a drunken reveler, and staggered through the doorway into the hall beyond. He lurched down the stairs, loudly boasting about his alleged accomplishments upstairs. He staggered out into the street, and as he expected the Kamlings who had followed him were on his trail once more. No longer feeling the need for secrecy, he strolled boldly along the roadways. He reached the Intrepid and signaled his teammates to open the hatchway.

Once inside the ship, he ran through the accessway to the bridge, yelling to his crew it was time to take off. He explained what he'd found as he settled into the pilot's seat, glaring at the Comm in annoyance when the expected message came in from the space traffic control tower.

"Frigate Nasontic," announced the voice from the tower, "Power down your engines. You do not have clearance to lift off at this time."

"This is the Nasontic," replied Laron, using the Intrepid's assumed name. "Our captain has had a family emergency. We must leave immediately."

"Stand by."

Arano looked around nervously. "I hope they hurry," he mumbled. "In about ten minutes, they're going to be very angry."

Laron glared at him. "Oh, no. What did you do now?"

Arano shrugged. "As I was saying, they have a large shipment of military hardware onboard that freighter. I just figured they might like a little confirmation their explosives are, in fact, functional."

Videre grinned wickedly. "And you didn't even invite me to the party. I'm hurt."

The minutes ticked by, and the group sat nervously waiting. Arano chewed absently on his fingernails, and Videre ran some unnecessary preflight checks. Laron, unable to control his nervous energy, paced the deck impatiently.

The Comm finally beeped again. "Freighter Nasontic, you've been granted emergency clearance for lift off. Follow the coordinates we're sending you."

Laron acknowledged the message, and Arano wasted no time lifting off. The ship raced away from the port, getting barely twenty kilometers into the air before Arano indicated the sixty-minute countdown on the grenades had expired. As if on cue, the Comm beeped once again, the nameless voice from the tower demanding they return to the spaceport, saying all traffic was terminated following an incident at the loading docks.

Arano chewed thoughtfully on his lip as they continued their flight from the planet. "Videre, are the shields functional?" he asked.

Videre checked his display. "Negative," came the reply. "Because of the nebula, shields are down, subspace communications and targeting computers are off-line. Scanners are minimally functional. There are at least six fighters outbound from the planet, unknown configuration, exact number hard to determine due to the interference. They're closing the distance between us with an estimated time to firing range of five minutes."

"Cut power to weapons, shields, and all computers except the navigation computer. Life support at minimum power. All excess power to engines, and give me maximum speed. Prepare for evasive maneuvers followed by total system shutdown on my mark."

Videre acknowledged the orders and made the necessary preparations on his control panel. Lain left his weapons station, his controls useless while the power was shut down, and strode to the emergency supply cabinet. He grabbed four sets of cold weather gear, brought them to his teammates, and donned his own protective suit in the process. Meanwhile, Laron retrieved several emergency air tanks, each containing enough compressed air for fifteen hours of usage on an average-sized Human.

Arano watched on his viewscreen as the nebula's gases surrounded the Intrepid, seeming to swallow it whole. Their increased speed had slowed the fighters' approach to the ship, giving Arano the time he needed. As soon the fighters' view of his ship was obscured, Arano executed a sharp turn to the starboard side. He cut all power, leaving only emergency lighting and a dangerously low life-support system operational. The artificial gravity system was also disabled, and the crew floated about the bridge for several moments until they secured themselves to the decking with the magnetic boots included in the emergency survival gear.

In this fashion, the occupants of the Intrepid made their way to the edge of the nebula. Arano counted on the fighters having a difficult time tracking them in a nebula while Intrepid's systems were powered down.

The impaired scanners, combined with a low energy signature, should effectively conceal their ship from its hunters. Inertia would carry them toward the edges of the nebula, with a nearly negligible speed loss from friction with the nebulous gases. Twice more during the next hour, Arano powered up the engines, made a slight change in their direction of travel, and powered the engines off again. The hours slipped by, and while they saw no signs of pursuit, they also didn't see the end of the nebula.

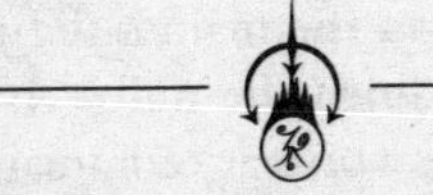

Alyna rolled the Summerwind on its side, allowing Pelos to bring both secondary plasma batteries to bear. Streaking low over their target, she held the ship as steady as possible while Pelos blasted away at two Rising Sun heavy artillery positions. His heavy barrage of fire silenced both artillery positions in small but brilliant explosions. Kish called out another target, an anti-aircraft battery, and Alyna adjusted their course to prepare for a run at their newest target.

For another hour, the ground battle raged. The Coalition's armored division thundered into Rising Sun's defensive perimeter, guns blazing. For a few tense minutes, the defenders held their positions, seemingly ready to throw back the assault. But finally, on the right flank, a Coalition tank platoon burst through the defensive lines and flanked the entrenched Bromidian soldiers. The soldiers held in reserve by Rising Sun's commanders left their positions of cover to fill the gaps in their crumbling right flank, but were cut down by the heavy crossfire coming from the Avengers in their Assault Class fighters. The Coalition artillery also inflicted a heavy toll, each exploding shell claiming Bromidian lives.

Soon, the entire Rising Sun defensive line collapsed on itself, falling back to the main building at the compound's center. Sporadic explosions rocked the compound, and Bromidian soldiers continued to fall prey to the incoming fire as they retreated across the killing zone. A large satellite communications array was mounted on the main building's roof, and numerous antennae lined the walls. It was immediately obvious this was a primary command and control center, and the Bromidian soldiers appeared ready to defend it to their deaths. The zone between the advancing Coalition forces and the retreating Rising Sun forces was littered with Bromidian dead, the ground covered with their thick black blood.

Minutes later, in a surprise move, all remaining Bromidian forces pulled back inside the main command center, causing a cessation of all incoming fire for the Coalition forces. As the long-range weapons pounded the command center in preparation for the final assault, the main ground forces held their positions, waiting for guidance from their commanders.

Suddenly, the entire building erupted in an enormous explosion, leveling all nearby buildings and damaging dozens of others. Alyna sat stunned in her pilot's seat, unable to comprehend what had happened. She activated her Comm to see if any of the commanders had an idea what caused the explosion. A cornucopia of conversation filled the channel in a chaotic flood of voices.

"... no idea what happened ..."

"We didn't hit it that hard ..."

"May have been a self-destruct of some sort ..."

"This is Admiral Quentin of the USCS Victorious. All systems just came back online. My command display shows all Coalition capital ships have their shields at 100%. Fighters' shields and weapons computers are still offline. Our gunnery positions report beam weapon targeting computers are functioning, but we're still unable to acquire a lock with the torpedo systems. Cancel the order to fall back. All fighter wings, engage your priority targets."

The commotion on the Comm continued, but Alyna stopped listening, her mind buzzing with what had just happened. The destruction of the command center, followed immediately by the Coalition fleet's recovery of most of their systems, was too much to be called a coincidence. There had to be a connection. And there was only one way for them to find out.

"Ground Command, this is Captain Marquat of the Avengers in the USCS Summerwind. I'm bringing my craft in near the blast site. We need to speak to any live Bromidians your troops find. I have to find out what was inside the building that was so important."

"Copy that, Summerwind," came the reply as Alyna guided her ship toward the battle-scarred ground. All around, Coalition tanks and infantry emerged from their places of concealment to cautiously continue their advance into the heart of Rising Sun defenses.

The Summerwind landed gracefully in a nearby intersection that appeared to be relatively free of debris.

Leaving Kish behind to monitor the progress of the fleet's battle, Alyna and Pelos exited the ship. They moved to a sheltered position behind the jagged remnants of a wall ground commanders had established as a forward base of operations. She checked in at the command post, then she and Pelos began their own reconnaissance of the area.

They'd walked but a short distance when Alyna and Pelos were summoned back to the command post. A tall, athletic-looking Human awaited them, the insignia on his collar indicating his rank of major. He greeted Alyna enthusiastically, and motioned for the Avengers to take seats. He rubbed his hand lightly through his neatly groomed blond hair and watched closely while Alyna daintily brushed the debris off her chair before settling into her seat.

"Captain Marquat, I'm Major Nadir, Eleventh Infantry Division. We were interrogating a captured Bromidian, and came across something that might interest you. We've found a Brom who claims to be a part of a secret resistance group fighting to overthrow the Bromidian government."

"Do you believe him?" asked Alyna, leaning forward in her seat.

The major laughed as he kicked at small pieces of debris near his feet. "I wouldn't believe a Bromidian if he told me his command center just exploded. You're free to talk to him, though. If you choose to believe him, well, that's up to you."

"All right," said Alyna, rising to her feet. "I think we'll at least see what he has to say. Even if you're trying to offer a deception, you can inadvertently reveal something of the truth."

Major Nadir motioned for the Avengers to follow, and they entered the remains of a windowless building that might have served as a warehouse at one time. They crossed a wide-open floor, the ceiling barely visible several storeys above them in the dust and haze. Since the room was empty, it was impossible to tell what purpose it might have once served. Major Nadir fell back to walk alongside Alyna, stealing occasional glances when he thought she wasn't looking. Alyna noticed what he was doing, but said nothing. She continued to follow him until they came to a series of doors, and the major indicated the rooms behind them were used as cells.

"Your man is behind the third door on the left," announced Major Nadir. "I'll let the guards know you have authorization to enter." He led the way down the hall and opened the door, stuck his head inside and spoke briefly with someone. He opened the wooden door wider, stepped through, and motioned for them to follow. Alyna entered the room first, the crumbling walls and gaping holes in the ceiling giving mute testimony to the savagery of the earlier battle.

Once Pelos had entered the makeshift cell, the major shut the door behind them and motioned across the room. Lying in the corner with his hands tied together behind his back was a Bromidian wearing a Rising Sun uniform, now stained dark with his blood. Major Nadir nodded to Alyna and seated himself in an empty chair.

Pelos moved over to the badly wounded Bromidian soldier while Alyna looked uncomfortably at the guard and the major, who watched intently. "Major Nadir," she started, "if you don't mind, we prefer to conduct our interviews in private. Sometimes the information we gather can lead to future Avengers missions, and we try to limit the number of people who have access to that type of intel."

"Well . . ." The major squirmed uncomfortably. "Technically, we're not supposed to leave a prisoner alone like that. Since he's in our custody . . ."

Alyna strode confidently over to him, and took both of his hands in hers. "Please? I'd consider it a personal favor." She trailed off, fixing the helpless major with her tight smile and a wink.

Major Nadir couldn't hold out any longer. "Okay," he agreed with a smile, "but just for a few minutes." He motioned to the guard, and moments later the Avengers were alone with the captive.

"Hurry," muttered Pelos quietly. "He's hurt pretty badly and he hasn't much time left."

Alyna nodded, and knelt at the soldier's side. "Would you like some water?" she asked softly.

The soldier laughed. "You can dispense with your textbook interrogator's techniques," he said roughly. "I've been trained as an interrogator myself, so I know all the tricks of the trade. I'll answer any question you put to me, but, as your companion said, I haven't much time. Ask quickly."

"Okay," replied Alyna, somewhat taken aback by the Bromidian's straightforward attitude. "You claim to be part of a resistance group. Is that true?"

"I'm not just claiming to be in a resistance group, I am in a resistance group. We call ourselves the Rystoria

Liberation Front." His body was wracked by a series of painful coughs, but he managed a Bromidian smile. "Not a very imaginative name, I know. But you have to understand our culture. We're raised from birth to be warriors, and have little talent for creating fancy slogans.

"The RLF is based at our homeworld of Rystoria 2, or Vagorst as the Bromidian High Command calls it. The reason we refer to our world as 'Rystoria' rather than 'Vagorst' is because we reject everything the Bromidian Empire stands for. The manner in which our military treats conquered worlds is a disgrace to our race. My organization cheered the freedom fighters on Leguin when they drove the Rising Sun task force from their planet."

"How did you end up fighting for Rising Sun if you're in the resistance movement?" asked Pelos suddenly.

"I was sent here as an infiltrator," came the reply. "I was attempting to gather intelligence to demonstrate a definite link between Rising Sun and the Bromidian High Command. Unfortunately, your task force arrived before I could finish my work, and what little I accomplished has been destroyed. I can tell you this, however: you were supposed to come here. The High Command decided Rising Sun had outlived its usefulness. This was to be a grand final battle, convincing everyone the threat was destroyed. It was all just a decoy, though, meant to lure your fleet from their true target, whatever it was."

"Was?" asked Alyna.

"Was," confirmed the Bromidian. "By now, their main objective, whatever it may have been, has been neutralized. But my time grows short. Let's move back to the resistance movement."

"Why hasn't the Coalition learned of this It? Our intelligence network should've informed us of this by now."

"Do you really think the Bromidian High Command would let news like that slip out?" raged the soldier. "The only information you'll gather from Rystoria is what the High Command wants you to gather.

"Now listen closely. Your special operations units will eventually need to make contact with us. We're rapidly spreading, and within a few weeks we'll have cells located on most of the occupied systems controlled by the High Command. Bromidian society isn't as monolithic as you may think, and we have sympathizers everywhere.

"On Rystoria 2, in the city of Anhyd, look for a restaurant with the sign of the raven out front. Tell them Zharnak sent you, and show them this." He handed Alyna a narrow black ring, embossed with intricate designs so interwoven they were difficult for the eye to follow. "This ring will let them know we've spoken. You'll still have to gain their trust, but it'll be a start." He paused as his body convulsed, leaving him gasping for air.

"There's . . . more. The reason Rising Sun destroyed their command center wasn't just to keep you from taking prisoners. There was technology there, technology they were afraid you'd find. Their entire strategy of conquest depends on it. The Beacon. You must discover its secret and destroy it, or the war is lost. You haven't much time"

His eyelids fluttered rapidly as another spasm rocked his body. Finally, the convulsions subsided, and he let out one long last sigh as life fled his body. Alyna stood and faced Pelos, shaking her head.

"I don't know . . . did you get all that recorded?"

"Yes," came Pelos' reply as he indicated his datapad. "If there's anything to what he said, we should be able to"

He was cut off by the sudden beeping of their Comms. Alyna retrieved hers, activating the link. "Captain Marquat."

"This is Kish. The fleet reports the battle is nearly finished. We suffered heavy losses early on, but once the fleet's systems came back online we defeated them rather swiftly. However, we just received two priority subspace messages. The first is from Captain Lakeland, and I'll brief you when you return. The other is from our outpost in the Navek system. Event Horizon has laid siege to Navek 6, and the whole system will be under their control within the hour!"

CHAPTER FOURTEEN

TWO DAYS LATER, ARANO'S TEAM STOOD REUNITED in their planning room on Immok 2. They'd read the mission briefings from each squad's separate missions and discussed the implications of each, awaiting the arrival of Captain Pana and his news on Dar Noil. Arano felt great relief learning his entire team had survived intact, and had no small amount of guilt realizing his greatest anxiety resulted from his separation from Alyna. He even felt a small surge of jealousy when he heard how the helpful Major Nadir had flirted with Alyna. He laughed heartily, however, when he learned how she'd used his attentions to gain a private audience with the Bromidian soldier, and then casually dismissed the major when she left.

He stood close by Alyna's side, closer than was absolutely necessary. Close enough, in fact, he frequently brushed her hip, or her arm, as he shuffled through the seemingly endless pile of papers before him. Alyna didn't seem to mind, so Arano stayed put.

"What was your impression of this Bromidian?" asked Videre. "Could he have been telling the truth?"

"I really don't know," replied Alyna thoughtfully.

"I've been going over the conversation in my mind since I spoke with him. If he was from one of the Coalition races, I'd say he was straightforward with us. However, since we've had limited experience in the interrogation of Bromidians, I don't know what body language to look for. He certainly had detailed information."

"And then there was his information about what was supposed to be the 'true target'," muttered Arano, a sarcastic lopsided grin on his face. "That seems a bit too convenient. 'I have some great information for you, but . . . Oops! It's too late to use it.' I'm suspicious of helpful intel presented too late to be used. He could've been a mole planted by the High Command, trying to get us to waste our resources attempting to contact a phantom organization. They might even be using this as a ruse to make contact with Coalition intelligence agents and blow their cover."

Discussion of the matter ended, however, when Cadron Stenat entered the room, followed closely by Imatt Deeps of the Galactic Bureau of Intelligence. Both grinned triumphantly, giving Arano a glimmer of hope that at least one of their dilemmas had been solved.

"I have more good news than you can handle," gloated Cadron. "First, have you noticed it has seemed quieter around here recently?"

"Well . . .," Arano began cautiously.

"Cono Vishturn was reassigned by the Grand High Councilor's office. Rumor has it Tient was unhappy with Cono's reports, probably because he started giving us glowing recommendations. At any rate, that's one thorn out of our sides."

"Amen to that," agreed Alyna.

"The next item is a little hard to believe at first. Agent Deeps and I were studying data on the security breaches, trying to find a pattern or a common thread. As I had mentioned before, no one had accessed more than a few pieces of sensitive data, making the pool of conspirators much too large to have avoided detection.

"We excluded several people from the pooling data because they were deceased, and decided to try another angle with them. What if they were either paid or extorted for the information, but were murdered after delivery? When we made a pool of those Coalition employees who died in the past three years, we made a startling discovery: although each had only accessed a small portion of the compromised data, together they'd accessed all the information. That's where Imatt Deep's contacts came in handy." He looked at Imatt, who sat nearby.

"My first step," Imatt told them, straightening his immaculate tunic top, "was to determine the date each person died and the manner of death. I can't explain why, but only people assigned to the Coalition Personnel office have access to this information. Of course, I have other ways of gathering data.

"Interestingly, all were victims of the Disciples of Zhulac. At first we thought the Disciples were actually spies for either Rising Sun or Event Horizon, and they murdered these people after getting the information they wanted. After all, dead men don't tell tales. This theory didn't hold up under closer scrutiny, though, since none of the people accessed the compromised data until the days immediately after their death.

That's where our idea hit a dead end."

"But how could spies have accessed the sensitive data after the victims' deaths?" protested Lain. "Even if these people had given up their passwords to the Disciples, there are still other security protocols in place."

Arano's eyes lit up in understanding. "When the virus attack on our computer told the system I was dead, I was still able to access the computer system for weeks. That means it was possible for the Disciples to be the ones who accessed the files. And the spy would have to have been a Coalition employee for them to have even gained access to the facility."

"Being an employee would get them inside," agreed Alyna, "and if they'd obtained passwords from the victims, they would've been able to defeat all the security protocols except the retina scan. I don't know of anyone who was ever able to bypass that protocol."

"I've got it!" proclaimed Kish suddenly, snapping her leathery fingers. "Think about it. The Disciples have been mutilating their victims, supposedly in keeping with ancient rituals. What if there was a deeper purpose? What if the eyes of the Coalition employee-victims were kept in stasis to be used later to defeat the retina scans? We proved on a deceased Event Horizon soldier a retina scan will work after death."

"That doesn't quite hold water," objected Lain, reptilian features contorted in thought. "They couldn't just hold a pair of eyes up to a retina scanner. The computer would never read them."

"What if the eyes were transplanted into another host?" suggested Kish. "We do possess the live organ transplant technology needed for such an operation, but it hasn't been used in over a century." She frowned. "Of course, the Biomek Company has recently been expressing interest in the field."

"That makes sense," Imatt said. "I've had some agents investigating Biomek recently because of their ties to Event Horizon. And as for the victims' passwords," he added grimly, "they wouldn't have to obtain them through torture. Dar Noil accessed the records of all of the victims, including their passwords. He gave the Disciples everything they needed."

"Including a host for the transplanted eyes," interjected Videre suddenly, his fur bristling. "Remember how bad his eyes have looked the past several weeks? The multiple eye transplants must have caused tissue deterioration in his own eyes."

"Wait a minute," Pelos rumbled, coming to his feet. "Let's assume this is all correct, which it appears to be. Event Horizon was behind the Disciples killings. They generated a serial killer story to hide the fact they wanted to kill Coalition employees in order to access sensitive information. So, why does Rising Sun seem to reap all the benefits of this intel?"

Imatt nodded enthusiastically. "There must've been a secret pact between the two organizations." He looked at the Avengers thoughtfully. "You people are really good at this sort of thing. There's a job waiting for you in the Bureau after this is all over, if you're interested."

Arano chuckled softly. "Our next move is to round up the Disciples. Our link to them is going to be Dar Noil. Let's hope Captain Pana found something for us. We need to locate the other members of this conspiracy."

"Now I know why the Disciples brought in Renz Hanne," muttered Pelos, rubbing his fierce beak. "Anyone could have ripped the victims' eyes out, but it would take a surgeon to remove them intact for a transplant."

"They really thought of everything," mused Cadron. "No wonder we hadn't made more progress on this case. We treated it as a serial killing spree, when it turned out to be something totally different."

"Let's go talk to Pana," said Arano firmly. "I have a bone to pick with Dar Noil."

An hour later, Avengers Team 5 was gathered with Captain Pana and Imatt Deeps in the Avengers' main planning room. They worked on a plan for Dar Noil's capture, and wanted to make sure the trap they planned was airtight. Dar Noil had a lot to answer for, Arano thought grimly, and would pay dearly. Arano found himself subconsciously flexing his fingers into fists, fingernails digging into the fleshy area of his palms as the anticipation built.

"This'll work just fine," agreed Imatt Deeps, tapping his finger on his notes. "With Captain Pana's team shorthanded, they don't have enough personnel for the assault portion of the operation. We can station two of his people at the Southwest corner of Noil's apartment building and two at the Northeast corner. Since there's no underground exit, he won't be able to slip out without being seen."

"Ideally," added Arano, "he won't even have a chance to run. If we can storm his apartment and have the element of surprise on our side, he won't know what hit him." He looked grimly at the Avengers under his command. "We want him alive, so our weapons will be set for stun. But if it turns into a life-threatening situation, don't hesitate to use deadly force. Your life is more important than a traitor's, and I want you all heading home tonight. Let's go."

Arano led a group of grim-faced soldiers out into the deepening night where they boarded a transport. Almost immediately they were underway, the transport's engines humming quietly as it carried its passengers to their long-awaited meeting with the traitor who had betrayed them so many times. Arano sat in silence, hardly noticing Pelos' Tsimian good-luck rituals. Instead, his thoughts were gathered on the present task and all Dar Noil had cost the Coalition. The mission at Codian 3: Noil told Rising Sun an Avengers team was enroute to assassinate General Handron. Fortunately, the leak came too late to stop Arano's team from succeeding, but had nearly prevented their escape. Task Force Blue's rendezvous at the Earth System: the betrayal there had resulted in the destruction of a Coalition task force, as well as an Avengers team. Noil had also planted the virus in the Coalition computer system, wreaking havoc and destroying what was thought to be the only copy of the Disciples murder video. Noil had also caused the original tape to disappear, and the courier in that case had likely been murdered. The list went on and on. Furthermore, almost 50 people had died at the hands of the Disciples, and Noil would wish he was dead before Arano was done with him.

The transport slid to a gentle stop several blocks from Dar Noil's residence, and the occupants stepped out onto the sidewalk. Lon Pana pulled out his FM radio and checked with the teammates he had left behind to confirm Dar Noil hadn't left his apartment. They answered in whispered acknowledgment and confirmed Dar was indeed still home, reporting he was occasionally visible through the windows on the building's thirtieth floor. Lon told them to hold their positions, and the group silently moved out.

Arano led his team forward, sticking to the shadows as he moved. His thoughts were totally focused on the mission, all ideas of vengeance and betrayal safely pushed away to a corner of his mind where it wouldn't disturb him. In the darkness he heard the low chirping of insects, the ones closest to him becoming still at his approach. He sweat freely in the cool but humid night air as his team neared its objective.

When they were within striking distance, Arano signaled a halt. He looked back at Lon Pana and nodded curtly. Lon nodded back and slipped off into the darkness to join his team in their surveillance positions. Arano gave Lon about a minute to get in place, silently counting off the seconds while he studied the building in front of him. It was a fairly standard apartment tower, thirty stories tall, made of steel and concrete. While it was located in a fairly well-to-do section of Immok City, the building had fallen into disrepair, with crumbling mortar in evidence on the lower floors. Arano tried to study the building's higher floors, but the upper reaches were lost in darkness. He drew a calming breath and signaled to his team.

With their senses on full alert, Arano's squad penetrated the front door of the apartment building, Imatt Deeps in tow, while Alyna led her squad in the back door. Moving through the lobby, Arano saw the building only had two lifts, one of them closed for repairs. He forwarded this information to Alyna, telling her to take her squad up the back staircase. Videre laughed wickedly at the thought of the trek up thirty flights of stairs until Arano announced his squad would take the front stairs. Imatt Deep would stay in the lobby until the Avengers notified him they were in position on the thirtieth floor, at which point he would ride up on the lift.

Creeping through the lobby, Arano pursed his lips when he saw the ornate furnishings, depicting a cost and a lifestyle far beyond what Dar Noil should've been able to afford on his Coalition paycheck. Intricately carved statuettes and priceless floor rugs hinted at an air of ostentatiousness that set Arano's teeth on edge. The signs of age on the building's outside weren't in evidence here. He shook his head in disgust, realizing how easily even a routine audit of personnel in sensitive positions would've shown how Dar lived well beyond his means, and might possibly have ended the investigation before so much harm had been done.

Arano led his squad tirelessly, energy fueled by the thought that here, finally, was his chance for a payback. Dar Noil was to be taken alive if possible, but he didn't have to be taken intact. A few bruises and contusions here and there, a couple of broken bones, who knows what could happen, he thought angrily. Dar Noil's acts wouldn't go unpunished, and street justice was one of Arano's favorite options.

Thirty flights of stairs later, Arano's team was in position. They'd made the ascension cautiously, not knowing what to expect, and as a result weren't winded when they reached the top. Arano held a whispered radio conversation with Imatt Deeps, telling him to move up to their location. Lon Pana announced in a terse message that Dar had just been spotted as he walked near an open window in his apartment. Arano's pulse sped up as the anticipation grew, and once again he forced himself to control his breathing, knowing he needed to stay calm if the operation was to go smoothly. He had toyed briefly with the idea of simply knocking on the door and pretending this was a social visit, but he'd quickly discarded the thought. Although Dar had been to a few of Arano's cookouts, Arano had never visited Dar at home before, and he didn't want Dar to think anything might be amiss. He wouldn't give his quarry a chance to destroy evidence or files he might have inside. Arano glanced down the hallway at Alyna's squad, feeling the sweat roll down his sides in the warm, stifling air of the confined hallway. He adjusted his grip on his pistol and edged forward, his squad right behind him.

The door to the lift opened, and Imatt stepped into the hallway, weapon in hand. Arano moved into position in front of the door to Dar's apartment, Alyna at one side and Imatt at the other. The rest of his team faced opposite directions down the hallway, providing security in case any of Dar's cohorts should come along. Arano performed one last check on his weapon, made sure it was set for stun, and looked at his companions. Each gave him a nod, and he sent a prearranged signal to Alyna.

He stepped back from the door, then delivered a powerful kick that smashed the lock from its moorings and sent the door sweeping open in a crash. Instantly, the raiders were inside the apartment, eyes searching the room for their prey. They found him standing near the open balcony door, mouth agape. "What" he began.

"Hands up, Noil," ordered Arano. "You're under arrest for treason and accessory to murder."

For the span of two heartbeats, Dar stood frozen in place. He started to speak, but apparently couldn't find the words. Then, in a blur, he ducked out through the balcony doorway, three stun blasts bouncing harmlessly off the hand-carved wood of the doorframe. With a roar of rage, Arano charged after him and was through the door before Alyna and Imatt could react. He spotted Dar Noil standing on the railing surrounding his balcony. Arano kept his pistol trained on Noil and moved cautiously forward.

"Stay back," warned Dar, his voice nearly hysterical with fear. "I'll jump, and I know you want me alive." Arano paused, and Dar drew himself up as he gained a small measure of confidence. "That's right, you need me alive. I can give you information you never dreamed of. But I want your word I can go free."

"No chance," answered Arano. He slid over to the nearest part of the railing and peered down at the ground, thirty floors below. "It's a long way down, Noil. You'd have a long time to think about it. I think you'd better start talking now before I go with my gut instincts and kill you where you stand."

"Stay back!" shrieked Dar, voice rising an octave as his fear returned to him in a rush. He looked wildly back and forth between Arano, who was standing near the railing, and Alyna and Imatt, who emerged from the door. "This is bigger than you think. This time, the Bromidians are going to win. With the Beacon in the Broms' control, the Coalition doesn't have a chance. There's still a chance for you to change to the winning side."

"I'm already on the winning side," replied Arano menacingly. "Either jump or get off the railing, because, quite frankly, you're beginning to irritate me. If I have to pull you off there"

But he never got the chance to finish. With a maniacal laugh, Dar stepped off the railing into the void and disappeared from view. Arano rushed to where Dar had stood, but could only watch helplessly as Dar accelerated toward the ground far below, his trip ending with a sickening thud. Arano stood motionless for a time, watching Captain Pana's team emerge from hiding to examine the broken body.

He turned to his cohorts and reentered the apartment, biting his lip in disbelief. The other members of his team cautiously entered the apartment at Arano's request, and he tried to force a smile. "Noil has been neutralized," he announced. "He's suffering from Sudden Deceleration Syndrome. It's usually fatal from this height, so we won't be getting any answers from him. Let's toss the apartment before the police show up."

They began a search of the dwelling, looking for

clues to connect Dar with the Disciples of Zhulac and Event Horizon. Minutes later, Arano appeared prophetic when the local police arrived and took charge of Dar's body (which Lon Pana had already searched). They attempted to take over the apartment as a crime scene, but Imatt Deeps overruled them. He told them it was a sensitive Coalition Government-related incident involving top secret information that might have been compromised. He promised to allow them in as soon as the Avengers were finished.

With the police on the site to help with crime scene security, Arano and Lon were able to dedicate their entire teams to a detailed search of the apartment. They were finished within a few hours, having gathered everything related to either the Disciples or the many security breaches suffered by the Coalition. They made a final sweep to ensure they hadn't missed anything.

Finally finished, the group exited the apartment, leaving the scene to be processed by the police officers. Arano, Alyna and Imatt were briefly delayed while they gave statements to the officers' supervisor. Once the formalities were completed, they boarded the waiting transport.

Soon they were gathered in Arano's planning room. With the invaluable aid of Cadron Stenat, they sifted through the evidence. Almost immediately, while his team was still studying the items seized from Dar Noil's apartment, Arano was called out of the room to meet with Laron for a debriefing of their attempt to arrest Dar Noil. When that meeting was done, Laron joined Arano as he returned to his planning room.

By that time, the information had been catalogued

for easier access. One of their biggest surprises was the discovery of a fourth conspirator, located in Immok City. He was a Padian named Caer Uldor, a man Arano told them was wanted in connection with several murders back on Leguin 4. He was an expert in stealth and surveillance who'd become disenchanted with the Padian way of life when, as an adult, he was refused entrance to the Whelen Academy. The fact adults were not accepted into a Daxia class at Whelen Academy seemed to be lost on him.

Another important discovery involved Dar's disclosure of sensitive information about the weapon and shield systems used by the Coalition in their warships. Arano had forwarded it to the Coalition military commanders right away, believing this was how Rising Sun had developed the technology that was the cause of the equipment malfunctions the Coalition experienced. He hoped the information would help engineers run down the virus more quickly, but doubted it. Arano still had reservations about the whole virus idea. Something didn't seem to connect for him, but he couldn't explain why.

What came as no surprise to anyone was the amount of sensitive information Dar had compromised. While it didn't encompass all the security breaches of the past few months, it came close. He certainly had a lot to answer for, and Arano felt cheated Dar had escaped by taking the coward's way out. Arano even entertained the brief thought he might have derived more satisfaction from Dar's death if he had fired his weapon at the plummeting body, hoping to take his life before the sudden stop at the bottom deprived Arano of his vengeance.

At any rate, the worst information leak in Coalition history had been silenced. Congratulations poured in from all over the Coalition military and government offices. Since the primary mission had been to neutralize the threat Dar Noil posed to the Coalition, everyone considered Arano's team successful. Even the Grand High Councilor had sent a moderately congratulatory notice, although Arano detected a strong hint Grand High Councilor Tient begrudged him even this small recognition.

The mission wasn't completed, however. Sure, Dar Noil was dead, and the Disciples of Zhulac had been effectively stopped, but there remained the matter of apprehending the remaining co-conspirators. Of the three other known members of the Disciples, only Caer Uldor remained on Immok. Intelligence agents had determined from information confiscated at Dar's house that Renz Hanne and Pronus had left the system and returned to their homeworld at Lican 2. Officials there weren't sure where the pair had gone upon their arrival, although they believed Pronus would try to seek refuge with the Kian, the secretive Tsimian group so similar to the Daxia of Padian fame.

Caer Uldor was their first objective; he was believed to be in Immok City. All they had to go on was a recent communication sent by Caer Uldor to Dar Noil earlier in the day, sent from Caer's home in Immok City. The difficulty with apprehending Caer was his Padian heritage. His danger sense, while nowhere near as refined as Arano's, would still alert him to an impending attack. For that reason, extravagant planning was needed. Arano already had an idea for the resolution of the problem.

Soon Arano found himself riding in an unmarked transport on his way to Caer's last known location, intent on making an arrest. In answer to a flurry of questions from his teammates and Imatt Deeps, Arano explained the abilities and limits of the Padian danger sense.

"The ability to sense danger, while inherent in Padians, isn't all that sophisticated," he explained. "Caer won't be warned very far in advance of an attack, although the greater the danger, the earlier the warning. It takes a decade of training for the Daxia to have such a well-honed danger sense. In his case, if we approach him to apprehend, not injure him, it'll lessen his ability to sense us. We apprehend people like this on Leguin 4 all the time. We must be prepared to defend ourselves if necessary, but we must put all thoughts of vengeance out of our minds. The more animosity you feel toward him, and the more you dwell upon those feelings, the sooner he will sense our presence. It's similar to predatory animals able to smell fear."

They spent the remaining time studying various photographs of Caer and refining their plan for his apprehension. Their plan had the advantage of simplicity: they would drive right up to his residence and rush the house in an all-out assault. The arrest warrant they'd obtained stated explicitly they weren't required to knock on the door before forcing entry. As Arano had explained, the more time they spent sitting outside his house waiting to make the arrest, the greater his chance of spotting them or receiving a warning from his danger sense. After a short ride, the transport turned onto Caer's street and the driver gave them a warning. The time had arrived.

They approached Caer's home, a tri-level dwelling remarkable only in its lack of outside decoration of any kind. It almost seemed as if the house's owner had gone out of his way to make it inconspicuous. There was a single tree in the front yard, but no shrubberies or flowers. The house itself was painted a plain off-white color, and the shutters were only slightly darker. The thick curtains completely covering the windows hinted whoever lived there enjoyed his privacy.

The transport rolled to a sudden stop in front of Caer Uldor's house. Alyna led her squad in a sprint to cover the rear exit, Imatt Deeps at her side. Arano charged directly for the front door, Laron Alstor and the rest of Arano's squad close at his heels. Laron, Arano noticed with annoyance, giggled almost uncontrollably as he readied the battering ram.

Arano took his position to the right side of the door, and Laron bounded onto the porch. Without slowing, he slammed the ram into the door, swinging the door wide open in a shower of splinters and nearly ripping it from its hinges. Arano was inside in a heartbeat, immediately searching for his quarry. Leaving his squad to pull security in the main entryway, Arano led Laron on a sweep of the house. The tension built with every empty room, every closed door opened to reveal no sign of their target. In a short time, the main floor was cleared and Arano announced he and Laron would check upstairs. In response, Alyna sent Kish and Pelos inside to cover the basement stairs.

With Laron covering him, Arano kicked open the first door at the top of the stairs. Inside he found signs of a hasty packing job, abandoned before it was completed. Using his voice-activated radio, he told his team what he'd found and indicated he believed Caer was still in the house. After a careful but speedy search of the room, he moved on. It took several minutes to finish searching the upstairs area, and still there was no sign of Caer Uldor.

Arano and Laron returned to the main floor and entered the basement stairwell. They edged down the stairs, and Arano cautiously tried to open the door. He wasn't at all surprised when it didn't yield, having been locked from the other side. Laron signaled to Pelos, who brought him the battering ram. Laron seized the ram, gave Arano a slow three-count, and drove the ram sharply into the door. This time, although the door splintered, it didn't open. Arano took hold of one side of the ram, with Laron still on the other. Together, they began a relentless pounding, each earsplitting blast further weakening the door's braces. Finally, the door simply split down the middle. It fell open, one side swinging uselessly on its hinges, the other still held in place by the large iron bar that had held the door shut.

A damp, rotten odor assailed their senses. Arano was taken aback momentarily, but he and Laron pushed forward resolutely. There was only a minimal amount of light in the main room, and they activated their flashlights and continued their search. Arano, gun in his right hand and flashlight in his left, extended his arms with the backs of his hands pressed together to better brace his weapon for firing.

Systematically, they moved down a hallway, searching each room without finding Caer anywhere. Minutes later, with only two doors left to try, Arano felt a sinking feeling in the pit of his stomach realizing Caer might have escaped their dragnet. However, when Arano approached the next door, his danger sense alerted him. Laron had worked with Arano long enough to recognize the warnings by the look on Arano's face, and Arano could tell by Laron's enthusiastic nod this case was no exception. They both knew their target was inside the next room. With Laron in place to cover him, Arano drew back and kicked the door open.

And in a flurry of movement, a man dressed all in black burst from the room, swinging a knife at Arano. Had the object of the attack not been a Padian, and a Daxia besides, the knife strike might well have been lethal. But Arano reacted as only the Daxia can, and in the span of a few heartbeats the man was on the floor, blood flowing freely from his nose, the result of a sharp blow from Arano's free hand. Arano secured the man in handcuffs while Laron watched the room in case anyone else emerged with a vengeance.

After the rest of the house had been cleared, Arano's entire strike team stood assembled in the living room as they interrogated Caer Uldor. Caer had been reticent at first, refusing to answer questions. Imatt Deeps took over the interrogation then, and Caer soon changed his attitude. Arano had seen some skillful interrogations in his time, but he'd never seen anyone on a par with Imatt Deeps. In less than an hour, Caer

Uldor practically begged to tell his story, and Imatt had never laid a hand on him.

At first, what Caer told them merely confirmed what they'd already suspected. Event Horizon operatives had established the four conspirators in Immok City. They were under orders to carry out a campaign of terror and espionage disguised as a serial killer's handiwork. Dar Noil, their point of contact at Coalition Headquarters, picked out the Coalition victims, and made sure no Padian victims were selected. His main criterion was their access to whichever area of information his Event Horizon contacts had asked for. Dar obtained the victim's vital information as well, such as home address and security passwords. If the victim was a random citizen, Caer was responsible for making the choice. Since they had no access to personal information on the random victims, Caer never selected a Human victim for fear he might accidentally select a Padian.

After the victim was chosen, Caer took over for the next phase of the operation. He stalked the victim for several days or even weeks, determining their habits and patterns, and helping to select the site for the attack. Since Caer was adept at surveillance, not one of the victims ever spotted him or even became suspicious. He seemed quite proud of that point, and even managed to slip in a comment about how he still had plans to attend Whelen Academy.

Once Caer conducted his reconnaissance, it was time for the attack. The Tsimians, Renz Hanne and Pronus, were responsible for this final step. Renz Hanne was picked for his medical expertise, and Pronus because he was a cold-blooded killer. Renz and Pronus got together and planned the attack, including the date, the time, and the place. With military precision, they carried out certain aspects of the attack the same way every time. They placed three vehicles in the area as a means of escape. They conducted complete rehearsals of each operation, each time throwing in different twists to account for almost any eventuality.

When the time for the attack arrived, Renz used a motion tracker to make certain no one was around. Once he gave the all-clear, Pronus ambushed and disabled their victim with a stun-stick. When the victim was secured in a spread-eagle position, his clothes were cut off and a gag forced into his mouth. The brand on the chest was applied by heating a metal rune with a small laser. The victim was again hit with the stun-stick, and Renz Hanne removed their eyes. If the victim was with the Coalition, the eyes were preserved in a cold storage unit and eventually transplanted into Dar Noil to enable him to access the targeted top secret files. Renz continued the ritual by removing the victim's tongue. The final touch was the administering of the poison, killing within a few minutes of ingestion. The Tsimians then collected their tools, checked the area with a DNA scanner, and left the scene, taking an indirect route to reach their getaway vehicle of choice.

The system had served them well for over two years, and it was only pressure from their contacts at Event Horizon that had caused their unveiling, according to Caer. He said the Event Horizon agent they usually spoke with told them the Disciples program's usefulness was coming to an end because the Avengers were making too much headway on the case. He wanted Caer and the others to step up the pace of the murders, getting as many more victims as they could before they were discovered. Caer was unhappy their last Human victim had actually turned out to be a Padian. He hadn't even really had a chance to stalk the victim. Caer was not surprised this one had escaped.

Imatt Deeps took custody of Caer, saying he needed information about Event Horizon's contacts within the Biomek company, who would also be held accountable in the Disciples murder spree. As Imatt left with the subdued Caer Uldor, Arano and his team continued scouring the house. The only item of interest they found was a reference to a house nearby, which appeared to have been the residence of the Tsimians, Renz Hanne and Pronus. Arano contacted Coalition Headquarters to brief their chain-of-command, and police officers arrived to secure the scene. Arano led his weary Avengers back to the transport for the short trip to the Tsimians' Immok City home.

The search of that house proved largely uneventful, although it yielded more information. They found the original version of the tape of the Disciples murder at Wolf Lake, the tape that had been stolen from a murdered courier weeks earlier. Their final windfall was a suspected location for Renz Hanne on Lican 2. It wasn't much, but was definitely a place to start their search for the elusive doctor.

As they were leaving, Arano received a priority call from Coalition Military Headquarters. He pulled the Comm from his belt and answered.

"Captain Lakeland, this is Commander Mendarle," began the message. "We just received word of your accomplishments with the fourth Disciples conspirator. Excellent work, Avenger."

"Thank you, Sir," replied Arano. "My team has put in a lot of work on this, and it's quite an indescribable feeling to finally see it all wrapped up. All we have to do is find the Tsimians, and we have a lead on that."

"Actually, it's why I'm calling you. I'm sending you some coordinates on Lican 2. According to an intelligence report we recently received, Renz Hanne was seen at this location. You're to take your team there immediately and apprehend him. Is Major Alstor still with you?"

Arano looked over at Laron, who wore a defeated expression and appeared about to run. The Major sighed, and nodded. "Yes, sir, he's with us. He's been rather useful on this operation." He winked at Laron, who gave him a grateful look. Obviously, the Major feared he would be put back into his office environment.

"That's fine, then. Until further notice, he's assigned to you as an advisor. Cadron Stenat has been pulled from your team. He has shown great promise in his efforts on your behalf and has been placed in an intelligence analyst's position.

"The Tsimians from the Disciples are your top priority right now. Neutralize them as swiftly as possible and get back here. In about two weeks, the fleet will have completed repairs from the battle at the Solarian System with Rising Sun. An attack on Event Horizon should probably come shortly thereafter. Any questions?"

"None here."

"Then get moving. Mendarle, out."

The Avengers completed a few short tasks at the Tsimians' former residence and returned to the transport, which left for the spaceport and their waiting ships. Major Alstor sat with an almost boyish look on his face, anticipation etched into his decidedly boyish Human features. Arano looked at him, rolled his eyes, and laughed.

"Laron, are you going to be okay?"

"Never been better," Laron laughed. "I was afraid I'd be sent back to the paper-pushing office. It just feels great to be back in the field again. I think I'm going to get myself demoted and get back out here permanently."

"How does Mendarle handle it? Look at his history: a decorated infantryman and a skilled pilot; in fact, he holds the record among active pilots for the most confirmed kills in fighter versus fighter combat. I just don't understand how he can stand being cooped up in an office when he could be out here where the action is."

"More money," Laron answered sadly. "He has always been materially oriented, and the promotions bring a higher level of pay. In fact, he hit the proverbial skids a few years back, so he jumped at the chance to take a promotion and its associated pay raise. It was the only way he could avoid bankruptcy."

"Some people just don't understand what this is all about, do they?" wondered Alyna. "They don't see there's more to this job than getting paid."

"And they end up behind a desk," agreed Arano as

the transport slowed to a stop next to their waiting assault class fighters.

CHAPTER FIFTEEN

ARANO EASED THE USCS SPECTER INTO THE DOCKing zone of the spaceport. With a hiss of its repulsors, the Specter settled obediently into its bay. Immediately, the countless dockworkers inevitably found in military spaceports emerged from unseen accessways to tend to the Coalition ship. The flight to Lican 2 had taken about 14 hours, and had provided Arano and Laron sufficient time to devise a basic strategy for the neutralization of the two remaining members of the Disciples of Zhulac. With the apprehension of Caer Uldor and his subsequent confession, the need for capturing the two operatives alive was less urgent. As a result, Arano had announced that weapons would be set to their "kill" settings, and resistance met with lethal force.

As he walked down the ramp from his ship and into the docking bay, Arano glanced to his right, waving at the rest of his team disembarking from the USCS Summerwind. They boarded a nearby transport and were soon on their way to the local security headquarters building for the Coalition forces in the Lican system. The residents of the city, Tsimians for the most part, strolled by without noticing the transport, lost in their own important errands. Arano noticed that, by and large, the city seemed to be a busy but orderly place. Various smells assailed his senses, from the sharp tangy scent of hovercar fuels, to the sweet aromas wafting from the local eateries.

After a ten-minute ride, Arano saw their destination in the distance, clearly marked as a Coalition military facility. There they hoped to secure the assistance, or at least the cooperation, of local law enforcement. They needed them for their two-pronged attack.

Arano's team was going after Renz Hanne with token assistance from the local police. They had a general idea of where to find him, and they'd all seen pictures; Arano had high hopes for a speedy resolution. It was a simple matter of following the trail, and eventually they would succeed.

For Pronus, however, the situation was more complex. Pelos had called in some favors with his Tsimian friends, and they confirmed Pronus had indeed sought refuge at the Kian's main compound. The problem was the Kian were even more secretive than the Daxia, and no one other than members and trainees were allowed inside. In fact, as Pelos had pointed out, anyone who failed the training was executed, preventing the dissemination of information about the Kian by a bitter, washed-out candidate.

Pelos had requested and been granted a meeting with a member of the Kian Council of Elders. Pelos believed the Avengers could convince the Elder Pronus had violated his trust by his acts of murder and mayhem, and the Elder would then turn Pronus over to the Coalition. Failing that, a new plan would have to be devised, but Pelos warned vehemently against using force to take Pronus from the Kian.

Their transport stopped at the security building's main entrance, and they were escorted into a meeting room. While not as well-equipped as their planning room back on Immok, the room at least had a computer terminal, a communications array capable of both local and subspace communications, and a large erasable pad useful for the planning of assaults. Arano looked around the facility, satisfied with their accommodations.

After a brief wait, the door opened to admit an enormous Tsimian concealed within a dark, heavy cloak. Pelos rose and greeted the newcomer in an oddly ritualistic fashion, dropping to one knee and bowing his head.

"Arise, my friend," ordered the Tsimian in a deep, formal voice. "Í am called Storoc. I am the Chief Elder of the Kian. Introduce me to your companions."

"Certainly, my Lord," replied Pelos, obviously familiar with Kian customs. "Our leader is Captain Arano Lakeland, who is also a Daxia." Pelos had made an earlier request to reveal this bit of information, and now Arano understood why. The effect on Storoc was obvious and immediate.

"Greetings, Daxia," he said, and nodded respectfully. "You and I are cousins in ways no family ties could accomplish."

"Thank you, my Lord," replied Arano, taking a cue from Pelos, who continued the introductions. Oddly, Storoc showed little interest in the fact all the soldiers before him were members of the elite Avengers, or even that Laron had been awarded the Golden Cross of Valor, and focused his attention on Arano, the Daxia.

"So, Daxia," growled Storoc, "you believe one of our brothers has committed atrocities against civilization, and you wish to extradite him. Tell me what he has done, and show me your proof. I will take the information before the Council of Elders, and we will have a decision before the sun finds its bed this evening."

Arano looked at Pelos, who nodded encouragingly. The plan called for Pelos to give the presentation, but Storoc's attitude toward Arano had changed that. Arano rose to his feet and nodded respectfully to Storoc.

"Pronus was recruited by members of the terrorist group, Event Horizon. He and three others were members of a conspiracy that worked to give sensitive classified information to Event Horizon, another terrorist group called Rising Sun, and ultimately the Bromidian High Command. Their methods were brutal. They concocted a story of a group of serial killers known as the Disciples of Zhulac."

"I've heard of their attacks," nodded Storoc. "Pronus was involved?"

"Yes, he was, my Lord," continued Arano. "He and another Tsimian, Renz Hanne, committed the actual murders. They saved the eyes from their victims and used them to defeat the retina security scans on our computer systems. That was how they accessed the information they stole. There were other victims, of course, who didn't work for the Coalition. They were murdered simply for the purpose of confusing our hunt. If all of the victims had been Coalition members, we would've found them sooner."

"And these other members of the Disciples," interrupted Storoc. "What of them?"

"One was a Human who worked in our building. He was the one who selected the Coalition victims and obtained necessary information about them. Another was a Padian who conducted the surveillance on the victims prior to the attacks. The Human is dead, and the Padian is in custody, having given a full confession. That leaves only the Tsimians. We will be hunting Renz Hanne ourselves, but as for Pronus"

"You didn't wish to violate the sanctity of our stronghold," finished Storoc. "A wise choice."

Arano presented Storoc with a stack of papers and photographs, detailing the information gathered over the course of the investigation of the forty-eight murders committed by the Disciples. They sat in silence for over an hour while Storoc sorted through the information, looking over some items intently and passing over others with a marked lack of interest. Finally, he gathered the items and rose from his seat, an ominous specter in his massive cloak.

"You have given me much to ponder, Daxia," he announced. "I will take this information to the Council of Elders, and I will return this very day with their response. Ordinarily, even in a case as extreme as this one, I wouldn't harbor much hope he'll be turned over to you, as members of the Kian are always being persecuted by those who don't understand us, or who fear us. But in this case, your word as a Daxia will carry much weight. We know you wouldn't lie, so the matter will be considered more objectively. Until then . . ." Storoc turned and left the room without another word.

The group turned their attention to the matter of locating Renz Hanne. According to the local law enforcement officers, Renz Hanne's family was now aware of his crimes, and had forced him to leave their family estate. Police intelligence reports indicated Renz was trying to keep a low profile by hiding in one of the local homeless shelters, biding his time until he had a chance to make his way to a spaceport. With Coalition authorities watching for him at every spaceport, it wouldn't be an easy task. Arano made the decision to split the teams into their two squads and assign each a number of the shelters. They would keep in touch by the subspace frequency on their Comms since there wasn't any need to hide their presence.

An hour later, Arano led Lain, Videre and Laron into their first shelter. With Laron and Videre covering the exits, Arano and Lain strolled boldly into the building, eyes searching the disheveled faces staring darkly back at them. They'd just missed the serving of the afternoon meal which might have facilitated their search by gathering nearly every resident into a single area. The shelter was not crowded, and a mere fifteen minutes later they'd completed their sweep of the building, coming up empty-handed.

As they left the building, Arano noticed the two undercover Coalition agents who slid quietly into their surveillance positions should Renz enter the building after they left. In this manner they completed the sweep of their targets by nightfall, and had nothing to show for it. When they met with Alyna's squad back at the security building, they sat down to discuss a new plan of action.

They'd barely started when they heard a knock at the door to their meeting room. Lain opened it, and another cloaked Tsimian, presumably a member of the Kian, entered the room wordlessly. He placed a box on the table in front of Arano.

"Daxia," he said, bowing respectfully, "Storoc sends his greetings. He was unavoidably detained by other matters or would have been here himself. The Council of Elders has made their decision, and your answer is contained in the box." Without another word, he left the room.

Arano pulled out a small knife, removed the bindings from the box, and opened the lid apprehensively. He stared wordlessly, shrugged, and sat down. "There's our answer," he told them, gesturing at the box. The Avengers crowded around and peered inside to see Pronus' severed head.

The break Arano needed came early the next morning. Kish was paging through local records, trying to find a location Renz might seek shelter. The business, called Med-Plus, had seemed innocuous enough at first, simply a series of warehouses clustered around an office building. The warehouses were mainly used for the storage of medical supplies, although non-perishable foodstuffs occasionally found their way into the storage units. What caught Kish's keen eye was the notice at the bottom of the company's description, indicating it was actually owned by Biomek.

Considering that company's involvement with Event Horizon and, indirectly, the Disciples, it seemed a likely place to continue their search.

Arano grumbled during the trip to the warehouses. He doubted the family had intentionally deceived the authorities, but believed Renz himself had probably misled them when he left their estate. Hopefully, if Renz was sheltered by Med-Plus, no one from that company had thought to stake out the shelters Arano and his friends had searched the day before. If they had, Renz would be alerted and less likely to make a mistake and give away his position.

There were four buildings to check, so Arano devised a different strategy. While he and Pelos checked each building, the rest of the team would pull security outside, making sure Renz didn't try to sneak past them. It would take longer, but it was better to waste time than allow their quarry to escape. Having Pelos with him was an added bonus; Pelos' Tsimian heritage made it easier for him to recognize Renz Hanne, also a Tsimian.

They gave their teammates enough time to settle into their positions before Arano and Pelos entered the first warehouse. Wearing the long coats and hardhats of licensed inspectors, they strode purposefully through the structure, seeming to take meticulous note of every detail of the warehouse's operation and pointing out safety hazards to nearby employees. As they'd expected, the workers gave them a fairly wide berth, none of them willing to have to take bad news to the supervisory staff.

This particular building had four floors, but was fairly easy to search because most of the floor plan was open. The crates weren't stacked very high, and Arano could easily see over the top of them. Although many of the employees cast nervous glances in their direction, Arano saw nothing out of the ordinary that led him to believe their quarry had spotted them. There were few doors in the building, leaving few hiding places for the fugitive. Of course, thought Arano glumly, it made the building less likely to be Renz's hiding place. Nonetheless, he and Pelos completed the search and in about an hour concluded Renz wasn't inside, and moved on to the second building.

The second warehouse was approximately the same size as the previous building, and upon entering noticed the floor plan was similar. Again taking up their guise of Coalition inspectors, Arano and Pelos moved with confidence among the employees, who cast only occasional glances in their direction. The primary difference was that the previous warehouse had contained primarily medical computers, and this one was predominantly stocked with medical supplies. They cleared the first two floors without incident.

They reached the third level, a cavernous room with several pillars to support the building's weight. Crossing the floor, Arano glanced into the far corner and noticed a Tsimian who appeared to be going out of his way to hide his face from the "inspectors". The brief glimpse alerted Arano he might've found their prey. He casually motioned to Pelos, and the two crossed the room, walking directly toward the cowering Tsimian.

The Tsimian shouted a startled oath, threw down his tools, and ran for the stairs. Abandoning their roles as simple inspectors, the Avengers raced after him, and Pelos radioed the others they were in pursuit of a possible suspect. Arano could hear Alyna directing the rest, keeping surveillance in place while providing assistance in the chase.

Arano entered the stairwell breathlessly and paused to take in the situation. A noise overhead caught his attention, and he saw a flash of movement on the stairs above him. Together he and Pelos flew up the steps, closing the gap with their quarry.

Arano heard the door above him slam shut, and his fears were confirmed when they reached the top of the stairs: the door was locked from the outside. Arano looked questioningly at Pelos, who nodded and took a few steps back. Pelos took several deep breaths and charged into the door, his massive strength blasting it from its hinges. Stepping out onto the roof, Arano heard a terrified cry, pulled out his laser pistol and turned to confront the Tsimian.

"It's over, Hanne," Arano told him. "The others are either dead or in custody. Why don't you make it easy on yourself and come quietly?"

"W-w-what?" asked the cowering man before him. "What're you talking about?"

Arano peered more closely at him, doubt clouding his thoughts.

"That's not him," confirmed Pelos. "He looks pretty similar, but that's not Renz Hanne." He pulled out his Comm, notifying the others about the situation and putting them back in their positions.

Arano took a step closer to the now-collapsed Tsimian. "Who are you, and why did you run from us?"

"Taron Accos," said the trembling Tsimian. "You

aren't with Sharun?"

Arano shook his head. "Who is Sharun?"

"A local moneylender. I needed cash in a hurry, and he was the only one I could turn to. I'm behind in my payments, and his hit teams are usually Humans or Tsimians. I thought you were here to kill me. You . . . you aren't inspectors?"

"Don't worry about it," Arano told him coldly. "Go back to work. Forget you saw us." Shaking his head in disgust, Arano turned and went back inside the warehouse.

Since their short chase had taken them out of the building, they had to start the search from scratch, this time from the top down. When they were back on the third floor, there were stares from the people working in the area who had seen them run outside, but their fear of inspectors prevented a confrontation. After a meticulous search, the second warehouse was cleared.

They entered the third building, which had smaller floors than the other two buildings, but six levels and many more doors. The open areas were stacked to the ceiling with crates, many labels warning of dangerous chemicals. Arano was not happy about the change of scenery, and was especially nervous about the tighter quarters. The building could prove to be a labyrinth, he thought, and knew the search would take longer. They'd examined perhaps half the first floor when a supervisor confronted them.

"Who are you, and what do you want?" demanded the short but stocky Tsimian, red armband denoting his rank, his beak clicking in anger.

"Inspectors from the Coalition Bureau of Storage

and Shipping," answered Arano with a pious sniff.

"And I assume you have identification to prove it?"

Arano and Pelos pointed to the ID badges pinned to their shirts, partially hidden by their long coats. The supervisor paled slightly, and backed away from the confrontation. The formerly haughty Tsimian actually seemed to shrink in height as he looked for a way out of the predicament. Sensing his advantage, Arano pressed the issue.

"Where's your office?" he asked arrogantly, leaning forward with his hands on his hips. The now-terrified Tsimian could only point to a small room in the nearest corner.

"We will see you there in two hours," stated Arano matter-of-factly, stabbing a finger at the trembling worker. "You've interfered with our inspection of this facility, and we'll want to know why. Usually, it means you have something to hide. I suggest you return to your office and get your paperwork together. We're going to check your records for the last six months. I hope, for your sake, that everything is in order."

The thinly veiled threat was more than the supervisor could handle. He turned, coughed, and practically flew to his office where he immediately tore into his filing cabinet. Arano chuckled, and he and Pelos moved on. Apparently, word of event went ahead of them, because there were no further incidents, and when Arano and Pelos were in the area, the supervisory staff had their noses buried in their work.

Searching the building took them twice as long as the other warehouses, but they finally reached the top floor. Arano retrieved his Comm, notifying Alyna their search was nearly complete and she should prepare to shift the surveillance teams one last time. About to terminate the conversation, he was interrupted by a nudge from Pelos.

"Viper!" hissed Pelos. "There he is! The Tsimian in the corner wearing the safety glasses and the blue lab coat. That's Renz Hanne!"

Arano followed Pelos' gaze to a Tsimian who appeared to be looking over some new construction plans, pointing out flaws to the smaller Tsimian who stood behind him, rubbing his beak and shaking his head in obvious irritation. The Avengers spread out and closed the distance between themselves and the last member of the Disciples of Zhulac. They were within thirty feet when their target looked up from his work.

Arano never knew what had tipped Renz off. Whether he read it in their eyes, or whether it was intuition, Renz instantly knew he was in trouble. With a speed born of anger and fear, he leapt away and ran for the stairway. Arano was closest, and swiftly caught up with him. In desperation, Renz pulled a pistol from a pocket in his cloak and fired at his antagonists. The Avengers were forced to dive for cover while Renz kept running.

One shot from Hanne's pistol struck a pallet of flammable liquids, and the resulting explosion was an inferno within moments. Shouts of panic arose from the warehouse workers, and fire alarms added to the din in the smoky room. Arano staggered back to his feet, the ringing in his ears making his head feel stuffy. Seeing Pelos resume the chase, Arano returned his attention to finding Renz. He caught a fleeting glimpse of the fugitive as he ducked through an open doorway and into the waiting stairway.

"Alyna!" Arano called into his Comm. "Target has been acquired, and he's escaping. We have a fire on the top floor, and he's in a crowd of employees heading down a staircase, southwest corner of the building. Subject is wearing a blue laboratory coat, black pants, and safety glasses. He's armed, so shoot to kill!"

"We're on it!" came the excited reply. As he replaced his Comm on his belt, Arano heard Alyna direct the other Avengers to close in on the location as she tried to cover all exits from the building. Gaining the entrance to the stairway, Arano spotted Renz in the crowd less than two floors below him. Arano tried to push his way through the crowd, but the workers were in a near state of panic, and his efforts were fruitless. He was forced to move with the crowd down the first flight of stairs until he managed to work his way over to the outside wall. When he reached the second floor, he smashed the window and climbed out on the narrow ledge outside. As he expected, a canopy covered the entrance twenty feet below. With only a moment's hesitation, he stepped off the ledge.

His feeling of exhilaration was short lived, and the sudden stop on the narrow canopy was more violent than he had expected. He lay motionless until the breath returned to his body before he rolled off the tarp, landing lightly on his feet. He couldn't see his quarry, but knew he had to be close; Renz would be hard-pressed to get past the perimeter of Avengers, even with the crowd.

Then his heart went to his toes. Right inside the doorway lay Renz Hanne's lab coat and safety glasses. Without the identifiers, Renz stood a good chance of slipping out undetected in the mob. Arano called his teammates on the Comm and alerted them to the latest development. He kicked the safety glasses savagely, and he was considering his next move when a call came in from Laron.

"Viper, this is Laron. One Tsimian has broken away from the main group and is running due south. I'm on the second floor of another building, so I'll try to maintain visual contact until you or Pelos get close."

"On my way!" Arano yelled, sprinting off at top speed, Pelos only a step or two behind. Arano soon spotted the Tsimian Laron had located, and knew once again he was hot on the trail. He notified his team without stopping, and settled into a steady pace, endurance currently more important than speed.

Renz glanced back, screamed in anger, and pulled out a laser pistol. He fired at his pursuers, shots flying erratically past his targets. Arano was concerned about innocent people getting hit by stray laser fire, but there was nothing he could do about it. Letting Renz go free was not an option.

Arano again pulled out his Comm. "Lain, how close are you? I'm at Fifth and Mirshat, still southbound."

"I'm about four blocks behind you," came the breathless reply. "This rifle is slowing me down."

"Get up here as quickly as you can," ordered Arano. "He's firing at us, and someone is going to get hurt. We're coming out of the tall buildings now, so you should be able to get a clear shot with your rifle."

"Got it." Lain replied simply.

The chase continued. Arano watched with satisfaction when Renz slowed and even seemed to stagger at times. Exhaustion was taking its toll at last. But Arano's excitement turned to dread when the unthinkable happened.

Driven to the point of exhaustion, Renz stopped at an intersection about a block ahead of Arano. Without hesitating, Renz shot the driver of a nearby wheeled vehicle, threw the driver's body in the street, and jumped inside. Arano procured his vehicle more gently, simply stopping and commandeering it. The owner wasn't excited about the prospect, but the look on Arano's face and the laser pistol in his hand were enough to convince him. As Arano got behind the wheel, Pelos jumped in beside him.

They sped off in pursuit, dodging in and out of traffic. Arano concentrated on driving while Pelos called out their location and direction on the radio. Arano knew Alyna would be in contact with the police by now; Arano had forewarned them about their operation. Before long, police vehicles would be involved in the pursuit, hopefully bringing the chase to a screeching halt. With the heavy afternoon traffic, Arano didn't want the dangerous race to go on any longer than necessary.

As they flew down a busy street, Arano looked ahead and saw traffic at the next intersection was congested, and neither vehicle would be able to get through. There was a raised median in the middle of the road and a curb to the right, and nowhere for Renz Hanne to go. Arano grunted in frustration, however, when Renz managed to drive his vehicle up over the median, through oncoming traffic, and back onto his side of the road. Arano followed,and the chase was on again.

About a kilometer ahead, the police had set up a roadblock. Arano smiled grimly when he saw the flashing lights on the cars blocking the road, and loosened his pistol in its holster. Renz slowed his vehicle, and Arano assumed he wasn't sure what to do next. Suddenly he veered left, drove over another curb, smashed through a police vehicle, and kept going on the wrong side of the road.

Arano had no choice but to follow him, adrenaline pumping as he faced oncoming traffic. Renz drove like a madman, not moving for vehicles heading directly at him, the drivers finally veering aside at the last minute to avoid a collision. Arano, his pulse pounding and his white-knuckled hands glued to the steering controls, dodged artfully through the chaos-filled roadway.

"I hate to take this risk," growled Arano, "but he's going to end up killing someone. Pelos, see if you can get a clean shot and disable that vehicle."

"Okay. It would be easier if you had stolen a hovercar instead of something with wheels."

"Next time, you steal the car," replied Arano calmly. Pelos grinned at him and leaned out the window, trying to take aim. But with their vehicle bouncing around as Arano darted from lane to lane to avoid oncoming traffic, Pelos found aiming to be nearly impossible.

At last, however, luck went their way. Renz turned into a small business park where there was less traffic.

Arano sped up, closing the distance to approximately ten meters. Pelos' first two shots were off their mark, but the third caught a rear tire, which exploded in a shower of smoke and rubber. Renz slowed, but didn't stop. A steady rain started to fall, making the chase even more perilous.

Renz made another quick turn, hampered by the loss of a rear tire and the wet pavement, and suddenly the combatants found themselves on a dead-end street. Pelos grabbed the Comm and announced the chase would soon revert to a foot pursuit. But once again, Renz showed ingenuity. He blasted through a warehouse's closed garage door and into a large utility bay. The two vehicles roared across the cavernous floor, and sparks flew from Renz' damaged tire as startled workers dove for cover. Pelos had to discontinue shooting, fearing he might hit a bystander. Moments later, they crashed through another garage door, bumped across a grassy field and into a nearby residential area.

Finally, with an explosion of steam, Renz's vehicle announced it had all it could take. When it ground to a halt, Renz leapt out and ran between two houses where he entered a stand of trees. Arano and Pelos cautiously approached, staying behind cover. Ordinarily they'd keep their distance, surround the trees, and wait for Renz to come to them, but there wasn't time. Before there were enough people to surround the trees, Renz could escape unseen. As they drew closer, shots rang out from the woods, coming uncomfortably close.

"Damn," swore Arano. "Okay, Pelos, you pin him

down from here. I'm going to flank him. We're definitely not going to be able to take this one alive."

Arano sped off to the left as Pelos fired wildly into the trees to keep Renz from taking an aimed shot. Arano dove behind a storage shed, rolled to his feet, and looked around. He stood next to a jumble of empty wooden crates, and stacked them to a height of roughly two meters, climbed to the top, and dragged himself onto the roof of the shed. Despite Pelos's cover fire, Arano knew Renz would keep a watchful eye on the storage shed at ground level, waiting for Arano to look around one side or the other. He hoped Renz wouldn't look up.

Arano crawled to the edge of the roof facing the firefight and peered out at the woods. It only took him a few moments to spot his opponent, crouched behind a large tree stump. He briefly toyed with the idea of waiting for Lain and his rifle, but feared Renz might shoot Pelos in the meantime. That left him with only one viable option.

He drew his laser pistol, braced it on the roof of the shed, and sighted in on Renz Hanne's position. At the moment, Renz was concealed by the undergrowth around him, so Arano took a steadying breath and waited. His patience was rewarded moments later when Renz rose to take an aimed shot at Pelos. From fifty meters away, Arano's pistol flashed its deadly laser fire, and Renz dropped lifeless to the ground, smoke rising from the gaping wound in the side of his head.

Gathered once more in the security building, the Avengers held a mission debriefing with Commander Mendarle via subspace radio. The Commander seemed extremely pleased with the outcome of the mission. He actually laughed when he heard both Tsimian Disciples had been killed. Arano wasn't sure how to take that, although he was glad his commanding officer could relax in these stressful and dangerous times.

Following the debriefing, the Commander became serious again. He said he'd come into some vital information, and another mission for Avengers Team 5 had already been arranged.

"This mission is top secret, involving highly sensitive information," he told them. "I can't send you this over the subspace channel since it's possible our codes are no longer secure, considering Dar Noil's unauthorized computer access. We can't risk having the wrong people intercept this message."

"A reasonable precaution, sir," agreed Laron.

"For that reason, you'll travel to the Earth system where you'll meet with Task Force Green. They're already patrolling that system, and they're aware you're on your way. Colonel Vines will rendezvous with you on the USCS Valiant, where you'll receive your mission briefing. Major Alstor will remain attached to you as an advisor. I can't stress enough the importance of this mission. Your success can mean the swift destruction of Event Horizon. Your failure means a protracted war. Commander Mendarle, out."

Arano turned to his companions. "While we head to the transports, I want to share with you some information that just arrived from a friend of mine who's with the Immok City Police Department. They located an apartment Pronus and Renz Hanne were using as a makeshift office for the duration of the Disciples murders. They located all the trappings used by the killers: the rune, the laser for heating it up, a stun stick, a motion tracker, a DNA scanner, and the assorted stakes and ropes they used. In Pronus' bedroom, they found the tongues of all the victims. It seems, like almost all serial killers, he kept a trophy from his victims to help him relive the moment of the kill. By the way, the police department also sends their congratulations and their thanks."

"I'm just glad it's all finally over," mused Alyna. "People were dying, and we were standing around feeling useless."

An hour later, Arano found himself in the spaceport hanger as his weary team boarded their ships for some much-needed rest while taking the long rift-drive jump to the Earth System. They received their clearance from the spaceport, and two Assault Class fighters launched toward the heavens.

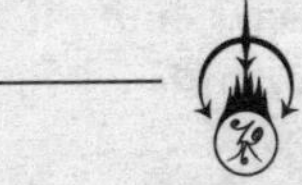

The flight from the Lican System to the Earth System took an entire day, and was the longest single jump that Rift Drives were capable of making. Arano spent the time rehashing old times with Laron. The friends had spent eight years together, most of that time in the Avengers. Although they still worked together, Laron's promotion kept him away, and the two spent less and less time together. Videre eventually complained the story Arano or Laron was telling had been told a dozen times before, but his half-hearted complaints did nothing to dampen the spirited conversation.

When they docked with the USCS Valiant, Arano realized, a bit guiltily, he hadn't even thought of Alyna during the trip. He acknowledged her with a smile when the squads from Avengers Team 5 filed into a nearby meeting room. Moments later, a stern but proud-looking Human entered. His enormous collection of medals gleamed brightly on his chest, and he carried himself with the self-confident gait shared by those who have faced the trials of combat and lived to tell about it.

"I'm Colonel John Vines," he announced as the group snapped to attention. "Take your seats. I prefer my meetings to be a bit more informal when the pencil-pushing desk jockeys aren't around." Arano smiled at the comment.

He began by introducing himself, gave a quick background of his military history and said he'd spent time in the parachute infantry, and later, commanding frigates. Arano introduced himself and his teammates, and Colonel Vines insisted on learning their backgrounds, as well.

"Here's what we have for you. In the Selpan System, at Selpan 4, we've discovered a secret Event Horizon outpost. It's a large station, as military bases go, but that's because Event Horizon sends its command staff there for R & R. There's an experimental, and highly illegal, weather control system set up outside the base on a hilltop. It allows them to give the officers perfect weather for every visit, and they grow crops at a tremendous rate.

"The base is also used as an Event Horizon Command and Control center. Coded messages are relayed to their outlying stations. The loss of this center would be a major blow to their forces. Additionally, we believe information can be found there concerning the President, and maybe even the location of Event Horizon's homeworld.

"Keep in mind, there's also a civilian population on Selpan 4. They aren't active members of Event Horizon, but they tend to support them, both financially and by providing them with equipment and supplies. If you're compromised, don't count on the civilians to help you. There are a few Coalition spies hidden in the civilian ranks, which is where our information comes from. They can help you, if you can find them. I'm giving each of you a packet with a series of recognition signs and passwords in case you need to make contact with an agent.

"Your mission is to enter the system in a civilian ship and destroy the Command Center. If you can obtain information from the center's computers before you destroy the place, great, but your primary mission is to destroy the facility. If necessary, you have permission from the Avengers Command Staff to destroy the weather control device as a means of distracting their soldiers from your true objective. Be advised, however, this will likely cause a massive weather disruption with destructive storms of unbelievable strength striking all over the planet. I'm not trying to talk you out of destroying the device; far from it, I believe you should destroy it. I just want you to be prepared for the aftermath.

"We have a ship waiting for you at docking port one-one-five. It's an Eagle Class freighter, loaded with medical supplies. It already has a shipping manifest and a due date at Antor, a civilian city adjacent to the base. From there, you'll have a seventeen-hour jump to the Selpan system. Land with the ship, disperse into the city with the crew, and conduct your mission. In the confusion afterward, you should be able to re-board your freighter and leave the way you came in. Any questions?"

There were none, and Colonel Vines gave the Avengers a vicious grin. "Give 'em hell!" he told them.

CHAPTER SIXTEEN

THE FREIGHTER DROPPED OUT OF ITS ARTIFICIAL wormhole in the Selpan System, cruising to the Antor spaceport right on schedule. They spent the first hour getting clearance from the port's security detachment to unload the cargo, and then the heavy work began. Arano's team spent the next few hours with the crew of the freighter, unloading the medical supplies destined for the nearby Event Horizon Base. Videre was inclined to grumble loudly about the work, and Arano realized Videre's grumbling fit the part they were trying to play. But it began to grate on his nerves. Finally, with the work finished, they headed for the bars, seemingly ready for an evening of carousing.

They divided into two groups. Alyna took her squad and headed into the forest surrounding the town, where they were to destroy the Selpan Weather Control Device. Arano took his squad and Laron toward the military base. Theirs was the main objective: the destruction of Event Horizon's command and control center.

After a brief, casual stroll, they reached the section of Antor frequented by members of Event Horizon's military. This area of town bordered the military base, and in fact was centered on the main gate. Soldiers and terrorists from Event Horizon issued through the gate and into the city in search of all manner of services. Everything could be found in town, from haircuts and uniforms to alcohol and other vices. Anyone with an eye for business and a commodity he could sell to a soldier had set up shop, and business was booming.

The streets were fairly clean, and the outsides of the buildings were well-kept. Soldiers and civilians alike bustled through the busy thoroughfares, filling the sidewalks to overflowing. To Arano's right, he saw a uniformed Event Horizon soldier holding open a door for an elderly woman, and Arano puzzled over the duplicity of that simple act. Here was a man who, on this world, showed respect for his elders, but had the same woman lived on Immok, or any other Coalition world, the same soldier would kill her without hesitation. Arano shook off that line of thinking, knowing it would accomplish nothing.

It took the group about an hour to locate a uniform servicing shop that was closed for the weekend. Arano posted his squad at likely locations near the back door as lookouts. Videre casually approached the back door, pulled a small tool from his pocket, and went to work on the lock. With the confidence of a trained professional, Videre picked the lock and was inside. Arano lost sight of Videre once he slipped into the darkened interior of the store, but knew Videre was working on the computer controlling the alarm. Shortly, Videre poked his head out the door, gave the thumbs-up, and he ducked back inside. He soon exited the building carrying a sack containing four Event Horizon uniforms.

Their next stop was a nearby motel, where they rented a room. It would serve as their base of operations, as well as provide them with a place to wait for Alyna's squad to complete their task. Arano checked his watch and saw they still had several hours to wait before the destruction of the weather control device. Leaving their new uniforms in the room, they broke up into two groups to conduct further reconnaissance of the border area between the city and the base. Arano and Laron headed south along the outer wall of the military installation, while Lain and Videre headed north.

Alyna led Pelos and Kish out of town, then turned and left the road, plunging into the forest. Using their satellite map of the area, she'd plotted several landmarks to guide her from their present location to the hilltop with the weather control device. It was located about a mile north of the city, but she'd led her squad out of town to the southwest, planning to circle around in an effort to maintain the element of surprise. She found it eerie to check her intelligence report and know at any given time what the weather would be like. In fact, a light shower was scheduled for that evening, and she planned to use it to her advantage. Her squad would hit the small guard outpost just after midnight, about 30 minutes after the rain. She hoped that complacency, coupled with the inclement weather, would make the guards less alert.

She got her bearings on the map and used her compass to set their direction of travel. With Pelos and Kish slightly behind her and to either side, she started out, and made for their first waypoint. The trees were similar to pine, and the wind whispered endlessly through the boughs. While the foliage in the tops of the trees was crowded tightly together, the slender trunks were spaced far enough apart to allow the small group to pass easily through the forest. The ground was covered with a layer of fallen needles, muffling the sound of their passage.

After about two hours of walking, they found their destination, a communications repeater tower. While Pelos and Alyna kept watch, Kish set demolition charges on the tower's support legs. They would detonate them when they set off the charges that would destroy the weather control device. From there they turned north and followed a firebreak toward their next stop, a small forest ranger outpost.

Alyna kept her team out of sight, about fifteen meters inside the wood line, avoiding detection but close enough to see the road. The traveling was more difficult, this part of the forest covered with pockets of a springy thorn bush which, when pushed aside, sprung stubbornly back into place. The sweet smell of wildflowers filled the air as Alyna pushed resolutely onward.

After another hour, they heard voices mingled with the tramp of booted feet. All three took cover and drew their weapons. Soon, the patrol came into view, walking boldly down the middle of the firebreak. They obviously didn't expect any trouble, laughing and joking among themselves, their weapons slung, paying no particular attention to their surroundings. As swiftly as they'd appeared, the soldiers disappeared into the distance, totally unaware of the soldiers hidden in the nearby thicket.

When the ranger's outpost came into sight, Alyna pulled her squad a short distance off to the east, and called a temporary halt. She allowed them a ten-minute rest, then she motioned them back to their feet.

The next leg of the trip took them considerably longer, their route taking them through hilly terrain covered with giant trees that blocked their view of the setting sun. The forest teemed with wildlife, mostly timid creatures that scattered into the underbrush at their approach.

Alyna glanced at her watch and checked the time against her planned timetable. It appeared they would reach their third checkpoint right on time. Almost as an afterthought, she checked the time schedule for the weather; the sky was already starting to cloud over in preparation for the evening's scheduled rainfall.

At length they reached their next stop, a noisy brook cutting a narrow trail through the ancient forest. They paused to fill their water bottles, then they pulled back into the trees a for another break. They had only another three kilometers to travel before they reached their objective, and Alyna wanted her team rested and ready. Settling back against an enormous tree, she gazed off into the gathering mist.

Arano and Laron emerged from the restaurant where they'd just eaten a late dinner. They continued to scout the town, studying the soldiers to learn their mannerisms and customs. In a couple of hours, they would pose as Event Horizon soldiers, and wanted to look the part. Videre had taken a special delight in picking out their stolen uniforms by rank, as well as by size. He'd appointed himself as a Sergeant First Class and Lain as a Sergeant, while Arano and Laron were given the rank of Corporal. Videre enjoyed outranking his superior officers, if only for a few hours.

Two hours before midnight, Arano and Laron retraced their steps to the motel. Groups of drunken revelers staggered through the streets, some singing in loud voices notably off-key. There were members of all races, even, to Arano's extreme distaste, a disproportionate number of Bromidians. The hate built within him, and he frequently found his hand subconsciously reaching for his knife.

Ladies of the evening called out to them as they passed, some of the more desperate ones showing a sample of their wares. The Avengers feigned interest but lamented they had to get back to the base. On the sidewalk in front of them, a soldier lay sprawled in an intoxicated stupor, oblivious to his surroundings. They stepped over the unconscious soldier, and continued on their way.

Arano and Laron returned to their room and changed into their Event Horizon uniforms. Arano wrinkled his nose in distaste at the offensive odors permeating their room, and found himself wishing they'd been a bit more discriminating when choosing their base of operations. As they finished, Lain and Videre also returned, and once everyone was dressed they sat down to compare notes and discuss their strategy. Arano and Laron had found no surprises in their area, but Lain and Videre had run across an interesting facility in one of the local bars.

"At first," explained Lain, "We thought the soldiers going into the back room were simply seeking . . . less than legal diversions. Later, we noticed that the soldiers going in weren't the soldiers coming out. It seems they have a secret entrance to the base in the back room of the bar. Sometimes soldiers have trouble arranging for a pass into the city, so they come through this bar. All you need is enough money and you can slip right through, no questions asked."

"But Lain," argued Arano, scratching his head. "I didn't bring that much Event Horizon currency along. Where do we get the money?"

"You're forgetting your place, Corporal," laughed Videre with a grin. "When I borrowed those uniforms, I also took out a small loan from the store. It seems the owner doesn't much trust banks and he kept a large amount of cash in a safe in the office. I didn't take it all, of course, but I grabbed enough to get us in through that secret gate. Back out again as well, if we can arrange it."

"Okay, 'Sergeant'," said Arano, rolling his eyes. "Looks like the 'backdoor' will be our way in. We get inside, get as close to the command center as we can, and when they start heading out in response to Alyna's attack, we blow the place. Questions?"

There were none, and Arano continued. "With

Sergeant Videre's permission, we can get started."

As he and his squad checked over their uniforms one last time, Arano mentally reviewed what he knew about Event Horizon. Following the formation of the United Systems Coalition in 2104, there was some dissension among the various races. The people opposed to the Coalition believed there was no need for such a government in space, and some were violently opposed to the idea. Eventually, a resistance group was formed with the intention of crushing the Coalition and bringing anarchy to the outlying systems.

Ironically, this anarchic group was ruled with an iron fist. No questioning of authority was allowed. The current leader, Tebran Mas, instituted public floggings for rule violators.

For decades, this group haphazardly attacked USC targets, and were so ineffective they were little more than an annoyance. But, around 2195, something changed. They had ships, they had technology, and they had organization. It was believed they were receiving help from somewhere, but no one knew the source. Now, he thought, all things considered, it was fairly obvious the Bromidians had a hand in their evolution.

Despite the possibility of overstating the obvious, Arano added one last bit of instruction. "While we're inside their compound, we must follow military doctrine to the letter. Videre will march us in formation everywhere we go, unless emergency circumstances dictate otherwise. Videre, we're counting on you to lead us there."

Their plans finalized, the group went through their equipment, making sure all was in working order. Lain paid special attention to the compact but extremely powerful "C-12" explosives he would use to demolish the command and control center. Next, he checked the detonators to be certain that they were in working order, then packed everything away. In order to look inconspicuous, the group traveled as light as possible and carried their smaller, less powerful laser pistols, more easily concealed within their clothing. At last, with equipment stowed in their backpacks, the four warriors departed their room.

Following Videre's lead, the Avengers retraced their steps to the nearby bar where Videre and Lain had found an alternate entrance to the Event Horizon Base. Posing as soldiers, they strode confidently into the bar, glancing disinterestedly at the patrons. The lighting was low, which suited Arano just fine. With a tip to the bartender, they were ushered without ceremony into a nondescript back room, and another healthy bribe bought them entrance to the base. The door slid shut with a grating sound that set Arano's teeth on edge, and they stepped out into the quiet, orderly streets of the military post.

The group formed up, Videre leading them, and with military precision marched down the neatly arranged streets, taking an indirect route to their destination. A light rain fell, and it occurred to Arano the rain had been indicated on his mission briefing sheet. The dampened streets cast eerie reflections back at the small group as they moved purposefully through the enemy stronghold.

Once within sight of the command center, they circled once to determine their best line of approach and the best place to hide. They stopped outside a storage building, and Videre put on a show of issuing blistering ultimatums to "his" soldiers before leading them inside. The building was deserted, so they set up their base of operations and established a guard detail. Arano checked his watch and saw they had less than an hour before Alyna's midnight attack. He chuckled to himself when he remembered the watch was given to him by a member of Transcorp, a company run by Event Horizon operatives. He turned and joined his team as they waited for the attack on the command center.

The time had come for the next phase of Alyna's task. While Pelos scooped up piles of moist soil, Kish started a meticulous examination of Alyna's uniform. At last, mind made up, Kish ripped Alyna's clothing around her feet, knees, and neck. Taking the dirt from Pelos, she smeared Alyna's uniform, face, and hands, giving her a haggard, disheveled look. Satisfied, the three took up their vigil, watching the surrounding trees for signs of the enemy.

"It's time," Alyna whispered. Without hesitation, Marnian and Kish stood and gathered their equipment, and moments later were ready to move. Alyna used her compass to set a heading toward their final destination and they moved out in single file, Alyna in the lead, followed by Kish, with Pelos bringing up the rear. They slipped through the night, gliding through the trees like ghosts. Alyna was glad she'd brought her team to their release point as early as she had. They were far enough from their objective to avoid detection by Event Horizon patrols, but close enough she was able to give her team an hour's rest before the assault.

The terrain sloped more steeply, slowing their pace as they neared their objective. They passed a bubbling, frigid pool of water released from an underground spring, paused for a refreshingly cool drink, refilled their containers, and moved on.

About fifty meters further up the slope, they reached the crest of the hill. From there they could see across a draw to the larger hill where the weather control device was located. In fact, from her vantage point, Alyna saw the guard outpost that stood watch over a nearby cave entrance. Within the cave was the weather control device's computer, a massive collection of electronics capable of unfathomable levels of computations. Atop the hill was a sensor array linked to a satellite relay system, which detected existing weather patterns and enabled the creation of new weather conditions.

Alyna turned to her teammates, indicated they would split up here, and moved on alone. At first, she continued to move stealthily, avoiding a two-man patrol that casually strolled by along a forest road. The scheduled rainfall began right on time, a slow, steady rain that effectively soaked Alyna to the bone. While the rain added to her disguise, making her appear even more worn and beaten, she shivered with the cold. With her breath steaming in the cool evening air, she found herself wishing she had brought rain gear.

When she was perhaps fifty meters from the guard

outpost, she dropped to the ground and noisily dragged herself through the underbrush, moaning theatrically. Thorns dug into her body, her torn uniform exposing the soft skin of her arms and legs to the ravages of the underbrush.

She had dragged herself over halfway to the guard outpost and was frustrated at the guards' incompetence, when she was finally spotted. All four guards emerged, gathering around her in a circle. Feigning a struggle to reach her feet, Alyna smiled inwardly. With the exception of the patrol she'd passed in the woods on her way in, she had the attention of the entire guard retinue. All the guards, that was, as long as their intelligence reports were correct. According to their data, the overconfident Event Horizon leadership felt their system was secure and impenetrable, and the guard post was more a symbolic gesture than an actual security force.

One man, apparently the leader, sauntered up to Alyna with a leering grin. "Who are you, and where did you come from?" he demanded.

"My name is Maleen, and my ship crashed several kilometers west of here. I. . .I was the only survivor. All my friends . . ." she broke off, sobs wracking her body. She glanced up and saw the look in her captors' faces; it spoke volumes about their intentions for her.

"Men, we need to get her inside. If she's the only one who survived this crash . . ." he paused and gave his soldiers a knowing grin, ". . . we'll need to get her inside and taken care of immediately. I'll clean her wounds, and you men prepare her . . . sleeping quarters."

They all laughed, and the leader drew his knife,

intending to hasten the removal of Alyna's already-ripped uniform. When he leaned close, a pair of shots rang out from the surrounding trees, and two of the Rising Sun soldiers fell dead. The leader looked up angrily, and Alyna's knife swept upward, neatly slicing open his belly. With a short scream, he collapsed gurgling to the earth. The sole remaining guard managed to draw his weapon, but twin shots from the trees silenced him forever.

Alyna rolled to her feet, and took in the situation at a glance. Pelos and Kish stepped into the open and swept the area for other foes. Then the Avengers moved without hesitation to the nearby cave mouth.

"I passed a mobile patrol on my way in," Alyna told them. "Did you see them?"

"They've been neutralized," Pelos told her, grinning. "I hate loose ends."

"All right. We have about an hour before this group misses their next radio check-in, and another fifteen minutes before the reactionary force can arrive. We need to be long gone by then. Pelos, it's your show. You take care of the computer, and I'll go up topside with Kish and set the charges on the array."

Alyna and Kish went to work. They circled the enormous dish with its spider-like legs as they attached the explosive charges. Despite their actions, the low hum of insects in the underbrush continued uninterrupted. Alyna crinkled her nose in protest as the odor of well-oiled metal mingled unpleasantly with the smell of their explosives. All the while, she kept a watchful eye on the surrounding forest, ever alert for more patrols from Event Horizon.

With her task completed, Alyna climbed back down the hill and returned to the cave where Pelos was diligently setting the charges. She looked at him curiously, her head cocked, obviously surprised he hadn't finished already.

"Sorry I took so long," laughed Pelos, "but I've never had weather control at my fingertips before. I was tempted to set off a snowstorm, just for fun, but I was afraid if Arano's squad was getting chased, it'd make evasion more difficult because of the footprints. So instead, I settled for the next best thing."

Alyna groaned. "You're getting as bad as Videre. What did you do?"

"Don't make me ruin the surprise. Let's just say any ships on the ground at their military spaceport are in serious jeopardy. I made certain my little distraction won't endanger Arano's team, though, so don't worry. Let's get out of here."

Arano and his squad emerged from their hiding place, Videre again in the lead, the time for their assault at hand. Moments before, scores of Event Horizon soldiers had poured from the command center, evidence Alyna's attack on the weather control device had been successful. As if more evidence was necessary, laughed Arano to himself. A few minutes earlier, a speechless Videre had called Arano's attention to the massive tornado sweeping across the military spaceport. Although it was over a mile away, debris from the spaceport had landed nearby, mute evidence of the tornado's power. Arano smiled inwardly; very few of the ships at the space port would be capable of flying in the next few weeks.

The general mobilization in response to Alyna's attack had, as expected, left the command center with only a skeleton crew. Videre was able to march the Avengers squad right through the front gates to the guardpost. They fell on the two hapless guards like a pack of wolves, and in the span of a few heartbeats the command center lay open before them.

Abandoning their guise as simple Event Horizon soldiers, they drew their weapons and moved inside the complex. They had to make haste, because once the initial shock faded, order would be restored and their mission would become infinitely more difficult. Arano briefly consulted a nearby fire evacuation map to get his bearings before he led his squad down a series of subhallways.

The interior of the command center was painted a uniformly gray color, although the floor was discolored from the passage of countless feet. At precise intervals, doors opened to either the left or right, and at every junction was a map indicating the major points of interest in the facility. Some of the doors stood open, and a glance inside told Arano the command center had indeed been evacuated in a hurry. Books lay open, half-eaten meals sat on tables, and some computer terminals were still activated, waiting with mechanical patience for commands that would be a long time coming.

Arano silently called a halt outside a doorway marked with a sign warning that entrance to the room beyond was restricted. He motioned for his squad to watch the hallway, and pushed the door open, Laron at his side. He pointed his laser pistol around the room, searching for enemy soldiers, but saw none. There was another door on the far side, but whether it led to an enclosed room or another hallway was unclear. He waved his teammates inside and pointed at the door, then motioned for Videre to secure as much information from the computer as he could.

Once his teammates were in position, Arano glided across the floor, Laron a step behind him, and listened at the door. He couldn't hear anything through the sturdy steel door, but as he reached for the doorknob his danger sense issued a warning. Laron saw the look in Arano's eyes and nodded, again knowing without words Arano sensed trouble. Arano gave a silent three-count and burst through the door.

Two soldiers in the room beyond looked up from their card game in surprise, apparently thinking a superior officer had caught them evading their responsibilities. Fear filled their eyes as Arano's pistol swung in their direction. Both reached for their own weapons, coming to their feet as they moved to attack. Arano's pistol hummed twice, and the first soldier fell dead before his pistol had cleared its holster. The second managed to get his weapon drawn and halfway pointed toward Arano before Laron's pistol sounded, eliminating the threat.

Arano made a quick check, realizing this was just a small antechamber with no other exits. Good, he thought. It will make security easier, only having to watch one entrance. Laron roughly searched the two soldiers, rolling the bodies over and checking their pockets. Arano stepped over to the table and seized a file marked "Confidential" one of the soldiers had been reading prior to their arrival. He made another sweep of the area to make certain nothing had been missed, and he and Laron returned to the main room.

Videre was grinning from ear to ear, feline muzzle showing its teeth in his delight. "We've hit a gold mine here, Viper," he said breathlessly. "I've found the location of their new headquarters building in the Niones System, the names of a few spies they have within the Coalition, and the dates and times for several terrorist attacks they have planned for the next month. There are also detailed lists of our planned military operations that have been presented to the Coalition High Council, in accordance with the new Defense Prelar's directive. Proof positive that loose lips sink ships, eh? But here's the big one: I've found the President!"

Arano's jaw dropped open in shock. "What? Where?"

"Navek System, in a local prison facility. We have to get word of this back to Coalition Headquarters immediately!"

Arano's head spun as he sat down to leaf through the file . He couldn't believe their fortune, finding all this information. They'd hoped to gather a few minor details about Event Horizon's operations, maybe even a few names. He'd known Videre's computer skills would enable him to get deep into their computer's secure information, but this . . .

Then he made a discovery of his own that chilled him to the bone. "You're not going to believe what I just found."

"What do you have, Viper?" asked Videre without turning from his work.

"Do you remember what that Rising Sun soldier told Alyna, and what Dar Noil told me, about something called the 'Beacon'? The full name is the 'Nebulatic Beacon.' We'll have to read the entire file to get all the details, and we don't have time for that. But, according to this, both Rising Sun and Event Horizon capital ships and starbases are equipped with this Nebulatic Beacon. Somehow, it forces our ships to drop their shields and shut down the weapons computers."

"And all this time, we were looking for a virus," mused Lain from where he guarded the doorway. "We thought the problem was in our computers, when all along . . . the Coalition has lost a lot of time on this."

"And ships," agreed Videre. "I'm done here. Lain, if you're ready to set your charges, I'll take over for you."

While Arano put the file in his pack, Lain placed the C-12 charges at strategic locations about the room. A few minutes later the explosives were set, and the team prepared to move out. A brief glance into the hallway showed the way was clear, so they holstered their weapons and moved out. They retraced their steps without meeting anyone, and exited the building without incident.

They were brought up short by a patrol of a dozen Event Horizon soldiers, the patrol's leader visibly shaken by the discovery the command center's gate guards were dead.

"You there," he commanded roughly. "How long

have you been inside?"

"Since sunrise," lied Videre, the apparent ranking member of the group. "Why?"

"We have two dead soldiers here, that's why," the soldier snapped angrily. "First the attack on the weather station, then this. No one leaves until we get this sorted out. We're all going back inside."

Arano swallowed hard. He realized how poor their odds in close quarters against twelve soldiers would be, but he also knew if they went back inside, their odds of surviving were even lower. Discovery of their identities notwithstanding, the explosive charges would detonate in just a few minutes, and the entire building would be leveled.

"But we were on our way to the spaceport," whined Videre obsequiously, trying to mollify the situation by playing on their antagonist's ego. "General Stontic has ordered us to help with the cleanup after that tornado came through today. His personal ship was damaged, and he's extremely upset."

The soldier suddenly looked less certain of himself. Apparently, Videre had gotten lucky, randomly pulling a name he remembered seeing in the computer reports inside the command center. He must've chosen the right name. "Well," the soldier stammered, "I'm not one to cross the general. Be on your way. Mind that you come and see me as soon as you're done so I can take your statements. Off with you."

Videre nodded, and formed up his squad. With the smooth grace of veteran soldiers, they marched off in the direction of the spaceport. When they were out of sight. Videre changed their direction and headed to the back door into the city. Since there was total mayhem in the Event Horizon base, Videre moved the Avengers at an easy jog, giving the impression his group had someplace important to go. Their feet splashed noisily in the puddles of water standing in the road, remnants of the evening's thunderstorm.

When they turned onto the street where they planned to exit the base, they saw the "secret" door blocked by a squad of soldiers. Obviously, diversionary side trips into the city weren't allowed under the current circumstances. They continued past the soldiers without slowing and turned the next corner, where Videre brought them to a halt.

"We have to get through that door," whispered Arano softly. "Any ideas?"

"I have one," smiled Lain. "Wait here."

Lain, strutting as if he were on a mission for the commander of Event Horizon himself, boldly crossed the street to an Event Horizon fueling station. Arano couldn't see what Lain was doing, but he trusted the dependable Kamling's judgment. They waited tensely for several moments, and then Lain came back across the street just as boldly, but a bit faster.

"Let's take cover," warned Lain as soon as he was close enough to whisper to his teammates.

Arano groaned as he and his friends crouched behind a large military transport. "What did you do?" asked Arano in exasperation.

Lain grinned, reptilian teeth gleaming in the night air. "They still burn fossil fuels in their engines. There was a truck with a plastic fuel container and a plastic cargo bed liner. I inserted a fuel pump hose into the container and turned on the pump." He was interrupted Videre snickered, trying not to laugh out loud. Arano and Laron looked at each other in confusion.

"What?" asked Arano impatiently, practically stomping his feet.

"When the fuel is pumped into the container," explained Lain, "the plastic cargo liner will cause the fuel to build up a static electric charge. It'll continue to build until the charge is great enough to spark between the pump and the cargo bed beneath the liner. When you have a spark inside a fossil fuel container . . ." he trailed off, grinning broadly.

Arano somehow managed to keep a straight face, despite the stubborn smile playing at the corners of his mouth. "That might draw those guards' attention from the door. How long will it"

He was interrupted by a cataclysmic explosion, shattering windows for blocks in all directions and throwing the Avengers squad to the ground, even behind the cover of the enormous transport vehicle. A huge pillar of flames leaped upward, chasing a mushrooming fireball into the evening sky. Shaken, Arano climbed to his feet, his head feeling fuzzy and his ears ringing. All four Avengers stood admiring Lain's handiwork while the Event Horizon guards left their position in front of the base's back door, leaving it unguarded.

By silent agreement, the group lined up in formation again, and Videre led them back to the door. The bartender on the city-side of the door seemed more than a little surprised to see men in Event Horizon uniforms step from the room at the back of his establishment. He gave them a queer look as they moved hastily out the front door and into the city streets.

"Let's move quickly," warned Arano. "If these people are Event Horizon sympathizers, that bartender might report us as deserters. By now he probably knows of the attacks on the base, so anyone leaving is going to draw suspicion. Let's get back to our hotel and get our civilian clothes. We'll head to the spaceport and get back on our freighter."

Alyna led her exhausted squad up the ramp of the freighter, nodding surreptitiously to the ship's captain, an agent in the intelligence service for the Coalition. Despite her squad's successful mission and the word she'd received that the attack by Arano's squad had also succeeded, she wasn't ready to relax. Arano's squad hadn't yet returned. Speaking to other crewmembers, she learned what had happened at the base. The last bit of news sent her heart down to her toes: an Event Horizon informant had spotted a group of suspected saboteurs leaving the base, and Event Horizon troops were in hot pursuit. She decided to give him a few minutes, and then her squad was going out to help.

Arano sprinted down a narrow alley, his squad close at his heels. Despite their change of clothes, they hadn't thrown off their pursuers. Even the detonation of the explosives at the command center hadn't distracted Event Horizon's soldiers from the chase. Exhaustion wasn't yet a factor for either side, and Arano's squad hadn't managed to open a sizable lead. Arano knew they would eventually be caught if they didn't change their plan; there were probably already Event Horizon soldiers maneuvered into position by radio, and the escape route would soon be closed. A desperate plan formed in Arano's mind as they turned down a darkened side street.

"This isn't working," Arano told them between gulping breaths. "I'm about to give you guys some orders you won't like, but you have to obey them. I'm going to fall back and cover you to slow down the pursuit. You three keep going, and I'll try to meet you at the freighter. If I'm not there in time, take off without me."

"Viper!" protested Videre.

"That's an order, Lieutenant! We have vital information that has to be returned to the Coalition. If we send it via subspace, there's a chance Event Horizon will know what we learned and we can no longer depend on our encryption codes. You must hand-deliver the data. Videre, you're in charge of my squad until I return. If you leave without me, have Alyna take the team and rescue the President before they move him. I'll meet with the spy network here and arrange for travel if I miss the freighter. Now, go!"

Arano removed the pack containing the information on the Nebulatic Beacon and tossed it to Videre. Then he ducked off to his right, and took cover behind an enormous tree. His teammates were clearly unhappy; all three hesitated and cast dark glances in his direction, but they followed his orders.

As they disappeared around the next corner, their pursuers came within range of Arano's pistol. He opened fire, his surprise attack catching the Event Horizon soldiers off-guard. Two of their number lay dying, and a third thrashed helplessly in the street, crying out in pain as he clutched his leg. The remaining dozen soldiers dove for cover, returning fire as soon as they were able.

Arano almost smiled to himself as he watched their futile efforts to engage him. His first target had been deliberately chosen, the shiny metal tabs on his shoulders marking him as the leader. In a totalitarian group like Event Horizon, when a leader is lost, the others tend to lose their cohesion and sense of direction. These soldiers were no exception, firing back at a target they couldn't see, none of them tried to maneuver for a better shot. Staying as low as possible, Arano backed out of the area, turned the corner, and ran on.

A shout rang out from behind him, calling for him to stop. A glance over his shoulder told him all he needed to know: another group of soldiers had spotted him. Paying no attention to where he was running, he nearly knocked over a young Human woman who stepped aside in astonishment. Regaining his footing, Arano ran on. The woman shouted at him and joined in the pursuit. When Arano glanced back again, he saw the woman trip and fall, slowing the soldiers behind her.

Ahead of him and to his right, Arano spotted a restaurant with a large outdoor courtyard. He vaulted over the low metal fence and darted inside. His hasty passage overturned several tables, spilling food and adding to the havoc he was trying to create. He cleared the doorway and, ignoring protests from the indignant host, pulled out his only smoke grenade. He removed the pin and tossed the grenade inside the doorway to the kitchen just as several Event Horizon soldiers entered the restaurant.

"Fire!" Arano bellowed at the top of his lungs. "The kitchen is on fire! Everyone out!" There were screams of panic as the patrons surged to their feet as one, pushing madly for the door. Arano melted in with the crowd heading out the rear exit, leaving the frustrated soldiers behind. He roughly pushed his way clear of the crowd and dashed off toward the spaceport.

Minutes later, a breathless Arano Lakeland pounded past the hangar, running toward the freighter. The ramps were closed, but at least they hadn't left. He pulled out his Comm, setting it to the air traffic frequency. He was about to contact the captain when he heard the tower give the freighter clearance to leave, saying if they weren't off the ground at once, they'd have to wait while Event Horizon inspectors checked the ship for escaped saboteurs. Arano slowed to an exhausted stop, put his Comm away, and swore as the freighter lifted gracefully into the sky.

CHAPTER SEVENTEEN

"WE HAVE TO GO BACK FOR HIM," ARGUED ALYNA, bravely fighting back the tears that threatened to run from her reddened eyes.

"Look, Alyna," Laron said soothingly, placing a comforting hand on her shoulder. "We can't go back. We wouldn't be able to leave the system, and we'd all be stranded. Arano ordered us to leave, and that's what we have to do. We have to get this intelligence back to the Coalition, and we have to rescue the President if we can. Arano is very resourceful, and I'm sure he'll find a way home. Now isn't the time for an emotional reaction."

"No?" she protested, her shoulders heaving with suppressed sobs. "Then when is?"

"When you're no longer in charge of Avengers Team 5," Laron replied smoothly. "Pull yourself together. Regardless of how you feel about Arano, he's just one man. We have to look at the big picture here. First, we take care of the business he assigned us. Then, if he hasn't returned, we go back for him. Until then, you need to be a leader."

Alyna nodded, anguish etched into her perfect

features. "Give me a few minutes, and I'll join the others," she said simply.

When Alyna returned to the room where her team had gathered, the ravages of her inner turmoil had been covered, and she was every bit the leader her team needed her to be. The leader Arano needed her to be, she added silently. She would follow his orders to the letter, and then she'd return to save him. Once again she was a professional soldier, keeping her emotions in check. She called everyone around the center table and presented Laron's plan.

"Okay," she told them, her voice steady once more, "here's our idea. Despite getting rid of Dar Noil and the Disciples of Zhulac, I still don't feel sure all our security leaks have been closed. I'd bet my eyeteeth someone in the upper administration is spying for the other side.

"For this reason, we aren't going to tell anyone other than Captain Pana what we've found out about the President. We'll give Lon our full report and leave at once for the Navek system. With only a few cosmetic modifications, Arano's ship, the Intrepid, can pass for a small freighter, and if we get into a pinch we can use it to fight our way out again.

"After we enter orbit, we can land in the large cave complex several clicks north of Labuk, the city where they are supposed to be hiding the President. We can sneak in, get the President, and sneak back out with no one the wiser."

"And then?" Pelos asked expectantly.

Alyna's lower lip quivered almost imperceptibly. "And then we go get Viper."

Arano sat down heavily on the bed in the modest hotel room he had rented. His physical exhaustion had reached the point he scarcely noticed the sparseness of his room, the furniture worn by the constant rubbing of the hands of those who'd stayed before him, or the wallpaper coming off the wall in a dozen places. He needed rest, but not without first trying to find help. When Colonel Vines had briefed Arano's team on the situation on Selpan 4, he had mentioned how and where to make contact with Coalition agents who were hidden there. At the time, Arano hadn't thought it would be necessary, but now the information was invaluable. The series of passwords assured both the agents and himself neither worked for the enemy, and he could then arrange travel out of the system.

His first order of business was to locate an agent, of course, which was fairly complicated. He knew of an establishment in another quarter of the city where a few agents were supposedly employed, but there was still the matter of picking them out of the crowd. He lay back on his bed, mulling over the proper way to go about the whole project.

A knock at the door brought him out of his reverie and on his feet, pistol in hand, gliding cautiously to the door. He looked out through the viewscreen and saw a Human female waiting patiently in the hallway. She had blond hair cascading down her back in a waterfall of curls, held firmly in place by a black band Arano noticed when she turned her head to the side. She was slightly shorter than Arano, and her tight-fitting blue jumpsuit accented her athletic body.

His brows furrowed with thought when he realized this was the same woman he'd nearly run over just hours before. With a flip of a switch, he activated the intercom.

"Yes?" he asked warily.

"Sorry to bother you, sir," she answered confidently. "I was told you were interested in employment as a computer consultant, and I wanted to talk to you about it. I hate to let a good opportunity pass me by."

Arano peered more closely at the viewscreen. She had just given him one of the passwords used when two agents in this system made first contact.

"I'm more interested in computer security," Arano said carefully.

"That's okay," came the reply. "The position is open to interpretation."

"Well, then," replied Arano, finishing the password ritual. "Perhaps I might be interested, if the money is right."

He concealed his pistol under his shirt and slowly opened the door. His contact entered the room casually, not saying a word until the door had been secured behind her. She turned to face him, smiling in disarming fashion. "So, Captain Lakeland, how are things?"

Arano looked at her more intently, recognition flickering at the edges of his consciousness. "Do I know you?"

"We went through the Coalition Military Academy together back in 2205. I had my hair shorter then, and

I've lost some weight. I'm not surprised you didn't recognize me." She held out her hand. "Wendra Banks. I'm with the Bureau of Counter-intelligence."

Arano accepted her hand, the memories coming back to him. "Ah, yes," he told her. "Now I remember. Your hair was quite a bit shorter, as I recall. When did you leave the military to become a spy?"

"About four years ago. This post has been really boring until recently. Once the war with Event Horizon got started, the place became a hotbed of activity. We've uncovered more information here in the last six months than in the previous six years. What brought you here? Wait, let me guess. The attack on the Weather Control Device and Event Horizon's command center. That has to be your handiwork."

Arano smiled, nodding. "Okay, so how did you find me?"

"After you nearly ran me over in the street, I knew I recognized you, but I couldn't put my finger on it. When I saw the soldiers chasing you, I figured you were with the Coalition, and it all came back to me. I delayed those soldiers a bit, and then I circled around to try to meet up with you. That ploy with the smoke grenade was brilliant.

"At any rate, I followed you when you sneaked out of the restaurant, and I saw you come up here. I thought I'd check to see if you needed a hand." She gave him a friendly smile, then moved to a chair and took a seat.

"What I need is passage off the planet and out of the system," he told her. "I stayed behind to delay the soldiers chasing us, allowing my team to escape. I need to catch up with them and get back in the war."

"I can arrange it for you," she told him, rising to her feet. "I have some contacts down at the spaceport. We can put you on a freighter as early as tomorrow morning. Let me go talk to some friends, and I'll come back tonight to let you know what I turn up. Don't leave the room. In fact, don't talk to anybody. Event Horizon has probably been nosing your picture around, and someone might be looking to cash in on a reward. I'll bring dinner back with me." She stepped closer, standing directly in front of him. "It's good to see you again, Arano," she said, and embraced him.

He returned the embrace, the sweet fragrance of her hair tantalizing. "You, too," he said simply. She stepped away, winked, and left the room. He locked the door behind her and lay down again to get some much-needed rest.

"Dropping out of the wormhole," Alyna announced, touching the controls that brought the Intrepid back into the emptiness of normal space. After more than eighteen hours in the wormhole, they'd entered the Navek system and were headed for the system's sixth planet. The Intrepid had been modified, with several cargo bays attached around her hull, concealing her impressive weapons array. The bays were filled with food and medical supplies, matching the manifest they'd been given in case they were scanned. In case of emergency, the bays could be easily ejected, exposing the massive armament arrayed on the powerful frigate. Continuing on their course, Alyna guided the ship into the frigid atmosphere of Navek 6.

The Intrepid glided low over the frozen wasteland, hovering over the ice fields with fluid grace. The skies were a leaden color of gray, the wintry cloud cover adding to Alyna's gloomy thoughts. The intelligence reports had said there was a likelihood of a heavy snowfall in about six hours, helping to obscure their tracks on their return trip, but hopefully not hindering their progress. Minutes later, the cave complex north of Labuk was in sight. Alyna guided the ship into the mouth of one of the larger caves, setting her down gently, away from the prying eyes of Event Horizon's scanners.

Alyna had ceded to Arano's wishes and taken command of the team, and she had left Videre in charge of Arano's squad. She attached Laron Alstor to Videre's squad, his addition making the unit a three-man squad once again. The team donned their cold weather gear and moved out onto the ice field.

The first thing Alyna noticed was the biting cold. Although the temperature was warmer this close to the equator, the wind that blew constantly had a decidedly frigid feel. With no trees in the hilly terrain, there was nothing to break the wind. About all that grew in that frozen wasteland was a species of scrubby bush, no more than a meter or so in height.

As she trudged along in front of her team, the frozen snow crunching underfoot, she saw the first snowflakes fall, pushed into a white blur by the blowing winds. Shrugging off her discomfort Alyna pushed on. She needed to accomplish the mission, the rescue of the President being of paramount importance, but she had another motivating factor.

Somewhere in the Selpan system, the man she loved had been left behind, possibly even in the hands of the enemy. The thought of what they might be doing to him right now distracted her from the mission and she tried to push it from her mind. She almost stopped dead in her tracks when she realized it was the first time she'd actually admitted her feelings for Arano went so deep. If only he would break out of his shell . . .

Shaking aside the personal thoughts, she focused on her plan. The main obstacle was a river, about a thirty-minute walk ahead. Although the air temperature was well below freezing, underground volcanic activity allowed the water to flow freely under the ice pack. In fact, at times the ice cover melted completely, exposing the running water to the open air. This was one of those times. A scan of the area when they flew over indicated the ice was less than two inches thick, and in places there was no ice at all. For that reason, Alyna's team carried inflatable rafts with them to cross the river. From there, they had about another two-hour march ahead of them before their attempt to penetrate the prison complex and find the President.

They reached the river without incident and found that, as expected, there was only a thin, brittle ice cover. Alyna and Videre removed the rafts from their packs and inflated them as their teammates watched the surrounding countryside for signs of trouble. Alyna's eyes scanned the hills while she waited tensely, her breath steaming in the night air. A herd of grazing animals trudged by, the first signs of life since arriving on the planet. Finally, with their rafts inflated and their paddles ready, they entered the river.

It only took the group about five minutes to cross the river. They hid their rafts in a dense patch of the scrubby bushes that dotted the countryside, and piled loose snow on top. That taken care of, Alyna got her bearings, and they headed off again in the direction of the Labuk prisons.

A knock at the door brought Arano out of a deep slumber. For a few heartbeats, he had no idea where he was or how he got there. But the disorientation passed, his racing heart slowed, and Arano remembered his situation. He climbed to his feet, pistol in hand, and moved to the door. Through the viewscreen he saw Wendra Banks standing in the hallway, her arms loaded down with the promised meal. He unlocked the door, opened it to admit Wendra, and locked the door behind her.

She set the food on the table, the smell reminding Arano he hadn't eaten all day. As they chatted about the times they'd had together at the academy, he brought them each a glass of water, and they sat down to their meal. While Wendra ate daintily, Arano devoured his portion, eating a second helping before Wendra had finished her first. Having eaten his fill, he pushed back from the table, waiting patiently as Wendra finished.

"I have something else, if you're of a mind," she told him, smiling. She reached into an unopened sack and produced a bottle of Tsimian wine. "This is my personal favorite," she said. "I save it for special occasions."

"None for me, thanks," laughed Arano. "That stuff goes right to my head, and I'd have a hangover for a week. I hate killing Bromidians while I have a headache."

"Okay," she laughed, putting the wine away. "Another time perhaps. Well, here's what I have for you. There's a freighter leaving for Karlac 3 tomorrow morning. The captain has always been friendly to the Coalition, and has agreed to help me. All I told him was that I have a friend who is having trouble with the locals and needs safe passage off the planet. He'll expect to be paid, of course. If you have him set down at the Coalition outpost on Karlac 3, I'm sure you could convince the base commander there to take care of your fare.

"We'll be meeting with the ship's first mate shortly after midnight. He'll take you to the ship and see to it you get out of the system safely."

"That was quick," Arano admired. "I wish the Coalition bureaucracy worked that efficiently."

They passed the next few hours in unimportant conversation, rehashing times together at the Academy and their separate adventures afterward, eating their evening meal when nighttime approached. Finally, long after the sun had set, Wendra indicated it was time to leave. They slipped out into the darkened streets, and Wendra led him on an indirect route to their rendezvous with the freighter's first mate. At the late hour, there weren't as many civilians on the streets, but there was an alarming number of soldiers, no doubt searching for the saboteurs who'd hit Event

Horizon's facility in such dramatic fashion.

As they continued on their way, Arano pulled his hood up around his face in the cool evening air. At one point, Wendra even doubled back on their tracks to ensure they weren't being followed, although Arano found the efforts to be a bit unnecessary. If Event Horizon knew where he was, they'd simply capture him rather than allow him a chance to escape. Despite Wendra's precautions, they arrived at their meeting on time.

She led him boldly up to a rather evil looking Kamling, leaning indolently against a light pole. "Arano, this is Accrom. Accrom, this is my friend, Arano. He's the one Captain Porzoff told you about."

Arano shook hands with Accrom, seemingly disinterested in the whole affair. "Give me your weapons," growled the Kamling.

"I don't have any," lied Arano, shrugging. Accrom moved to pat Arano down, but Arano pushed his hands away. "Don't touch me," he warned, drawing himself up as his muscles tensed for a fight.

Wendra stepped between them. "Come on, Accrom, do this for me," she said, fixing the Kamling with her pleasant smile. "He's okay. I promise he won't do anything evil to your ship."

Accrom, obviously less than happy about the situation, finally agreed. Arano barely had time to thank Wendra for her assistance before Accrom had started back in the direction of the spaceport, grumbling about something under his breath. Arano gave Wendra a final wave and moved off into the night.

They walked for several blocks before Arano felt

something was wrong. He'd been getting twinges of warning from his danger sense, but had put them down to the proximity of his enemies and the dangers of discovery. The idea lost validity when he realized that in this section of town there were relatively few soldiers. However, the warning grew and he became even more uneasy. Accrom, too, acted odd, looking about furtively and frequently patting something hidden under his shirt on his right hip. Arano drew a deep breath, pretending to scratch his side as he surreptitiously released the strap holding his concealed pistol.

The attack came without warning as they turned down a darkened alley near the entrance to the spaceport. Had Arano not been a Padian, the attack might well have been successful. Two Kamlings dressed in dark, tight-fitting clothes stepped out of the shadows to block their path. At the same time, a Tsimian burst from his place of concealment at the mouth of the alley, throwing himself at Arano. The Tsimian's roar of fury turned into a bellow of pain when Arano sidestepped the attack and brought his fist down smartly at the base of the Tsimian's neck. In one fluid motion, Arano drew his knife and planted it firmly between his attacker's shoulder blades.

The two Kamlings dropped their cudgels and reached for their laser pistols. Before either weapon cleared its holster, Arano's pistol had leaped into his hand and sounded twice, and the two Kamlings lay dead. He turned on an astonished Accrom, obviously shaken that his well-planned ambush had been so easily thwarted.

"Hands in the air," Arano ordered harshly. "I

know you have a weapon on your right hip, and if you make a move toward it I'll kill you where you stand. Now, who sent you?"

Accrom spat at Arano's feet, snarling in defiance.

"So," Arano said casually, "I guess what you're trying to tell me is that you've outlived your usefulness." He adjusted his aim, pointing the pistol directly at his foe's face. He wouldn't kill the man in cold blood, but he wouldn't let Accrom know it. It was gamble, but Arano believed he could win the confrontation.

"There's a very large reward on your head right now," Accrom said finally. "When Wendra asked me to help, I figured there'd be a reward out for you, so I got my friends here to help me. When I saw you, I recognized you from the pictures they've passed around. I have one in my back pocket, if you need proof."

"Well, sounds like you were trying to make a little extra money. How many others are involved in this? Your ship's captain? Wendra? Who?"

"Just us four," answered Accrom angrily. "The fewer people involved, the better. Get too many people involved and the reward money gets spread around too thin."

"Maybe you should have at least brought enough people to finish the job," Arano taunted.

He was about to ask another question when his danger sense again warned him of trouble. A heartbeat later, Accrom launched himself at Arano's laser pistol, and tried to wrench the weapon free. Despite the advance warning of the attack, Arano wasn't able to avoid Accrom's strike, and the antagonists were soon locked in mortal combat, both struggling viciously for control of the pistol. They fell to the ground, rolling side to side, vying for possession of the weapon. Taking a gamble, Arano took one hand off the pistol and reached toward the body of the dead Tsimian. Almost instantly he found what he was looking for: the knife sticking out of the Tsimian's back. He yanked the blade free of the Tsimian's corpse and drove it home in Accrom's neck just as the Kamling brought the pistol to bear.

Arano lay back for a few moments, gulping in the cool air while he contemplated what had just happened and what his next course of action should be. Finally, his mind made up, he retrieved and cleaned his knife, holstered his weapons, and started back toward his hotel room, hoping Wendra could shed some light on the situation.

As he stepped back onto the main street, a cry rang out from the other end of the alley. A quick glance told him someone had already found the bodies of Arano's attackers. While Arano had acted in self-defense, he didn't think the local police would be sympathetic to a member of the Coalition military.

He walked more quickly, trying to leave the area before a search could be organized. He knew his luck had run out, however, when a voice ordered him to stop. He took flight again and ran between two buildings, over a fence, and down a deserted side street. Once again, a full-scale foot chase ensued, with Event Horizon soldiers and local police officers calling to each other on their radios to coordinate the search.

He was about to turn down a street to his right when a quiet voice called out softly to him. He turned to find Wendra holding a door open and beckoning to him to hurry. He dashed across the street and through the open doorway. She silently pulled the door shut and slid the locks into place just as pursuing police officers arrived from both directions. Arano shook his head in wonder, realizing Wendra had just saved him from capture once again.

Alyna held up her hand, calling her team to a halt. Through the swirling white mass of falling snow, the fence that formed the perimeter of the prison compound was barely visible. Although the wire mesh of the fence was itself not much of a barrier, there would undoubtedly be other security measures in place, and she would leave nothing to chance.

With a short series of hand signals, Alyna positioned her team to provide security. Her first order of business was to scramble Event Horizon's sensors. She placed a small device at the base of the fence, and activated it with the press of a key. The machine hummed to life, providing a heavy electromagnetic screen to cover her team's breach of the perimeter. She was then able safely cut a hole in the facility's perimeter fence. She moved her team inside, keeping a close eye out for patrols as she went.

In the back of her mind, Alyna had a nagging feeling she'd left something behind. As her team moved cautiously across the compound, she realized the feeling related to Arano. He'd always been there with her on missions, but now he was missing and she didn't know when she'd see him again. She had to face the possibility she might never see him again, and the thought raised a cold feeling in the pit of her stomach. For a while, following the injuries she'd suffered during the raid in the Branton System, it had seemed he was going to stop hiding his true feelings. But it hadn't taken long for him to retreat into that emotional shell he hid behind. Forcing the thoughts back into the corners of her consciousness, she concentrated on the business at hand.

Alyna led her team around behind the facility to a large reservoir of heated water. Great tendrils of steam rose continuously from its black, mirrored surface. Feeding water to the reservoir was a system of drainage pipes, each approximately two meters high. Snow was collected from the roofs of buildings inside the facility, melted, and piped to this reservoir, where it was heated and pumped inside to be purified and used as drinking water. They had to carefully select which pipe to use, because the other two contained fresh sewage and were fairly offensive to one's sense of smell.

Eventually, using the enormous water pipe, the team made it into the prison's water purification facility. They exited the pipe, the other five soldiers securing the room while Alyna got her bearings. Water gurgled noisily through the countless pipes that traversed through the room, and the constant humming of the pumps added their own harmony to the cacophony of sound filling the chamber. Satisfied she knew where they were and which direction to go, she gathered her team and moved out toward the high security wing of the prison.

Arano sagged wearily into a chair in Wendra's living room, exhausted from the night's events. It had taken the two of them another hour of dodging Event Horizon soldiers to make it back to the relative safety of Wendra's apartment, and they had reached the limits of their endurance.

"How did you find me?" Arano asked her finally.

"Something about Accrom's demeanor set me on edge. If I had seen something more concrete, I wouldn't have let you go with him, but I didn't want to ruin your chance to escape the system just on a nagging suspicion. I followed you guys, keeping my distance. The route he took had me all but convinced he was up to something, and I was thinking of confronting him when the attack came. I have a few safe hideouts in the city, and you happened to run right to one of them. I just wish I'd said something sooner so none of this would've happened."

Arano waved the last statement aside, shaking his head. "I had the same feeling about Accrom, so I should never have gone along. You're right, though. I'll need to take chances if I'm to get off this planet. I simply need to stay alert, that's all. This incident could have cost me. I think just about everyone on that side of town was after me. I even saw a Bromidian chasing me at one point." Arano noticed Wendra seemed troubled by his last remark, but when she didn't respond, he shrugged and moved on. "So, any thoughts on my next move?"

"Why don't you get some sleep? I'll contact some of my friends and see what I can turn up." She turned on her hallway light, indicated a room for Arano to take, and entered her kitchen. Arano moved gratefully to the bedroom and slipped quickly into a deep sleep.

He had only been asleep a short while when he felt someone climb into bed with him. He knew without looking that Wendra lay next to him. She snuggled up close, burrowing her head into his shoulder. Arano noticed, nervously, that she wasn't wearing much in the way of clothing. She sighed contentedly, reaching up to gently stroke his face.

It was then that Arano realized how attractive Wendra really was. Her golden locks tumbled casually across one shoulder, and her slender, almost sheer nightgown revealed tantalizing curves. Although the baser side of his nature called to him, he forced himself to fight the urge. His feelings for Alyna notwithstanding, engaging in an intimate relationship could cause him to let his guard down. He had to keep his wits about him if he was to escape.

"Wendra," he said softly, "I can't do this."

"Is there someone else?" she asked, her eyes unreadable.

"Yes," Arano answered. He felt it was a simpler answer than the whole truth about his personal life, which even he didn't quite understand. He didn't know where his relationship with Alyna was, but he wanted to sort that mess out before he dove into anything else. Besides, he reminded himself sternly, his first duty was to stay alert and get out of his current situation and back to his team.

They fell asleep then, awakening hours later to the annoying buzz of an incoming call on Wendra's Comm. As she moved gracefully across the floor, her body faintly visible in the dimly lit room, Arano had to remind himself firmly he had made the right decision earlier. Wendra held a brief conversation on her Comm before she returned to Arano's side with a smile.

"I have a meeting set up for you," she told him. "We had an agent's cover compromised recently, and will be smuggling him off the planet later this evening. You'll meet with two of my cohorts. They'll take you to the safehouse where our agent is hiding, and the two of you'll leave on the same ship." She went on to describe the details, including how to recognize his contact agents, and the time and location of the meeting. They both agreed that this time, Wendra would stay back out of sight, watching for ambushes, and follow them to the safehouse to ensure nothing went wrong. Arano gathered his gear while Wendra prepared a quick lunch for the two of them.

Alyna gave Kish and Pelos a silent three-count and kicked open the door. All three Avengers were through the doorway in a heartbeat, each covering a separate area of the room. Alyna's compact, deadly laser rifle hummed twice, and two Event Horizon guards dropped lifelessly to the floor. The three veteran soldiers each indicated in turn their area was clear of enemy soldiers, and the Avengers team swarmed into the room.

There were few tables; most of the work performed here was done on computers. Along one wall, an enormous control panel blinked and hummed in mechanical precision, oblivious to the violence that had erupted in the room just moments before. Several smaller computers were in operation at different posts, but it was obvious the biggest computer was the room's primary system and would contain the information they needed. While Videre worked the controls, Alyna and the others set up a secure perimeter, keeping a watchful eye out for enemy soldiers.

"I've got him!" Videre called out triumphantly. "He's still here!"

"Videre, Lain, you go get him," Alyna ordered. "We'll keep you covered from this position."

Videre and Lain raced through a doorway in the back of the room and disappeared down the hallway beyond. Alyna waited tensely as the seconds ticked away . She cast frequent glances in the direction her friends had gone, inevitably followed by another look at her watch. She knew it was only a matter of time until some of the guards they'd dispatched went missing, or a body was discovered, and then all hell would break loose.

As if on cue, a warning klaxon sounded, echoing deafeningly in the confined quarters of the control room. "Intruder alert," intoned the voice on the intercom. "General Quarters. All guards to your posts."

Alyna swore softly to herself. They'd known that, eventually, the alarm would be sounded, but she'd hoped her team would be on its way out before the search for them was started. She watched as Kish set her explosive devices around the control room, and was counting on the detonation and resultant chaos to aid their escape. As Kish set the last of the charges, she heard running footsteps coming through the rear door, and Videre and Lain charged back into the control room, a tall, angry-looking Gatoan running with them. Although his face was battered and his fur matted and covered with filth, he still had a proud bearing.

"Thank Launyr you've come," the Gatoan said breathlessly, invoking the name of his deity. "They told me I was to be executed any day now because I'd outlived my usefulness."

"President Bistre," acknowledged Alyna. "We have to get out of here, right now. Are you able to run?"

He grinned, bearing his Gatoan teeth. "Think you can keep up?"

They checked the main hallway before sprinting across to another door leading to a less-used subhallway. At first, they were able to avoid the guards, who rushed about in a state of total confusion. One unlucky pair of Event Horizon soldiers charged blindly in front of the Avengers team, and were cut down by a vicious burst of laser fire. After Lain made certain the two soldiers were out of the fight, Alyna picked up the pace, leading her team back to their entry point at the storm sewers. It was where they hoped to gain their advantage. The soldiers hunting for them would check the normal exits, not expecting this type of an escape. She hoped their slight edge would be enough.

They were still a few floors above the relative safety

of their exit point when their luck ran out. An entire platoon of Event Horizon troopers was conducting a room-by-room search for the intruders, and found the Avengers by pure chance. With the smooth grace that comes from years of intense training, Alyna's team took up fighting positions and poured an intense barrage of fire on the hapless soldiers, all the while looking for a way to disengage from the fight. Siator Bistre had picked up a rifle from a fallen Event Horizon soldier, and the former-infantryman-turned-politician assisted his rescuers, firing upon the advancing enemy.

Laron called out over the din of the battle, and pointed to a nearby window. "Alyna! This is an outside wall!" Alyna glanced in his direction, nodded in confirmation, and continued firing. From behind her, she heard Laron's rifle blazing away at the window and its surrounding wall, opening an escape route for the embattled Avengers.

"No good!" Laron yelled with an oath. "We're about three floors up, and there's no ledge!"

As Alyna fought to think of an alternative escape plan, shots rang out from behind her team. Above her head, a portion of the wall exploded, showering her with debris. She bit her lip in frustration, a jumble of ideas running through her mind. She didn't need Laron's warning to tell her the team was surrounded. The situation was desperate, options quickly disappearing. She knew if she didn't try something soon, her team would be captured or killed.

"Laron!" she shouted. "What's outside that wall? Is there anything we could use for climbing?"

Laron glanced outside, peering through the gaping

hole in the wall. "Nothing," came the reply. "But judging by all of the steam coming up from below, I'd say the reservoir is right under us. Since I can't see the water, I can't tell how deep it is."

Alyna made up her mind in a heartbeat. "There's only one way to find out," she told him. Darting from her place of cover, she ran to the hole in the wall, looked out at the shimmering steam rising from below, and leaped out into the empty air.

CHAPTER EIGHTEEN

ARANO CASUALLY STROLLED DOWN A MAIN AVENUE in the heart of the city of Antor. Once again, he scratched at the phony beard, which continued to itch. With the rolling gait of a man who has someplace important to be, Arano followed his memorized course to his appointed meeting. All the while, he kept a wary eye on passersby. To his great relief, he received no warning twitches from his danger sense.

He turned left at the next corner, spotting a landmark that told him he was about a half-kilometer from his destination. As he neared the park, he received the slightest of warnings from his danger sense. He hesitated briefly, and then decided to deviate slightly from the plan.

The scheme he and Wendra had worked out earlier called for him to sit on a bench at the edge of a nearby park. His contact was to drive up in a transport and ask him for directions to the spaceport. They would run through a short series of recognition passwords to confirm identities, then Arano would simply get into the car.

Instead of going directly to his appointed spot,

Arano ducked into one of the nearby buildings. He rode the lift to the top floor and walked casually to the staircase. The door was unlocked, so he walked up the remaining flight of stairs to the roof. Again, the door was unsecured. He cracked the door open slightly, made sure the roof was unoccupied, and opened the door wide enough to slip outside. There was a fairly stiff breeze blowing, bringing with it the various smells from the industrial side of the city. Puddles from the previous day's rainfall dotted the rooftop, but the tar-covered surface was otherwise free of obstructions. Arano didn't know quite what he was looking for, but he also had a hunch this meeting was not what it seemed to be. He considered the possibility someone in Wendra's organization was working for both sides, selling information to the highest bidder.

Arano dropped into a crouch and moved to the edge of the building, keeping a close watch on the surrounding rooftops. At first, he saw nothing. But as the minutes dragged by, he saw what he was looking for. From an open window on the top floor of a nearby building, he saw first a glint of sunlight on metal, then what appeared to be a Human head peering down at the park. He pulled his binoculars from inside his jacket and focused in on the scene across from him. Moments later, his suspicions were confirmed when the man in the window shifted his weight, bringing his rifle plainly into view. Arano looked back toward the park and realized the bench was in plain view of the man in the window.

Arano had had enough. Too many people knew he was here in the city of Antor, and sooner or later his luck would run out. He stayed low in his crouch and moved back to the staircase. As he reached to open the door, he felt a sharp warning from his danger sense and knew he was in trouble. Somehow, the enemy knew he'd come up here, and was waiting for him in the stairwell. He was trapped.

Viper moved to the edge of the rooftop on the side farthest away from the park and peered over the edge. He was several floors up, much too high to jump, and there was nothing soft below to break his fall. As he was about to turn away, he caught sight of the ledge on the first floor beneath him, perhaps a foot wide. If he lowered himself over the edge of the roof, he would only have to drop a little over a meter to land on the ledge. The sculptured edging on the side of the building would provide him with a sufficient handhold to keep him from falling off. From there, it was a simple matter to enter through a window. He might still be discovered, but at least he would have a fighting chance.

He heard the jiggle of the door latch, and his mind was made up. He slipped over the edge of the building, kept a firm grip on the edge of the roof, and lowered himself as far as he could. He allowed himself one more glance down, then he dropped to the ledge below.

All things considered, it was a pretty decent plan. The only contingency Arano forgot to take into account was the condition of the mortar forming the ledge. He landed with a jarring impact, and the ledge crumbled away beneath him. With a gasp, he reached out reflexively toward the building, barely managing to secure a handhold as the remains of the ledge tumbled away beneath him. He dangled there for several seconds, hanging on only by one hand while he considered the situation. The structure of his handhold seemed secure, so he swung upward and got a two-handed hold on the wall.

He didn't know how long he could hold on this way, but he also didn't know where else he could go. The ledge had disappeared for several feet in each direction, making it as inaccessible as the ground below him. But if he stayed there too long, his hands would eventually tire, and he'd fall. For several long moments he hung there, unable to think of a solution to the predicament.

Without warning, the window above him slid open and a makeshift rope dangled down in front of him. Arano reached out, tested the rope, and grasped it tightly. He climbed the short distance to the window and slid gratefully through, then collapsed gasping on the floor and looked up. With a shock he realized that, despite the lack of warning from his danger sense, his rescuer was a Bromidian.

Alyna struck the water below with jarring force and drove deeply beneath the surface. She kicked hard, smoothly swimming upward until her head broke through to the steaming night air. She shouted to her team that she was okay, heard Laron acknowledge her call, and swam to the nearby shore. Fortunately, her pack was waterproof and contained an extra uniform, but she wouldn't be able to change clothes until the others came down and provided security. She heard a splash, then several more, and was soon joined by the other members of her team. By the time she'd changed her uniform, the team stood assembled, one member of each squad changing clothes while the others kept watch. Between Videre and Lain, they had enough extra gear to provide President Siator Bistre with a set of dry clothes.

Alyna got her bearings from nearby landmarks and led her team in the direction of the hole they'd cut in the fence on their way in. After they cleared the perimeter fence, Alyna set their course with a compass, and the team started out toward their ship. The snowfall intensified, blotting everything from view beyond fifty meters. Alyna felt her body temperature dropping, a result of her wet hair freezing despite the cap she wore. She had an odd, metallic taste in her mouth, and her limbs shivered with the cold. There was nothing to be done about it, so she pushed onward.

Alyna knew the storm limited the effectiveness of scanners, both the portable ones carried by ground troops and the kind mounted on airships. In addition, the intensity of the storm would block them from being spotted visually by their enemies. For once, she thought, having her intelligence briefing provide incorrect information worked out in her favor. This was supposed to be only a snow shower, but it had almost reached blizzard conditions. She picked up the pace, hoping to put more distance between themselves and their pursuers. She made a verbal check on her team and the President, lowered her head, and pushed on. The wind drove the falling snow, stinging her eyes and burying everything in its path.

When they reached the river an hour or so later, she found the flaw in their plan. The river had frozen over, and the new snowfall had obscured everything, making it impossible to tell where they'd crossed the river on their way in. Finding their inflatable rafts was comparable to finding the proverbial needle in the haystack. The group stopped for a few moments, resting and gathering their thoughts.

It was Laron who provided the solution they so desperately needed. He knelt at the river's edge, probed with his knife, then he stood and rejoined the others. "The ice here is about three inches thick. If we try to walk across it, we may end up falling through. If you go underwater, the current will pull you away from the hole you made, and you'll drown.

"Here's what we can do. One of us needs to backtrack for perhaps two hundred meters, wiping out our tracks. Don't completely hide our passage, just make it look like we tried to hide our tracks. When we cross the river, we will lie down on the ice and slide across on our stomachs, one behind another. Lying down on the ice will spread out our weight, and allow the thinner ice to hold us. The last person in line will continue to wipe out our trail. With luck, our pursuers might believe we were able to simply walk across the river. If they try to walk across themselves, they'll be delayed a bit when they fall through the ice."

"Why backtrack?" asked President Bistre. "What does that gain us?"

"If we simply crawl across," Laron answered, "they will be able to tell how we crossed, and follow suit. If we suddenly wipe out our trail on the river, they will still become suspicious. If they have been following a partially obliterated trail for some time, they won't give our river trail a second thought. Alyna, I'd like to volunteer to do the backtrack mission."

"It's yours," agreed Alyna. "We'll get started with the crossing, and you can clean up behind us. We'll form up on the far side of the river."

"Got it. By the way, getting on top of thin ice can be tricky. You have to dive forward across the top of the ice without landing too hard. You may have to wade into the river a short distance before the ice will support you. Even if we break through the ice here by the shore, it should be covered over by the time our Event Horizon friends arrive." Laron moved back along their trail, disappearing into the storm.

Alyna looked at her teammates thoughtfully, the details of the new plan coming to mind. "Okay, Kish, you're the lightest, so you'll go first. I'll be behind you, then Lain, the President, Videre, and finally Marnian. Laron will be along when he can. Let's do it."

Kish stepped lightly to the edge of the ice flow, crouched down, and dove low across the ice surface. It easily held her weight, and she crawled across the frozen river. Alyna allowed her to get a short distance out onto the ice flow, to avoid compounding the effects of their combined body weights.

When she was ready, she edged up to the riverbank. She dove out, but came down too hard with her knees and broke through the layer of ice. She stood up instantly, the savagely cold water already biting into her legs, gathered herself and tried again, this time sliding atop the ice. Shivering, she clawed her way across the frozen river, trying to ignore the numbing pain tearing at her lower body.

Arano followed the Bromidian to another of the nearby buildings, his head spinning in wonder. Humans were trying to kill him, and he'd been saved by a Bromidian. He wondered if he was being saved only to be captured, but he still hadn't felt any warnings from his danger sense. At first, he had assumed he hadn't felt a warning because he'd been in mortal peril while dangling from that wall, but now that the other danger had passed, he still felt nothing.

They climbed another short flight of stairs. The Bromidian glanced around, and then pressed a security card against a panel on the wall. The door slid open with a hiss, revealing a small, empty room with sparse furnishings and total lack of decoration. Obviously, Arano thought, the room was little more than a convenient place to hide.

Once inside, the Bromidian turned to Arano. "So, I take it you're the Human causing all the fuss? Event Horizon has all of their operatives out in force looking for you. They believe the rest of your team has escaped, but they want your hide. Nice job on their command center, by the way."

Arano looked at him curiously. "How do you know so much about me?"

"Sorry," the Bromidian laughed, a guttural sound in the dimly-lit room. "I guess I should explain everything to you. My name is Lentin. I'm an agent with the Rystoria Liberation Front. Have you heard of the RLF?"

"I've heard it mentioned," Arano answered cautiously. "A dying Bromidian soldier told one of my friends about it. I didn't know whether to believe it or not."

"Believe it," Lentin told him. "You need our help, by the way. Not just you, individually, but the entire United Systems Coalition. The Bromidian High Command has some surprises in store for you. You've already seen some of them in action, like the Nebulatic Beacon."

"We can deal with it," Arano countered.

"Deal with it? I can help you destroy it, forever." Seeing he had Arano's attention, he handed him a data disk. "This disk contains the location of the secret laboratory at Event Horizon's new stronghold. This is where the Beacon was developed, and all of the technical data on the beacon is stored there. The disk also contains information about the indigenous life there, a race similar to the Bromidians. You may find them useful."

"Latyrians," said Arano, his eyes narrowing suspiciously. "Why are you giving this to me?"

"The RLF doesn't have the resources to move directly against the forces of either Event Horizon or the Bromidian High Command. Our goal is to be a thorn in their side until the war starts between the Empire and the Coalition." He looked closely at Arano. "You know the war is coming, don't you? I can see it in your eyes. I also see hatred. You hate all

Bromidians, yes?"

Arano considered him a moment. "I'm a Padian," he said simply. "Rising Sun soldiers executed my parents and the woman I was to marry."

For a moment, Lentin could only stare at the floor in shame. "Rising Sun was developed by the High Command as a way of moving openly against the Coalition without having to declare war," he said in a quiet voice. "The atrocities committed against your people are but a few in a long line committed by Rising Sun. I offer you my deepest sympathies, and I pledge you my life." Lentin drew a wicked-looking knife from his belt and handed it to Arano. He knelt before him, head lowered in submission. "My life is yours, to take or to spare."

Arano stood silently for several heartbeats, a vast inner turmoil raging through his mind. He had no intention of taking the man's life. His confusion came from a revelation dawning in his mind. For how long had he hated all Bromidians just for being Bromidians, yet condemned Humans who felt the same way about Padians? He took Lentin gently by the arm, helping him back to his feet and returning his knife.

"Can you help me escape this planet?" Arano asked. "As you may have guessed, I'm stranded."

Lentin nodded silently. "Your first step is to avoid the Human, Wendra Banks. She's a free agent. She's also the one who sold you out to the Event Horizon secret police."

Arano's eyes narrowed. "You're certain?"

"I assume you got a good look at some of the men who are after you? Come with me."

Lentin parted the curtains on a nearby window, and Arano drew out his binoculars and pointed them in the direction Lentin indicated. At first he saw nothing, then noticed the lone figure standing by a street corner, leaning against a building. Arano instantly recognized him as the sniper he had seen earlier. Moments later, Wendra and a short Human walked up, Wendra shaking her head in confusion and the Human squinting up at the rooftop of the building where Arano had been rescued. Arano didn't need to hear the conversation to understand the sniper was furious with Wendra that Arano had escaped another trap, and Wendra and her companion had no idea what had happened to him.

"Why did she save me from those soldiers, then, on two occasions?" Arano asked, perplexed. "She could've just let them have me."

"No, because then she wouldn't have been paid by Event Horizon for turning you in. The soldiers would've taken credit. She was trying to turn you over to the secret police. She probably gave up on taking you alive, and may be settling for the lesser reward for bringing in your corpse."

Arano nodded in silent fury. "And you can help me escape?"

"Yes," Lentin answered simply. "I have a ship, and my crew members are from many different races. We won't be questioned. Bromidian ships are allowed to come and go at will."

Arano stood silently for a bit longer, his lips pursed in determination. "You know that I have to take Wendra down before I leave."

"All right," Lentin agreed. "Let's neutralize her, and then I'll take you to my ship. We must hurry, however. Your destruction of the Selpan Weather Control Device has upset the balances in the atmosphere. Many people warned them this might happen, but they built the device anyway. Deprived of a normal outlet for the pressures that build in the atmosphere, an enormous amount of turbulence has built out over the ocean. The destruction of the Device released the pressure and turbulence into the largest hurricane ever seen on any of the settled planets. The winds at its center rival that of the strongest tornadoes, and it has a diameter in excess of 900 kilometers. We must be on our ship before that storm arrives."

Arano's eyes were wide with horror. "What've we done?"

Lentin fixed him with a firm gaze. "You released the inevitable. Nature was not meant to be controlled. That device had less than a year left before the pressures became too great and the storm broke loose anyway. Now, let's take care of business and get out of here."

Alyna nearly collapsed from cold and exhaustion as she stumbled up the ramp of the Intrepid. She managed to drag herself to the pilot's seat, issuing orders as her crew moved automatically to prep the ship for takeoff. Her feet were numb, and she worried about the possibility of frostbite as the ship hummed to life, lifting from the surface of the frozen planet. Her fingers, stiff after spending so long in the snowstorm, worked numbly across her control panel as she started the launch sequence. The Intrepid emerged from its hiding place and launched for the lead-gray skies, but was swiftly met by a fighter escort consisting of four small, one-seat fighters.

"Standing by to eject the cargo pods and ready the weapons system," announced Lain.

Alyna hesitated, letting out a long breath. "Let's wait a bit, Lain. Keep the pods until we get a little further from the planet. If we dump the disguise too soon, they may send something more serious to deal with us."

Soon, the ship was rocked by incoming fire from the fighters swarming the Intrepid like a group of angry hornets. The shields held steady, and they opened the distance between themselves and the planet's gravity well. At a signal from Alyna, Lain ejected the cargo pods, bringing the ship's weapons to bear on the unsuspecting fighters. The enemy pilots' surprise was plainly evident in the almost total lack of evasive maneuvers as Alyna's crew systematically destroyed them. With minimal effort, the threat was eliminated. Alyna ordered the shields dropped, and as the Rift Drive engines came alive, the Intrepid slipped into the brilliant, swirling colors of the artificial wormhole.

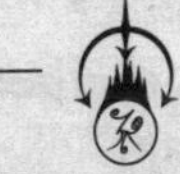

Arano had just gathered his few remaining possessions in Wendra's apartment when the door opened and Wendra entered, a puzzled look on her face. "You've got more lives than a cat," she commented with a smile. "I lost sight of you when you took a wrong turn on your way to the meeting. The next thing I knew, there were Event Horizon police and soldiers swarming the area. They were none too happy you escaped again. I guess we need a new plan."

"What now?" Arano asked her. "Every contact you've had so far has turned into a trap."

She drew up angrily. "If you'd followed instructions last time, this would all be over."

Arano nodded knowingly. "So, tell me. Was that sniper going to just shoot me in cold blood, or only if I tried to escape?"

"What sniper?"

"The one looking for me. The one you met with after I disappeared. Or should I have been more worried about the one who chased me up onto the rooftop of a nearby building?"

"They were there to cover you, in case something went wrong."

Arano laughed, shaking his head. "I can't believe you haven't figured it out yet, Wendra. I thought you were smarter than that." Seeing the perplexed look on her face slowly replaced by fear, Arano pushed onward. "Did it ever occur to you to wonder how I seemed to know, just in time, when one of your little ambushes was about to be sprung on me?"

"Now I understand," she hissed, backing toward the door. "You're a Padian!"

"And you're under arrest for treason," Arano told her coldly, drawing his pistol. With a scream, Wendra vaulted for the door, only to find it blocked by a Bromidian. She reached for her own pistol, but before she could clear her holster, Lentin had buried a knife in her chest. Her last breath gurgled and she collapsed to the floor. Lentin removed his knife, cleaned it on her shirt, and turned to face Arano.

"Would you consider that neutralized enough?" he asked with an insectoid grin.

"I'd say," agreed Arano. "Let's get out of here. I've already searched the place, and there's nothing here of any intelligence value. I think I'm ready to go home."

They headed toward the spaceport on foot, not wanting to chance paying for a ride and having the driver recognize Arano from the many photos passed around by Event Horizon. A heavy rain fell now, and the wind picked up as the massive hurricane drew closer. Arano could feel the air temperature dropping, a sure sign that they were under the leading edge of the massive storm encroaching upon the vulnerable city. He scratched at his annoying artificial beard and pressed forward.

As they strolled toward their waiting ship, the enormity of the events of the past few days came crashing down on Arano. One of the foundations of his adult life, indeed his purpose in life, had been eliminated. He'd always felt he could trust Coalition Intelligence agents, especially Humans and Padians. In this particular case, knowing the traitor before had made him trust her that much more, and had made him crash that much harder when she betrayed him.

Looking over at his companion, as the leading edge of the enormous storm raged about them, Arano was forced to confront the greatest conflict raging inside him. He'd sworn hatred of all Bromidians, hating them for what had been done on Leguin 4, both to Arano's' people and his family. But he realized now he had hated the Bromidians as a race, not seeing them as individuals. It had blinded him to the possibility that what had been done to his people was the fault of a small group of Bromidians, and not the fault of the whole race. He saw the distrust and hatred of Padians by a small group of Humans who'd disliked him simply because of who he was. He'd been angry these people hated him without knowing him, yet here he was doing the same thing to the Bromidian people!

They passed a small guard outpost as they neared Lentin's ship. The guards looked suspiciously at Arano, but a glare from Lentin was enough to allow them passage, and they reached the ship without incident. Minutes later, the ship blasted away from the planet's surface, and Arano was finally on his way home. He gazed out a viewport at the awesome beauty of the hurricane below, which Lentin had dubbed "Hurricane Viper" after Arano told him his nickname.

When he found himself alone in his private quarters, Arano sat for several long minutes, not moving, his thoughts again on his inner turmoil. When he confronted his personal demons, he began to see how his intense hatred for the Bromidian race had helped shore up the emotional wall he'd built, the same barrier that kept him from releasing his true feelings for Alyna. Reality came crashing in on him, and the wall crumbled. Somewhere, in the back of his mind, a part of him was relieved that no one was there to see his tears.

Lentin had flown Arano to the Subac system and left him at a Coalition outpost on Subac 2 Prime. From there, having identified himself, Arano was flown to the Immok System. He stood with the captain of the USCS Constitution, a Valkyrie Class light cruiser, as the ship docked at the star fortress orbiting Immok 2. The captain shook Arano's hand, congratulated him on his team's successful rescue of the President, and told him to enjoy the hero's welcome he deserved. Arano had laughed, saying the citizens of the Coalition didn't appreciate their military enough to do anything special for a soldier. Now, as Arano's transport lowered gracefully to the ground at the Immok City spaceport, he saw just how wrong he was.

A military band played the Coalition Anthem and a special song written just for the Avengers teams. A crowd of several thousand people had gathered, and the roar that went up when Arano stepped to the tarmac was deafening. Police vehicles circled the spaceport landing area, blaring their sirens and flashing their lights. Large fire suppression trucks from the Immok City Fire Department showered geysers of water into the air. When Arano approached an assembled group of generals, standing smartly at attention, he saw a well-dressed Gatoan standing to one side of the generals. Arano recognized him as President Siator Bistre.

Arano's head was spinning as he moved mechanically down the line of officers, shaking hands and saluting. He even received a fierce bear hug from the President, who again invoked his deity, Launyr, while expressing his thanks for Arano's selfless efforts in seeing to the successful rescue in the Navek System. He presented Arano with the Silver Cross of Courage, the second highest award the Coalition gave to its soldiers. Arano turned and saluted the Coalition flag while the military band once again played the Anthem. His eyes, however, scanned the assembled troops for one familiar face.

It didn't take him long to find her. As soon as the flowery speeches had ended, he roughly pushed his way through the assembled crowd, embracing Alyna in a way that suggested he might never let go. The only words he could bring himself to say were that he was sorry.

Late that evening, Arano and Alyna walked hand-in-hand up the stairs to Alyna's front porch. They'd enjoyed a night on the town, and gone for a long walk in a park near Alyna's home. During that walk, Alyna recounted the rescue of the President, and Arano told her all that had befallen him after his team had been forced to leave him behind. He even told her of his own inner turmoil when he was saved by a Bromidian, and how he had been forced to confront his demons.

But the night of relaxation was ending. They stood silently for a long embrace, and finally Alyna pulled back to gaze into Arano's eyes. He knew she could see the hurt and turmoil there, but he also knew she could see the love he'd finally found the strength to express. After an awkward silence, Alyna asked Arano to come inside. She'd barely finished her invitation before Arano had opened her front door and ushered her in.

CHAPTER NINETEEN

ARANO SAT IN RAPT ATTENTION IN HIS FRONT ROW seat as President Siator Bistre approached the podium. He was making his first speech to the High Council since his return two days earlier. While most members of the Coalition government had been overjoyed at his return, there were a few who didn't share that excitement. Grand High Councilor Balor Tient, for one, thought Arano with a smile. He noticed Alyna looking at him with raised eyebrows, obviously wondering what he found so humorous. He gave a short laugh and looked toward the VIP seating area where the Grand High Councilor sat fuming in silence, arms crossed and what appeared to be a permanent scowl etched into his face, obviously distraught to no longer be in charge of the government. Arano looked back at the podium when the President started to speak.

"Members of the High Council, friends, and especially, members of Avengers Team 5, I bid you welcome. Only a few days ago, I thought I'd never again stand before you, and it's only due to the bravery of these fine soldiers in front of me that I'm able to do so. I want you to know I was as outraged as the rest of you when our Prelar of Defense. . . excuse me, former Prelar of Defense, brought criminal charges against the members of Avengers Team 5 for undertaking my rescue mission without notifying the High Council beforehand. I've since dismissed those charges, and I've voided the law requiring the military to report all missions to the High Council prior to implementation. This was a ridiculous breach of operational security, endangering both the lives of our brave soldiers and the success of the war against our enemies."

Arano looked over at Balor Tient's entourage, a select group of High Councilors and their top advisors. Judging by their whispered conversations emphasized by harsh gestures, he guessed they were all having a bad day. Tient was unmoving, lips pursed and eyebrows furrowed as he glared at the President. Arano half-expected to see steam coming from the Grand High Councilor's ears.

"I've also ordered the Galactic Bureau of Intelligence to conduct a full investigation of the company called Garanth Construction, the builder of this wonderful new facility where the High Council members have their offices. The revelations that have come out about Garanth in the last two days have been disturbing, to say the least."

Arano nodded in agreement. Captain Pana's team had looked into more security leaks, and by feeding false information to members of the High Council, they'd tracked the leak back to its source. As it turned out, Garanth Construction owned all the buildings surrounding the new High Council building. Since all offices for members of the High Council had outside windows, it was a simple matter for spies in the surrounding buildings to use long-range listening equipment to pick up on everything discussed in those offices. This was especially damaging after the Prelar of Defense, who was a Bromidian, had forced the military to brief the High Council on planned military operations, which would, of course, be discussed in private in the High Council offices. The real shocker had come when it was discovered Garanth Construction was indirectly owned by Event Horizon. The possibilities of what secure information was compromised by this arrangement were staggering.

"We're also looking into the activities of the Bromidian Empire. Certain information has come to our attention indicating they may have been supporting both Rising Sun and Event Horizon. If this information is confirmed, the proper steps will be taken. Such actions must not be allowed to go unpunished.

"I've ordered the commanders of our military machine to pull out all the stops. Event Horizon must be destroyed, and we'll do whatever we must to see to it that future generations won't have to live in fear of these cowardly attacks on innocent civilians. We won't, however, feed military information to the High Council. Details of planned military assaults should be disseminated on a need-to-know basis, and you don't need to know."

The President continued to speak for another quarter of an hour, then the meeting was adjourned. Arano and his team returned to their planning room, where they knew their next mission was already awaited them. Alyna held on tightly to Arano's hand as they walked through the halls of the Coalition Military Headquarters Building, and Arano had no intention of letting her hand go. He felt alive, invigorated, and refreshed, as if he had been given a new shot at life. He'd felt this way since he confronted his feelings of hate toward Bromidians, and was beginning to realize the emotional toll his hatred had taken on him. The door to Team 5's planning room slid open with a hiss, and Arano led his team inside.

Colonel Vines was waiting for them, a packet of information in his hands. "Your team produced a gold mine of information in the Selpan system, Viper," he said simply. "We've been working on trying to find a fix for the problems caused by the Nebulatic Beacon, but it seems to be eluding us. We did find the reason Intrepid doesn't experience the shield and weapon system problems from the Beacon. The specs on your shields and weapons weren't yet in the Coalition computer system when Dar Noil accessed the information on our ships. Whatever it is the Beacon does, it's targeted at our ships directly, excluding all other ships from its influence. Unfortunately, very few of our ships have been retrofitted with the newer equipment, because the time for the overhauls takes so long.

"We do know the Beacon apparatus is extremely bulky and requires vast amounts of power. Nothing smaller than capital ships can carry it, although the bigger the ship, the greater the effects. This is why the destruction of that starbase brought a lot of our systems back online; the starbase was the major source of the transmissions from the Nebulatic Beacon in the Solarian system.

"Arano's informant gave us information tracing the development of the Beacon to a laboratory at a small outpost in the Niones System. You'll fly into the system, land in the jungle, and destroy the lab. Before you destroy it, we need you to recover as much information about the Beacon as you can. You may be able to enlist the help of the indigenous race on that planet, the Latyrians. They are physiologically similar to the Bromidians, although they are fairly primitive. They do have a few laser weapons in their possession for guard duty, but they mostly use longbows and hand-to-hand melee weapons. I've downloaded our information on them into Intrepid's computers.

"The Bromidians have enslaved the Latyrians, forcing them into manual labor in work camps. The Latyrians who don't work in the camps are forced to work as guards, patrolling the surrounding jungle to keep intruders away from the outpost. According to the information we've put together, the Bromidians pulled out some time ago and gave the outpost and its lab to Event Horizon."

The Colonel fixed the Avengers with a stern look. "We must know what the Beacon's weaknesses are. There has to be a way for us to bring it down. The time for a confrontation with the Bromidian Empire is fast approaching, and we need to be ready. In fact, we just received word the Bromidians have overrun two more systems."

He had to pause while the soldiers assembled before him registered their disbelief, the room filled with angry protests. Arano threw an unoffending file across the table, and Alyna buried her face in her hands.

Colonel Vines had to raise his voice to be heard over the angry Avengers. "They took the Trum System and the Drania System. Since there are no official governments in those systems, we can do little else other than issue a protest. We have no information about what happened to the people who lived in those systems.

"Trum and Drania are sparsely inhabited. The only reason for the Bromidians to take those systems is for use as launching points for a two-pronged invasion. The two systems are on opposite sides of the Coalition's territory, and control of them gives the Bromidian Empire a distinct advantage. We must be able to strike at them before they strike at us. To do that, we have to defeat the Beacon. We're depending on you."

"How do we enter the system unseen?" asked Arano quietly.

"We're going to send a surgical strike team in with you. Your team will take one ship, and I'm leaving your choice of ship up to you. When the fleet reaches the system, there'll be a brief battle, which will be carried low over the planet's surface. You'll simply duck out of the fight, and the other ships will leave the system. In the confusion, we believe you'll be missed. From there, you can move on the outpost. All rules of engagement are suspended. You're free to use whatever means are necessary to destroy that facility."

Arano expertly piloted the Intrepid through the battle playing out all around his ship. His teammates were at their assigned posts, monitoring systems and blazing away at enemy fighters. Arano flew like a man possessed, and hardly a shot from the enemy impacted his ship, and those few that did were turned away by the superior shielding systems. No fewer than six enemy fighters fell prey to the powerful weapons in the Intrepid before Arano received the signal it was time to hide. The battle raged ever lower, and Arano dove his ship into the cover of the jungle below, finding a clearing large enough to safely land his ship. Overhead, the battle carried on for a few more minutes, then slowly disappeared from view.

For the first hour, his team worked to assemble the camouflage screen. Between the visual camouflage, a netting system that would make the clearing appear to be another part of the jungle when viewed from the air, and a sensor-damping field to prevent sensor sweeps from finding them, they were fairly confident the ship wouldn't be discovered. That accomplished, the Avengers loaded their gear and began their assault on the outpost.

Arano assigned Videre to be the "point" man, and the team moved out in single file, Videre about fifty meters ahead. For the first hour, they prowled the heavily forested jungle terrain without incident, seeing no sign of enemy soldiers. The dense foliage slowed their progress considerably, and at times they were forced to cut their way through the tangle of vines and undergrowth. Colorful insects flitted in and out of view, ducking behind enormous trees in games of hide-and-seek. Small, unseen animals skittered about in the underbrush, never quite coming close enough to be seen. They had to pause once when Videre warned a rather large predator was enjoying an evening meal directly in front of them. Arano and Alyna consulted their maps, decided on an alternate path, and the team moved out again.

Arano was reviewing the plan in his mind when he heard the commotion in front of him. Videre cried out sharply, and the rest of the team came forward at a run. Two Bromidians were struggling with Videre, attempting to restrain him. Arano dove into the nearest and bore him to the ground where he finished the fight with his hastily drawn knife. He looked up, saw the other had been dispatched, and looked back at the Bromidian he had killed. While he considered his actions, he suddenly realized that killing Broms no longer held the strange feeling of satisfaction it used to.

His eyes widened slightly when he realized the dead soldier was not a Bromidian. The similarities were there, and at a glance was easy to miss the true identity of Videre's attacker.

"Latyrians," he said with a hiss. "Not quite as close to Bromidians as Padians are to Humans." He searched the body and, finding nothing of interest, stood up. "You okay, Videre?"

"I'm fine," Videre told him. He glanced down at his torn sleeve, some blood and a welt plainly visible. "They have retractable claws, one on the back of each hand. One of them got in a lucky swipe." He gave Arano a playful shove. "Why didn't you warn me, Mister Danger Sense?"

Arano laughed. "I wasn't in danger. Why would my sense warn me about you?" He stood up and brushed the dead leaves from his pants. "Let's move. They may have friends nearby."

They resumed their march, and within a few minutes Arano realized they were being followed. The first sign was a bellow of rage, presumably from whoever had discovered the bodies of the fallen Latyrians. Shortly afterward, when they crested a hilltop, Arano called a brief halt. He climbed up through the branches of a thickly-limbed tree and looked back over the valley they'd recently left. While the jungle obscured everything beneath its heavy foliage, there was a clearing about a kilometer from Arano's position, a clear swath cut through the jungle by a small but swift river, with a rope bridge Arano's team had used in crossing. As Arano peered down across the valley, he saw a group of at least twenty Latyrians cross the same bridge. He ran his fingers through his short hair while he considered their options. He slid lithely back to the jungle floor and informed his team of the developments.

"We need to start disguising our trail," he said shortly. "They appear to be tracking us, and they aren't very far behind. Move out as before, but try not to break through too many branches. I'll trail behind and cover our tracks. Alyna, we need to try a few changes in direction. Hopefully, that will throw them off."

They moved out again, Arano using all of his woodland skills to deceive the Latyrians tracking his team. Alyna made several radical changes in direction, all the while keeping the team heading in the general direction of the small Event Horizon outpost and the hidden laboratory inside. Late that afternoon, they drew within two kilometers of their objective. Arano maintained a tight vigil on the surrounding jungle, however, as he doubted they'd been able to lose their pursuers.

Arano paused long enough to set a few snares across their trail, leaving them well-concealed in the heavy jungle undergrowth. As the team continued toward their objective, Arano continued behind trying his best to conceal their tracks from the pursuing Latyrians.

They'd gone perhaps a half-kilometer when a blood-curdling shriek filled the woods. Arano knew without a doubt that a Latyrians had been caught in one of the snares, the spikes probably penetrating the tough Latyrian skin on an unsuspecting leg. He smiled grimly, knowing that while the Latyrians were still on their trail, they would move more slowly now. His increased confidence showed in the extra spring in his step as they closed in on the lab.

Alyna made another change of direction and guided the team down a steep slope to a gurgling brook. They waded out into the knee-deep, crystal-clear water, hoping the stream would conceal their trail completely and allow them to complete their mission undisturbed. They followed the brook for several hundred yards, finally emerging when they located a game trail. Arano began to believe they'd lost their pursuers while he finished concealing all traces of their passing. They moved carefully up the embankment and headed once again in the direction of the laboratory.

They called a brief halt in order to prepare for their reconnaissance of the target. They had basic intelligence information about the facility, but Arano and

Alyna needed to move up to within visual range of the target for confirmation. They wanted to be certain their planned method of entry would succeed, and a visual check beforehand was always best. Videre was in a noticeable amount of pain, the swelling in his arm having grown during the march. Kish tended to his injury while Arano and Alyna dropped their equipment in preparation for their reconnoiter.

Arano looked to Alyna to see if she was ready when they heard the sounds coming from behind them. The team immediately dove for cover, weapons at the ready. They didn't know if it was their pursuers coming up from behind them or another patrol, but they were nearly certain they'd been found.

The noises ceased, and the jungle fell silent. Even the natural sounds died away to stillness, and the ensuing silence was almost palpable. From the way his danger sense warned him, Arano surmised they'd been discovered and surrounded. He silently motioned to the other Avengers to face out, an indication to his team he believed the enemy was all around them.

Several tense moments passed and nothing happened, but no one relaxed. They all knew it was just a matter of time before the assault came, and they were ready. Arano found himself holding his breath, and he let it out softly. A quick check of his team showed the same tension in their faces: Alyna chewed on a fingernail, and Lain was finishing one of his battle rituals. The tension built until Arano felt like he would explode, and then a lone figure approached them, hands held up in front of him. He was a Latyrian, Arano thought, and a high ranking one, if the uniform he wore was a clue.

"Hold," the Latyrian said brokenly. "I seek a parley. We've tracked you since your battle with our sentries, and now we seek to talk."

Arano waived his team back, ordering them to stay behind cover. He lowered his weapon to the ground and came slowly into the open. "How did you follow us? I thought we were hiding our tracks rather well."

"You did. We saw no visual signs of your passing. One of your soldiers was stung by my sentry. We can follow the scent over a great distance."

Arano nodded as, unbidden, the memory of his attack by stinging insects came to mind. The entire nest had followed the hormones left behind by the first sting, allowing them to track him when he tried to outrun the swarm. The Latyrian soldier who stung Videre must have injected him with a similar hormone.

"My name is Vantir. I'm the leader of this patrol. We're of the Finlen tribe."

"I'm Viper," Arano told him, trying to keep things simple. "I'm the leader of this team of soldiers. What do you want from us?"

"You're here to attack the evil ones who hold the fortress in the next valley, yes?" Seeing Arano nod, the Latyrian continued. "We can't permit this. You must speak to our tribal elders. You'll come with us to our village."

"And our alternative?" Arano asked tentatively.

"We fight," the other said simply. "I have fifty warriors hidden around you. You wouldn't survive."

Arano considered the situation for a moment, then nodded to his teammates. They stood up, handed over their weapons, and allowed themselves to be pushed into a line. Without wasting any time, Vantir led them off into the jungle.

The path they followed was faint, and in places seemed little more than a minor game trail. For over an hour, the Latyrians led them in stoic silence over the hilly terrain. They even doubled back once or twice in what Arano assumed was an attempt to make the Avengers lose track of where they were. In this environment, Arano thought, it wouldn't take much to do just that.

As their forced march continued, Arano reflected on what they'd learned about the primitive Latyrian society from known history and from information obtained in the Selpan system. The Latyrians had lived in a tribal theocracy for over a millennium, with total governmental power resting in the hands of the priesthood. The father of their gods was Xaxil, and all tribes paid homage to him. To honor him, a statue was carved from a precious stone, deep blue in color, similar to sapphire. For several centuries, the ultimate power rested with whichever tribe possessed the Idol of Xaxil. Every few decades, a lower tribe conducted a raid, stole the Idol, and became the ruling tribe.

Such was still the case in 2097, when the Latyrians were discovered by the Bromidians. The Broms studied them for an entire year, learning what they could about the race that seemed so physiologically similar to themselves.

In the end, rather than exterminate the entire race, the Bromidians settled for enslavement. They sent a strike team to a Latyrian temple and successfully stole the Idol. The Bromidian diplomats then issued a blistering ultimatum: surrender to the will of the Bromidian Empire, or the Idol would be destroyed. The tribes held a council, and it was decided to give in to the wishes of their conquerors. Since that time, the Latyrians have provided labor and security at the research facility here on Niones 4.

They reached the end of their trek as they entered a crude village set on the edge of a lake. The structures were made of tree branches overlaid with enormous leaves, lending a medieval air to the scene. The roads were an unpaved mixture of dirt and mud which their captors trudged through without a second thought. The entire village exuded an air of a complete lack of technological advancement, reinforcing the belief that these were indeed a primitive people.

As they splashed along on the rain-dampened streets, Latyrian villagers emerged from their huts to stare in wide-eyed astonishment at the warriors bringing the Avengers team to the center of the village. There, seated upon a rickety wooden throne was a Latyrian wearing a varicolored headdress with long, streaming flowers. Arano's team was marched straight to the throne, where their captors knelt in obeisance before the Latyrian seated there. Arano bowed respectfully, and his teammates did so as well.

Vantir stepped forward, followed closely by two Latyrians carrying the confiscated weapons. "Lord Chieftain Mendan," he began, bowing his head respectfully. "We captured these outsiders attempting to attack the sacred fortress. We've brought them here, as you requested."

The Latyrian on the throne stared down at the Avengers assembled before him. "I'm Mendan, Chieftain of the Latyrian people. You risk much by coming here. If we had allowed you to get through, the Evil Ones would have destroyed the sacred Idol of Xaxil. That, we can't allow. What have you to say for yourselves?"

Arano stepped forward, bowed once more, and looked up respectfully at the Latyrian chief. "Your Grace," he began, hoping he used the proper form of address, "we mean no harm or disrespect to your people. Our quarrel is with the 'Evil Ones' you spoke of. We would see them destroyed and their influence driven from your lands."

The chief glared down at Arano, one hand thoughtfully rubbing his chin. "It's not your intentions that concern us. It's your actions. Had we allowed you to assault the fortress of the Evil Ones, they would have destroyed our Idol. If we allow anything to happen to the Idol of Xaxil, we will fall into Xaxil's disfavor. He will call down mighty storms and floods to destroy us all. This must not be."

Arano chewed his lip, an idea forming in his mind. "How do you know for certain the Idol remains unharmed now? Do you know where it's being kept?"

"Once each cycle of seasons, one of our elders is allowed to see the Idol. He is taken, blindfolded, to the Idol's resting place and allowed to confirm the Idol's continued safety."

"What if we were to rescue the Idol for you? Would you then allow us to continue with our mission?"

"If you take the Idol from the Evil Ones, then by our ancient laws you would become our ruler. We'd have no choice but allow you to do as you will."

"We have no intention of keeping your Idol. We wish only to return it to your control. Will you let us try?"

There was a long pause as Mendan spoke with his assembled group of advisors. Apparently, Arano's declaration of intention to return the Idol to the Latyrians had made quite an impression on several of the chief's advisors. A heated argument ensued, with Latyrians waving their arms in each other's faces, nearly shouting in anger. Finally, a compromise seemed to be reached, and the entire retinue returned to their seats.

The chief looked down at Arano once again. "You're the leader of this group?"

"I am," Arano replied simply.

"Then you must prove your intent. Denabin, God of Truth, will judge whether you're truly worthy of saving our people. You shall represent your soldiers during the Trial. One of our own will be chosen as your opponent. He'll be picked by one who opposes letting you do as you suggest. You two will vie for the will of Denabin. Win the contest, and you may do as you suggest, as Denabin will have smiled upon you. Lose, and we'll destroy you for trying to deceive us."

"It shall be so," answered Arano. "When do we begin?"

"You'll be taken to a secluded place where you can prepare yourself for the Trial. In a short while, we'll meet on the shores of the lake. There, Denabin will tell us the truth that hides in your soul."

The Avengers were led to a sheltered clearing overlooking the lake, and two dozen Latyrians stood guard around them at a respectful distance. The grass in the small meadow was almost knee-high to Arano, and under other circumstances he would've enjoyed the peace and serenity of the natural surroundings. In their current situation, however, he could think only of ways to escape their plight. The guards were far enough away to allow the Avengers to talk without being heard, but they were also too far away to overpower them without taking unacceptable losses.

As the team of soldiers gathered to discuss their strategy, Alyna was already planning their escape, studying the surrounding terrain. She estimated that if they could break through the ring of guards, they could reach the cover of trees and gullies beyond the village in a matter of seconds. It would be risky, but it would still be preferable to taking their chances with some primitive superstitious ritual. She whispered her plan to Kish, who considered it, looking speculatively at the proposed escape route.

With a start, she realized Arano, Videre, and Pelos were having a heated discussion off by themselves. She frowned, wondering what the three were up to. Arano seemed extremely unhappy, but he reluctantly nodded in agreement. He waved the rest of the team over to him and sat down, an obvious look of displeasure on his face.

"Here's the situation," he told them shortly. "There are more guards out there than you can readily see. Videre noticed some of them by pure chance. There are probably more than fifty Latyrians surrounding us right now. If we try to escape, we don't have a prayer, especially without our weapons. Even if we got away, what then? Without our weapons we can't assault the fortress, and Event Horizon would have soldiers crawling up our backs in minutes. Besides, we have no way of finding our ship without the Latyrians' help. Our best bet is to wait this thing out.

"Pelos, our resident racial expert," he acknowledged his lieutenant with a weak smile and a light-hearted attempt at humor, "has told me what to expect. I have to meet some type of tribal champion in single unarmed combat. If I defeat him, the Latyrians will stick to their word and allow us to try to rescue their Idol. If we succeed, we'll easily be able to get their assistance on our mission."

"You don't think they'll go back on their word?" asked Alyna suspiciously.

"Not a chance," answered Pelos. "They believe the outcome is pre-determined, not by skill or chance, but by the will of Denabin, their God of Truth. They wouldn't dare to go against the wishes of one of their gods."

There was no more time for discussion when a troop of Latyrian warriors stepped into their midst. "It's time," the leader said simply, motioning for Arano to move ahead. They were taken down to the lake shore, where a group of over 100 Latyrians had gathered. Seated in a semicircle on a raised platform were the tribal chieftain and his advisors, looking on in anticipation of the coming contest. No, Alyna corrected herself, they didn't consider this to be a contest. To them, this was a judgment.

Alyna and the others were taken to a nearby log and ordered to sit. From there, they would be able to watch the "judging." Soon, Arano and his opponent stepped out onto the sandy beach and faced each other while a Latyrian, presumably a priest of Denabin, performed a short ritual.

Alyna sized up the Latyrian Arano was to fight. She believed that while Arano would be the slower of the two, he'd at least be stronger. She knew Arano was going through the same thought process, and would probably use a defensive technique. If Arano allowed the Latyrian to initiate contact, his opponent's advantage in speed would be gone, and it would come down to strength and technique. Alyna was confident Arano held the edge in both of those areas.

The fight appeared ready to begin. Alyna wondered briefly what form the combat would take, if there were judges, and when someone would step in to end the struggle. Her contemplation of the matter ended when the two circled each other warily, each probing, searching for an opening.

Arano and his foe began throwing light, probing jabs, testing defenses and looking for a weakness to exploit. The Latyrian landed a solid open-handed blow to the side of Arano's head, sending him spinning, the hidden claw drawing a bright red streak on his cheek. Arano staggered back, agilely caught his balance, and retaliated with a kick to his opponent's thigh which sent the Latyrian staggering backward. The blows ceased for several long moments as the two injured fighters caught their breath, each rethinking their strategy. Soon they closed on each other once more.

The Latyrian made a quick grab for one of Arano's legs, but he dodged out of the way. Another attack, and again Arano avoided the grab. But this time, the Latyrian darted right back after Arano without pausing. He secured a solid grip on Arano's leg, attempting to pull him to the ground. Alyna's heart went to her toes when Arano began to fall.

But it was all a ploy. With a vicious attack that stunned even Alyna, Arano used his foe's momentum against him and threw the surprised Latyrian to the ground. Arano rained a furious swarm of blows upon the Latyrians head, and the two combatants slid into the lake. Gaining control, Arano forced his opponent face down in the water before rising up and slamming a double-fisted blow to the nape of the insect-like neck. It was apparent even from where Alyna stood the blow had stunned the Latyrian, maybe even knocked him unconscious. She almost cheered, knowing the fight was over and Arano had won. She resisted the urge to run out to where Arano stood, choosing to maintain her dignity.

Arano straightened, blood from the cut on his cheek flowing freely onto his uniform. But he wasn't finished. Without slowing, he forced the Latyrian's head under the water. As Alyna watched wordlessly, her mouth agape in disbelief and horror, Arano held him under water for a full two minutes, until it was obvious the Latyrian had died. He slung the body over one shoulder, carried him over to where the priest of Denabin stood watching in approval, and laid the body before him. Arano bowed respectfully, and a huge cheer went up from the onlookers. Arano was taken off to another part of the village, while Alyna and the others were taken to a small windowless hut.

And the waiting began again.

Videre sat down silently next to Alyna. "Do you want to talk about it?"

"About what?" Alyna snapped, dashing away her tears.

"What Arano did out there today. You seem to be pretty upset over what happened."

Alyna took a deep, shuddering breath before going on. "He'd won the fight. It was over. There was no need to drown an unconscious man."

Videre nodded, the whiskers on his muzzle twitching speculatively as he looked around the sparse interior of the hut. "You should really get all the facts before you judge his actions. Didn't you hear what he and Pelos talked about? Pelos read all our available information about the Latyrians before we came here. He put that knowledge to use this afternoon, and it saved all of our lives."

Alyna looked at him sharply. "What do you mean?"

"I'm sure you saw how unhappy Arano was with what Pelos told him, but he knew Pelos was right. In this primitive society, mercy is considered a weakness. Arano needed to show the chieftain, as well as the advisors, that we're not weak, and we have the ability to rescue their precious Idol. Additionally, in this particular contest, the only way Denabin's will can be shown is by the death of one of the fighters. For Arano to ask the chieftain to spare the man's life would have been to insult the ruling of Denabin, and we'd all be dead now."

Alyna nodded silently, letting it sink in. She hadn't considered that possibility, and felt mixed emotions about the incident.

"You still haven't heard about the origin of Arano's nickname, have you?" She shook her head. "He'll probably be angry with me for this, but I'm going to tell you anyway. You know that his nickname, Viper, comes from the name of the Padian god of autumn, Vyper. Vyper is important to Padian folklore because he brings the killing frost every year."

"I seem to remember Arano telling me about that," Alyna said in a quivering voice as she fought to get her emotions under control. "Something about the killing frost making the animals safe to eat."

"That's right," continued Videre. "Now, I need you to think back to the times when you were living on Subac 2 Prime. When winter was coming on, and you got what we might call the first good killing frost of the year, it seemed pretty cold, right? It seemed absolutely frigid. Later, when winter hit with full force, you found out what 'cold' truly felt like. Then, when the weather warmed back up to the 'killing frost' temperatures, it didn't seem very cold at all. You realized it was just cold enough to do the job, which in this case was making the animals safe to eat.

"Arano is the same way. Sometimes what he does will seem to be a cold, vicious act. Later, when you get deep into a war and see just how cold and brutal war can be, you realize Arano is just cold enough to get the job done. Like the killing frost. Like Vyper." He stood up and moved away, leaving Alyna alone with her thoughts.

Later that evening, Arano returned to the tent with an older Latyrian man. His facial wound had been dressed and cleaned, but was still much in evidence. "This is Enton. It was his son I contended with this afternoon in the Judgment of Denabin."

The Latyrian stepped forward. "Your leader, Viper, is a great warrior. He has honored my son by giving him a warrior's death. I'm forever in your debt. I pledge my life to your cause." He knelt, pressed his forehead to the ground, then stood and left without another word.

Videre caught Alyna's eye, and he nodded to her knowingly. She mouthed the words, "Killing frost," in return, almost smiling.

"They're going to help us," Arano began, "but first we must secure their Idol for them. The Idol is being held in a listening post concealed deep in the jungle about five kilometers from the research facility. We'll have to enter the post and get the Idol before the Latyrians will help us attack the lab.

"It seems the Latyrians have a knack for strategy the Bromidians and Event Horizon didn't anticipate. During the annual visits to see the Idol, the Latyrian chosen for the visit has left a small amount of stinger hormone behind, both in the room where the Idol is stored and at regular intervals during the trip through the jungle. We'll be able to have a Latyrian lead us right to the listening post by following the scent of the hormones they left behind. Enton has volunteered to lead that mission. Once there, we'll overpower the guards and rescue the Idol.

"A large strike force from the surrounding villages will assemble here, waiting for confirmation that the Idol is safe. As soon as it's in their hands, we'll all move on the lab. We must move with a purpose when we get there, because as soon as we make it apparent we're going to take the lab from Event Horizon, they'll start destroying information. We have to locate the details about the Nebulatic Beacon, or this whole mission will be for naught."

"When do we leave?" asked Alyna in a quiet voice.

"Now," Arano said with a grin.

CHAPTER TWENTY

THE LATYRIAN, ENTON, LED THE TEAM OF AVENGERS deep into the forbidding jungle. Arano marveled at the ease with which Enton passed soundlessly through even the thickest jungle growth. He finally decided it must have something to do with the softer Latyrian bones and extreme joint flexibility, enabling them to contort their bodies in ways beyond the abilities of the other known races. Arano and the rest of his team floundered along behind Enton, trying their best to emulate his silence but not quite succeeding.

Although Arano had no idea where they were going, Enton confidently led them through the trackless wilderness, making frequent direction changes but doing so with certainty. Arano surmised Enton was following the scent of the stinger hormones left behind by the tribal chieftain during his last visit to the Idol. It made sense that if Event Horizon didn't want the Latyrians to know where their Idol was, they'd take a meandering, indirect route, confusing any attempt by the blindfolded Latyrian to keep his sense of direction. As a result, the hormone markers left behind by the Chieftain would follow the same winding path, and the Avengers would have to do so, as well.

The listening post was some distance away, so the group walked for the better part of the afternoon before the outpost came into view. Arano motioned for his team to secure their perimeter while he moved in for a closer look with Alyna and Enton. The Niones sun settled low in the sky, turning the horizon to a ruddy haze as Arano studied the facility. There was no perimeter fence to keep people out, and no secure gate. Two Kamling guards patrolled the outside, walking an endless circuit around the gray concrete structure while keeping an eye on the surrounding jungle.

The building itself wouldn't take more than fifteen minutes to search, and they had the added benefit of the Latyrian's ability to follow the scent right to the Idol. Although he'd never seen it, Arano knew he would recognize the Idol immediately. Roughly a little over a meter tall, it was carved from a stone of a deep blue shade, almost the color of midnight. It would probably be fairly heavy, so they would have to pass it around between them during the return trip and share the burden.

They studied the facility for the better part of twenty minutes, discussing various strategies and making suggestions about courses of actions and conjectures about the strength of the obviously modest Event Horizon garrison hidden within. Satisfied at last they would learn no more by sitting there, they returned to their anxious teammates to finalize their plans for the assault.

"Our first task is to neutralize the guards outside without letting them raise the alarm," Arano said.

"Once we've accomplished that, we can get right up to the building and jam their communications by destroying their uplink tower. We can then force open the front door and deal with whoever is inside. I know this is really sketchy, and we normally have better intel on our target prior to an assault. But that won't be the case this time. We'll have to be flexible on this one and adjust to the changing situation as the mission unfolds.

"One other thing: we can't fail. There'll be no second chance here. If we're discovered and fail to recover the Idol, Event Horizon will either move it or destroy it. Either way, we won't be able to return the Idol to the tribes, and they won't allow our attack on their research lab. We must do this right the first time."

"Do you have a plan for taking out the guards?" asked Videre, leaning forward curiously.

Arano nodded slowly. "I have my sniper rifle with my equipment pack. I also have a device for silencing the report." He glanced over at Enton, whose Latyrian face was furrowed with confusion. "I normally don't like to use it; it lowers the accuracy of the weapon. Besides, the sound of the rifle is a great psychological weapon in itself. But in this case, we need to take these guards out silently.

"I need to be fairly close to use the rifle in this configuration. The best range would probably be about 300 meters. From there, I can eliminate both guards before they know what hit them. I'll wait until the rest of you are in position, and then I'll take them out. You charge the area and secure the door, and I'll meet you as soon as I can. Then we'll have to improvise."

"I'll stay with you to be your spotter," volunteered Alyna. "Videre, you lead the others as close as you can and wait for the shots. You won't hear when Viper starts shooting, so make sure you stay alert. Just wait until bodies start falling, then get up there as quick as you can. Enton, I think you should go with the others."

Enton nodded and left with Videre and the rest of the Avengers while Arano unpacked his rifle. It was a heavy weapon, and the silencer made it more unwieldy. When he was ready, he and Alyna began their own journey to find an area Arano could take his shots. He led her purposefully through the jungle, angling toward the terrain he hoped would provide a vantage point.

They found it on the downslope of a ridge overlooking the outpost. There was a fairly large tree with wide branches jutting out into the open air. One particular branch was large enough for both Arano and Alyna to take up comfortable positions side-by-side with a good view of their target. As Arano sighted his rifle, he felt his pulse quicken at the occasional touch of Alyna's arm while she readied her own gear. Again he wondered how he could have been blind to his feelings for her for so long, and smiled at the irony that he owed the revelation to a Bromidian.

Arano sighted his rifle on one of the unsuspecting guards as Alyna watched on with her spotter's scope. He allowed his breathing to become slow and regular, relaxing his body as he prepared for the shot. The guards stopped, and one of them retrieved something from his pocket. Arano moved his weapon's selector switch to the "fire" position, placed his finger on the trigger, and squeezed his finger gently backward. He hesitated when his danger sense issued a subtle call.

Alyna suddenly hissed a warning, causing Arano to stop short. She nodded at the facility's only door, and Arano swung his rifle in that direction. Two more Event Horizon soldiers emerged and shouted to the guards standing outside. Arano breathed a sigh of thanks to Alyna for her alert and timely warning. Had he taken the shot, at least one of the newcomers would have made it back inside and raised the alarm, both here and at the research laboratory. He bided his time, and in a few moments the new guards ducked back inside.

Again, Arano sighted in. He gave them a few minutes, waiting to see if the other guards would reemerge from the building, but no one came. Satisfied, he readied his weapon, slowed his breathing and relaxed. He picked out his first target, sighted in on his chest, and fired.

The weapon jumped in his hands, the resulting violent impact with the guard below them contrasting sharply with the rifle's deathly silence. With the speed of a cat, Arano chambered another round, sighted in on the guard looking at his fallen comrade, disbelief etched onto his face, and fired once more. The second guard collapsed beside the first as Videre and Laron led the other Avengers on a charge from their nearby place of concealment. While Arano gathered his gear, he saw Enton check the two guards, apparently satisfied they were dead. Arano and Alyna climbed down from their tree and joined their teammates at the entrance to the outpost.

"You're truly a great warrior," Enton greeted him. "Your actions this day will bring honor to my family and my tribe for generations to come." He turned, an angry snarl escaping his insectoid mouth. "Now, let us see to freeing our most holy artifact from the foul clutches of the Evil Ones." Arano accepted the compliment with a nod.

Pelos and Lain dismantled the building's cable connecting it to the uplink tower, effectively cutting off all communications. There were no subspace repeater towers in the area so communication would be impossible via the smaller hand-held units the soldiers inside might be carrying.

Lain roughly searched the fallen Kamlings and produced a bloodied security card. He placed it in a small depression next to the main door, and the door opened wide to reveal the hallway beyond. Instantly, Alyna's squad burst through the door, laser weapons at the ready, each checking an area of the hall. Alyna announced in a whispered voice that the room was clear, and the whole team moved inside.

"Kish, take the point," Arano ordered quietly. "Enton, follow her closely and tell us where to go. You have the scent?" Enton nodded, Kish took up the lead position, and the team slid along the hallway. The smooth, seamless walls had few doors along their length. Both the floor and the walls appeared to be made of concrete, giving the facility a bleak, war-like appearance. At the end of the hall, three doors awaited them, and Kish looked to Enton for guidance.

The Latyrian stood motionless before the doors, sampling the air. Finally, he indicated the door on the right and stepped back out of the way. Again, Alyna's squad led the way into the room beyond. This time, they found the room occupied by three Event Horizon soldiers, who leaped to their feet at the intrusion, reaching for their weapons. The Avengers were quicker, and their laser rifles rained deadly fire, ending the fight quickly. Arano's squad concealed the bodies in the nearby bunks, giving the casual observer the illusion the soldiers were merely sleeping. Kish again took up the lead position, and at Enton's signal they exited through a door in the far wall.

Voices came down the hall from a room behind them. Arano snapped his fingers lightly, and when he had his team's attention gave hand signals to establish fighting positions. Since there was nothing to hide behind, they all dropped to the floor. Alyna's squad faced forward while Laron and Arano's squad faced the source of the voices. Moments later, a Bromidian civilian and two Kamling soldiers from Event Horizon stepped into the hallway and right into a murderous rain of fire. All three fell immediately, dead before they hit the floor. Arano and Videre pulled the bodies back into the room the three had just vacated, while Lain and Laron continued watching the group's rear.

Arano rejoined the group with a smile, waving a data disk and a stack of papers. He brought his team in close and lowered his voice to a whisper. "These were on the Bromidian. He appears to be some kind of diplomat. The papers, and presumably the data disk, discuss possible changes to something called the Niones Articles, an alliance between the Bromidian Empire and Event Horizon!"

There was a brief but silent celebration while Enton looked on in confusion, and then the mission resumed. Enton led the band of fighters down another hallway to a solitary door, a sign identifying the room beyond was a storage area. The Latyrian sniffed the air around the door eagerly, and raised his hand in excitement.

"It lies within this room! The Idol is here!"

Arano nodded and motioned Enton aside. "Lain, Videre, Laron, you're with me. Alyna, your squad has security out here." Arano took a deep breath.

Flanked by Lain and Videre, Arano gave a silent three-count before pushing the door open. A lone Gatoan sat inside, asleep at the room's only table. Arano pointed to Lain and motioned at the sleeping soldier. Lain understood immediately: if the sleeping man awoke, he would die. Lain moved closer to the table and trained his weapon on the unsuspecting sentry while Arano and the others moved deeper into the room.

A locked cabinet stood against the far wall, its contents hidden behind the sealed doors. Arano motioned to Videre, who slipped forward. It took several minutes for him to check the cabinet for alarms and disarm the only one he found. He went to work on the lock next, and within seconds bypassed this final security measure. The doors swung open silently as Videre turned and bowed grandly.

Inside the cabinet was a statue standing perhaps a meter tall. With a color of the deepest blue, it was a breathtakingly beautiful carving of the Latyrian god Xaxil, the father of the Latyrian deities. The statue was exquisite, displaying every conceivable detail of the leader of the Latyrian pantheon. The figurine was so life-like Arano half-expected it to step off the shelf and lead them back to the Latyrian Village. Arano started forward, but he stopped and turned questioningly to Enton.

"No, Viper," Enton said to the unasked question. "I'm merely your guide. It was the battle prowess of you and your warriors that got us here. You've won the Idol, so you must retrieve it."

Arano nodded, taking a moment to stand in awe of the statue's beauty before he picked it up. He slung his rifle across his back and reached out reverently. The statue was heavy, he thought, too heavy for one person to carry the entire distance on the return trip. He hefted it over one shoulder, drew his pistol with his free hand, and motioned to the others. The guard at the table continued to sleep, and they slipped from the room without further pause.

Alyna's eyes flew open wide when she saw the Idol, obviously as taken by its appearance as Arano. The Avengers formed back up into their defensive posture and returned to their point of entry. They reached the exit without incident and slipped unnoticed into the surrounding jungle.

They'd only gone a few hundred meters, topping the ridge where Arano had taken his shots, when they saw the patrol of Event Horizon soldiers in the distance. They were still over a kilometer away, but the enemy soldiers moved along a road in the open, and it was easy to the group totaled over a hundred. Obviously, they weren't expecting any trouble.

Arano called a halt and brought his troops in close. "This patrol is heading right for the outpost. Once they discover what we've done, they'll head back to the lab and sound the alarm. They'll think the Latyrians have rescued their Idol, so they won't suspect Coalition involvement right away. We need to head back to the village as quickly as possible and warn them."

"Actually," mused Alyna, "this may work to our advantage. Event Horizon will most likely go on the offensive to try to steal the Idol back. If we can prepare the Latyrian forces and destroy Event Horizon's assault force, the lab will be left with only a minimal force to defend it. We should be able to take them out at that point and still save the data from destruction."

Arano smiled broadly. "I knew there was a reason I brought you," he told her, dodging the handful of dirt she threw in retaliation for his remark. "Okay, let's go. We've got a battle to plan."

The village erupted in celebration when they stepped from the jungle, Arano holding the Idol high over his head. Mendan, the chieftain, came forward and bowed deeply, a fierce gleam in his eyes.

"You have succeeded, mighty Viper! Indeed, Denabin spoke truly when he said you would save our people. Now, with the Idol returned, we can smite the Evil Ones who dared defile our most holy object. Our gods and our people demand vengeance, paid for in the blood of the infidels!"

"Lord Mendan, we must gather your council of warriors quickly to find a strategy for the coming battle," Arano said simply. "We believe the forces of the

Evil Ones know by now the Idol is returned to you, and they will come to reclaim it. Let us destroy them now, while they wallow in the open, rather than wait until they cower behind the walls of their fortress."

"There's much to what you say, Viper. It shall be so. But you need not ask this of us. You have rescued the Idol of Xaxil. By our ancient laws, you're now the ruler of all Latyrians! I've gathered about me representatives of all the tribes, and they pledge their allegiance to you. Let us destroy the Evil Ones together!"

Arano nodded uncomfortably, wondering how to get out of this one. It was one thing to help the Latyrians throw off the oppression of Event Horizon, but it was another to become involved in local politics. He'd hoped to simply give the idol back, but that wasn't working out. Pelos was their expert on primitive cultures, he thought silently, and would surely have a solution.

The most pressing matter was the coming battle. By dawn, Arano had gathered his team in the village's main hut, standing around a table supporting a crude model of the terrain surrounding the area. Together with Mendan and several other tribal chieftains, they hammered out their strategy for defeating the force they knew was coming.

Several hours into the planning session, a runner appeared to announce an Event Horizon force was on the move, but the earliest the force could arrive was in another six or seven hours. Arano explained to the assembled Latyrian chieftains the enemy force would most likely wait until close to sunset before beginning their assault.

It was well past noon when Arano summarized

their strategic situation. While they outnumbered the approaching force, the Latyrians used mostly primitive weapons against the laser weapons of Event Horizon. Their small number of laser rifles wouldn't be able to offset that advantage. Arano assured them the battle could still be won, but he explained it required greater guile and well-planned tactics.

"What it comes down to," he told the assembled group, "is a few basic guidelines. One element has already been accomplished: we've made the enemy divide his forces. The Evil Ones had to leave a garrison at their fortress, but they need a significant force out here to overwhelm you. This has left the Evil Ones with two armies, both weaker than the army as a whole.

"We want to let them come to us, instead of us taking the battle to them. They have better weapons from a distance, so we'll attack them in close quarters. An ambush is the key. We have the knowledge of the terrain, and we know the numbers on each side."

He pointed to an area of the terrain model. "We'll engage them here, hitting from the front with laser rifles and archers. When they stop to combat this force, we will hit them hard with swordsmen from the flanks. The swordsmen will be concealed close enough to the Evil Ones they'll be engaged in hand-to-hand combat almost instantaneously. At that point, their laser weapons will be as dangerous to them as they are to us because they won't be able to aim their shots when you're face to face with their ranks. Hit them hard, and hit them fast.

"If they follow standard tactics, they'll halt their army when they are still a few clicks away." Not knowing if his Latyrian allies knew what a kilometer was, Arano indicated a general area on the terrain model. "They'll have what is called a 'release point', an assembly location they won't leave until a designated time, then they'll all move out together for the final leg of their journey. My team will try to come up with a method to determine when they are going to leave; it'll help our planning to know what time to expect the attack."

The planning session broke up soon afterward, each tribal chieftain returning to his warriors and filling them in on the tactics for the coming battle. Arano entered the hut where his team's gear was stored, pulled some food from his pack, and sat down to await the time to take their positions. While he ate, he noticed Lain working at a portable scanner, a puzzled look on his face.

"Is that some type of Kamling battle ritual?" Arano teased him.

"No," laughed Lain, "just trying to work something out here. This scanner is picking up brief bursts of energy several clicks away, in the general direction of Event Horizon's forces. I can't figure out what's causing it."

"Keep me posted," Arano told him. "I don't want them surprising us with some new technology. The Nebulatic Beacon is enough to worry about."

He turned his attention to another important matter as Alyna sat down beside him, also trying to grab a quick meal. "You ready?" she asked him.

"For what?" he asked innocently.

She laughed, jabbing a playful elbow in his ribs. They ate in silence for several minutes, exchanging occasional glances. When he could stand the silence no longer, he set down his plate with a sigh. "Alyna," he said seriously, "I . . . I'm really sorry I didn't come to my senses sooner."

"Viper," she said, equally serious, "we've talked about this. You had some issues to work through, and it had to happen in your own time."

"I know, but I still feel guilty. I put you through a lot, and I wasted a lot of time. Now that I've finally come around, we can't even enjoy any time alone together because of the war. Who knows when we'll be able to"

"When the time comes, we'll still be together," she interrupted him. "After what I put up with to get this far, you're stuck with me now. So get your mind back to the present. We have a battle to win. How much longer before we move out?"

Arano peered at his watch, almost laughing out loud when he remembered once again it had been a gift from an Event Horizon operative during his mission in the Ervik System. It was just dark enough in the room that he couldn't see the numbers on the display, so he activated the watch's backlighting feature. But before he could give Alyna a response, Lain yelped excitedly.

"What did you just do? That was the same energy signature I've been reading from Event Horizon's soldiers."

Arano moved hurriedly to Lain's side, pressing the backlight button on his watch once more. Lain confirmed his suspicions with a nod.

"This is the watch I was given on Ervik 4," Arano

told him. "The man who gave it to me worked for Event Horizon. This must be the standard issue watch for their soldiers."

"We can use it to track their movements," suggested Kish.

"We can do better than that," countered Pelos.

"Uh oh," laughed Videre. "The head-shrinker is going to work his voodoo again."

"Think about it," continued Pelos. "They're only occasionally checking their watches right now. As the time for them to pass their release point approaches, they'll check their watches more frequently. This is only natural behavior; they'll be nervous and impatient. When they suddenly stop checking their watches, we'll know they're on their way. We can use the same technique when they stop at their final checkpoint before the attack. We can pass the word to our troops using our signaling system, and they'll know the time for the ambush has come."

"Pelos, you're really devious." Videre laughed. "You should've been a woman." He had to duck away when both Alyna and Kish turned on him.

Arano settled into his perch, peering down at the site of the coming battle in anticipation. One last time, he checked both the supply of ammunition for his sniper rifle, and the moving parts of the rifle itself. He looked over at Alyna, holding her spotter scope, laser rifle close to her side. The soldiers of Event Horizon were less than two kilometers away, ready to move on the Latyrian village. Arano checked his scanner and confirmed the energy surges had become more frequent. The time was at hand.

Without warning, the surges all but ceased. From his fighting position, Arano saw the Latyrian sitting with Kish Waukee stand and give the signal to his comrades that the enemy was on the move. Although it was an audible signal, only other Latyrians could hear it. An anomaly of the race allowed them to produce a noise beyond the hearing capabilities of all the other races, but could plainly be heard by other Latyrians. They'd employed this tactic capturing the Avengers. They used it now to entrap the "Evil Ones."

Eventually, the army of Event Horizon topped the hill in a loose formation. Arano bit his lip grimly as he thought to himself the army had come prepared for the wrong type of war. They thought they faced a primitive army using primitive tactics, not a well-prepared fighting force lying in ambush. The Latyrians weapons might be primitive, but they were about to give their enemy a lesson in modern warfare.

As one, the concealed ranks of Latyrian archers and the few Latyrians carrying laser rifles rose to one knee and fired. The enemy soldiers froze in their tracks, watching in disbelief as their front ranks collapsed under the onslaught. Far down below, Kish and Pelos were plainly visible as they worked the apparatus to jam the subspace radios used by Event Horizon's soldiers.

Arano opened fire, carefully picking out the highest-ranking officers in the center of their formation. With Alyna at his side pointing out targets, Arano was able to decimate the Event Horizon officer corps.

Just as the surprised army gathered itself to face the unexpected threat, the next phase of the ambush sprang into action. With an earsplitting roar, hundreds of Latyrian warriors surged from their places of concealment and charged howling into the midst of Event Horizon's soldiers. Laser fire crackled from Event Horizon's rifles, claiming as many hits on fellow soldiers as it did on the Latyrians. Wielding their light but incredibly sharp swords, the Latyrians devastated their foes.

When it must have seemed to the enemy leaders the situation couldn't get any worse, Laron, Videre, and Lain led another group of Latyrians in an attack on the enemy rear. The Latyrians in this group, picked up discarded Event Horizon laser rifles and fired on the exposed rear flank. The battle quickly turned into a rout, with some of the terrified enemy soldiers throwing down their weapons and dashing for the cover of the jungle. The Latyrian reserves made sure none escaped.

Arano had disapproved of this part of the battle plan. Part of civilized warfare called for the taking of prisoners when the time arose. However, this was the Latyrians' fight, and the Avengers primarily acted as advisors. Being a primitive race, both technologically and culturally, the Latyrians didn't agree with the Avengers, and were determined to wipe out the enemy to the last man. In a surprisingly short period of time, it was accomplished.

Arano gathered with the Latyrian leaders in a hastily assembled shelter to plan the next phase of the operation. The minimal garrison at the laboratory facility wouldn't expect an attack, and the army they'd just eliminated wouldn't be missed for some time. Their failure to check in with the base might arouse some suspicion, but in a jungle environment like this, communication lapses weren't uncommon. The Avengers and their Latyrian allies would definitely have the advantage of surprise, but only if they hurried.

It took them the better part of an hour to plan the assault on the lab, and the army moved out immediately afterward. They marched well into the night, arriving within sight of their objective shortly after midnight. They surrounded the base, breaking their army up into the four groups that would comprise the final assault. Once they were in place, Arano bade farewell to the chieftains and led his team closer to the base. The Latyrians would hold their position until they received Arano's signal. If they hadn't received the signal by sunrise, the attack would go on anyway.

The defenses protecting the little fortress weren't very impressive, in Arano's opinion. There were only minimal heavy weapons positions on the perimeter, and the fence was not well maintained. In fact, Arano's team could breach the fence with ease; the careless soldiers hadn't trimmed back the branches of a large tree, branches which now dangled well over the fence and into the courtyard of the besieged Event Horizon facility. Arano led his team up the tree and over the fence. The Avengers had penetrated the outer defenses undetected.

Arano gave a heavy, disgusted sigh as he examined the careless defenses Event Horizon had erected. Granted, it made his job easier, but seeing sloppy work by soldiers always set his teeth on edge. There appeared to be no monitoring devices, no cameras or motion sensors. The distance from the fence to their building was a scant thirty meters, nowhere near a large enough kill zone. The bushy trees that dotted the landscape between the fence and the building provided excellent cover for the Avengers to hide behind, and the lack of windows in the building prevented even casual observation of the invaders by someone inside the lab.

If the attitudes of the soldiers patrolling the perimeter were any indication, the Event Horizon commanders at the facility had no idea what had happened to their expeditionary force they'd sent to recapture the Idol of Xaxil. The soldiers on patrol walked about aimlessly in large groups, weapons slung over their shoulders, talking loudly among themselves. The Avengers easily avoided these disorganized groups and made their way to a side entrance.

The door was locked and warded by an alarm, but was otherwise unguarded. Arano motioned Videre forward to open the door and bypass the alarm. Laron stood by with Videre to provide security against whatever awaited on the other side of the door. At another signal from Arano, the Avengers took up defensive positions to watch for a chance encounter with one of the incompetent patrols. Videre disabled the lock, and he and Laron burst through the door. Laron stepped out and indicated that the way was clear, and the rest of the team filed inside.

Lain took up the lead position for the team as they moved deeper into the complex, and Arano was struck by the oddly alien architecture of the facility. The Bromidians had been the original tenants, and they'd only recently given the place over to Event Horizon. At regular intervals, pairs of signs were mounted to show the way to various areas,one sign displaying the information in the language of the Coalition, the other in Bromidian.

Lain used the signs to guide them directly to the control room. Remarkably, they didn't encounter anyone in the open hallways. Arano surmised it had to do with the odd hour. Members of anarchy groups probably weren't early risers.

Arano moved up to the control room door, his laser rifle held at the ready. Without further prompting, Videre and Lain flanked him, ready to make entry. Laron and Kish watched ahead down the hall, while Alyna and Pelos watched for signs of trouble from behind. Arano glanced over at Lain and nodded, gesturing toward the door with his rifle.

The door slid open with a hiss, and the three Avengers were through in a rush. There were a half-dozen soldiers inside, but not one of them even managed to get a panicked shot off.

"Clear!" called Arano. The statement was echoed by his squad members, and they stepped into the room cautiously, weapons still ready to fire . All four walls were lined with computer panels and terminals, some of them carelessly marked as containing sensitive information. Videre and Lain checked the bodies while Arano pulled the rest of the team inside. Once they had the room secured, Arano told Lain to get to work on the computer, where he would find the information so desperately needed by the Coalition. Arano and Laron set to work sorting through stacks of documents while Alyna had the others guard the door.

As Lain neared the end of his task, Videre left his guard position to set the explosives to destroy the control room, and which would probably destroy a good portion of the rest of the building as well. Arano continued paging through the sensitive information before him, amazed the data wasn't more closely guarded. There was more evidence pointing to an alliance between Event Horizon and the Bromidian Empire, as well as a high level of cooperation between Event Horizon and Rising Sun. One troubling bit of information pointed to someone high up in the Coalition, either in the government or the military, who was providing information to the Bromidian Empire. While no official name was listed, a vague reference was made to someone with the code-name of Kranton. Arano made a mental note to have Captain Pana check into it.

"Viper," Lain said with a smile. "I've got it. All the technical readouts on the Beacon are here on this disk. I think we have what we came for."

"Great job, Lain. Videre, you about finished over there?"

"Just finished, Mon Capitan." Videre replied with a mocking laugh.

Laron smiled widely. "Well, Viper. What do you say we get out of here so our Latyrian friends can finish the job?"

Arano nodded. "Let's go."

He lead his team back out into the hallway and again found it clear. They moved out in a hurry, trying to get clear of the building as quickly as possible. Soon they were back out through the side door and up against the fence. They didn't bother with subtlety this time, cutting a hole in the perimeter fencing with a laser cutter. When they heard the alarm, Arano gave the nod to an already giggling Videre, who detonated the charges in the control room.

The blast shattered all the windows Arano could see, and even damaged the outer wall in a few places. All signs of pursuit dissolved as the soldiers milled about, uncertain what to do next. Their question was answered a moment later when a now-familiar roar erupted from the surrounding jungle, and hundreds of Latyrian warriors burst from the concealing trees. They fell on the hapless soldiers of the "Evil Ones", decimating their ranks.

Between the explosion and the surprise attack, the Event Horizon soldiers were completely demoralized. Some attempted to retreat, but there was nowhere for them to go; Latyrians poured in from all sides, some swinging their deadly swords while others fired captured laser rifles. Almost before it had started, the battle was over.

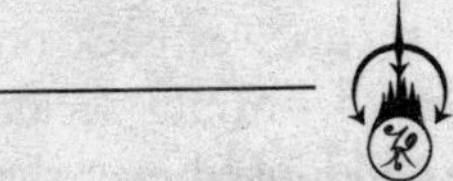

Arano took his spot in the pilot's seat on the bridge of the Intrepid. He thought back to the tremendous events that had befallen him in the past few days. He'd been stranded in enemy territory, nearly captured, and was about to fall to his death but was saved by a Bromidian. Then there had been the improbable alliance with the Latyrians, the rescue of their Idol, the defeat of the encroaching Event Horizon army, and the subsequent victory over the Event Horizon forces at their secret jungle laboratory. Following that battle, the Latyrian chieftains from the various assembled tribes had attempted to install Arano as their king.

Arano almost laughed out loud as the memory came back to him. He'd tried to turn them down, telling them he had other commitments, but the chieftains hadn't wanted to take "no" for an answer. It was Pelos who'd suggested the solution that saved Arano from becoming royalty. Arano explained to the assembled chieftains his mission to recover the Idol from the Evil Ones had been at the behest of Chieftain Mendan. The Idol, therefore, belonged with Mendan's tribe, and he should be the king. Arano said he would be the king's champion, although it was a moot point since Arano wouldn't be around to perform the duties of the position. The assemblage had agreed, allowing Arano to avoid his embarrassing fate. Immediately after the coronation of King Mendan, Arano and his team were escorted by an honor guard to the Intrepid.

And now they found themselves back on Immok 2, bearing the information that would decide the fate of the Coalition. Arano had looked over the data on the Nebulatic Beacon during the return trip, and felt certain he knew what the Coalition's next move would be. He definitely wasn't making any long-term plans.

CHAPTER TWENTY-ONE

THE MAIN PLANNING ROOM SETTLED INTO A hushed quiet as General Tamor entered the room, flanked on one side by an admiral Arano didn't recognize, and on the other by Commander Mendarle. A brief discussion between the general and his staff delayed the meeting for a few minutes, and Arano allowed his thoughts to drift back to the meeting in the High Council chambers the evening before.

Grand High Councilor Balor Tient had been in quite possibly the worst mood Arano had ever seen another living being suffer through. He surmised the Grand High Councilor must have gotten wind Captain Pana was investigating him as the source of the information leak mentioned in the papers Arano had recovered in the Latyrian jungle. Since Tient had been friendly to the Bromidians for years, he also was extremely unhappy about the Coalition's preparations to make war on his former comrades. The debate had been heated, President Bistre presenting the volumes of evidence proving the Bromidians had been behind the terrorist groups, Rising Sun and Event Horizon, as well as the heinous activities of the Disciples of Zhulac.

Balor Tient had tried several times to interject his opinion into the discussion in an attempt to curtail the High Council's march toward war, but to no avail.

In the end, the vote on a declaration of war against the Bromidian Empire had barely passed, the votes plainly running along the divided lines within the High Council. Tient had stormed from the chambers following the final vote count, and the United Systems Coalition was once again at war with the Bromidian Empire.

Several hours later, word was received that the Bromidians had responded by beginning their invasion of Coalition-held space. The two Bromidian task forces poised at the edges of the Coalition had struck simultaneously, taking the Branton System and the Eden System. They hadn't yet solidified their holds on these systems, and the Coalition was poised to strike back while the enemy was still in disarray.

"Soldiers of the Coalition," began General Tamor, "the time has come. For decades, we've lived under the shadow of the dangers posed by the Bromidian Empire. Now that the time of their invasion has come, we must take the opportunity to crush their military machine, once and for all. The Coalition Joint Command Staff has met and decided upon a course of action. It is dangerous, with our hopes balanced precariously between the skill of our pilots and gunners in the fleet, the courage of our ground forces, and the ingenuity of our elite units, the Avengers.

"Based upon information gathered during recent operations in Event Horizon territory, we've confirmed the source of our ships' system problems is a device called the Nebulatic Beacon. Through a series of complex calculations, the device sends out a signal that emulates the field found in a nebula, causing our shields and weapons guidance systems to malfunction. Our larger ships are less susceptible to the Beacon than our fighters, and they experience only minimal problems. However, the larger the installation the Beacon is in, be it a capital ship, starbase or even a planet, the greater the effect on our ships.

"During the recent battle against Rising Sun in the Solarian System, we encountered an especially powerful version of the Beacon. It depended upon calculations and power boosts sent by a Beacon facility on Solarian 3, rather than depending solely upon the signal from the main computer on Rystoria 2. When the computer facility was destroyed, the Beacon's effectiveness decreased sharply. Their capital ships still had functional Beacons, the reason systems in our fighters continued to malfunction following the destruction of their computer facility.

"According to our data, if we destroy the main computer on Rystoria 2, all the Beacons will stop functioning. They depend upon this computer for the calculations required to keep the Beacon running. Without it, they're nothing more than dead weight.

"This, then, is the general outline of our plan. The fleet will be divided into four groups. The first group will maintain its position as a home defense unit. Task Force Alpha will strike at the Bromidians in the Branton System, while Task Force Beta attacks the fleet in the Eden System.

"The greatest task falls to Task Force Omega. Our

recent victory in the Solarian System has opened a corridor for the Omega Force to launch a strike at the heart of the Bromidian Empire: their homeworld at Rystoria 2." He had to pause when the room erupted into surprised mutterings and protestations. He finally managed to bring the din back under control. "The High Council isn't aware of this plan. They know we will strike back against the Bromidian fleets in our territory, but we've told them nothing else. Our approval for this mission came from the President himself.

"President Bistre has brought us another surprise. He purchased a supply of the experimental plasma torpedoes. They've been used in a few skirmishes with astounding success. About three-quarters of the fleet will have them, but bear in mind they won't be effective until the Beacon is down and the targeting computers are back online. If past performance is any indicator, only ships larger than heavy cruisers will be able to use torpedoes at the beginning of the battles. At this point, just under ten percent of the fleet has been refitted with the newer weapons and shields systems, which are immune to the effects of the Beacon.

"I know what many of you are thinking: 'Why not destroy the Beacon first, and then engage their fleets?' The answer is simple. We want their fleets engaged in a battle when the Beacon is disabled. We believe the Bromidians will employ a reckless strategy that depends upon the Beacon for success. We'll set up a picket line of Thief Class Cruisers to prevent their escape once the Beacon is disabled, and we'll destroy their entire military machine in one grand action.

"The problem with our strategy is this: we will be

jumping in practically on top of their defenses. We'll be engaged in ship-to-ship combat within five minutes of our arrival. We'll have to conduct the battle for almost six hours before the Rift Drive engines in the capital ships will be cool enough to make a jump and escape the system. This mission will be do or die.

"One final note of importance: the fleet has been outfitted with several contingents of Firestorm Class Fighters. Besides the obvious benefits of these next generation fighters, we'll take advantage of their Rift Drive engines."

Arano pursed his lips as he considered that announcement, instantly seeing the benefit of such an action. With traditional fighters, there's a lull immediately after a Rift Drive jump while the assault carriers bring their systems back online. It takes a while to get the fighters launched, and during that time, capital ships are vulnerable. The Firestorms would be able to jump in with the rest of the fleet and provide fighter cover.

"That's it. Head back to your individual areas and meet with your commanders. You'll receive your orders momentarily."

The meeting broke up, and Arano milled around with the other Avengers team commanders as they filed out of the room. When he returned to his own planning room, his team was waiting for him, anxious for news of the coming battle. As he finished giving them his abbreviated version of events, the door opened to admit Commander Mendarle and Colonel Vines. Avengers Team 5 fell silent as the pair entered the room, their serious air speaking volumes about what was in store for the elite team of soldiers.

"Well, Viper," began Colonel Vines, his face solemn, "upon your shoulders falls the greatest burden."

"I had a feeling, Colonel," Arano replied.

"Your recent successes were partly to blame for your assignment to this mission. The primary reason was your team's contacts with members of the Bromidian rebel group, the Rystoria Liberation Front."

"Wait," protested Alyna, leaning forward in her seat. "My contact died. He wasn't able to report back to his compatriots to tell them about us."

"True," agreed Commander Mendarle, holding up one finger. "But Arano's contact was more involved, and he apparently spread the word when he returned. One of our intelligence agents was approached by the same Bromidian recently. We've arranged a meeting between your team and members of the RLF. You'll take the ring given to Captain Marquat by the RLF member in the Solarian System, and that shall be your primary means of recognition. The rest of the details will be included on your mission orders data disk."

Colonel Vines continued, smiling at Major Alstor. "Laron, you'll remain assigned to this team for the duration of hostilities. Viper, as I'm sure you already know, your mission is to destroy the Nebulatic Beacon. There's a window of opportunity for the operation that must be adhered to for the overall battle plan to succeed. I know this complicates matters, but it can't be helped. If you destroy it too soon, the Bromidian fleets will pull back to Rystoria 2, and we'd rather avoid another massive pitched battle like the one in the first Bromidian War. Destroy it too late, or fail to destroy it at all, and it may be our fleets that are destroyed. We're counting on you, Viper."

Arano nodded. "When do we leave, sir?"

Colonel Vines looked around, feigning shock. "You aren't gone yet?"

Following the instructions included in his mission briefing, Arano led his team into a restaurant called The Black Raven. An hour earlier, they'd arrived in the city of Anhyd, a small spaceport on the Bromidian homeworld of Rystoria 2. According to their information, they would be contacted by a member of the Rystoria Liberation Front. This side of town, while primarily populated by Bromidians, contained a fair number of members of the other races, mostly crew members on freighters docked at the spaceport. The wide spectrum of people allowed the Avengers team to blend in.

They entered the restaurant and found the main room full of customers dining on various foods. The aromas mixed into a tantalizing smell, reminding Arano just how hungry he was. He casually looked over the clientele, noting while the restaurant itself had a formal air, the customers tended to be dressed a bit more casually. He surreptitiously studied the low lighting level which would help the Avengers to maintain their anonymity.

Arano strode confidently up to the host, a Bromidian busy checking over a list of names. After a few moments, he gestured impatiently without looking up. "You have a reservation?" he asked.

"Yes, we do," Arano replied smoothly. "Actually, we're here to meet someone for dinner. I believe the reservation is under his name. Zharnak."

The host started almost imperceptibly. "Sign here," he instructed, his eyes finally coming up from the podium as he offered the sheet he'd been reading. Arano signed the book as instructed, the intricately wrought black ring on his right hand catching the eye of their host. "This way, please."

He led the group deep into the restaurant, through a side door, and into a back room where he instructed them to wait, offered to bring beverages upon his return, and left the room. They seated themselves around the plain wooden table at the center of the room, and Arano passed the time studying their surroundings, a mixture of Bromidian architecture and artwork collected from various worlds. Seeing the questioning look from Laron, Arano shook his head to indicate he felt no danger threatening their safety. The host returned briefly, brought the promised refreshments, and left again without saying a word.

The door on the far side of the room slid open with a loud creak, and another Bromidian entered. He sat down in a vacant seat and glanced at the Avengers.

"I'm called Amon," he finally announced in his guttural Bromidian voice. "Don't tell me your full names; I don't want to know them. Just give me something to call you by."

Arano proceeded with the introductions, using only their first names (and his own nickname) as Amon had requested. "Is this room secure?"

"Yes, Viper. All employees here are trusted

members of the Rystoria Liberation Front. We have dampening fields in place around this whole quarter of the city to prevent electronic eavesdropping. The Bromidian Empire believes this to be a natural effect of machinery operating in the area. We can speak in safety here.

"Lentin told me you're the Human he rescued in the Selpan System. Is this correct?"

"It is," Arano said simply.

"Very well. I understand you're here to destroy the computer controlling the Nebulatic Beacon. Since the Coalition was instrumental in the destruction of the laboratory on Niones 4, we owe you a debt of gratitude. We're willing to repay your assistance by helping you here." Seeing Arano's raised eyebrows, Amon gave a short laugh, his insectoid face contorting into a semblance of a smile. "Yes, we've already heard of the attack on their lab. Your secret is safe, however. Since the Latyrians were so thorough in the elimination of the Event Horizon forces there, the Bromidian High Command has no idea there was outside help. The only reason we know is because we have a few agents living among the Latyrians. Bromidians would've spotted us fairly easily, but the other races have a harder time telling us apart."

"So, what do we do next?" asked Laron.

"From here, I'll take you to our stronghold outside of town. We'll meet with the leaders of the RLF to plan our course of action. For the last few months we've staged hit and run attacks on their patrols and supply transports. We've amassed a fairly substantial cache of weapons and supplies, so we should be able to pull off something significant with your help.

"It's important you're persuasive when you speak with our ruling council. I believe we now have the capacity to pull off a major assault, but there are those on the council who are more conservative on these matters.

"We need to move against the High Command soon. If we wait too long, they'll find our stronghold and crush us." He paused briefly, taking a deep breath.

"Lentin has become a trusted agent with your Coalition military commanders," he continued. "He has been entrusted with the knowledge you're planning a major offensive to coincide with the destruction of the Beacon computer. He had to be told, in order for him to understand why the timing of the Beacon's destruction is so important."

"When do you want to start?" asked Alyna.

"Not until after dark. Enjoy the dinner I've ordered, and once the sun has set, we'll leave." He seemed to consider the matter further. "It might be a good idea for you to avoid being out in the sun for prolonged periods here. Our atmosphere has always had a thin ozone layer, and in times past my people lived mostly underground. Extended exposure to the Rystorian sun can be bad for you."

The group ate their dinners and talked about the issues facing the RLF. Amon briefed the Avengers on their strengths, including the types of equipment and weapons they'd managed to amass during their raids. By the time darkness fell and Amon announced it was time to leave, the outline of an idea had formed in Arano's head. He would need a terrain map to complete his plans, but had a good start on the tactics for the coming battles.

Arano stood before an enormous hologram depicting the land features of the area immediately surrounding the Rystoria Liberation Front base, extending over 100 kilometers across. His teammates stood silently off to one side, watching as Arano and several members of the RLF's ruling council discussed the feasibility of attacking the well-fortified base holding the Nebulatic Beacon computer. The council seemed split on whether or not the idea should even be tried.

"Perhaps Viper could explain how it is that a force like ours can defeat the army guarding this fortress," complained one Bromidian. "They outnumber us four to one, they have soldiers with better training, and they have better equipment and more supplies. Besides, they are fortified behind their walls. We cannot defeat them."

An argument ensued, the shouts rising until no one could be understood. Arano whistled to get their attention, then stepped forward. "It's true we don't have the capability to attack them inside their compound. Until we weaken their forces, we can't accomplish our mission. All it means is we have to change our way of thinking and put a new plan into action.

"Perhaps it would help if I gave you a little of my background. I'm a Padian, and I'm a member of the Daxia." He had to pause as the murmurs of approval and respect rippled through the room. "I was present when Rising Sun invaded my planet. I was also part of a force, smaller than yours, which drove Rising Sun away in defeat. Our odds were worse than yours, yet we succeeded. You'll succeed, too.

"The first thing you must remember is that this is a war. We have to maintain civility, but we don't have to engage in a fair fight. In fact, during the coming battles, we'll never be in a fair fight. We'll ambush their convoys, using hit-and-fade tactics, and generally make a nuisance of ourselves. We'll never attack their strengths, but instead will attack their weaknesses. Rather than attack the enormous garrison inside the fortress, we'll start eliminating every soldier, every patrol, when they leave the base. They will continue sending out larger and larger patrols to ensnare us, and we'll destroy each one. Eventually, they'll be weakened to the point we can mount a successful attack on the city."

"What do you recommend?" asked Hawan, leader of the RLF.

"First, I need to see your arsenal to know what we have to work with. But you can start by placing snipers around the fortress. Keep them mobile, and use two-man teams. Their purpose isn't to single-handedly win the battle, but rather to harass the enemy. Morale will drop in a hurry when they find out they aren't safe in their own stronghold." He paused, studying the terrain in the hologram, the fortress clearly depicted northwest of the RLF base. "There are wooded hills on three sides of the fortress. Your snipers will be invisible in there. If the enemy sends out teams to sweep through the trees, we'll have reactionary forces standing by to stop them. After they lose a few patrols trying to clear out the forest, they'll give up."

The discussion continued, and a few more ideas were proposed as the night went on. Arano and Laron took a tour of the armory, while Alyna and the rest of the team set up their own equipment in what served as their sleeping quarters. By the time Arano and Laron returned to the others, Arano had a good idea what their first major assault should be. A brief explanation to the ruling council led to the plan's approval. The Avengers grabbed a few hours of sleep, gathered what gear they needed, and moved out with the RLF forces, disappearing into the night.

Dawn came silently, the Rystorian sun climbing almost grudgingly over the ridge to Arano's right. He shifted his weight, bringing his prized sniper rifle around to a more comfortable position. He glanced at the two Bromidians sitting beside him, Rystoria Liberation Front soldiers who were part of the upcoming sniper teams. They were there to observe the way Arano and Alyna interacted, learning the nuances of the sniper and spotter combination.

Alyna checked her scope as Arano continued his whispered conversation with the future snipers. His position had been carefully chosen, a clearing on the north side of a ridge, overlooking the steep drop-off formed by the cliff beneath him. From this vantage point, he had a clear view of the bridge spanning the chasm before them, the same bridge that would be used by a Bromidian convoy carrying weapons and supplies to their fortress, over twenty kilometers away.

Down below, near the wide, empty clearing where the bridge connected to Arano's side of the cliff, Videre lay in wait with his trainees, members of the RLF who would become "experts" in the use of demolitions. Videre had formed an immediate camaraderie with the two soldiers, Rontil and Pent. He explained, in brief, the finer points of their task as they placed the explosives on the bridge supports. Rontil and Pent already had some experience in the use of explosives, and were enthusiastic about learning what they could from Videre.

Their wait was rewarded when the Bromidian convoy came into view and rolled onto the bridge. Hawan had objected to the next part of Arano's plan, which called for an attack to eliminate most of the Bromidian soldiers guarding the convoy, feeling they were too badly outnumbered. After Arano reminded him about not engaging in a fair fight, and explained the finer points of his idea, Hawan agreed.

As the lead elements of the convoy reached the far side of the bridge, Rentil reached for the detonation controls. "Now?" he asked enthusiastically.

"No, no, no," said a smiling Videre, shaking his head. He reached out and slapped Rentil's hand. "Patience, my child."

Pent could barely contain his laughter. "When do we blow them up?"

"Viper will give me a signal. We want to wait until most of the supplies are on this side of the bridge. When we set the explosives off, the army on this side will still be small enough for us to defeat, and our artillery will keep the army on the other side of the gorge from joining in the fight. Then, we grab our prizes and run for it."

The three sat silently while the convoy rolled across the doomed bridge in single file, rumbling endlessly across the enormous structure. The lead vehicles reached the far side, and they spread out into a defensive posture, their occupants looking disinterestedly toward the wall of trees surrounding them on three sides. Soon, the supply transports made their crossing, gathering in the center of the defensive perimeter they reached the other side. The tension built, Videre perspiring in nervous anticipation as the moment for the ambush drew near.

Arano announced the time had come with a single shot, killing the driver of a vehicle nearing the end of the bridge and effectively blocking traffic. Videre grinned broadly and motioned to Pent and Rentil. The Bromidians detonated their charges, which exploded with several staccato blasts as the bridge collapsed, section by section, into the gorge, taking the hapless military troops with it. As the soldiers of the Bromidian Empire stared in wide-eyed astonishment at the rapidly disappearing bridge, Laron sprang the rest of the ambush.

With a hail of laser blasts, the soldiers of the Rystoria Liberation Front opened fire on the Bromidians who had crossed the bridge. Arano responded by picking out targets one at a time, eliminating Bromidians who exposed themselves to his deadly rain of fire. Next to him, Alyna's rifle hummed away as she fired off burst after burst of laser fire.

The Bromidians on the far side of the gorge gathered their heavy equipment to come to the aid of their embattled comrades. The RLF artillery opened fire on them, scattering the soldiers who attempted to fire their heavy weapons, destroying several weapons platforms in the process.

Minutes later, the guns fell silent. The enemy soldiers on the near side of the gorge had been eliminated, and those on the far side of the chasm were forced to fall back. Several Bromidians from the RLF dashed from cover, seizing vehicles and equipment as quickly as they could. Once they'd obtained everything they could use from the shattered convoy, the attackers disappeared back into the trees. As suddenly as it had begun, the battle was over.

Late that evening, Arano, Laron and Alyna gathered with Hawan and the ruling council to plan their next move. Two other major successful ambushes had been accomplished that day, both resulting in heavy losses for the Bromidian Empire, while the RLF suffered only minimal casualties and secured large amounts of weapons and supplies. The sniper teams were in place, wreaking havoc among the Bromidians who thought they were safe within the protective confines of their fortress. One team had assassinated two generals out surveying the remnants of an ambushed patrol that had just limped back to the fortress. This particular action had resulted in several sporadic patrols emerging from the fortress in a vain attempt to silence the snipers. Some of those patrols even managed to return to their base.

Arano studied the latest intelligence reports. Judging by the troop movements inside the fortress, it appeared a major sweep of the area was in the works, with the Bromidians preparing to send out a large force in an effort to eliminate the RLF forces. It was what Arano had hoped for, and not a moment too soon. A runner had just brought him a message that had been passed through the RLF intelligence network. Current events had forced the Coalition's hand, as the remaining Event Horizon fleet massed to join the Bromidian Empire fleet in the Branton System. Coalition Command wanted to begin their final offensive before it happened; they stepped up the timetable for the final attack, and needed Arano to destroy the Beacon computer in 24 hours.

He intently studied the piles of information before him, but couldn't seem to put together a viable plan of operation. He'd counted on having more time to weaken the garrison at the fortress before mounting his final assault. The problem was he needed more troops to work with. He had enough to pull off several harassing raids on the main Bromidian patrol. He also had sufficient forces to pull the Bromidians away from the main fortress and permit a major strike on the base. He didn't, however, have enough additional troops to conduct the diversions and still be able to pull off the attack on the base with any degree of certainty. If he pulled enough troops away from the other RLF force to make certain of victory against the fortress, there wouldn't be enough soldiers left in the other unit to draw the main force off. They would pose only a minor annoyance, and the Bromidians would never fall for it.

Laron leaned forward, staring the shimmering terrain hologram, his eyes narrowing. "What type of facility do they have here?" he asked Hawan, pointing at a building perhaps fifty kilometers from the main fortress.

"It's a hangar for their airborne transport ships."

"Are any of those ships armed?" Laron asked excitedly.

"No," replied Hawan, shaking his head. "And they store nothing of value there. We've never bothered attacking it, because there's nothing useful. If we tried using unarmed transports to move around in for any length of time, we'd get shot down."

"Wait a minute," Arano said breathlessly. "Let me see your equipment list again." Arano perused the list breathlessly while the others stood by, waiting to see what had Arano all worked up. After several long moments, he solemnly laid the sheet out in front of him.

Laron looked at him suspiciously, his shoulders slumping. "What do you have in mind now, Viper?"

"Laron," Arano told him, "you're going to love this."

Captain Lon Pana led the remnants of his Avengers team into the hangar of the USCS Constitution. They conducted a final inspection of the fighters they would fly in the coming battle, the new Firestorm Class Fighters equipped with the powerful plasma torpedoes. It would be an extremely dangerous mission for his team, he knew. A fighter escort mission was always dangerous, but in this particular case, they knew going in they wouldn't have functional shields, not to mention having their torpedo guidance systems off-line.

He sighed, walking around his ship to check the torpedo launch tube. It all depended on Arano. If the Beacon was shut down during the battle, the Coalition ought to be able to turn the tide of battle and annihilate the Bromidian fleet. If the Beacon were functional for the whole battle, however, it'd be another story. Probably a story written by the Bromidians, Lon thought grimly.

His team was assigned to Task Force Omega, which would strike at the heart of the Bromidian Empire. Their assault on Rystoria 2 would determine the outcome of the war. The other two task forces had important missions as well, but without the victory in the Rystoria System, the other battles would be nearly moot points. He only wished his team could go in larger ships. He wanted to take the Assault Class fighters, but with only four active team members he couldn't fly both of the ships.

"Captain Pana."

The voice came from behind him, and he turned to meet the lieutenant who'd entered the hangar. "Yes, Lieutenant?"

"Your new orders," came the reply, as Lon accepted a stack of papers. The messenger saluted smartly and exited, leaving Lon to peruse the documents.

His team gathered around him as he suddenly burst out laughing. "Arano, I could kiss you!" he shouted. Seeing the perplexed looks of his teammates, whose slack-jawed expressions signaled they thought he'd lost his mind, he explained further. "Arano made arrangements to keep us out of fighter duty. We'll still provide an escort for the mission, but we'll fly his new ship. It looks like the Intrepid will make the final battle after all."

CHAPTER TWENTY-TWO

ARANO PADDED ON SILENT FEET, ALERT FOR SIGNS of danger in the surrounding forest. Small birds sang cheerfully among the branches of the trees, oblivious to the warlike party traveling beneath them. There was a stiff breeze blowing in their faces Arano knew gave them a double advantage. Not only would the rustling of the leaves help to conceal the sounds of their passage, but the scents of their bodies and equipment were carried away from their enemies.

Arano smiled to himself, amazed the leaders of the Rystoria Liberation Front had been so easily convinced to go along with his plan. It was shaky at best, but Arano felt it would work. There had been time to provide the RLF soldiers with rudimentary training in the areas they needed to make the mission successful, and then they were underway. So far, there had been no sign of the enemy, and he hoped it would stay that way.

He hadn't had much sleep in the past few days, but the adrenaline rush kept him energized. He knew his entire team would feel the effects of fatigue in the next few hours, but he was still confident they could function and succeed. In times of peace, they trained to the point of severe exhaustion to overcome the mental barriers that prevent most people from going past their physical limits. In times like these, the training paid off.

Fortunately, the RLF soldiers participating in the battle hadn't been pushed to the same limits Arano and his teammates had. The soldiers were tough, but they weren't prepared to hold up under the same rigors. They had courage, though, he thought grimly. They'd brought every able-bodied soldier in their command who wasn't involved in other aspects of the fight against the Bromidian Empire, leaving their base camp virtually unguarded. If the assault failed, the RLF was finished. Arano glanced to his rear, eyeing the soldiers speculatively. The RLF would fight viciously, like a caged animal. For them, as well as the Coalition, this was do or die. There could be no failure, and there would be no second chance.

They reached their final checkpoint about an hour after midnight, a dirt road stretching off into the darkness, both to their left and their right, as far as they could see. Arano called a halt and put out security, gathering with the leaders for one final conference. Arano, Alyna, and Hawan went forward on their own, and crossed the remaining distance to the hangar in about half an hour.

The forest remained unchanged, an endless sea of rough-barked trees and sparse undergrowth. The area teemed with small furry animals, scurrying about as they gathered food and kept a nervous eye on the newcomers. The hangar itself was situated in an artificial clearing, the trees removed long before. A tarmac stretched along for well over a kilometer, and a number of large, metallic buildings lined one side. There was very little activity Arano could see.

The three soldiers studied the area for several long minutes, noting the positions of weapons emplacements as well as the locations and habits of the patrols protecting the hangar. Satisfied they'd learned all they could, they turned to leave.

Arano became still, waving Hawan and Alyna into places of concealment before finding one himself. His heart raced as he sat waiting, eyes on the nearby trees, his danger sense shrieking in warning. He heard the sounds of booted feet as a patrol tramped carelessly through the undergrowth toward his position, and he silently swore in frustration at the turn of events. If they were discovered and the alarm sounded, the garrison would be alerted and the RLF would have no chance to overrun the hangar. On the other hand, if they eliminated the encroaching patrol, their disappearance might still alert the garrison. He clenched his jaw and waited helplessly.

The patrol drew closer, and Arano heard their subdued conversation. There were four of them, he saw, and they seemed to be passing by oblivious to the group hidden in the darkness just yards away. One of the Bromidians slowed, as if he noticed something near Alyna that drew his attention. He turned in Alyna's direction, and Arano slowly drew his knife. One of the other Bromidians said something unintelligible to the Brom who'd broken off from their group and he stopped, shrugged, and returned to the patrol. It disappeared silently into the darkness.

Arano breathed a silent sigh of relief, letting the air slowly escape from his lungs as he relaxed his tense muscles. The irony of the situation was not lost on him: just a few short weeks ago, he would have been bitterly disappointed to have lost an opportunity to kill that Bromidian. Now all he felt was relief. He sheathed his knife, waved to the others, and they resumed their trek back to the waiting army. They encountered no more patrols, and made it back to the base camp without further incident.

After a short conference with Hawan, the Avengers led their RLF soldiers into the night. With Arano's squad walking the point on the assault force's left side, and with Alyna's squad ahead on the right, the group moved cautiously toward their objective. As they slid stealthily through the pine forest, Arano found himself wishing belatedly they'd brought some Latyrians with them for the assault. Their uncanny ability to make and hear sounds beyond the hearing spectrum of other races was ideal for sending signals between the various units of their force.

They walked on into the night, still meeting no patrols. Apparently, the Bromidian leaders were deceived into believing the main RLF objective was the fortress, since most of their recent activities were in that area. Or, at least, so Arano hoped. If this were the case, the Bromidians would mass their forces near the fortress, leaving the hangar without the benefit of reserve forces. Arano's soldiers could quickly overwhelm the garrison at the hangar, but they would allow the garrison to send off a distress signal. It would draw the Bromidian patrols away from the fortress, bringing them to the rescue of the soldiers at the hangar. It would also reduce the forces protecting the fortress, making it an easier target. Providing, of course, Arano's plan for getting the RLF soldiers from the hangar to the fortress succeeded.

About two hours after midnight, the first Bromidian defensive position appeared ghostlike in the distance. Arano signaled a halt, motioning for the leaders to spread their units out to their pre-designated areas. The Avengers gathered, waited fifteen minutes to allow their detachments to get into position, and moved forward slowly. Arano led his squad, including Laron, toward the nearest Bromidian weapons emplacement, knife in hand, while Alyna took her team to another bunker further to the north.

Arano's targeted emplacement had two heavy laser rifles mounted in its front protective wall, and had been affixed with overhead cover to offer some protection from artillery airbursts. Had they tried to fight their way through such defenses, they would have lost over half their army. Because there weren't enough soldiers stationed there to put out effective patrols, it enabled the RLF forces to sneak up on the outer defenses and take them out silently.

Arano edged up to the rear entrance of the bunker and motioned for Lain and Laron to watch for other soldiers. Videre gave an almost imperceptible nod, and they eased into the bunker. There were three soldiers inside, and all rose to their feet in surprise. Arano buried his knife to the hilt in the chest of the first Bromidian solider, barely slowing as he charged another. With a low Gatoan roar, Videre wrestled the remaining Bromidian to the floor. He slashed his knife across his enemy's throat and held him down as the life fled from his insectoid body.

Arano tackled the remaining soldier just as the Bromidian's laser pistol cleared its holster. With one hand on the soldier's weapon, Arano rained blow after blow on the Brom with the other. The combatants slammed into crates filled with supplies, knocking them over and sending both fighters to the ground. They stayed locked in their death embrace, the Bromidian fighting to free his weapon and Arano trying to hold on until Videre could help him. The Bromidian put his free hand on the weapon, and Arano saw his opening. He grabbed a knife from the Bromidian's utility belt and drove it into his stomach, twisting the handle and ripping it upward. There was a wet, tearing sound, and the Bromidian's struggles ceased.

While Arano caught his breath, Videre went to the opening in the bunker that faced away from the hangar. He whispered softly, and a group of RLF soldiers materialized out of the darkness. They swept into the bunker and moved efficiently about the room as they collected the heavy weapons and the associated power packs. Arano climbed to his feet, made sure Videre was all right, and moved back out into the forest. He saw the relief in Alyna's eyes when he emerged unscathed from the bunker, and walked casually to her side.

"We'll be ready to leave here in about ten minutes," he said, checking his watch. "We're right on schedule."

"Are you sure about our mode of transportation

from the hangar to the fortress?" Alyna asked. "It seems a bit risky to me."

"I doubt they'll fire on their own transports until they're certain we're in them," Arano replied breathlessly. "If we land the craft in or near the fortress, the Bromidians will figure us out and turn their artillery on us. They might also shoot down any transports that were slow to arrive."

"Yes, but the alternative you have proposed is a bit hazardous. These RLF soldiers don't have the proper training. We could lose a large part of our force to injuries."

"I don't think so," Arano disagreed. "Bromidians have a tough exoskeleton, which should help to protect them. Besides, the most dangerous part is the landing, and we trained them pretty hard on that part."

Alyna nodded in silent agreement, looking off into the darkened forest. In a few minutes, the force was ready to move again. They slipped forward, moving into their final positions. The RLF soldiers carrying the newly acquired heavy weapons brought their burdens to the edge of the treeline and mounted them where they could provide fire support for their comrades attacking the hangar. Arano knew that to both his right and left, other RLF groups had moved to the edge of the trees with similar weapons. At last, the strike force stood ready.

Lon Pana sat silently in the deserted cockpit of the Intrepid. He checked the navigational computer, which showed they still had another seven hours before they exited the wormhole and stepped into the largest battle of their lives. His team had spent the majority of the rift jump running through battle drills to familiarize themselves with the controls and weapons systems on Arano's vessel. Satisfied his team was ready, Lon had sent them to their quarters to try to get some sleep, while he sat in the cockpit mulling over the coming battle.

He would much rather have gone with Viper to the ground battle on Rystoria 2, or Vagorst, as the Bromidians called it. In fact, most of the other Avengers teams were already on the ground there, smuggled in on freighters by the Rystoria Liberation Front. Even now those teams worked to disrupt communications by destroying the Bromidians' subspace repeater towers. A few of them were also trying to destroy ground defense installations in an effort to aid the fleet once it arrived. Lon's team couldn't participate, though, since it wasn't at full strength. He would have to be satisfied with what he had. At least, he thought grimly, his team didn't have to go through the coming battle in fighters. Arano's ship would give them a fighting chance, especially since its systems were unaffected by the Nebulatic Beacon.

He rose to his feet and strolled through the ship, checking on their weapons stockpiles. They'd converted several rooms into cargo bays and filled them with plasma torpedoes. Since the ship would have its missile systems operational through the entire battle, it seemed prudent to carry a generous supply of extra warheads. To aid in the loading of the added torpedoes, Coalition Command had assigned four extra crew members to the Intrepid. The soldiers served only in the capacity of loading torpedoes into the torpedo bays as it became necessary. An additional soldier would operate the Intrepid's Disruptor Beam.

He completed his inspection tour and returned to the bridge and again seated himself in the pilot's chair. He ran through what diagnostics he could, although the shields and weapons systems couldn't be tested until they'd exited the wormhole. Content he had done all he could to prepare for the battle, he allowed himself to catch a few hours of sleep.

Arano checked his watch one last time. He allowed a few extra minutes to be certain he'd left enough time for the other elements of his army to get into place, but could wait no longer. He motioned to the soldiers around him, and they took aim on the defensive emplacements around the hangar. Moments later, Arano's sniper rifle fired, the report echoing across the valley, and a Bromidian sentry fell lifeless from his lookout tower. Instantly, the forest erupted in laser fire as the RLF army poured a hail of incoming shots on the unsuspecting defenders. From some distance behind him, Arano heard the heavy artillery commence firing, and it wasn't long before the shells shrieked overhead and impacted among the enemy positions. Explosions erupted all along the enemy front, blasting debris, equipment, and at times, Bromidian bodies into the air.

A radio squawked to Arano's right, and he could hear the radio operator calling in directional adjustments for the artillery unit. The explosions from the incoming artillery rounds walked across the open tarmac, finally landing on the Bromidians' two heavy weapon emplacements. Eruptions of fire lit the night sky as the heavy laser cannons exploded, showering white-hot fragments of metal in all directions. With the heavy weapons down, Arano readied the next phase of the assault.

He removed a red signaling flare from his pack and activated it, sending a bright scarlet streak rocketing upward to illuminate the night. At the prearranged signal, the RLF soldiers on Arano's right shifted their fire toward the western end of the hangar area, while the forces to Arano's left swept across the tarmac from the east. They met with fierce resistance, more than the planners had expected, and the assault quickly bogged down.

At Arano's side, Alyna laid down her rifle, switched to her spotter's scope, and activated the night vision function. Arano knew without looking she was scanning the area where hidden Bromidian soldiers were firing on the assaulting RLF units. She waved the radio operator to her side, indicating the area where the Bromidians lay in hiding. After a hurried radio conversation, the artillery guns launched another salvo, this time shifting their points of aim slowly in the direction of the fierce combat at the tarmac's eastern end. Arano knew it was delicate work; make too big an adjustment, and you risked moving the shots too far and hitting friendly troops, but adjust it too slowly and your assistance might come too late.

Lain and Videre took up a new fighting position using special projectile rifles equipped with armor piercing ammunition, and the Avengers swept their powerful infrared scopes back and forth across the Bromidian-held areas. Even the enemy soldiers well-hidden behind crates weren't safe as armor piercing ammunition blasted through heavy cover to take Bromidian lives. Slowly, the assault team inched forward as the Bromidian defensive lines crumbled.

Arano pulled a yellow signaling flare from his pack and activated it, launching his second beacon into the night. At that signal, the artillery units stopped firing and the assaulting force advanced further into the compound, the lull in incoming fire allowing them to move without worrying about friendly fire accidents. Simultaneously, Pelos, Kish, and Laron led a second assault force onto the compound, driving directly to the hangar itself. More heavy fighting followed as the Bromidians inside fought to protect what little ground they still held. It was a valiant effort, but to no avail, as the superior tactics and overwhelming firepower of the Avenger-led fighting force finally overwhelmed the defenders, and the hangar facility was theirs.

"Ten seconds to wormhole exit," announced Lon, sitting up straight in the pilot's seat as his pulse raced. He touched a few more controls, and the Intrepid returned to real space, right on time and in formation with the massive assault force sent to attack the Bromidian homeworld. After a short delay, all systems came online and his gunners charged their weapons. He activated the scanners, immediately locating the juggernaut of a fleet guarding Rystoria 2. Silhouetted against the planet itself was the massive star fortress built by the Bromidians in direct violation of the Treaty of Rystoria.

Lon snorted in disgust. If the Coalition bureaucrats had acted when their intelligence agents had first told them about the construction of this star fortress, they could have stopped the Bromidians from completing it. Now it was up to the fleet to destroy it.

Lon scowled as he studied the scanner readout, lines of concern creasing his countenance. The Bromidian fleet didn't rush out to meet them as they'd hoped. Instead, they hovered protectively around the planet and the star fortress, almost daring the Coalition fleet to come within range of the massive installation's weapons. Lon knew the fleet would have to take that dare, and he received confirmation almost before the thought was completed.

"This is Admiral Modian of the USCS Striker. All ships, move into attack formation and begin the assault." When the broadcast didn't end there, Lon rolled his eyes, knowing the admiral was about to reiterate what the entire fleet already knew. Admirals were like that sometimes.

"When the Beacon activates, other than the refitted ships, only our battleships and heavy cruisers will have functional shield and weapons systems, so all other capital ships need to stay close. Fighter Wing One will protect the capital ships, Wing Two will attempt to destroy their fighters, and Wing 3 will do as much damage as possible to that star fortress. Luck to us all."

"All right, people," Lon announced. "Lets go make some Bromidian space debris." Grasping the pilot's controls, Lon accelerated ahead with the other ships in Wing 2, driving out to meet the incoming Bromidian fighters. At a sharp command from Lon, the torpedo gunner sighted in on the closest enemy ships. Before the Intrepid was in range of the Brom's weapons, four enemy fighters had fallen victim to the plasma torpedo barrage. Two Firestorm Fighters formed up on Intrepid's wing to protect them should enemy craft attempt an assault from behind. With its massive weapons array blasting, the Intrepid waded through the storm of Bromidian fighters, wreaking havoc as it went.

Laron trotted from the waiting transports across the battle-scarred tarmac to where Arano and Alyna made final arrangements with Hawan and his ruling council. "We're all set," he announced. "All equipment is loaded, and everyone's parachute has been inspected twice. Any time you're ready . . ." He trailed off with a grin.

"I still don't know about this," began Hawan slowly. "Parachuting out of a perfectly good transport just doesn't seem like a good idea."

"We do it all the time," Viper reminded him. "There'll be a few minor injuries, and maybe one or two of your people might be injured to the point they can't fight. We'll still do better than we would by trying to land near the base where they could turn their heavy weapons on us. We could lose a third of our force."

"What happens if my parachute doesn't open?" asked a nervous member of the council.

"We've been over this," answered Alyna soothingly. "That's why you have a reserve parachute. You'll have plenty of time to open it."

"How long?"

"The rest of your life," said a straight-faced Videre, ignoring the scowl from Arano.

"Enough talk," shouted Hawan, raising his rifle. "Onward, to victory!" His troops answered with a deafening roar that shook the hangar.

Arano nodded solemnly. "Let's go," he said simply. They followed him out into the night, walking up the ramp of the nearest transport. The door closed behind them, and the engines hummed to life. The craft vibrated slightly as it lifted from the tarmac, swinging gracefully in a circle before heading in the direction of the waiting Bromidian fortress. A cheer went up from the soldiers onboard Arano's transport as the RLF members shouted battle slogans and pounded their fists on each other's backs.

Arano thought about their current tactical situation. By now, the fleet had engaged the enemy overhead. Word of their attack on the hangar should've reached the Bromidian soldiers in the area, and their large force out patrolling for the RLF army was, no doubt, already enroute to the hangar. When they arrived, the token force Arano left behind would begin firing artillery and heavy weapons at them, and then would simply slip away into the woods, leaving behind the booby-traps they'd painstakingly installed. By the time the Bromidians figured out the RLF force they were looking for was no longer there, it would be too late for them to be able to stop the assault on the fortress.

The RLF soldiers and the Avengers would insert by parachute close to the fortress, breach the wall, and hold a portion of the base. With their defensive perimeter set, Arano would lead his Avengers into the main building where they would set explosives to destroy the computer controlling the Nebulatic Beacon. Then it would be up to the fleet. His thoughts drifted to the battle, which by now must be raging up beyond their sight . . .

"Picking up traces of nebulatic emissions," announced Captain Pana's computer operator. "Our scanners indicate most of the ships in the fleet are losing their shields."

"Okay, people," announced Lon. "This is the moment of truth. Most of our fleet is helpless right now. The smaller ships and fighters can't even use their targeting computers. Let's make a difference."

The Intrepid zoomed through the enemy fighters, making short work of those coming closest. A few tried to slip in behind them, but the fighters providing Intrepid's escort were able to dispatch the threats. While the battle had started well for Wing 2, the tide was turning. Without the benefit of their protective shields, they were easier prey for the Bromidian fighters swarming all around them. Coalition fighters exploded at an alarming rate. Lon bore down, adjusting auxiliary power to the weapons and ordering his gunners to fire faster. Intrepid's shields were holding, but it wouldn't last. Lon knew the time was coming when he would have to take a few chances. His pulsed raced as several dangerous options raced through his mind.

He checked his battle scanner, and slammed his fist on the armrest as he watched four frigates, two light cruisers, and a heavy cruiser from the Coalition fleet flash briefly and disappear from his scopes. The fleet was suffering heavy losses, and Lon wasn't sure how much longer they could hold out. "Damn it, Arano, where are you?" he swore softly.

As the fleet closed the distance between its ships and the planet ahead of them, the star fortress opened fire. In addition to the massive armament of beam weapons, no fewer than ten torpedo bays fired torpedoes in rapid succession, aiming at the larger ships in the fleet. Lon knew even the battleships, with their shield systems intact, couldn't handle that type of barrage for long. Again checking his scanner, he realized the same thought must have occurred to Admiral Modian onboard the USCS Striker, a Titan Class Battleship, the largest ship in the Coalition fleet. The Striker was changing its course, swinging heavily about to face the star fortress.

Like the proverbial meeting of the immovable object and the irresistible force, the clash was indescribable. They seemed evenly matched. The Striker rapidly closed the distance between them while the fortress shifted all its outgoing fire toward the ship presenting its greatest threat. Both suffered a weakening of their shields, and it wasn't clear which would have won the battle if there had been no other ships involved. The Bromidian reserve fleet, apparently held in check for this very purpose, now joined the battle, concentrating their fire on the oncoming battleship. Still piloting his ship through a swarm of fighters, Lon watched his scope in wide-eyed disbelief as the Striker's shields finally failed completely. Torpedoes and beam weapons found targets on the ship's vulnerable hull, and explosions rocked the Striker from bow to stern. It appeared the ship was doomed, a thought confirmed by Lon's scanner a few moments later.

Rather than abandon ship, Striker's crew worked feverishly, firing all remaining torpedoes without the benefit of the targeting computers destroyed by the hail of enemy fire. Meanwhile, the admiral seemed to have his own fate in mind for his ship. The Striker set a collision course, accelerating as she went. The Bromidians on the fortress probably realized what was happening, but there was nothing they could do. The battleship was crippled, out of the fight, but she wouldn't be completely destroyed so easily. Despite the Bromidians' best efforts to stop it, the Titan Class Battleship rammed the star fortress, destroying both of them in a soundless, blinding explosion.

Lon bowed his head, unable to express his grief. He took a deep breath, straightened in the pilot's chair, and gripped the controls with renewed determination.

Arano's parachute carried him imperceptibly closer to the ground below, just another paratrooper in a sea of countless others. The only sound reaching his ears was the occasional creak of his harness. As was the case on every jump, he had the sensation of flying. The fierce adrenaline rush born on the wings of anticipation inside the craft had once again given way to a strange sensation of peace. Even in the midst of battle, he was struck by the beauty and serenity of the scenery about him while he drifted gracefully to his landing. He struck the ground with a jarring impact, rolled, and lay motionless for a few brief seconds before climbing out of his parachute harness.

He jogged in a low crouch to his assembly area, directing the RLF soldiers into defensive positions when they arrived. Before long, his entire Avengers retinue was present, and the last few stragglers from their Bromidian fighting force had made it to the assembly point. A quick head count revealed that, as Arano had predicted, very few injuries had been sustained. The transports weren't so lucky, however. All were destroyed within minutes of releasing their cargo of paratroopers, again proving to the RLF leadership their Avenger advisors knew what they were talking about.

Once assembled, the army moved out at once. They didn't have far to go, but time was critical to the success of their mission. While onboard the transport, Arano's navigator had picked up several subspace messages from the Coalition fleet, and their situation appeared bleak. Arano pushed resolutely onward, determined to do his part to bring about an end to the war.

After a brief march of approximately three kilometers, they stood within sight of the walled fortress. They were at the edge of the killing zone, still within the cover of the trees, but with the thick layer of clouds overhead they were nearly invisible to the Bromidians manning the walls. The sun was just beginning to brighten the eastern horizon, and the troops would need to act with haste.

Videre led a small group of RLF soldiers ahead under cover of darkness to the outer wall. They moved like shadows as they placed explosives at regular intervals along the base of the wall. Videre followed behind them, inspecting their work and approving of what they'd done. When they were finished, the group pulled back to the cover of the forest.

"All set, Viper," Videre told him.

Arano checked his watch. "Anytime you're ready, Videre . . ."

Videre gave him a tight grin as he pulled the detonator device from his pack. The army took cover behind trees, rocks, and whatever else they could find. Arano closed his eyes to calm himself, knowing the moment of truth had arrived. He wiped his sweaty palms on his pants, and he took a comfortable grip on his weapon. He watched patiently as Videre typed in the final security codes to activate the detonator.

A tremendous explosion rocked the brightening skies, shattering an entire section of the wall and sending it crumbling to the ground. An enormous pillar of smoke belched skyward, obstructing their view of

Videre's handiwork. As one, the RLF soldiers rose from their places of concealment and rushed forward, running at top speed for the breach in the Bromidian fortress' defenses. A few Bromidian soldiers appeared atop the wall, near the edge where the wall had fallen. Arano couldn't make out details as only their silhouettes were visible. Then there was no more time for thought as laser fire poured down at Arano's troops. RLF soldiers dropped in their tracks when an occasional shot found its mark. They valiantly returned fire as they ran, but there was no way for them to take aim without stopping, and their shots had little effect.

They reached the relative safety of the shattered remains of the wall, and clambered through. The Bromidians stationed above wouldn't have a clear shot, giving the RLF forces at least a brief respite. A detachment was sent to both sides of the gap with the intention of sweeping the walls clear of Bromidian soldiers. It was accomplished after a brief but violent firefight, and Arano signaled for the heavy weapons to come forward. From the cover of the trees, the remainder of the RLF force rolled forward, carrying with them the bulky heavy weapons, artillery pieces and heavy laser cannons, items too bulky to be safely carried across the open field with incoming fire.

The seven Avengers rushed around their perimeter, establishing a secure area and setting up their heavy weapons. Sections of the destroyed wall were stacked in orderly rows to provide the raiders with safe fighting positions. Snipers and a security detachment were placed atop the walls to provide additional cover fire for the troops below. Once they were brought into place, the artillery pieces lobbed occasional shells into the fortress interior, more to give the Bromidians something to think about than in an attempt to cause any real damage. As their position became more secure, spotters joined the snipers atop the heavily damaged wall. The spotters warned the troops of approaching enemy units, and also directed the fire coming from the RLF artillery cannons.

Arano gathered his team and stood silently before Hawan. "Well, this is it," Arano told him. "There's nothing else we can do here. Hold this position as long as you can. We'll go do what we came to do, and hopefully the fleet can send us reinforcements soon enough to save our hides."

Hawan made a strange sign with his hands. "Luck be with you, my friends." With that, he turned and saw to the finishing touches on his defenses.

Arano turned to Videre. "Are your explosives ready?"

"All set," came the reply. Again, Arano noticed all traces of the joker in Videre had disappeared, replaced by a serious and highly trained soldier who was there to do a job. "I set a fifteen-minute timer on the dial. Press the yellow button, enter the security code, and the countdown starts. If anything happens to the timer device, I have a backup."

"Suicide button?" asked Laron quietly.

"Yes. Press the red button, and the detonator is online. Hold the button down, and nothing will happen. Release it, and the bomb goes off. Suicide for the one who uses it. It also has a failsafe, should the user be compromised and unable to release the button. Twenty minutes after the suicide button is pressed, the diodes will overload and short out, detonating the bomb."

"Let's do it," Arano told them, leading the way through their perimeter and into the heart of the fortress.

A warning beep from the Intrepid's computer told Lon more ships were emerging from the wormhole. And not a moment too soon, he thought. This was the remainder of the Coalition fleet, including the Thief Class Cruisers, sent to finish off the Bromidian fleet. Their arrival was supposed to coincide closely with the destruction of the Nebulatic Beacon, thereby giving the Coalition the upper hand in the battle, but the change in the timetable had thrown everything off. Now the best the new fleet could hope to do was save some of the original ships from destruction. Over half of the initial wave of Coalition ships had been destroyed, while the Bromidians had suffered losses equaling a quarter of that number. The rapid loss of Coalition ships had only accelerated the destruction of the Coalition fleet, as the Bromidians had been able to concentrate more firepower on the remaining ships. For the moment, at least, the new arrivals had thrown the Bromidians into a state of disarray.

A group of three frigates menaced a Coalition heavy cruiser, firing volley after volley into the heavily damaged ship's unprotected hull. Had all of its systems been on-line, the cruiser would have dealt with the frigates, but as things stood the cruiser was in trouble.

Lon shifted course, bringing the Intrepid around for a run at the frigates. He signaled to his torpedo gunner, who immediately worked on a torpedo lock.

Lon dodged the Intrepid through a sea of enemy fighters, all the while closing the gap between his ship and the frigates. Two torpedoes left their firing tubes as the torpedo gunner targeted the next frigate. Lon's plasma battery gunners worked desperately to keep the enemy fighters at bay, and they drew heavy losses from the small ships trying to intercept them. Meanwhile, the Coalition trooper Lon had assigned to the Disruptor Beam fired on a small group of Assault Class Fighters, momentarily disrupting their internal systems and leaving them easier prey for the group of Coalition Firestorm fighters attempting to eliminate them.

The Intrepid fired another pair of plasma torpedoes as its targeting computer shifted to the third frigate. The first two torpedoes had already impacted, resulting in devastating damage to the frigate. A hull breach was evident, and the ship listed helplessly and began to lose power. Before the third pair of torpedoes was launched, the second frigate had gone the way of the first, taken out of the battle, at least for the moment. As the third set of powerful plasma torpedoes found their marks with a pair of brilliant explosions, the Coalition heavy cruiser that had been in trouble only moments before went on the offensive, firing its weapons at point blank range and wreaking havoc on its three attackers.

"Lon," shouted the navigator, "I'm picking up an intense level of nebulatic emissions coming from the surface of Rystoria 2. We haven't seen anything of this magnitude before."

Lon frowned, heart pounding in his chest as he checked his own scanner. The Intrepid still had all systems functioning, and her shields were sitting firm at 52%. His blood ran cold when he surveyed the remainder of the fleet. All Coalition ships not refitted with the new systems, including the two Command Class Battleships, had lost their shields and targeting systems. In fact, most of the fleet was losing power, their weapons systems shutting down completely. Most of the fleet smaller than light cruisers had lost so much power they were losing life support. Within two hours, the crews on those ships would be dead.

Then another warning beep sounded, and a check of the scanner confirmed Lon's fears: another fleet had arrived, but this one was not friendly to the Coalition. Event Horizon's fleet had come, joining forces with the Bromidian fleet already engaged in battle. Lon felt the cold grip of fear realizing the extent of their enemies' deception. The Coalition had been led to believe the Event Horizon fleet would be in the Branton System, assisting the Bromidian forces there. The advantage of numbers was now solidly on the side of the Bromidians. Lon knew if Arano didn't destroy the Nebulatic Beacon soon, the Coalition fleet was lost.

Without a whisper of warning, the firing stopped, and the combined enemy fleets pulled back, reforming their battle lines closer to the Bromidian homeworld. The subspace Comm beeped, and a Bromidian face appeared on the screen.

"Coalition soldiers," the guttural voice began, "I am Admiral Vishtok of the Bromidian Empire. Your fleet is lost. The Nebulatic Beacon has assured you do not have the means to defeat us. Surrender your ships now, and we'll spare the lives of the crews. Refuse, and you'll be destroyed. You have five minutes."

Then a new face appeared on the screen, this one Human. "This is Admiral Solute of the USCS New York. All Coalition ships: stand by for further instructions. Those of you experiencing equipment problems switch all power to your weapons systems. Shut down all other systems except your engines. All other systems, including life support, are to be turned off. The Bromidians will execute us all if we surrender; it isn't an option. We'll fight to the end. Admiral Solute, out."

As one, the enemy ships leaped forward, weapons firing. Within moments, the Coalition ships hummed to life once more, the air inside them slowly depleted of oxygen as life support systems were shut down. The Coalition ships charged recklessly, their crews aware that if they didn't win this battle quickly, they wouldn't survive.

CHAPTER TWENTY-THREE

"THIS IS THE BUILDING," WHISPERED ARANO. THE structure was enormous, stretching five stories above the ground, and at least that many underground, while covering several acres. The entire outside of the building was sheathed in a strange white rock Arano found similar to quartz. In broad daylight, he thought, the Rystorian star would reflect off this surface, painfully so for those not used to the planet's thinner atmosphere.

While the other Avengers stood watch, Videre moved forward and went to work on the locking mechanisms holding the door shut. He swiftly disabled the alarm and the lock, gaining access to the building. They moved inside cautiously, Videre and Lain weighted down with the various components for the bomb they hoped would destroy the Nebulatic Beacon's computer.

They crept down the hallways of the cavernous building, following the instructions provided by the intelligence operatives of the Rystoria Liberation Front. The walls of the building's interior were made of a plain white rock, but the floor was made of more of the quartz-like rock. Unlike most military buildings Arano had been in, the hallways tended to curve sharply and unexpectedly, leading him to believe this was not originally a military facility.

The route they followed was not the most direct; they stuck to the less-commonly used hallways, helping them to avoid detection. More than anything, a combination of stealth and speed would make the mission a success. A little luck wouldn't hurt, Arano thought. Although he had never been a devoutly religious man, Arano found himself praying to the Four Elementals that he would succeed, saving countless Coalition lives. The thought of what could happen if he failed was too devastating to consider.

There was no more time for stealth when they turned a corner and came face-to-face with three Bromidian soldiers on some nameless errand. The Avengers responded with instant violence, laser rifles blazing, and the threat was eliminated in the space of two heartbeats.

"Let's go," shouted Arano, leading his team away at a dead run. The use of laser weapons had more than likely alerted the Bromidians there was something wrong, and this was where the search would begin. Arano referred to his directions, turned down a pair of subhallways, and slowed his team to a more cautious pace.

They descended three flights of narrow metal stairs, finding themselves within striking distance of their target. They were close enough that, if necessary, they could detonate the bomb where they were, with a reasonable chance at successfully destroying the computer. However, Arano didn't want reasonable; he wanted certain. The little band pushed onward, staying alert for more enemy sentries.

They found trouble around the next corridor. A large Bromidian patrol, probably enroute to determine the origin of the earlier skirmish, stumbled across their path. The Avengers dove for cover, spraying the area with laser fire as they assessed their situation. Too many Bromidians, Arano thought grimly. There's no way we can fight through in time. He consulted his map and found another way around.

"Lain, Videre, you're with me!" he shouted over the din of the firefight. "The rest of you keep them busy! We're going to try another route!"

He backed away from the firefight, Lain and Videre on his heels. They passed through a door in the side of the corridor and dashed down another hallway and beyond the Bromidian soldiers. Frequently consulting his map to assure he was on track, Arano led his squad to the computer room.

A silent three-count later, they burst through the doorway, laser rifles firing once again. When they were done, four Bromidian soldiers lay dead and the room was theirs. In front of them, a computer of stunning size and complexity sprawled in electronic bliss, happily chirping away to whomever would listen. From behind it, a series of thick cables emerged and raced to the ceiling where they disappeared, presumably on their way to the satellite array on the roof.

"I've got the door," Arano told them. "Do your stuff."

As Arano leveled his rifle at the closed doorway,

Videre and Lain planted their series of explosives at key points around the Nebulatic Beacon computer. They were nearly halfway done when the door opened to admit two Bromidians. Arano's laser rifle sounded in rapid succession, and the Broms crumpled to the floor. Arano dragged their bodies off to the side before resuming his vigil.

Finally finished with the explosives, Videre and Lain worked quickly to connect the explosives to the detonator. "Viper, we're all set," Videre announced.

"Good," Arano acknowledged. "Set the timer and let's get out of here."

Videre nodded, tapping several keys as he entered the codes necessary to start the countdown. He frowned when he tried the codes a second time, then stood up angrily, slamming his fist on the table.

"Videre, talk to me," Arano pleaded, his eyes still on the doorway.

"Something has happened to the timer. It won't activate. I"

He trailed off, turning the timer device over. A single hole was burned into the bottom, evidence of a hit from laser fire. "It's been hit, Viper. It's finished."

Arano felt a strange, euphoric calm come over him when he realized what he had to do. He moved woodenly to the table where Videre had been working on the detonator. He stared silently at the red suicide button for a few moments, then turned to his teammates.

"Get out of here," he told them sharply. Seeing them hesitate, he continued. "That's an order, Lieutenants! Get the Hell out of here! Alyna is in charge now. I'm giving you fifteen minutes to get clear of the building, and then I'm activating the suicide button."

"But" began Lain in protest.

"Starting right now!" Arano roared, pointing at the door. "Get out! When this bomb explodes, the whole building will come down!" The Avengers stared at each other in horror as they backed slowly out of the room. "Please," Arano told them softly. "Tell Alyna I love her."

He watched his teammates depart, the door sliding silently shut behind them. He checked the time on his watch and eased into the chair next to the detonator. He experienced a morbid fascination with what he would feel when the bomb exploded. Probably nothing, he thought with a short laugh. The force released by the bomb would level most of the building. He would be dead before he felt anything.

Arano realized he only had two regrets. His first was that he would never know the identity of Kranton, the remaining Coalition member who betrayed them to the Bromidians, and would therefore not have his chance for revenge against the shadowy figure. He almost laughed. Obviously the traitor was Grand High Councilor Balor Tient. He'd made no secret of his dealings with the Bromidians. It would have been a simple matter for him to provide the Bromidians with sensitive information. He only wished he had a chance to deal with Tient himself.

His other regret was one he could readily have changed, and it was the one regret he most wanted to change. He and Alyna would now be forever denied their chance to have a life together, an he felt a sharp pang of anger at himself. He knew the chances had been there, but he'd been so consumed with his hatred he'd failed to recognize what was in front of him. He had been given one other chance at happiness, his fiancé back on Leguin 4, but she'd been murdered by members of Rising Sun. Oddly, he found he could no longer even picture her face. His thoughts drifted back to Alyna, and he realized that, in their brief time together, they'd somehow managed to build the beginnings of what could have been a lasting relationship. He sighed, once again checking his watch.

That was when the door slid open and several Bromidian soldiers rushed in, rifles trained on Arano. He stared at them in defiance and reached surreptitiously for the suicide button. His hand had barely moved when one of the Bromidians fired a stun-blast, knocking Arano to the floor. An obviously high-ranking Bromidian soldier entered and sneered disdainfully at Arano.

"So, Human," he said with distaste. "This is what you had in mind. You have failed."

As Arano waited for sensation to return to his stunned body, he looked up at his captors with undisguised hatred. He tried unsuccessfully to speak but gave up in disgust. Arano realized he'd have to stall for time, waiting for the stun to wear off so he could activate the bomb.

The Bromidian's scowl deepened, and he turned to one of his cohorts. "Send Kranton in here. Let him talk to this cretin."

Arano's pulse quickened. It appeared he would get his chance to kill the traitor after all. Once the effects of the stun beam wore off, he would dive for the suicide switch, putting himself back in control of the situation. In fact, he'd give Balor Tient a few moments to gloat, and then snatch victory from Balor in a blinding explosion. He would have laughed if he were able, and suddenly realized he might have become a bit unstable.

There was a commotion out in the hallway, and the door opened once again. But it wasn't Balor Tient who walked through the doorway. Arano could only stare in disbelief when he found himself face-to-face with Commander Mendarle.

Lain and Videre slowed as they neared the area where they'd separated from their teammates. They were greeted with an ominous silence, and the fear their team was lost danced tantalizingly around the edges of Videre's thoughts. He decided to take a chance, grabbing his Comm and activating it on the secure FM channel.

"Alyna, this is Videre," he whispered cautiously.

Anxious moments passed, and nothing happened. He repeated his call, fear rearing its ugly head when he imagined the worst. He nervously fingered the Comm as the silence continued.

"Alyna here," his radio finally squawked. Videre and Lain looked at each other with relief, and Videre told Alyna he and Lain were coming in.

A staircase and two doorways later, they were reunited with their team. Videre felt a stab like a knife when he saw the look of elation on Alyna's face fade to one of horror as she realized Arano wasn't with them.

"Where's Viper?" she asked desperately.

"I'm sorry, Alyna," Lain told her gently. "The timer mechanism was damaged in the firefight. Arano stayed behind to activate the suicide switch. He's going to activate the bomb in about eight minutes, sooner if he's discovered. He gave us orders to get out of here before the building comes down. We have to leave."

Tears were instantly evident in Alyna's eyes when she turned to Major Laron Alstor. He returned her gaze, his own eyes swelling when he read her intention. His shoulders slumped in defeat and he nodded to her. "Thank you, Laron," she said quietly. Without another word, she took a look at the map in Lain's hands and dashed off down the corridor toward the room where Arano waited for his final countdown.

"How could you just let her go?" asked Pelos in shock. "She's going to die if we don't bring her back."

But Videre was already shaking his head, holding Pelos from charging after Alyna. "Didn't you see the look in her eyes? She died when we came back without him."

It was a grim group of warriors that turned toward the exit. They moved quickly, haunted by both the loss of two teammates and the knowledge that at any minute the bomb could explode, bringing the whole building down with it. They met only token resistance on their way out, and each group of Bromidians was dealt with in an explosion of violence fueled by rage and tempered by the flames of grief and anguish. None could stand before them. Minutes later, they stood within view of their way out.

"Commander Mendarle," Arano said in disbelief. His muscles cramped, another side-effect of the stun. "How" He tried to phrase the question but couldn't find the words. He struggled to move his body, but the blast from the stun rifle was just beginning wear off.

"Well, Captain Lakeland. Not quite who you expected to find? You were expecting the Grand High Councilor, no doubt. Well, don't be too disappointed. He had a bigger hand in this than I did. I'm more of a pawn." He turned to the Bromidians milling about behind him. "What are you fools doing? Do you think this man made it in here alone? There will be others. Leave two men here to guard the prisoner, and find the rest of the intruders!"

A strange tingling feeling began in Arano's limbs, and he knew the stun effects were dissipating at a faster rate. He had serious thoughts of activating the button, killing himself but taking a traitor and the Bromidian computer with it. It would be so nice to let go, he thought. He'd been through so much, his body ached, and he just wanted to rest. His side ached where the stun blast had hit him, and ironically it was the pain that brought him to his senses.

He had six teammates who depended on him to stall the Bromidians long enough for them to escape. He had to stop the search party that was about to go after his friends.

"You're too late, Mendarle," Arano laughed. "This

bomb will destroy everything in this building, us included. By now, my team is in the hangar, stealing a ship. Before your Bromidians can get to them they'll be on their way out. The bomb's timer only has about six minutes left before detonation, so you'll never deactivate it in time"

A Bromidian raised his rifle and pointed it toward Arano, but Daton Mendarle waved him off with an oath. "You idiot! He probably has some type of suicide switch on that detonator. If you shoot him, the bomb will go off. Find his team in the hangar and bring them here. He won't detonate it if his precious Captain Marquat is in the blast zone. We can make him defuse the bomb."

A desperate hope dawned in Arano's chest as the Bromidians filed out of the room, leaving only two sentries behind. He was certain the Commander knew the bomb could not be disarmed once it had been activated, if he even believed the timer had been set. Arano also figured the Commander wouldn't believe the team's exit plan called for stealing a ship. Daton moved closer to Arano, casually bringing up his pistol.

"You know, Lakeland, what the worst part about working for the Bromidians is?" He turned to face the two Bromidians who had stayed behind. "It's so hard to find good help." Without changing his expression, he casually gunned down the two Bromidians, watching emotionlessly as they tumbled lifelessly to the ground. He turned to face Arano. "So, now what do we do?"

Arano shook his head in confusion, the events of

the last few minutes almost too much to comprehend. Obviously, Daton was the traitor known as Kranton, but just as obvious was the fact that he had just double-crossed the Bromidians. Arano slowly dragged himself to his feet.

"Arano, please," said the commander, uncharacteristically using Arano's first name. "You've got to understand. I was not a willing participant in all of this. I was a loyal Coalition soldier, but the Grand High Councilor took care of that for me. I allowed him to blackmail me, and this was my reward. I'd tell you my whole story, but there isn't time. Your team will be out of the building soon, and we can set off your explosion. I need you to listen carefully.

"Look. I'm beyond rehabilitation. Even if we, meaning the Coalition, win the war, my crimes will be discovered, and my name will be disgraced. I want to spare my wife and children that final humiliation. Here." He pulled a data disk from his pocket and set it on a nearby table. "This disk contains all the information you need to nail the Grand High Councilor. He was selling out to the Bromidians for money and power, thinking he could prevent a war between the two powers by making the Bromidians a great enough threat that we'd be afraid to fight them. All he accomplished was to make them even bolder than before. He must not get away with it."

He gave Arano a direct look. "I can tell by the display on the timer that it has been damaged. I want you to let me be the one to set off the bomb. You take this disk and go deal with Balor Tient. See to it he pays for his crimes. If you have to expose my name in the process, then do so. He must not be allowed to go free." He picked up the detonator, not even hesitating for a moment before pressing the suicide button.

Arano stared at his former leader in wonder, trying to decipher what lay behind his cold, dead eyes. It was a risk he wanted to take, but he was afraid to do it. To put the defeat of the Bromidians in the hands of a traitor . . .

"Arano. I know you have no reason to trust me. I know your vaunted danger sense won't help you here. You have to listen to your heart. And if you're going to put your trust in me, the time is now. We'll be found here soon."

Arano licked his lips and considered the matter. His head spun as he tried to focus his thoughts. He looked at the commander once again, saw something there he hadn't seen before, and made up his mind. He limped over to lean on the table. With his free hand, he picked up Daton's disk and put it in his pocket.

"One more thing," Daton told him. "I'm only giving you ten minutes to get clear, once you leave the room. After that I can't guarantee your safety, so you'd better hurry. Take this." Daton tossed Arano a security card. He caught it and held up to the light. "That card will get you through any door in the complex. When you leave this room, use that card to activate the lock, and then destroy the control panel in the hall. That'll keep them off me for a few minutes longer and get you to safety. Now, go!"

Arano stood locked in place, staring at Commander Mendarle, then turned and left the room without a word. Once outside, he activated the lock with his security card, and destroyed the panel with a blast from his laser rifle. He checked his watch, gathered his bearings, and dashed off down the hall. Reaching the stairs, he ascended two at a time as he raced against the clock in his effort to escape the building. He paused to check his location, and decided he could save time by taking a different way out, now that he had his security card. He opened a nearby door, stepped through hurriedly, and looked around for signs of the enemy as the door slid shut behind him.

He hesitated when he thought he heard someone calling his name. Alyna? No, he thought, it wasn't possible. The rest of his team would be outside by now. He made his way to the exit once again, but something stopped him. It had to be Alyna, he thought. He decided to take a few extra seconds to be certain before he made his escape. Arano slid the door open again and stuck his head through the doorway, looking for the source of the voice.

And there was Alyna, her beautiful face ravaged by tears as she rushed over to the open door. They met in a fierce hug, both of them openly crying. She tried, unsuccessfully, to form a question, but Arano put a solitary finger to her lips.

"Later," he told her. "We have to get out of here, now!" He took her by the hand and led her away.

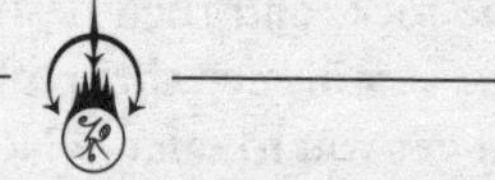

Commander Daton Mendarle looked at his watch. Almost time, he thought. He relaxed in anticipation of the now-inevitable, blissful relief from the personal hell his life had become, a life wracked with intense feelings of guilt. The relief he wanted so badly would come with the lifting of his finger. How many times had he thought of doing this before, only to stop himself at the last minute? Now he could erase it all, with one last act of courage for the Coalition in the process.

Courage, he thought bitterly, a self-loathing scowl on his face. When had he lost it? He should have faced the Grand High Councilor long ago. When Balor Tient had first come to him with his damning pictures, he should have confronted Balor. Instead, Daton had sold his soul. What had he been thinking? Each time he allowed himself to be blackmailed by Balor, he gave the Grand High Councilor more ammunition for his acts of extortion. What are a few photos of his marital infidelity compared to proof he'd sold secrets to the enemy? Now he was stuck, and his reconciliation could not happen. At least, not in life . . .

A pounding on the door brought him back to the present. Apparently, the game was up, and the Bromidians had come for him. He checked his watch, decided he'd waited long enough, and straightened himself to his full height. "May God forgive me," he said quietly, and released the button.

"Task Force Omega, this is Admiral Solute of the USCS New York. The Nebulatic Beacon is still up, and our losses are unacceptable. We have to assume the attack on the Beacon has failed. Prepare to retreat. We'll have to run a fighting withdrawal for about an hour until our capital ships are able to activate their Rift Drives. Any ship about to have total life support system failure should jump out as soon as its rift drives are capable."

"Too late, Admiral," interjected Lon, activating his own Comm. "This is Captain Pana, of the Intrepid. My scanners are still working, and I'm picking up a Bromidian picket line of Thief Class Cruisers. We can't escape."

"I copy that, Intrepid. We'll have to try to take the Beacon down ourselves. We'll lose the fleet coming that close to the planetary defenses, but if we can destroy the Beacon, we won't have died in vain. All fighter groups, form up into escort formations. Let's make this . . . wait! Something is happening on Rystoria 2!"

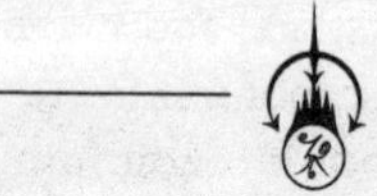

Arano and Alyna sprinted through the open doorway to the outside just as the first echoes of the tremendous explosion below reached their ears. The entire building shuddered and buckled as its support system was destroyed by the unbelievable force of the blast. Fortunately, Arano's sense of direction hadn't failed him, and the Avengers came out of the building on the side closest to the defensive perimeter set up by the Rystoria Liberation Front forces. Without slowing, Arano led the way through the maze of the city, finally emerging near the outer wall and nearly collapsing in exhaustion when he reached the RLF's sentry lines.

He leaned on Alyna for support and limped his way to the center of the encampment, to the delighted surprise of five Avengers who'd arrived only minutes earlier. Triumphant shouts filled the air as the group gathered around Arano and Alyna, celebrating their miraculous escape from the jaws of death. Arano sketched in the details of what had happened, telling them of the ultimate demise of their traitorous commander. They marveled at the unbelievable luck of timing that Alyna had seen Arano when she did.

"Congratulations, my friends," said Hawan, coming over to shake their hands. "My scouts report the entire building has collapsed. You've done what you came to do. Now, we have to prepare. There are two forces moving against us: the patrol they sent to intercept us outside the walls, and another force from within. We must see to our defenses."

"The Beacon is down!" shouted Admiral Solute. "I say again, the Beacon is down! All ships, commence battle plan Charlie!"

Like leaves before a shifting wind, the tide of battle turned. The Coalition ships powered up their shield and weapon systems, bringing life support back online and turning the battle against their Bromidian opponents. Although they were now outnumbered, they fought back viciously, their plasma torpedoes wreaking a deadly toll on the Bromidian fleet. The disintegration of the Bromidian forces accelerated as their numbers dwindled, and they fell into disarray.

The USCS New York led a charge against the Bromidian flag ship, firing a deadly barrage of plasma torpedoes as the New York's escort ships opened fire with a rain of fire of their own. The flag ship shuddered, small eruptions breaching its surface, and then exploded in a brilliant flash, sending a rapidly expanding ball of fire into the void of space.

Not knowing what else to do, the leaderless Bromidians attempted to retreat. It only hastened their demise, as the Coalition Thief Class Cruisers activated their neutrino fields, preventing the Bromidian Rift Drives from functioning. The Coalition ships fell on the confused and disarrayed Bromidian fleet like a pack of dogs, decimating the remaining ships.

"There's the signal from the Admiral," announced Lon. "All fighters in Wing 2, this is Captain Pana of the Intrepid. We've been given the go-ahead. Follow my ship to the Bromidian capital. We have some Avengers to rescue."

Laser fire erupted from within the city and without as the Bromidian forces closed in from all around the embattled forces of the Rystoria Liberation Front. It was over two hours since the destruction of the Nebulatic Beacon, time enough for the Bromidians to gather in force and move against their invaders. All the soldiers of the RLF could do now was fight back. The Bromidians would take no prisoners, and there was nowhere left to run.

Arano positioned himself atop the tallest building

inside their defensive perimeter, Alyna at his side. She spotted Bromidian officers among the ranks of their attackers, and Arano followed each sighting with a single shot from his sniper rifle. He knew he wasn't killing many Bromidians, but he also knew the effect on the Bromidian forces would be felt beyond the number of officers he killed. As always, the death of their leaders was devastating to them, and slowed their advance noticeably.

"Viper, this is Lain," came the voice on the Comm. "We've got Bromidians breaching the perimeter on the northwest side. We've stopped this charge, but they're massing again. We've lost too many soldiers. One more charge and this line is finished."

Arano swore softly in frustration, biting off several oaths with deadly shots from his rifle. Had he escaped certain death, only to die anyway in a needless battle after his mission had been accomplished? He gathered his equipment to go to Lain's aid, and heard the roar of ion engines. He glanced up and saw one of the most beautiful sights he had ever seen: the Intrepid flew in low, leading a pack of Firestorm Class Fighters as they assaulted the Bromidian ranks. A roar of triumph went up from the encircled RLF forces as the Bromidians broke and ran. In minutes, the battle was over.

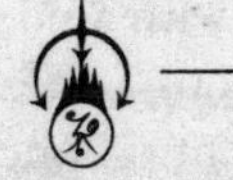

Arano stepped from his quarters onboard the Intrepid, returning to the bridge where his team awaited the dissemination of information from Commander

Mendarle's data disk. Instead of a briefing, Arano chose to play the disk for them, or at least the commander's soliloquy regarding his treason. He sat in his captain's chair, inserted the disk into the slot next to him, and brought the video up on the main screen. Commander Daton Mendarle's face appeared, troubled and worn.

"My name is Commander Daton Mendarle of the United Systems Coalition. I'm currently in charge of all Avengers teams, a position I've held for the past three years. I spent four years on Avengers Team 1, Squad A. When I was promoted to Major, I took over command of Teams 1-3, and I was promoted to Commander two years later. In addition to being in charge of the Avengers teams, the last promotion put me on the Coalition Security Council, making me privy to sensitive information.

"Hopefully, by the time you view this, I'll be dead. Use the information contained in these files to discredit and arrest the Grand High Councilor. He has been working for the Bromidians from the start, and has been the greatest source of our security troubles. I've paid the ultimate price. Please do not let him escape.

"For me, it started three years ago. I was in deep financial trouble from a gambling habit I developed. Grand High Councilor Tient somehow knew of this, and he came to me with a side job to help me out. It seemed a simple enough task: transport one Human female to a settlement on one of the outer planets in the Sol System. I was told the woman was in a position to do the Coalition a great favor, but she needed protection from assassins. During the long flight, we ate dinner and had a few drinks. Before it was over, she had seduced me and we ended up sleeping together. She secretly taped our encounter and sent the video to Tient. He threatened to show the video to my wife if I didn't help him out. His requests seemed simple enough: send this team here, don't send that team there.

"I should have realized he was keeping track of these 'favors'. Before long, he had enough evidence to prove I was giving special favors to certain people, in violation of Coalition procedures. In fact, he had enough on me to get me thrown in prison. I should have realized that when you go along with an extortion plan, you only end up giving your antagonist more leverage against you.

"Before long, I was giving him and his contacts state secrets that Tient wouldn't normally be privy to. In fact, I met with one of Balor Tient's contacts on Karlac 3, but we were interrupted by Captain Lakeland. I don't know how he found out, but he almost caught me. And when Dar Noil struck at the Coalition computers, I knew ahead of time about his plans to do it. I was instructed to allow it to happen. I didn't stop to think about the lives that could be lost. And when we lost an entire task force because information about their movements was leaked out by Noil . . ." He trailed off briefly as he began to sob, then regained his composure.

"I finally told the Grand High Councilor I was finished with him. His threats against me no longer held any sway. That was when he issued his ultimatum: fail to obey his commands, and he would have my wife and kids executed by his secret police force. I continued to do his work, but I've been looking for a way out. This is it. I have data on this disk detailing the bribes he has accepted and the favors he granted for them. I also have proof he has been giving away technology to the Bromidians in the foolish belief that if everyone was equal, we could all be friends. I couldn't convince him it would just encourage the Bromidians to go to war.

"Well, this is it. My secret is out, and my life is forfeit. Please take care of my family, and see to it that no harm comes to them. Good luck."

The screen went blank. Arano sat silently for a few moments, running several courses of action through his head. Finally, his mind made up, he activated his Comm and contacted Admiral Solute on the USCS New York.

"Admiral Solute, this is Captain Lakeland of Avengers Team 5."

"Captain Lakeland! The Coalition owes you and your team a great debt of gratitude. Not only did you accomplish your mission, giving us our chance to win the battle, but you succeeded despite last minute changes in the timetable. Great job, Avenger!"

Arano briefly sketched in the details of the raid on the building that used to house the computer for the Nebulatic Beacon. He explained how the timer for their explosives had been damaged during a firefight, so he'd stayed behind with the suicide switch.

"Then how is it that you're here?" wondered the Admiral.

"Commander Mendarle came in and relieved me. He . . . had been working undercover for some time, attempting to penetrate their intelligence network to discover the identity of the traitor in our midst. He informed me, prior to this mission, he would be at the Bromidian base and would provide assistance if possible. We hadn't anticipated he'd take it this far."

"Mendarle is dead? This is quite a shock. Did he tell you what he found out?"

"Yes, sir. Grand High Councilor Balor Tient was our leak. I have all the proof here on disk. I'll send you a copy shortly."

"We must give Commander Mendarle the Golden Cross of Valor for this selfless act."

"Uh, sir . . . his last request to me was that he not receive any award for this," Arano lied. "He felt he owed it to the Coalition and didn't deserve any commendations. I believe we should honor a dying man's last wishes."

"Well, we need to do something for him," growled the admiral.

"What about his wife?" replied Arano, snapping his fingers as though the thought had just occurred to him. "Why don't we see to it she never has to work again?"

"Excellent idea, Captain."

The conversation continued as Arano discussed some of the highlights of the evidence against Grand High Councilor Tient, and Alyna moved silently closer to Laron.

"Laron," she whispered, "I'm a little surprised Arano is letting a traitor like Mendarle get away like this. I know he's dead, but now it's like he never did anything wrong."

"If Arano let everyone know what Mendarle did, his wife and kids would be disgraced, and his kids would never be able to get into the military. This way, his family is taken care of. I'm sure Arano will look into the matter to be certain Mendarle's wife was not part of the scheme, but I think justice has been served. Especially since Arano prevented the presentation of posthumous awards to a traitor."

Alyna thought about that for a bit, and then smiled. Laron looked questioningly at her. "The killing frost has come again," she told him. "He's only as cold as he has to be."

Captain Arano Lakeland signed off his Comm, then turned to face Laron and his team. "Okay, everyone," he told them. "Let's finish here and go home."

Arano awoke with a start, momentarily disoriented and unable to remember where he was. When his head cleared, he recognized his quarters aboard the Intrepid, and there was definitely no mistaking the slumbering form lying next to him. He leaned over and kissed Alyna's cheek, noticing with a grin she was still sleeping. He lay back down and gently slid his arm around the woman he loved, but sleep wouldn't come. He allowed his thoughts to drift back to the battles in the Rystoria System, and his mind naturally returned to the titanic conclusion.

Following the arrival of the Intrepid and its fighter escort, the RLF had requested Coalition transports. When they arrived, the RLF soldiers boarded immediately, asking the Avengers to join them. They'd flown to the Imperial Palace, and swiftly overwhelmed the few remaining loyal troops.

With Hawan in the lead, the RLF forces swept through the palace to the throne room. Emperor Vagorst VIII sat on his throne, looking disinterestedly at the armed group invading his throne room. Hawan had strolled deliberately up to the throne without bowing. "Vagorst VIII of the Imperial Bromidian Empire, your reign and that of your lineage is at an end," Hawan had told him. "The people shall rule from this day forward." He had drawn his long knife, and with a single thrust vacated the Imperial Throne.

The Bromidian homeworld was in a state of chaos as the new government was hammered out. Coalition forces were present to help restore order, but the forces of the Rystoria Liberation Front left no doubts about who was in charge. They worked on the details of the new government's structure, to be based, curiously enough, on the Padian government. The Padians had a Representative similar to that of the Coalition, but the Padians had taken a long hard look at the problems of the Coalition before establishing their own set of laws. The Bromidians apparently felt the Padians had done well.

The Bromidians had been defeated again, and this time they installed a new government. Arano's entire team had survived countless missions during the past few months. Commander Mendarle had faced the ultimate justice for his crimes. That left only one matter to be dealt with. Grand High Councilor Balor Tient wouldn't escape Arano's wrath.

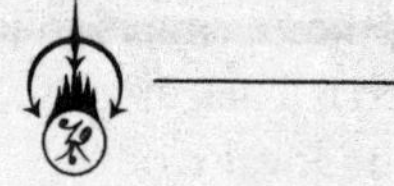

Balor Tient stormed down the hallway to the door of his penthouse condominium. He entered the security code, and the door slid obediently open. He stepped through with an oath, still in a foul mood over the way events had turned out. The Coalition had somehow won the war with the Bromidians, and Commander Mendarle was missing, presumably dead. If he'd leaked any information about Balor's doings, Mendarle's family would suffer the consequences.

He moved through the darkened room, gliding across the floor to the kitchen. With a sudden outburst of anger, he hurled a vase across the room, and felt a perverse measure of satisfaction when the vase shattered against the far wall. He activated the lights, poured himself a glass of wine, and turned toward the living room to watch the evening news.

When Balor stepped back into the now-lighted living room, he dropped his wine glass with a startled oath. Captain Lakeland of the Avengers sat in his recliner, looking at Balor with an annoying grin. Balor recovered from his shock and swore at him before returning to the kitchen to retrieve a towel.

As he wiped up the mess, Balor looked over at Arano with a snarl. "What in the hell are you doing here?"

"Unfinished business," Arano replied coolly. "You sold out the Coalition to the Bromidians and cost us countless lives, both among the civilians and the military. The time has come for you to face to the music."

"Sorry, Captain," laughed Balor. "You do realize,

of course, that before a member of the High Council can be tried for this type of crime, there must first be an impeachment by the High Council Ethics Committee. I own most of the members of that panel, and even if they approved an impeachment you'd never get it through the vote by the entire High Council. Besides, if it looked bad for me, I'd just leave the system and live elsewhere. You'll never land me in jail, Captain."

"I can honestly say I never had any intentions of putting you in jail, Tient," Arano said in a voice as cold as death, and rose from his chair, drawing his knife.

Balor froze in the act of cleaning up the spilled wine and broken glass, terror striking at his heart. "What . . . what are you doing? You plan to just murder me in cold blood? You'll never get away with it!"

"No, not murder," replied Arano in a calm, emotionless voice. "Perhaps you're not aware of the law that authorizes any member of the military at or above the rank of captain to execute anyone who that officer can prove has committed the crime of treason? I can kill you, here and now, and show my proof at a hearing they'll have for me in a few days." Arano issued an ugly bark of laughter as he took a menacing step forward. He paused, tapping his knife against his cheek. "Ironically, you were the one who passed this law in the first place. I call it poetic justice."

"I know of that law," replied Balor, regaining his composure, "but it doesn't fit this situation. When a group of Councilors insisted upon adding that ridiculous measure, I made them add the stipulation that it can only be used in time of war. So even if you had the proof, it's too late for you to take action. The war is over."

"Wrong," replied Arano, the cold, vicious grin spreading across his face. "The cease fire doesn't take effect for another hour. Your time has come, Balor."

As Arano started forward, Balor made a desperate run for the nearby Comm, hoping to call for help. His fingers hadn't quite reached the Comm when Arano caught up with him.

EPILOGUE

ALYNA SAT UNCOMFORTABLY BESIDE ARANO, LOOKing up at the enormous crowd of Padians who were watching the ceremonial greeting between the Coalition officials and the Padian leaders. The last time she had witnessed this event, she'd been pleasantly anonymous in the crowd with Arano's aunt. This time, at Arano's insistence, she was out on the stage with the clan leaders. She squirmed in her chair as she sat in silence, mesmerized by the incredibly ugly costumes worn by the visiting Coalition officials and trying not to laugh at the strange rituals they performed at the start of the ceremony. She glanced over at Arano, and plainly saw him fighting to keep a grin from showing, his shoulders twitching with suppressed mirth. When it was over, she followed Arano into another room, where the Padian leaders would hold a private meeting.

When she entered the room, she was surprised to see the Padian clan leaders convulsed in uncontrollable laughter, several of them parading around in mocking imitations of the rituals performed by the Coalition officials. A group of Padian women, presumably the wives of the clan leaders, were already at work on the next set of costumes and were quite obviously going out of their way to make the costumes as ugly as possible. Alyna looked questioningly at Arano, whose smirk had been replaced by the same outright laughter as the other Padians.

"Alyna," Arano said, laughing so hard tears streamed down his face, "the whole ceremony is a sham. You don't think we're that simple, do you? We're a little brighter than what the Coalition gives us credit for. We decided long ago these Coalition types take themselves too seriously. This is our way of taking them down a notch. We spend months designing the most embarrassing costumes and rituals we can think of, and then we sit back and watch the show."

Alyna didn't know how to answer that. She joined in their laughter when she realized there was definitely more to the Padians than met the eye.

Captain Arano Lakeland gathered his mound of paperwork, data disks, and other items he needed for his day-long seminar on unconventional warfare. Since the conclusion of the Second Bromidian War nearly six months before, Arano had become a highly sought-after consultant by civilian security firms and military leaders alike. Some had suggested Arano should retire from the military and make a fortune as a full-time consultant. He had turned the idea aside without a second thought. There remained too much before him in the military to cast it all away.

Following the death of Commander Mendarle,

Major Alstor had assumed the interim position as leader of the Avenger teams, a position made permanent a month later by Laron Alstor's promotion to Commander. Arano had followed in his friend's footsteps after the promotion. His earlier footsteps, that is, by turning down the offer of a promotion to Major, knowing it meant a permanent office job, taking him out of the field. Laron himself had turned down the promotion more than once before finally accepting the offer.

Arano had investigated the extent of Commander Mendarle's treason, finding his family was in no way involved, and was in fact completely ignorant of his dealings with the enemy. Arano kindheartedly allowed it to stay that way, not wanting to add to the new widow's stress. He also followed through on the corruption found in the office of the late Grand High Councilor Tient. His investigation resulted in the arrest and conviction of seven of Balor's aides on charges including bribery, extortion, and treason. The house-cleaning didn't stop there, either; several members of Balor's secret police force, Midnight Sun, were found to be a part of the conspiracy against the Coalition. Arano didn't rest until the investigation was over, and everyone even remotely involved brought to justice.

He sighed, seeing how anti-climactic events had become. Months ago, he was involved in a titanic life or death struggle against Rising Sun, Event Horizon, the Bromidian Empire, and the traitors within the Coalition. Now he was reduced to the mundane task of teaching others about the finer points of unconventional warfare. He picked up his duffel bag, made certain he hadn't left anything behind, and turned to leave.

"Alyna," he said on his way out the door, "if anything comes up, you know where I'll be. I want to get this over with today, so try not to contact me unless it's something important."

"Just get going," she laughed. "I think we can handle it here without you."

"Say 'hi' to our friends in Midnight Sun, if you see them there," added Videre. Arano rolled his eyes and left.

A short time later, a courier arrived at their door. "Captain Lakeland?" he asked.

"He just left," replied Videre. "Is there anything we can help you with? He's likely to be gone all day."

The courier seemed confused for a moment, looked back at the package, and seemed to remember something. "Not Captain Arano Lakeland. This package is for the other Captain Lakeland."

Captain Alyna Lakeland blushed, realizing even after a month of marriage she still couldn't get used to her new last name. She accepted the package from the courier, who saluted and left. The package contained results from her last doctor's appointment, confidential information that couldn't be sent over the Comm. She looked over the medical report, pulse quickening. Then she rushed over to the Comm and activated the link to her new husband.

"Lakeland," came Arano's voice as his face appeared on the screen. "What's up, Alyna?"

"Where are you?" she asked him.

"I just got into the transport. We're getting ready to leave the building."

"I know you didn't want to be bothered with anything today, but something came up I thought you might be interested in. You're going to be a daddy."

After a moment of stunned silence, Arano was out of the transport and dashing through Coalition Military Headquarters to be with his wife and his unborn child. The duffel bag, and unconventional warfare, were forgotten . . .

DARK PLANET

CHARLES W SASSER

Kadar San, a human-Zentadon crossbreed distrusted by both humans and Zentadon, is dispatched with a Deep Reconnaissance Team (DRT) to the Dark Planet of Aldenia. His mission: use his telepathic powers to sniff out a Blob assault base preparing to attack the Galaxia Republic. Dominated by both amazing insect and reptile life forms, and by an evil and mysterious Presence, Aldenia was once a base for the warlike Indowy who used their superior technology to enslave the Zentadon and turn them into super warriors to deploy against humans.

The DRT comes under attack not only from savage denizens of the Dark Planet, but also from the mysterious Presence, which turns team member against team member and all against Kadar San. The Presence promises untold wealth and power to any member of the team unscrupulous enough to unleash the contents of a Pandora's box-like remnant of Indowy technology. The box's possessor poses a greater threat than the entire Blob nation, for he is capable of releasing untold horrors upon the galaxy.

Kadar San finds himself pitted against a human killer, an expert sniper, in a desperate struggle to save both the Republic and the human female he has come to love. Like all Zentadon, however, Kadar San cannot kill without facing destruction himself in the process and he has no choice but to kill. In order to save the galaxy, Kadar San must face the truth . . . No one will leave the Dark Planet.

MORE THAN MAGICK

Rick Taubold

What if you were told you have a power you don't know about? What if you were told that you have to use it to save the universe from a major baddie? What if no one will tell you how you are supposed to do this?

A recent college graduate, Scott Madison is half-heartedly considering his future when he reads an ad on the dorm bulletin board. He ends up taking the job with Jake Kesten, Martial Arts expert and Ph.D. math whiz, and finds himself busting computer hackers for the government. It's an interesting job, if a little rough at times. Still, it's just a job.

Then Jake and Scott get a visit from what, apparently, is an old friend of Jake's — Arion. Scott thinks Arion dresses a little funny, what with the robes and all. But then Arion proclaims himself an Adept at Magick. Before Scott can even roll his eyes, he finds himself whisked away to another world where he joins his fellow adventurers, all plucked as unceremoniously from their own home worlds. Their mission? To save the Elfaeden and their friends, the Crystal Dragons. Their secret weapon? Scott Madison. Who is about to discover that there is something, indeed, MORE THAN MAGICK.

ISBN#0974363987
ISBN#9780974363981
Gold Imprint
US $6.99 / CDN $8.99
Available Now
www.ricktaubold.com

shinigami

django wexler

Shinigami:
In Japanese folklore, a spirit that collects the souls of the dead.

At age fourteen, Sylph Walker died in a car accident. That turned out to be only the beginning of her problems . . .

She and her sister Lina awake to an afterlife, of sorts — the world of Omega, ruled by cruel, squabbling, and nearly all-powerful Archmagi. When Lina finds a magical sword of immense power, she becomes the unwilling epicenter of the conflict. The sisters are forced to join the Circle Breakers, rebels sworn to prevent the tyrants from expanding their rule.

Lina, bearing the ancient artifact, is hailed as the Liberator — the latest in a long line of heroes expected to destroy the Archmagi. Sylph finds herself at the head of the rebel armies fighting to take back the land and the lives of its people. But what kind of a land is it? Is Omega really the world that lies beyond death? And who is the legendary Lightbringer, a being greater even than the Archmagi?

ISBN#1932815716
ISBN#9781932815719
Silver Imprint
US $14.99 / CDN $18.99
October, 2006
www.bloodgod.com